IN THE
SHADOW

MARLEY BRANT

Cover photo: photocosma/Cosma Andrei/depositphotos

ISBN: 0615653758
ISBN-13: 9780615653754
Library of Congress Control Number: 2012941676

Incarnat Books, Marietta, GA

m a r l e y b r a n t . c o m

For Damie

*…and all those who recognize that essence
and family have no veritable definition…*

*To the extraordinary group of magnificent eccentrics
who are my heart and soul*

Although the characters in this story are real people,
and most of the events actually happened,
this is a work of historical fiction.

This is

.........how it might have been.........

It was a nightmare....a horrible, horrible nightmare...

Bobby stood on the side of the porch from which the Union soldiers had just stepped down. This couldn't be happening. They were wrong. They had to be wrong.

Yet from inside the house he could hear his mother's wails, his sisters sobbing.

He watched as the men struggled to lift a body from the back of a buckboard. He frowned. Why were they doing this? Why were they putting his ma, his family, through this? Maybe they thought this fella looked like his pa....but...no, he would never believe it for a minute. The Yankees always got everything wrong. John had told him that over and over.

He watched as the captain in charge walked ahead of the men carrying the body.

"Ma'am?" he called. "Where would you like us to put the body?"

Just like that. "The body." They weren't showing any respect. That proved they were wrong. If the man who was shot was really his father, they would have to show respect. His pa was respected by everybody who knew him. The way they were acting proved it wasn't his pa's body they were delivering.

Jim had helped Bursheba inside and now, ashen-faced, walked back outside. In shock, barely looking at the soldiers, he motioned inside.

"In here," he all but whispered. "Bring my father in here."

"No, Jim, it's not Pa…" Bobby assured him. "It's not Pa."

Jim looked at Bobby, his expression blank. He turned back to the soldiers and again motioned inside.

As the two soldiers mounted the steps, awkwardly holding the body and carrying it in through the door, Bobby looked at the face of the man they bore.

He ran down the porch steps and vomited onto the ground.

John's horse thundered into the yard.

"You Bluebelly sons-of-bitches!" John screamed as he jumped to the ground and ran toward the group of soldiers that stood beside the buckboard. "You damn Yankee sons-of-bitches!"

He ran up to the first soldier in his path and struck him with all the anger a young boy could contain. The soldier flinched away from him and the others moved to push John backward.

"Lay off, boy," one of them quietly ordered. "We're sorry about your pa and all but don't you be hitting Union soldiers."

"I'll kill you!" John continued to strike out and kick at them. "I swear it, I'll kill every last one of you!" he swore through tears of anger and anguish.

"That's enough." the Captain grabbed John by the neck and roughly threw him to the ground. "Don't threaten people who have authority over you, boy. We've had a belly full of you Youngers. Now you lay off before we either throw you the hell somewhere you don't want to be or leave you lying inside next to your old man."

John sprang to his feet and lunged at him. Within a second the soldier reacted, grabbing his revolver and slamming the barrel against the side of the boy's head.

John reeled with the force of it. As the bile rose in his throat, he tried to protest but instead lost consciousness and fell bleeding to the ground.

"We're done here," the captain informed his men with a nod. They mounted their horses and rode slowly, confidently, down the road.

It was a nightmare…and he just wanted to wake up.

CHAPTER 1

Missouri, 1860

"J ohn, you're cheatin' again!" Bobby threw down his cards in disgust and glared at his brother.

The two boys hunkered atop the hay, playing pitch. The soft light from the lantern threw gentle shadows on the walls of the barn. One of the horses whinnied at the sound of the boy's agitation. Outside, the hot August sun was sinking low in a Western Missouri sky streaked with gauzy night clouds. The cicadas made themselves known but otherwise the night was quiet. It was the end of the day. Assigned chores had been completed and supper had been consumed with vigor; and now Bobby and John were just plain bored.

Fact of the matter was that Bobby didn't even want to be here with John let alone be cheated by him. It wasn't like John was his first choice as somebody to pass time with. He'd rather be with his oldest brother Dick but Dick was off with their father at another politics meeting. Dang, if it wasn't one meeting, it was another. Politics was all everybody talked about these days and it sure took up a lot of his pa and Dick's time.

"What *is* politics anyway?" he had asked.

"Why son, it's the fabric of communal life," his pa had answered. "When you have two or more people gathered, there will be some element of politics."

That didn't answer his question but he didn't say so. He was tired of hearing that word anyway. He didn't understand any of it but he knew people paid attention to what his pa and Dick thought. He knew his father had been mayor of their town of Harrisonville right around the time he was born. Now he owned a livery, a dry goods store and was in charge of some others things too. People were always asking his opinion.

"My father is a very important man," he'd heard his brother Cole boast. "He owns miles of land, he's a successful business-man *and* he serves on the Legislature. It doesn't get more important than that."

Their ma got annoyed with Cole when he boasted, but that didn't stop him from doing it. And his pa seemed to like it when Cole talked him up; even though his pa always told them they should be humble. That was confusing. Which way should it be? And he didn't understand what the legislature was any more than he did the word politics. It was something to do with men getting together to talk things over, as far as he could figure. Sounded real boring but his pa told Bobby and his brothers that taking an interest in their community and serving as an elected official was something "to which they should aspire."

"Does that have something to do with dying?" he'd whispered to John out of earshot of his father.

"That's *expire*, stupid." John didn't feel the need to go any further than that.

Bobby shrugged. He was used to being dismissed.

He'd heard a little about people who got elected. Their grandfather was a judge up north on the Jackson County Court and his Uncle Coleman was some kind of important out in California. He knew that he was supposed to be proud of his kin so he guessed he was, although he didn't really know why. Now his sisters were saying that Dick would probably be a judge or congressman one of these days too.

"Aw, Dick just wants to be a big shot like Pa," John shrugged when Bobby mentioned that. "Being a judge and a congressman ain't no big deal."

Bobby didn't think John knew much about those things either but he hadn't said so 'cause he didn't feel like arguing.

"Well, maybe he will be, maybe he won't, but Pa is real proud of Dick."

"Pa is proud of all of us, not just Dick." John rolled his eyes. "He's proud of himself too. He owns *thousands* of acres of land, spread out over *two* counties."

More business about the land his pa owned. It seemed like that came up a lot. Bobby didn't know why they needed all that land anyway but by the way they talked about it all the time, even he knew that having it was important to his pa. There'd been sixteen of them in the Younger family; his brother Alphae had died as little more than a baby, just after John was born he'd been told. Now, half of his sisters were married and had gone off with their husbands to their own houses. His pa had given some of them parcels, if their husbands would let them take it and Pa was kind of annoyed when they wouldn't, but there was still a lot left over.

"Owning Missouri land is golden," Pa often reminded him and his brothers. "The land will be handed down to the five of you and you will always enjoy its living legacy."

Whatever that meant.

"A legacy is bestowed. It's something to be remembered by after we're here and gone," Dick had told Bobby later when he asked.

"Shouldn't we be thinking about that around the time we're fixin' to die?"

"The end of your life is for reviewing what you've done up until that time." Dick had smiled. "You need to do right and moral things so when you get to the end, you have lived a good life and people will remember you for that."

John had again rolled his eyes when Bobby told him what Dick had said. Nothing new there. John didn't have much respect for

Dick, or for anyone really. But to Bobby, if Dick said that was the way it was, that was the way it was. John was just jealous of Dick because everybody liked him. A lot more people would probably like him by the time he died. Bobby had heard his pa say that Dick was smart and well-educated and that the fact that he came from a wealthy and respected family was important. His pa knew beyond a doubt that Dick would someday be a "man of distinction". That phrase might have been lost on a boy Bobby's age but he understood it because he had asked Dick and his pa to tell him exactly what that meant.

His brother Cole had sneered when he heard the answer. Nothing new there either.

"The hell with being known as a man of distinction," Cole later scoffed. "I want to be known as a man of action and results."

Bobby didn't see why you couldn't be all those things but he didn't want to say so to Cole because Cole would just mock him like he always did. Cole didn't like Dick and he wasn't like Dick. Dick treated Bobby like he mattered. He never ignored his questions or made fun of him for asking to have things explained to him. Being the youngest of the five boys and the next-to-the-youngest of all his brothers and sisters, nobody else gave a hoot about what he thought. Come to think of it, no one *ever* asked him what his opinion was. They never paid any attention to anything he had to say. Except Dick. Dick *cared* what he thought.

But Cole? He never cared. The way Bobby saw it, Cole thought he knew it all, knew everything there was to know. And nobody ever had to ask twice for Cole's opinion. He'd give it to you whether or not you asked for it or even cared what it was. Cole was a whole lot different from Dick. Dick had good sense. Cole would get something in his mind and he wouldn't let go of it just because that was the way he wanted it to be. And he would just go off and do whatever he felt like doing without thinking it through. Bobby had heard his father say that a bunch of times.

"The boy is just impulsive, Henry," their mother would sigh.

"Well, being impulsive is going to get him in some serious trouble someday," his pa would say as he took a big puff on his pipe.

4

It wasn't that Cole wasn't smart. He probably was, but Cole's way of sharing facts was to tell them from a place that made you think that only he had the information and you were just plain stupid.

"You should figure this stuff out on your own, Bobby," Cole told him more than once. "I don't have time to tell you all the things I know."

That was kind of a funny thing for Cole to say because Cole liked to hear himself talk. But that was Cole. And Bobby thought that it was odd how Cole would try to act like Dick when Dick wasn't around and always be ticked at Dick when he was in the same room. Cole might try to be like Dick but Bobby thought that no matter how hard he tried, Cole was just who he was.

Now John was starting to act like Cole and Bobby didn't understand that at all. John was *always* complaining about Cole. He shook his head. Sometimes his brain hurt from thinking so much. He always thought about things too much. Now here he was thinking about thinking too much. He'd come to the barn to look for something else to do besides thinking. He figured he'd probably find John in the barn putting together one of his schemes or whatever it was that he did out here. With John you never knew. Just when you thought you had him figured out, he'd surprise you. The only thing surprising was that it *wasn't* surprising the things John got up to, if that made any sense.

"Halloo? Did you hear me? I said, of course I'm cheatin'," John smirked. "I always cheat."

The hand with the cards dangled and with the other he picked at his teeth with a piece of straw.

"If you wanted to win, you'd cheat too."

"Cheatin's not right," Bobby muttered, his pale blue eyes narrowing. "You're going to hell, if you keep doing that."

He had rolled up the pant legs of his trousers and his shirt sleeves. It was *hot*. Maybe not as hot as hell, but hot. He slapped at his legs. Skeeters. All summer long they buzzed and bit. He hated them.

"I figure I'm probably going to hell anyway," grinned John as he pushed his dark, tousled hair out of his eyes. "So why not enjoy myself?"

John liked that idea. He was never going to be a leader like Dick. He wasn't going to be as popular as Cole and he wasn't going to be as smart as their third brother, Jim. Bobby was younger than he was and he didn't count. So why bother to put effort into things that weren't going to matter anyway? With the family as big a crowd as his was, if you didn't draw attention to yourself you could pretty much do what you wanted.

Bobby frowned. He couldn't understand how someone could just shrug off something as important as going to hell. The Youngers were Christian people, not people who went to hell. What made John think that was where he was going to end up anyway? And John seemed to like the thought of going to hell. What the heck was wrong with him?

He watched John flick the cards into the air one by one.

"Gotcha thinkin', don't I?"

John smiled. He loved to get Bobby stirred up; it wasn't hard. Bobby thought he knew all about what was right and what was wrong. Dick had filled his head with all those high and mighty ideas. All that talk was only a waste of time. So even though he actually liked his little brother, it was always fun to stir him up.

"No. I'm not lettin' you get my goat," Bobby decided. "You're just messin' with me."

"You make it easy, Bobby. So easy."

"Shut up."

With that Bobby dismissed the notion of John going to hell and put his mind on other things.

"Why do you think Pa and Dick have been going to so many meetings? Do you think somethin' is goin' on that we don't know about?"

"Yup, I know there is." John spit into the dirt. "There's been a bunch of fellas comin' by Pa's store to talk to him. I listened in the other day and heard 'em say there might gonna be a war."

"A war?" Bobby had heard the word used before but he wasn't quite sure what it meant to them. "What kind of a war?"

"A war where people want something the other side has, they shoot at each other and some of them die."

"Why would Pa and his friends be talking about *that?*"

John rolled his eyes. "Because the Kansans are idiots. And they want our land. And our Negroes. And our money. And our lives."

"Why?" Bobby frowned. This was all news to *him.*

"Because they're idiots, I just told you."

"So they're gonna come here and kill us?" *That* couldn't be right.

"They'll try," John dismissed. "Try to leave us in a steamin' heap of bloody guts. But we'll shoot 'em and kill 'em first."

"I don't wanna shoot anybody..."

"You will," John predicted. "Wait and see."

CHAPTER 2

Henry and Dick Younger stood outside the barn after put-ting away their buggy and horses. Bobby sat on a barrel at the barn's door, tapping the heels of his boots against the wood. He'd been thinking about what John had said and he was ner-vous. In contrast, the rhythmic thumping seemed to sooth the animals, who offered only an occasional exhale or soft padding. The stars were high in the sky now and a subtle breeze whispered through the Sweet Gum trees that surrounded the building. The light from a lantern threw a yellow glow.

John swung from a long rope he had fashioned to hang from the rafter in the barn. He might look like he was otherwise occu-pied but he could hear every word that was said. He wasn't about to be left out of *anything* if he could help it.

Henry pulled his pipe out of his pocket and placed it between his teeth. He didn't think to light it. His distinguished profile fell in shadow against the slats of the barn as he stared up into the night. The day's local election and the way things were headed troubled him. Neither he nor Dick had engaged in any conversa-tion on the way home.

"Pa, do you think it's a given that Kansas is going to elect Jim Lane come January?"

The handsome features of the younger man were formed in a frown. Dick too was disturbed by the night's agitated rhetoric among the men of their community.

"I'd say there's a very good chance, son," Henry replied. "And there's only going to be more trouble if that happens. Jim Lane hates Missouri. If that fool comes into more power, I'm sure that there's nothing but conflict ahead."

"Why can't they just work it out, Pa?" Bobby had heard that many times when there were arguments between his sisters. None of them wanted to be nice to the other one but after they said they were sorry and everything, things went back to normal.

"It's a matter of politics, son. Some very complicated politics."

There was that word politics again. Bobby let out a long sigh. There was no use in asking questions. All he was ever going to hear was the same old thing.

"May I, Pa?" Dick asked.

Henry nodded. He admired the relationship between his oldest and youngest sons. He knew Dick enjoyed mentoring Bobby and he was good at it. As for this issue, Dick was an educated man; he could articulate the matter in a way that Bobby would understand.

Dick sat on a bale next to where Bobby perched on his barrel. He ran a hand through his dark hair and his eyes gazed intently into those of his brother.

"It goes back to the year you were born, Bobby. When Kansas and Nebraska were declared territories of the Unites States it was decided that the people in each area could choose whether or not they wanted to hold slaves. There's a lot of disagreement about that. Most people who live in Kansas want it to be a Free State, without slaves. There are many in Missouri who think those Kansans are now unfairly trying to use a heavy hand to influence the people of Missouri to see things their way."

"Kansas has got *nothin'* to do with Missoura, I say." John called out. He didn't know anything about it but he knew his comment would fluster Dick.

"What's at issue, John…" Dick turned to the barn.

"What I want to know is, just what is a slave?" Bobby interrupted. He had heard the word mentioned a few times when he'd been at his pa's livery. As far as he could tell it had something to do with the dark-skinned people, people like Suze. Suze was his mother's helper and everybody in the family loved her as if she were family. What could any of this have to do with Suze?

Henry motioned to Dick that John's comment could wait. He lit his pipe and drew in a long breath of tobacco which he then let out in a sweet-scented stream.

"Slavery is a system where individuals are compelled to work for someone."

"What's compelled?"

"That means they're *forced* to or they get in a lot of trouble, really *big* trouble." John eased himself down from his rope and walked over to the others. The conversation was getting interesting and he wanted to be a part of it.

Henry glanced at John. He was going to have to choose his words very carefully.

"In the case of slavery, men and women have been bought from someone so that they can work for the people who bought them."

"How can you buy a person?" Bobby frowned. That sounded just plain crazy.

"Just hand over the money," John smirked.

Henry narrowed his eyes at John in response that his comment was not welcome.

"It is an unfortunate system that has been employed for many years," Dick picked up, ignoring John.

"Is it just the Negroes that are bought?"

"Of course it is, stupid." John sneered. "The Negroes and you."

"John, don't talk to your bother like that," Henry directed. "Be quiet for once." He and Dick exchanged glances. "Yes, it pertains to the Negroes, son."

"Was Suze bought?" He wanted to know more about *that*.

"No, Suze wasn't bought. She came to me from my father."

"How, if she wasn't a slave?"

11

"Her mother was a slave." Henry took another pull on his pipe. "We rely on a handful of Negroes that I inherited from my father to help us with our farming and to assist your mother with the things that she does to tend to our family. Suze is one of those people."

"So she's compelled."

"No, I wouldn't say so. We consider the Negroes to be simply employed. They are paid with food, lodging and clothing and they are free to leave if they so desire. The buying and selling of slaves, unlike the time and custom of my father and the tradition of my father's home state of Virginia, is a practice that many reject and one that I find obsolete and distasteful.

"Is there going to come a time when you're going to sell Suze, Pa?" His pa wouldn't do that, would he? He loved Suze. He didn't want her to go away to be with someone else.

"No, son. I would never sell Suze. The people that I have inherited as slaves are treated with the same respect as any other of the people that our family knows. We deal with people fairly; judging and treating them by their personal character and the way they respect and behave toward us."

Bobby nodded, relieved. He'd heard that kind of talk before, from both his pa and his ma, about respecting people and treating them fairly. He sighed. Here he was again with an awful lot to think about.

But what about what John said before? What about war?

"And slavery is why that man in Kansas is going to make trouble?"

"It has something to do with it, Bobby." Dick let out a long breath. It was a thorny subject. "The matter at hand here in Missouri has less to do with slavery and more to do with the resentment of people being told what they can and cannot do by a government thousands of miles away. Emotions are running high on both issues."

"I'll say they are!" Although John knew little about all this, he knew that people were gettin' fuming mad at the Kansans and that wasn't any less than hoppin' hoppers exciting. At least something was going on around here.

"Is there going to be a war, Pa?" Why not come right out and ask it? John had explained that word well enough. So even if he didn't understand a lot of what had just been said, Bobby did understand that. "Are the people from Kansas going to have a war with us?"

"Bet your bony butt they are!" John smiled.

"John, I'm not going to tell you again! The next time you pipe up there are going to be consequences."

"Okay, Pa," John smiled. He'd made his point.

Henry turned back to Bobby. "Son, there are many Kansans and Missourians who believe that a certain order needs to be established, that the constitution and laws of the United States must be endorsed to protect and serve *all* people. Those who are more headstrong need to be reigned in."

Henry looked into the darkness of the night. The issue seemed straightforward yet it had an underlying complexity that John and Bobby weren't mature enough to understand. The dissent was growing greater. Almost everyone was now involved in a battle of wills, whether they liked it or not.

He was unhappy with the wave of negative activism and he opposed it. He was known as a Conservative Unionist and had been elected to the border legislature with the intent of offering input that would move things away from confrontation. Even so, his livery and dry goods store were sometimes targeted by marauders from Kansas. It had all been minor but Henry realized that with intricate politics sometimes came a lack of reason.

"Tonight's election confirmed that the people of this community aren't in favor of Lane's interference but they're reasonable people." Dick preferred to believe the best in everyone and hoped that was true.

"This is the United States of America. People vote and the majority rules," Henry added. "If that goes against what any individual wants, well they have the next election to try to sway the vote to their opinion as to how things should be."

"So everybody has to do what the most people want." Bobby nodded.

"If what they want is reasonable."

"And what if it's not?" John asked in an attempt to stir the pot.

"Then you protest."

"How?" Bobby asked.

"You get in a war with them!" John crowed.

Henry exhaled. He was much too tired from the day's activities to be having this talk. He was pleased his son had questions but he'd had enough of all this for the time being.

"You don't harm your neighbors because you disagree with them or you simply want you own way." Dick shook his head. "Vigilante justice is never acceptable."

As Bobby started to ask another question, the sound of hoofs pounded on the hard ground leading up to the barn. The four of them watched as Cole slipped smoothly off his horse and approached, tether in hand.

Cole Younger was already imposing, even at the age of sixteen. He wasn't lean and distinctly handsome like his older brother; Cole was appealing in a rougher, more casual way. Tall, with a thickly muscled body, Cole was self-confident and charismatic. Young ladies were attracted to his shock of dark red hair and his piercing blue eyes and his friends enjoyed his candor and his way with a tale. Cole was on top of the world and ready to take on whatever crossed his path.

"Hey, Pa." Cole nodded to Dick and ignored John and Bobby altogether. He looked back at his father. "Things are getting pretty hot out there, aren't they? Some of those boys are *riled*! They're ready to *go*!" He grinned.

"I hardly find it something to be amused about, Coleman," Henry frowned.

Color rose in Cole's face. He and his father were two completely different people when it came to matters of individual will and independence. Cole didn't like being told what to do and he certainly didn't like being told how to think. Those Kansans and Unionists were way off base as far as he was concerned. He should have known better than to expect that his father would agree with the way he viewed the matter.

"People taking the issue into their own hands isn't the way to handle this situation," Dick began.

"Wasn't talking to you, Dick. Nobody asked you what you thought."

Cole glared at his brother. The golden boy always had an opinion about everything and it made Cole resent him even more that their father always agreed with Dick. Cole was almost seventeen and he wasn't a fool. Just because he saw things differently didn't make his opinion count any less. Maybe he wasn't as educated as his brother yet but he was just as smart as Dick, probably even smarter.

"Don't start in Cole," Henry sighed. "It's late. We all need to get some rest."

"I don't have the right to voice my opinion, Pa? The only opinion that counts around here is his? I'm goddamn sick of hearing his opinion!"

Bobby stared at Cole, his eyes big as saucers. John grinned.

"Coleman! That's enough! I'm not going to hear that kind of talk. You respect me and you respect your brother."

"The hell I will!" Cole retorted. "I respect you Pa, but I'm not gonna kowtow to his every word like everybody else around here does."

He continued to stare at his brother.

"Let me tell *you* something, Dick. People taking *the issue* into their own hands is the *only* way this *issue* is going to get settled. You think Missourians are just gonna stand by and let those damn Kansans take free rein of our land? Once we drive 'em back up into their own state and settle some scores, they won't be pushing their positions down our throats anymore!"

"Always trying to settle things with violence." Dick shook his head. "You'd think you'd learn."

"Oh, I've learned all right. I've learned that standing up for yourself is the only way to get what you want. I'm not letting *anybody* push me around. Not them Kansans, not *anybody*."

15

Henry had long ago realized that reasoning with Cole was a losing battle. God knew he tried to get the boy to reign in his explosive emotions but now that Cole was practically a grown man he didn't seem to have any more influence over him.

"Cole, this is a conversation for another time." Henry put his arms around the shoulders of his two oldest sons and waved Bobby and John over. "Let's finish up what we need to do and go in to bed."

Bobby hesitated to get down. He knew Cole was going to try to have the last word.

"It's always him, isn't it Pa. You're never going to side with me over him." Cole shrugged off his father's arm. "You can go to hell, Dick."

He turned away from the two men and took his horse into the barn.

"Pa…" Dick began. This wasn't something their little brothers should be hearing without a more reasonable rebuttal.

"I'm tired, Dick." Henry shook his head and started toward the house. "I'm going to bed. We'll have Cole's conversation another time."

Dick stared into the barn. Cole was so damn stubborn and hot-headed. Why did he always react rather than explore issues and come to sensible conclusions? He didn't want to argue with Cole. Yet it always seemed to come to that. He started to walk away and remembered Bobby sitting on the barrel, his eyes still large.

"It'll be all right, Bobby. Don't worry about me and Cole. We're brothers, we'll work it out. Come on, let's go in to bed."

Bobby jumped down. Dick put his arm around him and they walked toward the house. John decided that the show was likely over so he might as well head in too.

Cole watched them disappear into the night, seething with anger and resentment.

"You can go to hell, Dick," he repeated. "And I hope you do."

Bobby quietly entered Dick's room, his footsteps light as to not draw the attention of their father.

Dick's long body lay in bed with the soft glow of the lantern casting shadows over his sleepy face. A book lay open, propped on his knees. He smiled when Bobby entered the room.

"Can we talk more about slavery, Dick?"

"We will, Bobby, but not tonight." His father was right. They'd all had enough of that discussion for the time being.

"Okay. What book are you reading?"

"It's titled "A Tale of Two Cities," Dick smiled. "It takes place in France."

Bobby had a hard time imaging what life might be like in France. That was a long way away, across an ocean. Dick had once told him that. He wasn't even sure just where it was. All he knew was Missoura.

"What's it about?"

"It's about the politics during a time they call the French Revolution."

"Politics," Bobby groused. "We got enough *politics* going on around here without reading about other people's *politics*."

Dick sighed. His brother had already learned to dislike political issues and the acrimony they sometimes wrought. Things had been so peaceful and positive when he had been that age.

While it was true that politics seemed to be playing a prominent role in the lives of the family and their neighbors right now, he could only hope that reason would prevail and things would not escalate into a situation from which there would be no return. Yet he sensed that was likely not possible and it broke his heart. The division, even within families as was evidenced by his brother Cole's reaction tonight, was inauspicious and disturbing. The possibility of a civil war was not farfetched. Politics could be, and often were, deadly. And here stood his little brother already having to question and deal with such things.

"You're right, Bobby." Dick managed a smile. "Reading about love and commitment is much more satisfying."

"Love…" Bobby dismissed the notion that anything having to do with love was something he would be interested in. John said love made people act dim-witted. "I wouldn't want to read about love."

Dick chuckled. "Not even about the love of a family? The love of a big brother for his little brother?"

Bobby shrugged. He loved Dick and all but he didn't really want to read about something like that.

"There is nothing, Bobby, more important than the love of family. There may be politics; there may be things that happen in life over which we have no control. There will be good times and there will be bad. But nothing is more important than family. Don't ever forget that."

Bobby nodded. His other brothers and his sisters sometimes teased him and made him mad but he guessed he loved them just the same. They would always be around, he figured, just like Dick would always be there to answer his questions and teach him things. He guessed that was pretty important.

"Get off to bed now, little brother."

Bobby turned and Dick watched the boy's retreating back. Bobby was a smart and sensitive boy. There was so much promise. The world would be his oyster if life didn't get in the way.

Dick prayed to God that it wouldn't.

CHAPTER 3

B obby had been awake long before the crack of dawn. He'd tossed and turned last night thinking about slaves, bad feelings, and war. When he saw the darkness of night begin to fade he figured he might as well just get up and be done with it.

He was now pitching hay beside John and relishing the sweet smell of the dried grass as he drew in long breaths of it. He didn't mind his morning chores. His father had taught him that there were simply things that needed to be done every day in order to keep things moving along so they could enjoy the fruits of their labor. What he would really like to do is plant his own small crop garden 'cause that would *really* be the fruit of his labor. He wanted to talk to his pa about that but now didn't seem to be the time.

Henry walked into the barn where his youngest boys already had his horse reined and his buggy ready to go. Truth be told, he'd rather be pitching hay alongside his sons than heading into town to face another day of the heated agitation of the men who would stop by the livery to argue with one another. What he really wished was that he could take the time for a lengthy and pleasant ride through his fields; to get away from anything connected to the Kansas issue. A nice daydream but he had a business to run.

"Morning, boys," he waved absently.

"Mornin' Pa," John greeted. He leaned on his pitchfork. "Can I go with you today?"

John had been thinking about that since the second pitch. He hated chores. Especially in summer when all they got you was sweaty and made you stink. He wanted to go to the livery or to the store, where something *interesting* might happen. Where he could find out what was *going on*.

"Not today, John. I want you to look at that western fence today. Properly repair that break your horse caused."

Henry had not been happy that John had been racing his horse so recklessly that the horse had a broken a piece of pasture fence.

"That won't take long. I can head in after I'm done."

"Not today." Henry raised himself into the carriage. "I want you and Bobby to tend to the tack today."

"Okay, Pa," Bobby nodded.

John sneered at him and made kissing noises.

"Oh, and Dick's not feeling well," Henry mentioned as a second thought. "So be quiet when you go in the house."

"What's wrong with him?" Bobby asked.

"His stomach is bothering him. I'm off now. You boys stay out of trouble."

Henry clicked his tongue and steered his rig out of the barn.

"My stomach's bothering me too," John complained. "I'm sick enough to puke. I'm sick of doing chores and wasting time hanging around here when there's better stuff to do."

Bobby decided to ignore him. John was always complaining about something. He had wanted to see what John had to say about slavery but now he wondered what was wrong with Dick. Dick never got sick.

He put down his pitchfork and walked toward the house.

"Hey! Do what you're supposed to be doing so we can get this over with," John directed.

"I'm gonna go see what's wrong with Dick."

He walked into the kitchen where his mother was rinsing out a cloth from a bucket of water. She glanced at Bobby as he came in but he could see she was thinking of something else.

Bursheba Younger's face was drawn and tired. She hadn't much sleep last night. Bursheba was a compassionate wife and mother who put her family above all else. She couldn't imagine living her life any other way. A mother's instinct was strong, she mused. She somehow knew that one of the children was ill. She had checked on the youngest ones and found all but Bobby sleeping soundly. When she had raised an eyebrow at him, he had pretended she had awakened him. She could tell he wasn't ailing. She thought perhaps she was just sensing his restlessness. She didn't look in on the older children. They deserved their privacy. And then this morning Dick had called to her and told her he had awful pains in his stomach.

"What's wrong with Dick, Ma?"

"His stomach hurts," she replied. "I'm not sure why."

Bobby followed her as she returned to Dick's bedroom. The room was dark when she entered and Bobby stood in the doorway. The bedcovers were clutched in Dick's hands and his eyes were closed. His pale face was damp with sweat.

When Dick heard his mother come in he opened his eyes.

"Mother, I'm really in pain. I think I need a doctor."

"I think so too, son," Bursheba agreed. "I'll have Bobby go for Doctor Allen," she told him as she turned to direct her youngest son.

She didn't have to ask. Bobby was already out the door and running for his horse.

Henry had been summoned home and Doctor Allen was talking to him in the parlor. Bobby stood outside Dick's room listening to their conversation. He was worried. His mother was biting her lip and wringing her hands. The doctor was talking about removing something from Dick's body. He peered into the bedroom again. Dick looked terrible.

"Ma?" he whispered. "What's wrong with Dick? He's going to be all right, isn't he?"

Bursheba put her arm around him and squeezed his shoulder.

"I don't know Bobby...but he's in God's hands."

Bobby slipped into the room and approached the bed.

"Dick?" he whispered.

Dick tuned his face toward him. He hated to see the worry on his brother's little face.

"I've been praying that you're gonna be okay. I've been praying."

Dick reached for Bobby's hand, nodded and managed a small smile.

"I love you, little brother," he whispered.

"Let Dick rest now, Bobby," their mother instructed. "He needs to rest."

Bobby backed out of the room.

They buried Dick Younger two days later. They never knew exactly what it was that caused his death. Doctor Allen said it was likely that his appendix burst.

Bobby couldn't understand why God would take away such a good person, such a good brother. It didn't seem right that one day you were reading "A Tale of Two Cities" and the next day you were dead. Who was going to answer his questions and help him think things through now? Why did God think it was a good idea to have Dick die?

Maybe this was because of what Cole said. He knew that maybe he'd be going to hell for what he was thinking but right now all he knew was that he hated God. God was just plain mean.

Dick's death devastated his sisters and brothers. Dick had been the one they looked up to, the one that they all loved the most. Dick set such a strong example and was such a positive presence in their lives that his absence was incomprehensible.

Cole was particularly stunned. He'd cursed his brother to hell the night before Dick died but of course he didn't really mean it. He made sure to tell that to Bobby, who looked at him like he was the devil himself.

"You can't really curse someone to hell," Cole tried to explain.

"You did," Bobby accused.

"But I didn't mean it! A person doesn't have that kind of power over life and death."

"Well, you did it and now Dick's dead."

It took their mother to finally get through to the boy that Cole's words had nothing to do with Dick's dying.

"Sometimes things happen over which we have no control, Bobby."

It hurt her so much to see her little boy in such pain.

"It was just Dick's time to go to be with the Lord, whether or not we understand, whether or not we wish it didn't happen."

Bobby pretended he accepted that, hugged his ma and all, but it didn't make him feel any better. He wanted Dick to be there with them, plain and simple.

But as much as each of them grieved their loss, no one was more affected than Henry. Every day he would rise after a fitful sleep and ride his horse out to the far reaches, where he would stare off into the distance thinking of the young man who had been taken from him. He'd never known anguish so acute. Henry loved each and every one of his children but Dick was his firstborn son. The relationship they'd shared was extraordinary. The potential lost substantial.

"Frank," he asked his younger brother. "I'm just not up to making business decisions. Would you mind tending to the store and the livery for the time being?"

Frank didn't mind. He knew his brother was in tremendous pain.

Cole had offered to take care of things while his father took time to recover from the shock of Dick's death but Henry had dismissed him out of hand. He didn't have to say it, but Cole was not Dick and he didn't have Dick's aptitude for business. Henry's grief was so excruciating that he was completely unaware that his refusal to allow Cole to step up into a position that reflected his father's trust and faith in him had broken Cole's heart.

"Even with him dead he's always going to be Pa's favorite," Cole seethed to Jim. "None of the rest of us should ever think otherwise."

What could Jim say? He knew Cole was right.

CHAPTER 4

Five months after Dick Younger died, Jim Lane was elected to serve Kansas in the United States Senate. The rumors of Lane's potential power proved true. Within months President Lincoln appointed Lane a Brigadier General in the Union Army and Lane raised his troops. There were plenty of men who wanted to join in and have their say. A man named Charles Jennison headed a Calvary unit and worked in tandem with Lane. It was becoming clear that neither was a friend of those who lived along the Western Missouri border counties.

John and Bobby had been fishing in the creek and now they sat eating cornbread under a wide-armed Sycamore tree. It was a tranquil day, with only the melodic voices of various wood warblers attesting to the existence of the area's wildlife.

"They call Lane's men Redlegs," John told Bobby, staring north into the distance.

"On account of those red leggings they wear?" Bobby asked.

John didn't answer.

"And those men grouped on horses?" he continued. "They're in with Lane. They're called Jayhawkers."

"Why's that?"

"Don't matter. Stay away from them. They're sons-of-bitches."

Their father should've talked to them about all this and both of them wished he would. Henry knew it too but he just didn't have the emotional energy.

Bobby knew that John didn't really know much more than he did about the politics – that word *again* - so he decided to ask Cole.

"Is this about slavery still?"

"It's about we're going to have to kick their ass," was Cole's curt reply. It didn't much matter to him what his little brother knew about it. He had more important things on his mind now than explaining things to a little kid.

The bitter opposition between Kansas and Missouri only grew stronger. That summer Henry's livery was raided of saddles and reins and various other accouterments and, worse of all, forty horses.

"How much did they take, Pa?" Cole questioned, his face dark with anger.

"About $4,000 worth of assets."

"What are we going to do about it?" Cole was ready for the fight.

"Nothing at this point," Henry absently responded. "It's only a handful of hooligans."

Cole shook his head and walked away disgusted.

Henry didn't even notice. It would likely not be the last time that his business was looted yet he still refused to address the issue.

Bobby wondered when somebody was going to give them some straight-on answers. Was all this going to get better or worse?

"No, things aren't gonna get better," John whispered with excitement in his eyes. "They're gonna get worse, comin' toward us fast as you can say "John was right". Just you wait and see."

John *was* right. The formalized War Between the States that had been launched in America's southland was now reaching the wilds of Missouri. When troops led by Confederate General Sterling Price defeated Union forces down at Wilson's Creek, Price's soldiers were cheered by those further up the state that was only just beginning to feel the War's effect.

Jim Lane was furious at the hoopla. As soon as Price passed through, Lane led over 1,500 Jayhawkers and Redlegs into Missouri, where they laid waste to thousands of acres of farms and property.

Just for the hell of it.

Bobby tried not to think about the way Cole raged about war and fighting to Jim the night before. Jim didn't say anything back to Cole but Bobby watched John twitch he was so excited. All the talk of Kansas and war scared Bobby. But he didn't think anybody wanted to hear any of that and he didn't want to come off like a baby.

Right now he was helping his mother in the kitchen. She said she wanted to make more room in the pantry but as far as he could see she was just having him move things around and he didn't see where there was any purpose in that.

"Just humor her, Bobby," his sister Sally advised. "She's still grieving."

Bobby knew that; he didn't need Sally to tell him. He still couldn't believe Dick was dead. Well, he believed it because Dick wasn't there anymore. Almost every day he would think of something he wanted to ask Dick about. But Dick wasn't there and he never would be again. Without Dick to ask and his father acting strange, there was no one to explain all this stuff. He heard the angry talk in town but when he brought it up with his brothers, Cole wouldn't take the time to talk to him about it and John just made things up as he went along. He'd tried talking to Jim but Jim told him to ask their pa. But his pa didn't want to talk about it either.

"It'll all work itself out, son," he'd always say.

That didn't seem to be happening.

Bobby heard Cole and his sister Josie's husband, John Jarrett, talk about how the Confederate Army was taking on as many Missouri boys as were interested. But some of the boys wondered if the Army could get done what those boys could do on their own.

"They're told what to do and how to do it but just think what damage we could do if some of us boys fought for what is ours on our own terms," Cole boasted to his friends. "We'd have a bigger stake in it. That would make a real difference. We'd put those sons-of-bitches in the dirt, where they belong. The end."

Someone other than Cole and his buddies was thinking the same thing and he was doing something about it. Where the Kansans had been fueled by the leadership of Lane and Jennison, it took a silver-tongued young man from Ohio to bring together the angry young men of Western Missouri ol' Charlie Quantrill got them up and runnin' in no time. He taught them the nuances of fighting guerilla-style and they caught on fast, real fast. Quantrill's men may have been called Irregulars but their enemies knew them for what they were: Bushwhackers.

Quantrill's new troops were single-minded. They were infuriated by their possessions being looted, their land destroyed and their family members run off or killed. As they gathered through word of mouth, the raiders associated with Quantrill quickly increased in number. Most of them knew each other one way or another but even if they didn't, they quickly bonded and that bond was pure and simple: vengeance.

Maybe their methods were right, maybe they were wrong. Didn't matter. They were doing everything they could to stand against those who tried to force their will on down-to-earth people who didn't much appreciate that kind of treatment.

Quantrill was good at exploiting the loathing and fear that hung low over the families in the border counties but it wasn't Quantrill's manipulation that attracted young men to throw in with him – it was unadulterated hatred.

As all this bubbled over a slow boil, Henry was slowly starting to recover from the loss of his cherished son (although some people would later say that he never could and never did). His heart wasn't in it but he knew that it was time to return to his business. His wife and the children still at home deserved as much.

He sat on the porch smoking his pipe with his younger brother Frank. Bobby sat on the top step. It was a crisp November night and the air whispered with the imminent onset of winter. The men wore their coats; the boy only his long sleeves.

"Have you given any thought to moving west, Henry?" Frank asked. "I have. Maybe now is the time to go out there and start a new life. It worked for Coleman. He's prospering. And none of this business is going to touch California."

"I couldn't do that, Frank." Henry was shocked that Frank would even suggest such a thing. "I'm happy that our brother is doing well out there but Missouri is my family's home. I need to watch over my land and all I've accomplished."

"But aren't you worried about your children? It's getting pretty rough."

Henry looked down at Bobby. The boy took such an interest in everything and was hanging on his every word.

"Of course I'm concerned for my children but they need me to stand strong and reinforce my sense of duty and the ethics with which I have raised them. I can hardly turn my back on our neighbors."

"Then you've chosen to stand for which side?" Frank had been having a hard time understanding Henry's refusal to endorse one side or the other.

"I don't feel the need to take a side, Frank. We, *as a community*, need to work through this problem together. Taking sides isn't going to move that line of thought along. We are citizens of the United States of America. Dividing ourselves into sectors based on opinion will only serve to weaken and break us."

Henry believed that, he truly did.

"I refuse to be labeled either a Unionist or Confederate. That declaration will be for others. I will commit my energies to conducting my business, and my life, as usual until this wretched situation is stabilized."

Many of the men of Harrisonville believed that a more active involvement from Henry Younger would benefit Cass County but they were sympathetic to what he had experienced with the loss of his son and they couldn't complain. Henry gave generously of his resources to any and all of those who were put in a position to need them and he offered his services, regardless of their political affiliation.

"No," Henry restated. "We need to remain here and support those who need a hand."

This was the first time in a long time that Bobby had heard his father talk about what was going on. He had so many questions but didn't know if he should ask them.

"Have you heard about this Quantrill fellow?" Frank asked. He was looking for Henry's opinion on the issues too.

"Of course." Henry waved his hand. "He's a dilettante. He brings nothing to the table other than trouble."

"But John Jarrett likes him, Pa." Bobby decided to speak. They could ignore him if they wanted, but he was going to at least take a chance somebody would pay attention to him. "John says that Quantrill is just what we need around here. Cole says it too."

Henry had heard a credible rumor that John Jarrett was very active with that group and he disapproved of his son-in-law's involvement. Jarrett seemed somewhat undisciplined, a man who seemed to follow his whim. Henry didn't like the influence Jarrett seemed to have on Cole.

"We're not going to concern ourselves with Mister Quantrill, Bobby," Henry dismissed. "It isn't honorable to seek vengeance outside the law."

And that was that. Any thoughts Bobby might have had to explore the topic came to an abrupt end.

CHAPTER 5

C ole saddled his horse. Martha Mockbee was having a birthday party. He thought that was a little foolish in light of
everything that was going on but he liked Martha and her family
had been friends of the Youngers for a long time. Even so, he
was annoyed that, like his own father, Mister Mockbee refused
to formally acknowledge the War or take a side. It was late into
'61; things were hotter than ever, sure not be 'being resolved'
as his pa liked to preach. Ah, shit…he'd better not think about
that or he'd get riled up and that wasn't a good idea tonight.
He really didn't want to go to a party, of all things, but he and
his brother Jim had been asked to chaperone their sister Sally
and their married sister, Caroline. And it was a true thing that
the girls shouldn't be out at night on their own. So, if for nothing other than his sisters' safety, Cole had agreed to accompany
them. A party, for God's sake…didn't these people have more
important things to concern themselves with?

"I can do it, Cole," John had said earlier. "Let me drive em."

"Nobody wants a *child* around, John." The kid was always yam-
mering to go along. It didn't matter where or what for. "Forget
it."

"I'm not a child." John glared.

"Well, you're doing a good job passing for one," Cole dismissed.

31

"Maybe you should put on your party dress," Bobby teased. "Then you'd fit right in."

"Shut the hell up." John took a swing but Bobby was fast on his feet as he stepped backward.

Cole just shook his head and led his horse out of the barn. He'd be glad when the time came that he didn't have to be bothered by his little brothers.

"Hey, Cole," came a voice from the shadows.

Cole jumped. He looked behind him to see his brother-in-law standing there.

"For God's sake, Jarrett....you startled me."

"It pays to keep on your toes." John Jarrett smiled as he lit a smoke. "Especially with all the riff-raff out there on the loose."

Jarrett knew his father-in-law didn't approve of some of his views and likely considered him part of the riff-raff but he didn't much care. His part in this thing was necessary.

"Where're you off to?"

Cole stopped to cinch his saddle. "Mockbee's. Party for Martha."

"A party?" Jarrett lifted his eyebrow. "Shit-fire. Don't these people know there's a war goin' on?"

"It's her birthday," Cole offered in explanation.

"Oh, it's her *birthday*," Jarrett smirked.

Cole blushed. He knew Jarrett was right to have scorn for the event.

"Yeah, I know, but my pa wants me and Jim to take Sally and Caro."

"Smart thinkin'. Ya never know who's hiding out there in the woods."

Jarrett watched Cole finish his task. Cole didn't know that Jarrett had been assigned the job of recruiting him to join the Quantrill men. It was well-known that the kid had a simmering kind of temper but more importantly he had a strong penchant for righteousness and revenge. He'd make the perfect guerilla. Jarrett had been talking up the organization to Cole ever since he himself had joined.

"The boys are gonna be just a ways up the road tonight. You should come and talk to them."

Cole was tempted yet he knew his responsibility to his sisters had to come first. But he didn't want Jarrett to think his hesitation had anything to do with lack of commitment to the Cause… or a lack of guts.

"Maybe later," he shrugged.

"Yeah, maybe later."

Jarrett's tone suggested that he thought Cole was maybe afraid to throw in his lot with Quantrill's boys. Cole started to respond when Jim walked into the barn.

Jim didn't care much for his brother-in-law's involvement with Quantrill, even if he didn't know that much about it, but Jim wasn't one to reveal how he felt about things. He nodded politely at Jarrett.

Jarrett smiled at Jim. Jim had a different temperament from Cole but he had to admire the boy. Jim was quiet and didn't speak his mind much. He always had his nose in a book. But there was a levelness about him and he was pretty reliable. He had good sense and he was loyal to his family. Probably more than any of them. Jarrett considered that if the War went on any length of time, which it likely would, Jim might also be one to consider bringing into the fold. He was young, only fourteen or so, but he was a big kid…maybe a little down the road….

Jim felt Jarrett's scrutiny and self-consciously moved to hitch a horse to the buggy.

"You're taking your horse?" he asked Cole.

Cole nodded.

Of course he would, if for nothing else than a statement of his adulthood. That was fine with Jim. He'd ferry the girls. He knew Cole resented having to go to the party but Jim didn't mind. He loved his sisters and wanted only what was best for them. If it interfered with his own plans, so be it. He and Cole were miles apart on that kind of thinking.

Jim glanced over at Cole and Jarrett. He knew that Jarrett had been talking to Cole about joining up with the guerillas because

Cole had bragged about it to him. As far as Jim was concerned, that would be a huge mistake. Those boys were vicious. If Cole got involved with them it would be dangerous and surely wouldn't benefit him in any way. To say nothing of the hell there'd be to pay when their father found out.

As Cole moved toward his horse Jim noticed that Bobby had followed him out to the barn.

"You're lucky you're going to the dance, Jim." Bobby wished he could go along. Not to be with the older boys, with their big talk, or the girls in their stupid dresses, but just to be doing something.

"If you say so," Jim shrugged.

"I can't do *nothin'*."

"Anything," Jim corrected.

Bobby sighed. Even Jim was more interested in correcting his grammar than listening to what he had to say.

"Pa won't even let me ride my horse off the property. That stinks. What am I supposed to do with my time?"

"You could read," Jim suggested.

Bobby rolled his eyes. He was talking about something *fun*.

"I just wish all this was over." Bobby looked at the ground.

"We all do, Bobby."

"I know."

He sat on a hay bale and looked at John Jarrett. He didn't understand why some of his family didn't seem to like Josie's husband. He seemed all right. His gaze returned to Jim. He wondered if Jim liked John, because he had never known Jim to not like anybody.

Bobby's thoughts were interrupted by the appearance of Sally and Caroline. Dressed in ruffled dresses, the girls were anxious to board the buggy and be off to the Mockbee's to enjoy time with their friends.

"You girls look lovely," Jarrett remarked.

"Thank you, John," they replied in unison.

"I'll see y'all later," Jarrett nodded. "Have a nice time."

He turned back into the shadow from which he came and disappeared into the night.

Martha's party was just what the young people of the area seemed to need. There was so much discord and instability that it seemed like months since they had been able to dance, laugh and enjoy each other's company. They were kicking up their heels and putting aside all their concerns and fears, even if it was just for the night. Paper chains hung about the room and an assortment of treats were placed on tables. The atmosphere pulsed with the excitement of the young women.

Sally and Caroline stood with a group of their closest friends. Ben Lykins was keeping them all entertained with his silly jokes.

"What do you call cattle with a sense of humor?" Ben's eyes twinkled.

"What?" everyone yelled in unison.

"Laughing stock!"

They all groaned.

As they laughed they were approached by a man dressed in the attire of the Militia. The cluster of young people quieted and guardedly scrutinized the soldier. He had already drawn their attention by approaching one girl after another to ask that they dance with him. He'd become increasing annoyed when, one by one, they turned him down. They had no idea who he was and why he was even at this party. There had been talk that maybe he should be asked to leave.

Now he was addressing Sally Younger.

"How 'bout *you* dance with me?"

"Thank you, sir," Sally primly replied. "But no."

"Well, I say yes," he insisted.

"I suggest you might want to leave, Sir," recommended Ben Lykins. "Clearly the ladies are not interested in dancing with you tonight."

"Well now, don't they all think they're *special*," the soldier spat. "C'mon and dance with me and I'll show you *special*," he leered at Sally, roughly pulling her arm.

It happened quickly.

Out of the corner of his eye Cole saw the soldier's hand grab his sister. In a matter of seconds he was across the floor.

"Get your hands off my sister!" he demanded, yanking the man's arm away.

The soldier's face colored as he stepped back and glared. How dare this overgrown...*farm boy*...touch him? He was Captain Irvin Walley and he was Missouri Militia. He wasn't going to be spoken to like that. Who did this kid think he was? Oh yeah...he might've seen him around John Jarrett, before Jarrett went deep. And Jarrett was with Quantrill's louts, he was sure of it. Bushwhackers. The criminal scum who hid in the woods and sneaked around ambushing *real* soldiers.

"You one of those sneaky-shit raiders, boy?" Walley sneered. "Where's that coward Quantrill and his stinking spineless school-boys hiding this week? Where is he, boy?"

Cole's anger was palpable. This man had no business here at a party of friends. Especially because, if nothing else, he was with the state Militia and they were little more than a bunch of rotten Yankees. Cole clenched his fists and held his tongue. He knew that this was not the time or place to get into it with this damn *cadet.* Not with the girls around. He wouldn't put his sisters in the middle of something like that, although he would love to knock the arrogant bastard on his Bluebelly ass.

"I don't know what you're talking about," he hissed through his teeth.

Walley glared at him. "You're a liar!"

Cole's fist shot out and struck Walley square in the mouth, knocking him to the ground.

"Nobody calls me a liar!"

Walley struggled to his feet and grabbed onto Cole. The two grappled; arms straining, faces red. Soon Walley was again on the floor.

His hand quickly went to his sidearm.

Joe Worth kicked at Walley's hand, knocking the gun loose.

Cole was restrained by two of his friends while several others dragged Walley up on his feet.

"You're leaving, soldier," one of them told Walley as they pushed him in the direction of the door.

Walley pushed them off.

"Unhand me!" The command of his voice made the young men back off. Walley straighten his coat and glared at Joe Worth. "Hand me my weapon. Now!"

Silence.

Looks were exchanged and an unvoiced agreement was reached. As Joe Worth stepped forward to offer Walley his gun, butt first, a wall of bodies separated Walley from Cole.

Walley held his glare while he holstered his gun. He finally turned on his heel and walked toward the door. He stopped there and turned to face the room.

"This isn't over," he announced before walking out the door into the night.

Cole was livid. He hadn't wanted to be part of a public squabble. That was the last thing his father needed to hear. Damn that Yankee!

He brushed off his clothing as his friends clapped him on the back. He was too concerned about the consequences to stand in his glory. He pushed them aside to look for Martha Mockbee amidst the throng of young people who by now were excitedly discussing what had just happened.

"I apologize, Martha," he addressed his hostess.

"I don't believe that was your fault, Cole," she replied.

Martha secretly rather liked the idea that the Yankee had been put in his place. As long as no one was hurt, she would enjoy everyone talking about what happened at "Martha Mockbee's party".

Cole turned to tell Jim that they would be leaving. Sally and Caroline had already gathered their cloaks. They issued hurried apologies to Martha, who hugged them in understanding, and the four of them were soon out the door. Jim rushed ahead to fetch the buggy.

"Cole, how could you!" moaned Caroline as she watched Cole mount his horse.

Cole didn't bother responding; he was still seething.

Jim helped his sisters up into the buggy and turned to Cole. Cole frowned at him, ready to be angry at his brother for chastising him too.

"Cole, I don't think you had any choice."

Jim considered himself a gentleman but the soldier had not only called Cole a liar but had grabbed their sister's arm. He couldn't fault Cole for his reaction.

"Thank you, Cole." Sally blew Cole a kiss. "I appreciate your standing up for me."

Caroline looked at her sister in disbelief.

"It was the honorable thing to do," Sally pronounced. "Father will be proud of Cole."

Cole didn't know about that.

CHAPTER 6

Henry was sitting in the parlor when the young people arrived home. He found solitary solace in the pleasantly decorated room, especially in the nighttime hours after most of his family had gone to bed. He had been reading but comfortably enfolded in his easy chair, he had fallen into a light sleep. He awoke when he heard his daughters enter the house.

Caroline was staying over and she and Sally quickly crossed the floor to kiss their father goodnight. They had agreed on the way home that it should be up to Cole to tell him about what happened at the party. They rushed upstairs but waited at the top to hear what their brother was going to say.

By the time Cole and Jim entered the room Henry was tapping his pipe and preparing to retire to bed.

"Did you young people have a nice time?" he asked.

Jim looked at Cole. He was going to keep his mouth closed.

Henry was the father of fourteen children and he had long ago learned to read the signs when any of them had become involved in some foolishness that made it uncomfortable to face him.

"What is it?" He looked at Cole, instinctively knowing that the trustworthy Jim had not likely been involved in whatever it was that had them both looking grim.

"I'm sorry, Pa." Cole began. "I didn't start it…"

Henry sighed. "Oh Coleman, what have you gotten yourself into now?"

"It really wasn't his fault, Pa."

Cole looked at Jim with surprise. He couldn't recall the last time Jim had defended him to their father, if ever.

Henry was just as taken aback as Cole and quickly realized that whatever it was that happened was out of the ordinary.

"Stop beating around the bush and tell me what happened. Cole?"

As Cole recounted what had transpired at the party, Henry grew increasingly troubled. Surely Cole, of all people, knew the instability of the area and recognized that the Militia was not of a collective mind to be challenged by anyone, let alone a young man of seventeen. Cole might be big and dominant for his age but he wasn't, whether he liked it or not, truly an adult. At least not in Henry's mind.

John hadn't been asleep and was listening to every word of the account of what happened at the dance from the stairwell, just beyond where his sisters had stopped.

Bobby crouched beside him, awakened by John's tug on his arm.

"Bobby! Cole punched a Militia man! C'mon!"

Roused out of their sleep by the scampering of their brothers, Emma and little Retta stood by their bedroom door.

Bobby inched forward. Their father didn't look pleased about it but his older brothers told him plenty of times to stick up for their sisters. Just because it was a man in the Militia shouldn't mean that he should get away with being rude to Sally.

"He didn't leave me any choice, Pa," Cole was saying.

"That's showing 'em, Cole!" piped John.

"John, go back to bed! You too, Bobby. This doesn't concern either of you." The last thing Henry needed to think of was John and his unquenchable need for excitement. He watched as John and Bobby reluctantly returned to their room. Emma and Retta followed behind.

"Coleman." He drew his hand over his face. "You've confronted a member of the Militia. Do you realize the consequences this could have?"

Whether or not it was appropriate, Cole's action would likely have an adverse aftereffect. Certainly for Cole, perhaps for the family. He let out a long breath.

"Cole, you were not wrong to come to the aid of your sister...."

Cole couldn't believe his father was actually approving of what he had done. He nodded his head vigorously.

"That damn Bluebelly..."

Henry put up his hand to stop Cole from speaking. "*But...* you've made yourself, if not this family, a target for unpleasantness."

Cole stopped talking. He knew his father was right.

Henry paced the room. He had to think how to handle this. He had to decide quickly what would be best for his family and what would be best for his son.

"Cole," he decided. "I want you to leave immediately and go up to the Jackson County farm. The Kimberlins will take you in."

"Pa..." Cole protested. "I'm not running scared from any Yankee!"

"You'll do as you're told, young man." Henry grabbed Cole's shoulder. "From what you have told me of the impulsiveness and manner of that soldier he is *not* going to let this matter go. Like it or not, the Militia is the authority around here and this man *will* have his say. It's best for you to go up to Jackson County, have nothing more to do with him until he leaves the area with his unit, and lie low until this matter blows over."

"But Pa..." Cole shook his head.

"I'll hear no protest, Coleman. This is how we're going to handle it." Henry turned to Jim. "Jim, help your brother gather some things. Cole, you need to leave immediately."

Cole looked down, frustrated and defeated.

"Son," Henry said gently. He reached out and squeezed Cole's shoulder. "It's for the best."

Jim ran upstairs then joined Cole in the barn. He helped Cole throw some clothes and a bedroll up on his horse while Henry went upstairs to raise his wife and tell her what had happened.

"Runnin' away like a damn coward!" Cole raged. "What does that say about me as a man?"

"Pa's just protecting you and the family," Jim reasoned. He knew that the less said to his brother, the better.

"Against what? One goddamned Yankee? I should find that son-of-a-bitch and have it out with him right here and now!"

Cole crossed the barn and reached behind a stack of tack. He pulled out a small wooden box. He opened the lid. A .36 caliber Navy Colt revolver sat nestled inside.

"You're taking that?" Jim whispered. "It's against General Fremont's orders for a civilian to be armed!"

"To hell with John C. Fremont and his damn orders. I'm not going out there without a gun while some Yankee bastard is looking for me!"

He walked over to the wall and grabbed his father's Greener shotgun.

"Might as well take this too."

"You're doing the right thing, Cole!" John stepped out of the shadows. "Those Yankees are sure enough gonna have guns and they'll shoot you dead if you don't shoot 'em first!"

Cole ignored him.

"Are you crazy, Cole?" Jim knew his brother was impulsive but this was just looking for trouble. Serious trouble.

"Maybe so, Jim," Cole coolly replied. "But I'm crazy and armed."

CHAPTER 7

B obby hadn't said anything as John pitched himself out their bedroom window and shinnied down a tree. He knew there was no way that John wasn't going to be involved in this. As he leaned on the sill of the open window, he watched Cole place the rifle across his saddle. Cole was going to be in trouble now. Wait until Pa found out about that. Just *wait* until Pa found out about that.

Cole was not gone more than twenty minutes when there was a pounding on the door. Bursheba looked at her husband with alarm. She had recently lost one son and the thought that another was in danger terrified her.

John had run back, climbed up the tree and entered through the window before his father could catch on that he'd gone out to the barn. When he heard the horse approaching, he joined Bobby at the top of the stairs. This was the most exciting things that had happened around here in a long time.

"Cole took a gun with him!" he whispered to Bobby.

"I know." Bobby's heart was thumping

Bursheba asked Emma to take Retta back to bed and since they both were sleepy that hadn't been an issue. Now the older girls and Jim stood with their mother.

"Open up!" yelled someone from outside.

Henry put his finger to his lips, crossed the room and opened the door.

On the other side stood Irvin Walley.

"We're here for your son, Sir!" Walley demanded.

"My son is just going to bed," Henry gestured at Jim. "The younger ones are already there."

"We're looking for *Cole* Younger," Walley announced. "It'd be best for your family if you just hand him over."

"Now why would you be interested in Coleman?" Henry questioned. "He doesn't have anything to do with the military."

"He's a spy for Quantrill," Walley accused. "You'd best fetch him right now."

"A spy for Quantrill?" Henry asked incredulously. "He's just a boy."

"He ain't no boy and you damn well better believe he's a spy for Quantrill. We'll take him by force if we have to."

Bursheba, ashen faced, stepped forward.

"My son Coleman is not even in this house. You're scaring my children and I'd like you to leave right now."

"Bursheba..." While Henry wished that his wife would let him handle this he wasn't surprised that she spoke up. She was a fiercely protective mother.

"Give us Cole, ma'am. Now. And then we'll leave." Walley was clearly enjoying the discomfort he was causing. He would have his payback against that arrogant upstart.

"As my wife said, he's not here." Henry had heard enough. "I'm asking you politely to leave."

"I don't care what you're asking," Walley countered, thrusting his chin forward.

"Have it your way, then." Henry stepped forward. "I'm *demanding* that you leave."

Walley only grew all the angrier. First the kid, now his old man. He began to shoulder his way past Henry and into the house.

"We'll just see for ourselves!"

44

As Henry resisted, one of Walley's men ran up to the porch. "There's a lantern still burning in the barn, Captain!" he shouted excitedly. "Looks like he maybe just left from there!"

Walley looked at Henry with contempt. He turned heel and walked toward the barn. He paused, looking over his shoulder.

"This isn't done, Younger," he spat through clenched teeth. "Not by a long shot."

Armed with the revolver and on the run from the Militia, Cole Younger was now an outlaw. It bothered him that his father was going to be disappointed in him when he found out he had taken the pistol and shotgun, but that was nothing new. Hell, his father was always going to be disappointed in him. He would never live up to Dick and that was a fact. But whether or not his pa would approve, he sure wasn't going to go off to Jackson County without being armed. Back at the party Walley had been close to shooting him. If Tom hadn't kicked the gun away he might be laid out in the family's parlor with ice blocks at his feet by now. He knew those Militia boys; Walley would be gunnin' for him. And he was not going to be faced against without a weapon, regardless of what his pa thought, regardless if it was legal.

As he rode north, his mind played over the events of the evening. It was interesting that Walley would think that he was a spy for Charlie Quantrill. He didn't even know where those boys were. Nobody did for sure. They were likely somewhere nearby, since Jarrett had been around to talk with him earlier and had so much as told him so. Cole remembered Jarrett mentioning that if he ever wanted to find him, a good place to start was in what they used to call the Woolley Creek area up behind the old house. But for God's sake, Jarrett warned him, don't breathe a word of that information to anyone.

Cole was almost at that location now. He began to consider the possibilities. There was no way that he could turn back from taking the gun. He'd already done it. He wasn't a spy for Quantrill but if he was going to be accused of being associated with those boys why the hell not? Why the hell not up and join with 'em? There would be a bad situation when his father found out that he had the gun. His pa was too honorable to just ignore the fact that Cole had broken the law. So he'd be in deep trouble anyway. He was almost eighteen. He wasn't a boy who could be taken behind the barn and whupped. He was a man, damn it.

Yeah, why the hell not? If he was going to be accused of being a Quantrill man, he might as well *be* a Quantrill man.

It surprised him that they weren't that hard to find. They were just where Jarrett had told him they might be. Sure, he heard the click of a number of gun hammers but they seemed to have sized him up pretty quick.

"Who goes?" had been called out to him as he sat on his horse.

"Cole Younger," he had responded.

He wasn't told to approach the group. John Jarrett came out to him.

"What're you doin' up here, Cole?" Jarrett smiled. "Thought you were at a party."

Cole slid off his saddle and to the ground. As he explained to his brother-in-law all that had transpired in the last few hours, Jarrett began to smile.

"Ya done good, kid. You put that Yankee bastard in his place. On the floor."

Cole had been startled by the guffawing that came out of the darkness. They must have been listening to the exchange.

Jarrett put his hand on Cole's shoulder. "C'mon and say hello to the boys."

Cole had never felt more like a man than when he sat alongside the small band of six. They may have been few but they looked like they would slit your gut and eat your liver without thinking twice. He recognized a couple of them. They were Jackson County boys and he figured so were the others. He was a little nervous but when Jarrett informed the others that "this is the kid I've been telling you about" he felt ten feet tall. But he knew better than to show any signs of cockiness less they think he wasn't impressed to be in their company.

And he was impressed. These boys didn't just talk about facing off against Yankees the way Cole and his friends did. They took it to heart and laid claim.

By the end of the evening the group of Bushwhackers had decided they'd give the kid a shot and see if he was all Jarrett thought he might be. They'd have their eye on him, though. He wasn't to think otherwise for even a minute.

They needn't have worried.

Cole never looked back.

As to Henry's stance on the matter, he drew further into himself when he heard about Cole and the gun. He couldn't bear the thought of losing another son so he dismissed it from his mind as best he could. He preferred to live in an emotional world of his own design. He took care of the needs of his family but he still refused to acknowledge that the War was bit by bit, day by day, destroying Western Missouri. As he continued to mourn Dick and worry over the safety of Cole and his involvement with the Irregulars – oh yes, he'd heard - he seemed to move through his life almost as an apparition.

John was pleased that his father allowed him to work afternoons at the livery now, as it allowed him a chance to interact with the men who frequented it and listen to their talk about the War.

"Cole's lucky." John wished he was old enough that he could be out there raising hell with his brother.

"He better be careful, that's all." Bobby didn't know what to expect. The way Cole shot off his mouth at the drop of a hat could get him in even more trouble than he was in. When John told him that Cole had taken not only one weapon, but two, well that had seemed an even more foolish and dangerous thing to do.

"Aw, he'll do just fine. He ain't afraid of nobody."

"Just sayin'."

Bobby tried not to think of what might be happening to Cole. He'd turned his attention to his school work and the time he worked helping his father at the dry goods store. It gave him the opportunity to keep an eye on his pa; who still wasn't acting right. Everybody in the family was trying to help him get over Dick dying and his worrying about Cole but he just wasn't the same as he was before all that happened. Nothing was the same.

He guessed it might never be ever again.

CHAPTER 8
Summer, 1862

The floral trellis tablecloth was rich with bone china bowls filled with the fundamental food needed to invigorate the family which sat before it. Bobby was restless as he looked around the table at his brothers and sisters; since his schoolteacher called off their classes whenever she felt they might be "exposed to danger", he was stuck at home with his sisters a lot. He was tired of their chatter and he didn't want to listen to it now. It still seemed odd that Cole wasn't there, saying something he shouldn't and making somebody mad. And John was going to get them both in trouble if he didn't stop flinging peas at him. Jim watched John, rolling his eyes but, as usual, not saying anything. Bobby elbowed John and John shoved him.

Henry heaped more potatoes on his plate. He'd heard the reports of Quantrill's activities, although he was sure that they were exaggerated. His neighbors were far too consumed and anxious with all that. He realized that the reality of war was of grave concern to each and every one of them, but he didn't see the reason why they shouldn't all just go about their lives as best they could. That was just what he intended to do. He cleared his throat and all activity at the table stopped.

"I'll be leaving on a business trip," he announced.

Bursheba looked at him in surprise.

"The unpleasantness has affected the store and I need to bring in some new items that will excite our customers."

"Can I go, Pa?" John leaned forward in excitement.

"Not this time," Henry replied. "I'm going to New York."

"Henry!" Bursheba was shocked. He was going to leave them in the middle of a war and travel to New York? What was he thinking?

"Pa, that doesn't sound safe..." Jim began. Jim knew his father had removed himself from the reality of the War but he had to realize that traveling cross-country to New York was dangerous.

Bobby stared at his father. This couldn't be a good idea even if it was his father's. He'd been studying the map Dick gave him and he knew that New York was a long way from Missoura.

"Pa, you can use me on that trip." John wasn't deterred by Henry's out-of-hand refusal to let him accompany him. "I can be your lookout!"

Bursheba was alarmed at John's offer. The fact that one of the children would even consider that he would need "a lookout" was frightening. She never questioned her husband's business decisions but surely he couldn't be seriously considering this.

"Henry, there are certainly enough goods for our neighbors here in Missouri," she appealed.

"I've decided. I'll leave the day after tomorrow. It'll be fine, dear. I'm clearly no threat to anyone and I'm sure I'll be left alone to go about my business."

Bobby frowned. From what little he knew about the War he figured *everybody* was in danger, especially if they left town. John had told him that a bunch of times. People were acting crazy, John said. You never knew who was your friend and who wasn't. There were men fighting right around here every day. That's why they couldn't have school and his pa had told him he couldn't ride his horse through the woods. His ma was always telling them to be careful and to come home at any sign of trouble. What his pa had just said didn't make any sense. And New York was so far away. How did anyone even get to New York?

"I'll be taking a coach and it will be safe." Henry nodded as if reading Bobby's mind. "Please pass the peas, Jim."

Further discussion of the issue had clearly ended.

Bobby sat on the porch. He couldn't understand why his father wasn't concerned about a trip to New York. His pa had even seemed cheerful as he told them about it and that didn't seem right. There was a war going on and people were dying every day. His pa didn't know for sure he would be safe. And he wouldn't be there to watch over the family if something bad came up. Like John always said, what the hell?

Suze had come to tell Bobby it was time to go on up to bed. He didn't hear her when she came out on the porch. She sighed. Here was that little boy sitting there looking out at nothin'. Mizz Bursheba had told her what Colonel Younger had planned and even she was concerned about it. There was nothing she could do or say – that wasn't her place – but for the life of her she couldn't understand why he would leave his family to travel east what with all of this trouble goin' on. No wonder the boy had that little frown on his face, the way he did when he was thinkin'. She sat on the porch next to him.

"It's a nice even' out."

Bobby turned to look at her. He'd known Suze since he was a baby; his whole life. She was like one of his older sisters. He trusted her to tell him the truth.

"Do you think Pa goin' to New York is peculiar, Suze?"

"I can't say as I understand it, but your daddy needs to do what he thinks he needs to do."

"But who's gonna take care of us while he's gone?"

"I s'pose we'll all take care of each other."

Bobby figured that's all she was going to say about it. He knew that she didn't have a say in family stuff anymore than he did.

"Suze, can I ask you something?"

"You can ask me whatever it is you want to ask."

"What do you think about the War?"

That was a good question. Suze had been born into slavery and she knew no other way. The Youngers always treated her right and she got along well with each and every one of them. They were family to her and she loved them. Still, the Federals said they were fighting for the Negroes. That the Negroes ought to be free men and women just the same as anyone. She agreed with that, sure she did, but her home was with the Younger family.

"I dunno," she answered honestly.

"Well, I know that a person shouldn't want to own another person." He had given that a lot of thought. "But Cole thinks that's not all the War is about. He says it's about our rights as individuals. But Negroes are individuals too."

"Yes, we are."

"You feel like an individual, right?"

She felt enough like an individual to be sittin' here talkin' to Bobby, a little white boy, but this conversation was one he should be having with his father.

"Yes, I feel like an individual. But I was born into the Younger family same as you. I love my family. There's no place else I want to be."

Bobby thought about that.

"If I had to fight for you Suze, I'd do that."

She loved this boy's heart.

"I know you would."

By May, Henry had completed his trip – somehow without any incident or discord – and returned to Harrisonville with an enticing variety of commodities for his friends and neighbors. His trip, and his making it home alive, was the talk of the town. Henry hoped his success would demonstrate to one and all that they could continue their lives without succumbing to hate and destruction.

His neighbors knew otherwise.

Despite the fact that his son and a couple of his sons-in-law fought for the Confederate cause, Henry remained neutral in his own politics. He had been generous in selling horses to soldiers regardless as to which side they were aligned but his livery had been raided several times in his absence and this wasn't an issue that he could ultimately ignore. His supply of the animals was running especially low since the latest theft.

"I'll be going up to Kansas City," Henry told his family. "I need to liquidate some of the livery's equipment so that I can replenish the supply of horses."

"Is that safe, Father?" Sally asked. Not another trip. They had worried so over the last one.

"It'll be fine, Sally. I'll travel with a few of my men. I traveled all the way to New York and back without incident, surely I will be safe on a short trip up to Kansas City."

"Can I go, Pa?" John really liked the idea of this one. He loved going to Kansas City. That was *the city*.

"No, son. I need you here."

Although he was concerned for the safety of his father, Bobby couldn't help smirking at John.

John narrowed his eyes. His brother would pay for that later.

"He's not himself, Suze," Bursheba whispered in the kitchen, away from the ears of her children. "Putting himself in harm's way again isn't responsible. He could send some of the younger, single men."

"I'm sorry, Mizz Bursheba."

What else could she say?

CHAPTER 9

Henry's trip up to Kansas City was once again, surprisingly, without incident. He was pleased that his business transactions had netted him a substantial amount of money. He needed it. The recent raids had been particularly aggressive and he had lost a lot of inventory. He had mouths to feed.

He glanced over at the young men who accompanied him. They had been loyal and hard-working under trying circumstances, he mused. They deserved some enjoyment.

'Why don't you three stay in the city overnight," he told them, as he handed them their wages. "Here's a little extra for a hotel and a meal. I'll go back to Harrisonville on my own. The sooner my family sees me, the less they'll worry."

He tucked his profit into his money belt, boarded his buckboard and began his trip home. He was actually happy to be alone. Not having the others around would provide him with an opportunity to contemplate a few things without interruption. One of the things on his mind was that he knew that it was time that he stepped back into the leadership role he usually assumed. Perhaps his good counsel could help mend his community. They would all work together and come up with a plan to resolve this terrible situation. He would think of his approach to the problem while he traveled.

Just south of Westport as he headed out of Kansas City, Henry felt as if he was being followed. He looked around but there was no one behind him.

A mile or so down the road he again heard the soft pad of hooves. He began to grow a little uneasy. If someone was in his close proximity, why didn't they simply approach him? The thought crossed his mind that someone may have known that he had a great deal of money in his belt and they might be entertaining thoughts of robbing him. Well, he would just hurry home. There was little else he could do. He clicked to his horse.

As he approached an empty and lonely stretch of road he began to grow increasingly nervous. He definitely heard horses behind him and there were several. Yet when he turned he saw nothing. He must be letting his mind play tricks on him.

"Colonel Younger!"

Well now, he was not imagining it after all. He pulled up on his reins. Surely bandits would not know him and address him in so formal a way.

He turned in his seat. He was relieved to see that the voice calling to him was not one of a brigand after all. Seven Militia soldiers were on the road behind him. He waited as they approached.

"Gentlemen," he greeted.

Two of the men rode up to the buggy while the others remained back a few yards.

The man on the left looked familiar. When he stopped a few feet in front of the buggy, Henry recognized him. It was Irvin Walley, the man who had threatened Cole.

"Don't you know better than to be out all by yourself, Colonel?" Walley questioned with a smile. "These are dangerous times. Why, you might encounter some of those Quantrill boys."

Henry sighed. He didn't want any further trouble with this young man.

"I'm just a businessman on my way home to my family, Sir."

"I'm guessing your son Cole isn't one of those family members at home?" Walley smirked. "You wouldn't happen to know where Cole is, would you? Perhaps he's over there peeking out from those bramble bushes or maybe yonder, hanging upside down from a tree limb."

Walley and his friends laughed.

"I don't know where my son is at this moment and I've got no quarrel with you men."

Henry raised his reins, anxious to move on. These soldiers were looking for trouble and he wasn't going to have it.

"Good day," he dismissed. He clicked to his horse and began to move forward.

Walley moved his horse so that it was blocking Henry's buggy. His face reddened in a manner familiar to Henry from the night he had shown up at the Younger house demanding Cole.

"Hey now, I didn't say we were finished here. You show some respect to the Missouri State Militia!"

"My respect, Sir." Henry touched his hat. "Now if you don't mind…"

"But I do mind." Walley retorted. "I *mind* that your cowardly son is with that group of low-life bushwhackers lying in wait to ambush honorable Union soldiers and the proud servants of the Militia. I *mind* that so many of you yellow-bellied West Missourians are hiding and protecting them; letting them do your dirty work for you. I *mind* that your family members seem to think they're better than Irvin Walley and don't have to answer to me. I *mind* that State and Federal soldiers are lying dead in their graves while Cole Younger's *pappy* goes about his business as if he didn't have a care in the world!"

"Captain Walley…." Henry began. When was this man simply going to go away and leave him and his family alone? He threw his hand in the air. The man wasn't about to pay attention to anything he might say so why bother to even reason with him. The soldier's resentment about whatever he thought he was entitled to begrudge didn't entitle him to insult Henry, and Henry wasn't going to sit here and listen to him. He clicked his tongue again and the buggy began to move away.

"So you see Sir, I do *mind*!" Walley shouted from behind him.

Before he could be stopped by those with him, Walley grabbed his gun, aimed it at Henry and pulled the trigger.

Henry Younger was likely dead before his body hit the ground.

As he lay in the dirt, a black puddle of his lifeblood spread slowly beneath his head. That would be the only testament to his fate that Henry would be able to give.

CHAPTER 10

Cole and Frank James sat eating sandwiches in a corner of a Kansas City bar room with their hats pulled low over their faces. Earlier they happened upon a pair of Kansas stragglers that were so unnerved at the sight of them that one of them had dropped a handful of coin. Cole and Frank decided they'd use it to buy a decent meal.

Cole and Frank had become fast friends through their association with Charlie Quantrill. They called each other "Bud" and "Buck" and spent most of their free time in each other's company, same as they were doing this afternoon. They had the Quantrill experience to bind them, but the two young men were quite different in personality. Where Cole was loud and outspoken, Frank was quiet and rarely voiced what he was thinking. Where Cole was a man of words, Frank was a man of action. Cole had already demonstrated to those who led him that he was capable of sound strategic planning. Frank was making his mark as one of the most deadly of Quantrill's men. He didn't bother engaging his enemies; he'd merely shoot them full of holes and spit on their dead bodies before they had the opportunity to do it to him. Sharing a mutual hatred of Yankees and all they stood for, Cole respected Buck James as he did no other. Frank was a person who *understood*.

Now here they were, chewing on some god-love-it meat in a half-way decent wayside station.

There was a stir when two Militia officers came in and sat down at the scarred wooden bar.

Cole tensed.

"We won't even look their way," Frank murmured.

Frank's long, lean body slumped in his chair, his small but scrutinizing eyes scanning the room. He wasn't handsome. His nose was too large, his chin too prominent on his narrow face. What he lacked in appearance he more than made up for in smarts, you had to give him that. He quoted the Bible and Shakespeare equally; Frank was a self-educated intellectual. Perhaps his outwardly calm demeanor made people come to the wrong conclusion. Frank's anger boiled just below the infrequent tight smile he sometimes displayed. Let there be no doubt; Frank James was an uncompromising young man.

"Unless any more come in, we've got them outnumbered."

"No, we don't."

"They'll think we do. That's what's important."

Cole nodded and continued chewing.

"Lieutenant!"

A young soldier ran up to the man at the bar. Cole thought he looked like he was thirteen. Both sides were already having to dip into a shallow pool for recruits.

"There's been a shooting!"

The two men at the bar laughed.

"Well, no kidding, private," one of them snickered. "I believe there's a war on. There ought to be quite a bit of shooting."

Both men laughed again.

The soldier became flustered. "No, Sir. I mean, yes, Sir. I know there should be shooting Sir, but there's been a...exceptional shooting."

The lieutenant lifted his eyebrows. "*Exceptional.* That's a big word, private."

"Yes, Sir." The young man struggled to deliver his information without making a bigger fool of himself. "A civilian was shot."

The lieutenant shrugged. "Sometimes it happens."

"But this one...some men in the fifth regiment were down south of Westport and they ran into Younger's father..."

"Younger's father?"

The lieutenant didn't know what this boy was going on about but he wished he'd finishing delivering his news so that that he and his buddy could get back to their whiskey.

"Yessir, *Cole* Younger's father. You know, with Quantrill?"

"I think I know who Cole Younger is Private." The lieutenant rolled his eyes. "But I believe it's that *sumbitch bushwhacking* Cole Younger that you're referring to."

He smiled at his friend and raised his glass.

"Steady, Bud," Frank whispered to Cole. "We don't want to start something that isn't necessary."

Cole's eyes narrowed as he watched the three men. What did his father have to do with anything? It wasn't like he was involved in the War.

"Yessir, that *sumbitch bushwhacking* Cole Younger. These men ran into his father, Sir and...well, they *shot* him, Sir. He's *dead*."

Cole's face paled and his hand clenched his drink so hard the glass shattered. Although uneasiness had come over the patrons of the bar room when the two soldiers had come in, there was still enough noise that Cole's action went unnoticed. He started to rise.

Frank pushed him back into his seat. "It's probably a pack of lies, Bud. They're likely just stirring up trouble with that nonsense."

"I wanna hear it just the same, Buck."

Cole again began to get to his feet and Frank again pulled him down.

They watched as the lieutenant threw back his drink and the three men walked out of the bar.

Frank continued to hold his friend's arm. "Thomas Jefferson wrote that 'he is less remote from the truth who believes nothing than he who believes what is wrong'. There's better ways to find out the truth, Bud."

Now Frank rose and nodded that it was safe for Cole to do so.

As all eyes turned to them, the two men pushed their way out the back door.

Mrs. Washington Wells and the teenaged Sam Wells had gone to Westport for supplies and had taken the southern road on their return home. It had been a busy day and Mrs. Wells was anxious to put it behind her. Sam whistled while he drove their buckboard.

"You carry a fine tune, Sam," she complimented.

The boy smiled. Not too many people called him Sam these days. He had asked that his friends call him Charlie in honor of Charlie Quantrill.

"Goodness, Sam. Someone has abandoned their buggy," Mrs. Wells declared, motioning to the horse and buggy which stood empty near a grouping of Blackgum trees. "Now why would they do that?"

"Seems peculiar, ma'am," Sam agreed. And not a good sign. Maybe there had recently been a skirmish of some kind. Maybe there were still some soldiers in the area. He sure as heck didn't want them to become quarry, too, if that was what had become of the driver of the buggy.

"Whoa," he ordered their horse.

He didn't want to go waltzing into some kind of situation. He put his hand to his eyes and looked around him.

"Damn," he whispered.

"Sam!"

Mrs. Wells didn't like him to use colorful language. She began to scold him when she saw that his gaze had been directed to the road ahead.

"Oh!" She saw now what had caused Sam to exclaim.

A body lay in road.

"Sam, someone needs our help! Lift me down, please."

"Ma'am, hold the reins. I'll go."

Sam handed the reins to Mrs. Wells and quickly climbed down. He ran to the body and carefully turned it over. The man was clearly dead. Sam started to return to the buggy but stopped. The man on the ground looked familiar but he couldn't place him.

"He's dead, ma'am. There's nothing we can do for him."

"Oh!" Mrs. Wells repeated. "Help me down, Sam. We need to move the poor man's body out of the road."

Mrs. Wells was a kind woman and it was understandable that she would refuse to leave someone laying in the road, even a stranger.

Sam helped her down from the buggy and walked with her to the body.

"Oh, Lord have mercy!" she exclaimed. "It's Colonel Younger!"

Now Sam remembered. Mr. Younger ran the dry goods store and a livery in Harrisonville. That was why he looked familiar. *Cole Younger's pa*. Wooo-ee. There was sure gonna be hell to pay for *somebody*.

"I'll stay here with Colonel Younger, Sam, you take yonder horse and ride back to Westport," Mrs. Wells directed.

"Ma'am," Sam frowned. "I can't leave you here. There might be Militia or bushwhackers in the area still."

"Bushwhackers wouldn't have hurt Colonel Younger and damn the Yankees," Mrs. Wells spat. "You ride back to Westport and find that Colonel Peabody. He's in charge of the *Yankees*. You tell him what we found here. You tell him that Colonel Younger has been murdered. You tell him Mrs. Washington Wells is with Colonel Younger's body and expects his timely arrival."

Sam couldn't believe what he was hearing. He knew she was a Confederate supporter, but he had never heard the distaste she held for the Yankees until now. He hadn't, in fact, ever heard her angry nor have anything bad to say about anyone.

He quickly considered and decided that she was likely safe – even Yankees wouldn't hurt an old woman. The best thing was to quickly do as she directed and just as quickly get back here to take her home. He unhitched Mr. Younger's horse and rode off at a gallop to find Colonel Peabody and deliver Mrs. Washington Well's very firm instructions.

CHAPTER 11

This wasn't happening. Bobby stood on the side of the porch from which the Union soldiers had just stepped down. This couldn't be happening. They were wrong. They had to be wrong.

Yet from inside the house he could hear his mother's wails, his sisters sobbing.

He watched as the men struggled to lift a body from the back of a buckboard. He frowned. Why were they doing this? Why were they putting his ma, his family, through this? Maybe they thought this fella looked like his pa....but...no, he would never believe it for a minute. The Yankees always got everything wrong. John had told him that over and over.

He watched as the captain in charge walked ahead of the men carrying the body.

"Ma'am?" he called. "Where would you like us to put the body?"

Just like that. "The body." They weren't showing any respect. That proved they were wrong. If the man who was shot was really his father, they would have to show respect. His pa was respected by everybody who knew him. The way they were acting proved it wasn't his pa's body they were delivering.

Jim had helped Bursheba inside and now, ashen-faced, walked back outside. In shock, barely looking at the soldiers, he motioned inside.

"In here," he all but whispered. "Bring my father in here."

"No, Jim, it's not Pa..." Bobby assured him. "It's not Pa."

Jim looked at Bobby, his expression blank. He turned back to the soldiers and again motioned inside.

As the two soldiers mounted the steps, awkwardly holding the body and carrying it in through the door, Bobby looked at the face of the man they bore.

He ran down the porch steps and vomited onto the ground.

John's horse thundered into the yard.

"You Bluebelly sons-of-bitches!" John screamed as jumped to the ground and ran toward the group of soldiers that stood beside the buckboard. "You damn Yankee sons-of-bitches!"

He ran up to the first soldier in his path and struck him with all the anger a young boy could contain. The soldier flinched away from him and the others moved to push John backward.

"Lay off, boy," one of them quietly ordered. "We're sorry about your pa and all but don't you be hitting Union soldiers."

"I'll kill you!" John continued to strike out and kick at them. "I swear it, I'll kill every last one of you!" he swore through tears of anger and anguish.

"That's enough." the Captain grabbed John by the neck and roughly threw him to the ground. "Don't threaten people who have authority over you, boy. We've had a belly full of you Youngers. Now you lay off before we either throw you the hell somewhere you don't want to be or leave you lying inside next to your old man."

John sprang to his feet and lunged at him. Within a second the soldier reacted, grabbing his revolver and slamming the barrel against the side of the boy's head.

John reeled with the force of it. As the bile rose in his throat, he tried to protest but instead lost consciousness and fell bleeding to the ground.

"We're done here," the captain informed his men with a nod. They mounted their horses and rode slowly, confidently, down the road.

As angry as he had been with the politics of the War and the presence of the Union forces in Western Missouri, Cole couldn't contain himself with the diamond sharp hatred he now felt for the State Militia and the Federal government. He hated them for all they represented and he hated them now for the cowards they were. Without reason they had killed a good man – one who had taken no side and who had no enemies - and then they gun-butted his grieving son, a boy. The vendetta Walley had launched against him was not only outrageous; it wouldn't be tolerated. Walley obviously wanted to make this a personal war and that was what he was going to get.

Of course if Cole's plan was successful, it wouldn't much matter what Walley thought.

Walley was proud of himself for avenging his humiliation at the hands of the Younger family and he didn't see any reason why what went down on the Independence Road should be kept secret. His vanity and self-satisfaction, however, looked like it might cost him. When confronted with his crime, Walley claimed that Henry Younger, being the father of the guerilla Cole Younger, was obviously not only an enemy of the Union but also a threat to it. He also claimed that the killing of the senior Younger was in self-defense. His men would back him.

Evidently, so would the Missouri State Militia. Rather than hold Walley accountable out of hand, Brigadier General Benjamin Loan called for a trial to be held in Independence. At that point the men who accompanied Walley on the road the day of Henry Younger's death would have the opportunity to tell their story. Irvin Walley, unlike Henry Younger, would get his day in court.

"They're going to let that bastard go Scot free!"

Cole was beyond furious when he learned through word of mouth of this latest affront to his family.

"They're going to let his men tell his side. Those lying sons-of-bitches will back him up!"

Although he didn't know Henry Younger, Frank James was as outraged at the murder of Bud's father as the rest of Quantrill's men. It could have been any of their fathers, any member of their families.

Frank's father, a circuit preacher, had taken off for California many years before, ostensibly to bring the Good Word to those seeking their fortune there. Though Frank sometimes wondered if his father's leaving had more to do with his wanting to get away from the acid tongue of his mother, he had been a good man and Frank loved him. He could only imagine how he would feel if it had been his defenseless father that Walley killed.

"Ya gotta kill 'em, Bud. All of 'em. You know that, don't you?" he mused.

"Of course I do," Cole agreed. "They're not getting away with this. They're going to die. Every last one of them."

Frank wanted to be there to watch Walley die, oh yes he did, but when Quantrill called on Frank to help with a special mission, Cole was on his own. That fact didn't alter his plan. There were more than a few of his new friends who offered to ride with him to face-off with the detestable men who had broken the rules of combat by an act of sheer murder. Cole selected five of them to accompany him.

They would be *his* jury.

Before long, by listening to the constant human telegraph within the guerilla network, he knew the whereabouts of those he sought and moved forward with his plan to annihilate them.

He found them on the road to Independence where they were indeed headed to testify on Walley's behalf. His retribution was quick.

As he later walked amid the brutal carnage of their last encounter with anyone named Younger, Cole realized that Walley wasn't among the bodies that lay before him.

That was a fact that Cole Younger would regret until his very last day on earth.

CHAPTER 12

Henry Younger was laid to rest out at the Hardup Cemetery. When it was safe, when no one might threaten his resting place because of his son Cole's affiliations, he would be moved back home to lay under the Sycamore tree next to his son Dick.

It crossed Bobby's mind that maybe that was where his father really wanted to be all along.

Obviously Cole couldn't attend his father's funeral. His enemies would be watching closely; ready to capture and bring him in…or worse. Yet even their best efforts to carefully observe the comings and goings of the Younger family didn't detect Cole's visit to his mother during the dead of night a few days after the burial of his father.

Bursheba heard the whispers of what had happened to Walley's soldiers on the Independence Road and she knew she would not have been in any way able to prevent it. She also knew that the hideous vendetta of Irvin Walley would not end with her husband's death. A vicious circle of retaliation had been set into motion and there was no way it would terminate without someone backing away from it.

"If you don't stop this here, son, it will never end." She sat in her bedroom chair with Cole on his knees before her. He held her hand.

"Ma, that Yankee scum has to pay for this! Pa deserves that much!"

"Harming Mister Walley..." She refused to acknowledge his rank. He had in no way acted with the nobility of an officer. "It won't bring your father back. What it will bring is more pain and more sorrow. And Cole, I don't know how I could face that."

"But Ma..."

Bursheba closed her eyes and prayed for the words that would reach her son. She knew his loyal character and she knew that what she was asking him went against all that he stood for and all that he believed. She opened her eyes and squeezed his hand.

"Please, son. I'm begging you. To respect the goodness and reputation of your father, don't bring him dishonor. Promise me, Cole; please promise me that you will end your efforts to... deal....with Mister Walley. For your father's sake, for mine. For the sake of our family."

When all was said and done, only the profound love of a son for his mother allowed Bursheba to extract that assurance from Cole. Cole would abandon his plans to kill Irvin Walley. Granting his mother a pledge that he would never have agreed to had it been a request from anyone else, Cole promised his mother that unless he encountered Irvin Walley in the field of combat he would not make any further effort to avenge his father.

Cole left his mother sitting in her room. There was nothing else he could say to her that would bring her comfort. He joined his brothers in the parlor where the room was cloaked in dim light and faint shadow.

"You have to kill him, Cole," John urgently whispered from where he lay on the daybed. The pain in his head was still so great that he was barely able to lift it. But he knew what had been asked of Cole; they all did. "You have to finish it."

Cole walked over to John and patted his shoulder. It killed him, it absolutely killed him, to see the boy hurt so badly from the hand of a man both older and more physically powerful. If it was possible, his hatred of his sworn enemy grew even stronger just from looking at John's pale and determined face. But Cole had made a promise to his mother and now he needed to find the words to explain it to the boy who had so bravely stood for their father.

"John, I know you want revenge. So do I."

"Then don't let Ma make you promise to let Walley go free of this, Cole," John begged. "Don't let her make you promise!"

Cole looked at his little brother, wrapped in the gloom of the room, of the house, of all within. Cole had witnessed firsthand the horrors of the War; the lengths men of both sides would go to impose their will on others, whether they were right or wrong. He'd seen the power of might and the power of partiality and hate. He had taken a stand for what he believed; they all did, both Confederate and Union. He strongly supported the belief that here in Missoura, the issue wasn't really slavery but the demand for a rigid control. It hardly mattered anymore. Regardless of the issues, brutality occurred each and every day now, both sides involved. Rather than trying to reach a compromise or allowing each other to choose the way they were going to live their lives, it had come to this. This was the United States of America and it had come to this. And it was because of that intolerance and hatred, because of this war, that his family was in this position. Like so much of the talk, and so many of the actions, the killing of his father had been personal; not an act of war but an act of pure and personal vengeance. How could he explain that the man who had murdered their father was going to be allowed to go unpunished?

"Cole made a promise to Ma, John."

Bobby had been sitting quietly on the floor, his back against the legs of the hunter green winged chair where his father had once enjoyed reading periodicals. Over the past year he had watched everything he loved and enjoyed turned upside down and because he was the age he was he hadn't been able to do a thing about it. He wanted that man to pay for taking his father away; he wanted Walley to be lying dead in a hole just like his pa.

But a promise was a promise and this one seemed like the right thing to do. He knew his father wouldn't want revenge in his name. He knew in his heart that was true.

"You can't go against Ma, Cole."

Cole's lips grew tight as he nodded at his youngest brother.

Jim sat in the corner of the room. He knew about the vicious altercations between the Militia and Quantrill's men but the malicious murder of his father didn't make any sense to him. It was beyond his understanding how anyone could consider his father, a man of peace and compromise, a threat. He had not agreed with Cole's dedication to "The Cause", as Cole put it. He didn't believe that taking matters into your own hands could amount to anything other than more of the same but he questioned now if maybe his way of thinking had been wrong.

"What we want and what Ma needs are two different things, John." Cole spoke quietly. "Ma has lost her son and now her husband. Every day she worries about me and my safety." He closed his eyes and exhaled. "She needs to not worry about me doing in Walley and then his boys coming around here to take their revenge on one of you. I need to honor Pa and I need to honor Ma. I need to let this go."

"But Cole…" John couldn't believe that he was hearing Cole back down from something so important, whether or not it was to honor their ma and pa.

Cole put his hand up. "But I promise you, John, one way or the other, we'll have our revenge on these Yankees. I *promise* you that. They've made it personal and so will we. This war ain't over. Not by a long shot. We'll have our opportunity and when it comes we'll *take* it. I promise you that. We'll *take* it."

As Cole started to leave Jim motioned to him that he would like a word.

"Be quick about it," Cole encouraged. "Every minute I'm here is more dangerous for the family."

Jim looked at his feet.

"What is it, Jim?" Cole demanded. "I've got to go!"

Jim took a deep breath.

"Maybe I should go with you, Cole."

"What are you talking about?"

"Maybe I should go with you and fight."

Cole couldn't believe what he was hearing. Jim was the level-headed brother. The peacemaker. The one most like their father now that Dick was gone. Growing up he had often mocked Jim for fighting his battles with words rather than with his fists.

"*You?*"

"I'm just as capable as the rest of you." He raised his chin and stared down his older brother. "I can fight."

Cole started to laugh but then realized that Jim was dead serious. He didn't have time for this ridiculous conversation. Jim was no more a fighter than Cole was a pig farmer.

"Jim, your place is here, protecting Ma and our sisters.' He hugged his brother. "That's just as important as fighting right now. I gotta go."

With that Cole was out the door and into the night.

Bobby overheard the conversation and was relieved that Cole had said Jim shouldn't go with him. They needed Jim here. What would they do if Jim wasn't here?

He watched Cole slip through the back woods. John could think what he wanted and be upset that Cole wasn't going to hunt down Walley but Bobby knew that Cole was a man of his word. He would keep his promise to their mother. That was the right thing to do. But if Cole said the matter wasn't settled then the matter wasn't settled. That was the way Cole felt and it was now the way that he felt himself.

Bobby Younger had never known or understood hatred but by everything that he was and all that he had yet to be, he knew it now.

CHAPTER 13

Bursheba Younger had six children still at home and she knew she must go on giving them her loving best. Only two years ago her family had been intact and everything had been lovely. The future she envisioned for her children, which was once so promising, was not this. It was not anger, it was not murder. It was not war. Like Henry, she had seen her sons' futures as contributors of innovative thoughts through public or private service. Her daughters would marry well and both the Fristoe and Younger names would continue to represent honor and esteem. She now questioned if that future would ever come to fruition and in her darkest moments she doubted that it would.

Their beloved Dick, once so bright and shiny, now lay in a grave she could see from her bedroom window. The husband she adored lay in his own dirt-covered cavity. Her married daughters and their husbands were struggling, trying their best to make their way during this dire season of abhorrence and distrust. She had closed her eyes and ears when Josie's husband John had first begun to talk of intimidation and retribution. Henry had stepped in and clearly instructed John that such talk was not welcome in their home. Now it was the talk of all her friends and neighbors.

Cole, her volatile boy, was off God knows where doing God knows what. She feared now not only for his safety but for his life. Her other three sons were made tense, troubled and angry by the malicious actions of those around them. Her small daughters were fraught with fear. How could she explain this time, these horrible events, to them? How could she teach them not to hate those who were dedicated to the destruction of their family? She didn't know. God help her, she didn't know. Yet somehow she must find a way. She could not turn her back on everything that was good, everything that was moral and principled. Her devout Christianity firmly established that she teach her children that they love and respect their neighbors, not that they fear and hate them. For the first time in her life she didn't know quite how to do that.

She sat in the parlor reading her Bible deep into the night, seeking to find the words that would bring her encouragement and direction in the harrowing days that she knew were to come.

Cole did the only thing he felt he could do; remain focused on driving his enemy out of Western Missoura. As the War grew even more ferocious, Cole rose in the esteem of those with whom he served. By now many of the Irregulars were joining forces with their brothers-in-arms and enlisting in the Confederate Army. Cole chose to enlist and he was appointed a First Lieutenant under the command of General Joseph O. Shelby.

But while Cole's star continued to rise, things only got worse for the Younger family.

On one of his trips back to Harrisonville to see his family, Cole was met in the barn by an agitated Bobby.

"Put my horse up, Bobby." Cole handed him the reins. "I've got to be careful that the Yankees don't see me here."

"Something happened, Cole." Bobby took the reins but didn't move.

'What do you mean something happened?" Cole demanded. "What happened?"

"Something happened to Sally, Cole. She's been crying in her room since the other night when the Yankees were here."

"What Yankees? Here for what?" The hairs on the back of Cole's neck stood up.

"Sally had some of her friends over. Ma told John and me to stay in our room and amuse ourselves. Ma said Sally has been so nervous about the War and that she needed to have some time to just be a girl."

"For God's sake, get to the point!"

"Well, the other girls came over and they were talking and singing in the parlor. John and I put pillows over our heads so we didn't have to hear them."

"Bobby! Never mind what you and John were doing, why were the Yankees here?"

"We heard them ride up. We looked out the window and there were about six of them. John got out that old revolver he found last summer. He doesn't have any bullets for it but he figured maybe the Yankees wouldn't know that and he could scare them off."

"What happened!"

Would this boy ever get to the point? If John pointed a gun at a group of Militia, God knew....

"Is Sally all right, Bobby?"

"I'm trying to tell you, Cole." He was telling the story the only way he knew how. "Ma wouldn't let the soldiers inside the house so the girls went outside."

"Why did they do that? That's dangerous!"

"They didn't want to but Sally was afraid the soldiers would cause trouble for Ma."

"And what the hell happened, Bobby!"

"Well, John started down with that old revolver but Ma saw him and she took it away. But she was really upset, Cole. The girls weren't friendly with the soldiers so they didn't stay long."

"They left without a problem?"

"I guess so."

"Then what is wrong with Sally?"

"Well, after the soldiers left, the girls came back inside. They wanted to go home."

"And?"

"Sally wasn't with them. They were all asking 'Where's Sally? She was with the Captain.'"

"Where was she?" Cole's blood ran cold.

"She finally came back in but she was crying. Really crying. *Hard* crying."

"Why was she crying?" If he didn't hear what had happened to Sally in the next sentence his head was going to explode.

"I don't know, Cole. I asked Ma later but she wouldn't tell me."

Cole stormed out of the barn. He climbed the stairs two at a time to Sally's room.

Bobby didn't know what had happened to his sister but he knew it was probably something awfully bad. Damn those Yankees, damn them.

Sally lay on the bed staring out the window.

As infuriated as he was that the enemy had dared entered his mother's house, he only had to look at his sister to realize that she had been more than just intimidated by a soldier.

"Sally, what happened?" Cole chewed on his cheek, trying to be as gentle as he could under the rage he felt. "Bobby told me about the Yankees being here."

"I'm afraid to tell you, Cole." She couldn't look at him. She knew what the outcome of her brother's knowledge of the hateful and despicable act she had been subjected to would be.

But he knew. She didn't have to say more than that.

"Be brave," he told his sister through gritted teeth. "That man will never bother you again."

Cole made sure of that. Gathering twelve of his guerilla friends, he quickly located the soldiers. As they reached the top of the hill and looked down at their enemy, Cole instructed those with him to not, *do not*, shoot the captain. That was the man who had victimized his sister and that act would be *his* pleasure.

When it was all over, Cole walked up to the man's bullet-ridden body and spit on it.

"Sally, I've kept my word."

That winter the son of the appointed sheriff of Cass County was killed during an encounter with some of the guerrillas and the sheriff swore out a warrant for Cole's arrest.

"I'm damned if I do, damned if I don't!" Cole railed to Frank James.

"That's what happens when you make a name for yourself," Frank smiled.

CHAPTER 14

Cole's reputation, rightly or wrongly, continued to grow and cast a long shadow over his family. He remained in the area during the winter of 1862. His current assignment only caused his family more anxiety. The Union soldiers were now making routine visits to the Younger home in their attempt to capture him. Jim was constantly being accosted with the accusation that he was a spy for Cole and the guerillas.

"Do you think it's time for me to join up?" Jim asked his brother that January.

"No, I don't, Jim. Ma and the girls need you here. And God knows what trouble John might get into. You need to keep an eye on him. Bobby will do fine."

Jim nodded. He had anticipated Cole's answer.

"I think we need to move the family further north to one of the tenant farms. They might be safer there if they aren't where the Yankees expect them to be."

"You do that," Cole agreed.

By February the Militia found them.

"Well, well, Mrs. Younger," the Union captain touched his hat. "We've missed you."

Bursheba clutched her arms. She had been fairly confident that attempting to hide from the soldiers would not be successful but for the sake of her children she needed to at least try to escape their scrutiny.

Jim hid in the backwoods. He and Cole had decided that the best way for him to avoid the soldiers was by trying at all costs not to be present when they came with their questions. Bobby had seen the men coming up the road and had run to tell Jim as he worked out back cutting wood.

"They're here!" he warned.

Jim didn't need to ask who "they" were.

Now Bobby stood by his mother's side. He might be just a boy but he'd protect her in any way he could.

"Captain," she addressed the man who sat before her on his horse. Five other soldiers watched in amusement. "How may I help you?"

"You could tell us where your son Cole is, ma'am," he smiled. "In fact, while you're at it you can tell us where your other son is too."

"My son is out tending to our business and I'm sure you know by now that I have no idea where my eldest son might be." Bursheba refused to dignify this constant inquisition by having the names of her sons bandied.

"Mrs. Younger," the captain sighed. "Why don't you make it easy on yourself...and your other children," he nodded at Bobby. "Just tell me where they are."

"Sir, I've given you my response."

The captain glowered. It was the same song and dance every time he encountered this woman. He'd had enough.

"I see." He looked back at his men. "Mrs. Younger doesn't know where her boys are. That's a shame."

He turned back to Bursheba.

"Ma'am, I'll get on with my business then. It's my duty to inform you that under the Militia's General Order Number Three, all persons who knowingly harbor, conceal, aid or abet by furnishing food, clothing, information, protection or assistance whatever, to any emissary, Confederate officer or soldier, partisan ranger, bushwhacker, robber or thief, shall be promptly executed by the first commissioned officer into whose hands he or they may be delivered, or under whose control he or they may be placed."

Bursheba gasped.

Bobby stepped in front of her.

"Leave!" the boy ordered angrily. He was tired of these men trying to push his mother around. "You get out of here right now and leave my mother alone!"

The officer ignored him.

"The houses at which these persons received food, protection or assistance in any way," he continued, "shall be destroyed."

He turned to his men. "Make your preparations."

The soldiers dismounted from their horses and began to gather kindle.

"Mrs. Younger, I've decided you and your youngest pups will live. But I'll be damned if Cole Younger and his brother will have a house to return to and hide in. Go on in and gather what you can carry. Make it quick."

He waved his men forward.

"We're going to burn this house to the ground in ten minutes."

CHAPTER 15

Spring was ostensibly for rebuilding and new beginnings. The on-going war made that impossible. Bursheba returned home to Harrisonville with her family. She attempted to dissolve most of Henry's business interests to raise the money which would make it possible to take care of her children.

Whenever any of Cole's men came through looking for food or supplies, Jim helped them however he could although it made his mother nervous.

"It's not that I begrudge those young men food and clothing," Bursheba explained to Jim. "It is dangerous for our family to provide for them. We have seen how far the Militia will go to intimidate us."

"And every other family whose son, brother, husband or father chooses to stand against them, Mother. They need what little help we can give them. Without the support of their families they'll starve."

Bursheba had no argument for that.

The degree of hatred rose on both sides. Frank James' little brother Jesse was now riding with the Irregulars under the command of the ruthless "Bloody Bill" Anderson, who was aligned with Quantrill and the Confederates. The men of this command were not in any way dedicated to the wartime "honor" of Cole

and many of his comrades. These men were ten-times more brutal and suffered no one they perceived in any way as their enemy.
If the Union forces thought Quantrill and his men were tough,
wily and ferocious, the nefarious actions of Anderson and his
men were that times ten.

"Remember what you're fighting for," Frank advised Jesse.

"Well, we ain't slitting throats for the hell of it," Jesse smirked.

"You sure about that?" Frank questioned.

"There's no mistaking that we're serving 'The Cause'," Jesse
smiled. "We ain't taking no shit from any bull-headed, interlop-
ing Bluebelly sons-of-bitches."

As the War raged on, the number of young men who
aligned themselves with the guerrilla movement grew in number and intensity. Union Brigadier General Thomas C. Ewing
was ordered to put the guerillas out of business altogether or
at the very least render them unable to continue their unremit-
ting assault against the Federal forces. Ewing's first decision was
ill-conceived at best. In an effort to cut off his enemy from their
seemingly endless supply of food, shelter and assistance, Ewing
decided to arrest their daughters, their sisters, whoever the hell
it was that was sustaining them. This coddling of the enemy was
going to end right here, right now.

Bursheba sat in the parlor. She had never felt so alone. Josie,
Caroline and Sally had been rounded up like cattle. Good God,
was there no sense of humanity left? What possible crime could
the Yankees state against her sweet daughters? The Yankees. Dear
Lord, even she was now referring to the Militia by that demean-
ing term.

She looked at her boys standing together by the hearth.
John's face was rigid with anger. Bobby's was arranged in a glare.
They had once been so full of fun and adventure and now they
were full of nothing but animosity and loathing. She couldn't
blame them for feeling that way. What counsel could she possibly
provide that would make it any different?

Bobby came over to where his mother was sitting. Caroline's husband George had been to talk with the boys. George told them not to cause trouble with the Yankees or they would make things even worse for their sisters. It was best to let the soldiers take custody of them and then they'd find a way to bring them home without antagonizing those who held them.

"Ma, George said we shouldn't break the law." Bobby looked into the weary face of his mother. "But is there even law anymore?"

"There's no damn law. Only what the damn Yankees *say* is law." John had been quiet long enough. He had grabbed the rifle Cole had hidden in the boards over Jim's bed but his mother told him she couldn't bear to see it in his hands and to please, please not give her yet another thing to worry about. Then George had come to the house and warned him outright.

"If you show that rifle you will be arrested yourself. Then who will be here to protect your mother?"

Jim had asked him for the rifle and hid it again, this time where he could easily reach it.

John was so frustrated. If he was old enough, he would be out there kicking butt. But he wasn't, so all he could do was stay here and hate every one of those stinkin' sons-of-bitches.

"That's true, isn't it Ma?" Bobby knew what John's opinion on all of this was but he needed to hear it from his mother. "The only law is Yankee law."

"Oh, Bobby." She took his hands. "Nothing is the same as it used to be. It's hard to define anything at all these days. I only know that no matter how people treat us, how mean they sometimes are, we have to stay true to ourselves."

"But none of that matters to them. No matter how we go along with what they want us to do, they just keep changing things and getting meaner."

"I know, son. That's why it's important that we react in a way that shows them they aren't going to change who we are, regardless of what we are put through. We must always meet those who want to harm us with courage and a strong commitment to what we believe as Christians, what we know to be true. That in the end it is God who judges us, not our enemies."

"I don't have a problem judging our enemies." John wasn't giving up his argument. "They all stink."

By the end of the day over a hundred women had been imprisoned. Of course this only served to infuriate the guerillas even more. They began to make their plans to storm the jail.

But their efforts weren't required after the three-story building collapsed. Several women were killed outright. Others suffered broken limbs and God knew what all.

Caroline, Sally and Josie were bruised and battered and by the time Henry's brother Frank was able to return the three women to their homes, they said they didn't know how they all could possibly go on.

"We have to go on," their uncle told them. "We're fighting for our lives now."

John pounded one fist against the other as he paced the barn. His face was set in a mask of fury.

"I've had enough, Bobby!" he spat. "We've all had enough!"

"I've had enough too." Bobby couldn't believe what had happened to his sisters. Since when were they part of the fight? They were *girls*. They hadn't done anything. "But there's nothing we can do about it. No matter what we think, there's nothing we can do about it!"

"I don't know if there is or there isn't," John growled. "But there's gonna come a day when we sure as hell can and I'm gonna ride that bull like he ain't never been rode."

He dug deep into his pocket.

"I've got something for you. I've been holding on to it."

"What is it?"

John held out two shiny buttons.

Bobby looked at the buttons and up at John.

"They're from Pa's waistcoat. I took 'em off it before he was buried."

"Why?"

"There's one for me and one for you."

"I don't understand."

"These are to remind us of those stinkin' sons-of-bitches Yankees and what they took from us, in case we ever get soft. What they took from our family. You keep this button…" He placed one in Bobby's hand. "…and you remember all they took from us." He spit on the ground. "You remember all them Bluebelly bastards took."

The guerillas had had enough too. Injuring and killing innocent women was in no way acceptable to the men of Quantrill and Anderson. As it so often was by this time, it wasn't just war; it was personal. It was now their turn to throw down their fury.

Over three hundred guerrillas rode into Lawrence, Kansas that warm morning in August. They had been whipped into such frenzy that self-control and any kind of reason were quickly cast off. Throwing aside any semblance of decency, those who rode west that day held fast to the attitude that this was revenge, pure and simple.

It was a blood bath.

"My God," Cole later expressed to John Jarrett. "Men were killed right in front of their wives…their mothers…their children! Some of them were only boys…"

"You can't let it bother you, Cole," Jarrett responded. "That's justice. Our women were wives, and mothers, and children too and they weren't treated any better."

Cole understood that yet he had witnessed some brutal and hideous battle during his time at war but the vicious slaughtering of civilians that day was not what he had signed up to support. If this was justice, justice was not only bitter but unspeakable.

"Cole and the boys really showed 'em!"

When John heard of the atrocities at Lawrence he was thrilled.

"They gave them a big fistful of the shit we've had to put up with!"

"It doesn't make sense to me." Bobby was troubled by it. "Why buck up against the Yankees by doing to everyday people like they've done to us? They should have just fought the Militia. The people they killed were just *people*. They weren't soldiers."

"Some of them were. Besides, hitting the soldiers that hard takes a lot of planning. It's not something they can just go out and do."

"They've been doing it, haven't they? Cole said the guerillas and the Confederate Army have the Yankees on the run."

"It's complicated."

"You always say that when you don't have a good answer."

Bobby drew circles in the dirt with the stick he was holding.

"The Yankees have got to be really mad at what just happened. It'll be hard to get to the Quantrill men so now they'll just punish as many regular people as they can. Something bad is gonna happen. You wait and see."

CHAPTER 16

September, 1863

B obby was right and he wasn't the only one thinking about what price the Missourians would pay for the vicious act of a few. Even so, no one expected what came next.

General Order Number 11 demanded that entire counties, some 30,000 people, leave their homes and abandon their properties within fifteen days. Those who could prove their loyalty to the Union could stay within the confines of the military stations or they could relocate to designated areas of Kansas. There was to be no objection.

"As if quibbling was a choice." Jim had suffered in silence these past few months but he was damn tired of it all.

The Union didn't care what Jim or anybody like him thought. Those dirty Rebs would surrender their crops to the Militia and whatever the Militia couldn't use or didn't want would be destroyed. End of subject.

Bursheba knew it was just a matter of time before she and the children would again be forced from their home. Thank God Henry had purchased so much land all those years ago. She moved her family to yet another house once leased by tenant farmers.

Jim took to the woods as the Militia hunted down the guerrillas and those they suspected of aiding and abetting them. He promised his mother he would find somewhere for her to go where she wouldn't be found.

"To hell with that!"

John wasn't having it.

"We're not going anywhere. You go do what you need to do Jim, but Ma and the rest of us aren't going to be run off of our own land. Not again!"

Jim knew John had seen enough to mature him beyond his physical years and his objection wasn't unreasonable. John didn't want to leave and Jim understood that. In a better world he wouldn't be telling his brothers and sisters they had to move along again. Had he or Cole been able to stay to defend the family, they would feel the same.

"We've gotta stay, Jim," Bobby agreed.

He too had seen too much. It pained Jim that Bobby had been robbed of his boyhood.

"We can't just keep running from them. They're gonna do what they're gonna do anyway."

Emma and Retta started to cry. Sally had already been placed with relatives up north to ensure that she would be far away from the Militia soldiers and any of their unwanted attention. But the little girls, only eleven and six, needed their mother.

Bursheba looked at her daughters. She didn't know how much more of this they would be put through.

"Listen to Jim, boys," she begged. "We don't know what they'll do. They've already burned one house. If we don't cooperate this time they may hurt us."

"Ma is right," Jim agreed. Nothing was guaranteed.

"Then you'd better find us a place to stay quick, Jim."

John was tired of the Yankees and everything they had put his family through just because Cole was off being "Cole the Conquering Hero". The War wasn't exciting anymore, it was just hard. Their mother had been in bed sick when the new order had been read. She had not been well for weeks and worry about her children only weakened her.

"I'm not taking Ma and the girls to join all those other people on the road going nowhere."

"I'll find somewhere to stay," Jim promised.

But he didn't get the chance.

The next day the Militia arrived at the Younger house. It wasn't the same captain that had previously ordered her to burn her home but it might as well have been. The five soldiers rode up to the front of the house.

John and Bobby stood on the porch defiantly. They each held a large rock behind their back. They would defend their family this time.

Even if they weren't the same men, the resolve of the Youngers was known to them.

"I'd put those rocks down right quick if I were you, boys." The captain pulled his revolver and aimed it at the boys.

Bobby had never had a gun pointed at him. He let his rock drop to the ground.

John stared hard at the soldier without moving.

"Now." The soldier cocked his gun.

Bursheba had risen from her bed and as she stepped down onto the porch she struggled to place herself between her sons. She put her arms around them and bore down on John's shoulder.

"Do as the man says, John," she whispered. "Please don't make this harder than it already is."

John reluctantly threw the rock off the side of the porch.

The soldier glared at him a minute before lowering his gun.

"Mrs. Younger, why haven't you complied with Order Number 11?"

"I'm not well," Bursheba told him. The soldier had only to look at her face to know that she was telling the truth. "I have no place to go and I have my four young children. It's impossible for me to leave. Please…"

The captain refused to be moved by either her condition or her words.

"Mrs. Younger," he announced officiously. "You refuse to obey Military Order Number 11. We are going to burn your buildings."

"Please, Sir...I'm ill," she begged.

It made Bobby sick to his stomach to know that not only had his family been placed in this position again but that his wonderful and brave mother had to be embarrassed like this.

Bursheba saw that there would be no amnesty for her. "If I could have just one night...," she asked.

The captain looked at the frail woman in front of him. He listened to the soft cries of the little girls and observed again the strong resolve of the two boys. He had a wife and children himself. This was a hell of a war. God only knew what he would do if it was his family standing there under these circumstances. Yet he had orders and he had responsibility which he could not deny.

"All right," he sighed. "Mrs. Younger, you may stay the night and make your plans. You will leave in the morning."

"Thank you, sir, thank you." Bursheba nodded in gratitude to the soldier."

"Don't thank me. Your family won't be excluded from the orders of General Ewing," he answered. "You will leave in the morning but you will also, by your own hand, set fire to your buildings."

The next morning John and Bobby placed kindling along the sides of the house as Jim gathered more. John was furious, Bobby resigned.

"I'm going to light this," John informed his brother. "I'm not letting Ma do it."

"I'd rather we do it too John, but Ma needs to do it." Jim was going to see to this and then leave. He was only a magnet to the Militia. "She doesn't want to place that burden on us. I don't exactly understand why she feels that way but we need to let her do what she feels she needs to do."

"None of us can do what we feel we need to do."

"This can't last much longer." Jim, as articulate as he was, was at a loss for words.

"Remember what Cole said, John," Bobby seethed.

This wasn't right. Their mother was sick and there wasn't a thing they could do to help her stand against the Yankees. He wondered what it would be like if his pa were still living. Would Pa stand up to them? Of course. He wouldn't allow all this. But his pa was a man, not a boy. There was nothing they could do.

"I have a hard time remembering everything that Cole says, Bobby." John didn't care what Cole had said.

"He said this wasn't over. We have to wait for our opportunity to get back at them."

"Yeah, well, when's that gonna come, Bobby? When everything we have is gone? When there's nothing left to take or nobody left to kick?"

"It won't be like that."

Bobby refused to give up. It surprised him that John was talking that way. John was always the one who was the maddest.

"I'm telling you this." John threw a rock and watched as it bounced across the dirt. "If a chance comes along for me to get back at 'em, they won't know what hit 'em."

John always talked big. Usually Bobby ignored it. That wasn't the case this time. He agreed.

"I want to leave, Jim."

They turned to see Emma standing with little Retta.

"I want to leave Missoura."

"Shut up, Em!" John commanded. "After all those boys are fighting and dying for? We're *not* leaving Missoura! This is *our* home!"

"You'll go with Ma to Waverly for now – stay with Aunt Nancy." Jim hated to see this. How much longer was this going to go on?

"I want to go home, Jim," the little girl cried. "And I don't even know where that is anymore."

Jim, John and Bobby made a bed in the back of the remaining farm wagon. They helped Bursheba out of the house and stood beside her as she silently lit their kindle and the wood began to burn.

Suze's heart broke as the boys lifted their mother into the wagon. She got in the back with Emma, and Retta. John and Bobby took the reins.

As the flames roared and began to engulf the house, none of them looked back.

The lives of those involved in military actions, and those who struggled just to survive, continued amidst paranoia and fear. Things would never be the same as they were just a few short years ago. Jim had been in charge of the family for a while now. It wasn't a position he thought he'd ever hold, even in his wildest dreams.

He wasn't unhappy when Cole told him that he was going to Texas on Confederate business. That was fine with him. It made Bursheba and the children less of a target. Even so, Jim decided that when Quantrill returned to the area in the spring, he would become one of his guerillas. This war needed to end. It was time for Jim to stop hiding from the Militia and participate in the effort to bring all this to its obvious and dreary conclusion.

When the time came, Jim kept his vow and was welcomed by Quantrill as a scout. His mother had at first been horrified but she realized that without Cole and Jim around the family's level of safety actually rose. Jim argued that he would be far safer surrounded by men with guns and Bursheba allowed her son to sell her that notion.

Yet in the end, the fact that Cole and Jim were out of the area and no longer an immediate threat to them did little to lessen the Militia's attention to their family. They had suspected all along that Jim Younger was working with the guerillas whether he was officially aligned with them or not. Through scout reports of their own they soon found the family in Waverly.

Within minutes of their arrival at the farm, the house of Aunt Nancy Campbell was in flames.

John and Bobby had been fishing behind the property when they saw the fire shoot up into the gum trees. They ran to confront the soldiers.

"Damn you, Bluebellies!" Bobby cried, throwing himself against the leg of the last soldier to mount his horse. "Why can't you just leave us alone?"

A man in sergeant's stripes shoved him roughly to the ground.

"It's not our fault you Youngers haven't learned the lesson General Ewing's been trying to teach you."

The soldiers spurred their horses as they followed the road.

It was just business to them.

Bursheba was anguished at the price her sister and her family had paid for offering her family shelter. Yet she knew of nowhere else to go than to the farm of yet another sister in Missouri City. It seemed pointless to attempt to hide from the Militia but the only alternative was complete surrender. She knew her two young boys would never allow that to happen. None of them were willing to turn Cole and Jim over to their enemies. That was an impossible thing to ask, even for the safety of their mother.

On the Confederate side of that business, the efforts of the guerillas were starting to unravel. Bill Anderson and his men were surprised by troops and while most of them escaped with their lives, Anderson was not among them. Now that was a surprise.

Quantrill took what remained of his private army to Kentucky. Jim wasn't happy about leaving his family behind but he was by now, out of desperation, finally a fighting member of the guerilla organization and he didn't want to run from that. When it was all said and done, he wanted it known that he was one of those who had stood up to the forces – Federal and Militia – that had murdered his father, terrorized his mother and caused the destruction of his family's home and livelihood.

He wanted people to be able to say that while Cole Younger may have been a leader among courageous men, Jim Younger had also done what he could.

CHAPTER 17

As Quantrill and his dwindling band of guerillas neared Lexington, Kentucky on a cloudy May evening, it was decided that they would put up for the night at the home of Confederate sympathizer Jeremiah Wakefield. Only hours after the men fell asleep in the barn, the tracks of their horses were noticed by a Union captain as he and his men passed along the nearby road.

Whether out of fatigue or a sense of hopelessness, the guerillas had neglected to post a picket. The fighting men of Quantrill had finally been caught with their guard down. By the time the Union soldiers were through laying waste to the barn, Charlie Quantrill lay with his face in the dirt. The rebel leader was taken to the Lexington military prison but was dead within days. Command decided that those who had survived that last battle would be taken to the Alton Federal Prison.

Jim Younger was among them.

Less than a month later, General Robert E. Lee surrendered at Appomattox and that was the end of it.

Cole wasn't in Missoura to see his Cause go down in flames. He hadn't been standing in battle or anywhere near either his associates or his enemy when the end came. He had been sent out west on a scouting mission. Cole wasn't among his impassioned collaborators when he heard the news; he was in California enjoying a brief visit with his father's brother Coleman, his namesake. Now that was a surprise to him.

So this was it then.

"What do we do now, Mama?" Retta asked. "We don't have Cole or Jim to tell us. Where are we going to go now?"

"We have a strong family, Retta." Bursheba didn't know the answers to those questions. "We'll do what we have to do. One day at a time."

"Quit your whining," John directed his sister. "We'll get through this like we been getting through."

The Younger family would have to regroup to face the next chapter in their lives. It wasn't what they expected or what they wanted, but one way or another their lives *would* go on.

"You were a little hard on Rett," Bobby later told his brother. "She can't help it if she's scared."

"We can't let our weakness show. If the Yankees see it, they'll take advantage of it."

"What more is there for them to take advantage of?"

Bobby wasn't scared anymore. The time for that had long passed. But he was concerned about his mother and sisters. They'd been through a lot and they still had more to go through.

"They'll think of something new. You don't think just because they won they'll leave us alone do you?"

"No, I'm not stupid. We'll just lay low and deal with whatever they come up with next."

"Now there's a new idea," John said sarcastically. "Seems to me we've been doing that for a few years now." He threw a stone across the field. "Goddamn Yankees."

Bobby nodded. It was one of the few times he agreed with John.

He hated them too.

Yet Bobby still questioned what the Union wanted at this point. It had gone on so long and those who were left were so tired. Nobody had much of anything left.

"When are they going to stop? Just let us all be?" he muttered to Dick Hall, the husband of their sister Belle.

"What fun is there in that? Those in power want to punish those who dare disagree with their opinions and plans." He sighed. He was tired of it all too. Especially as a family man. "They want to make the Confederates pay for rising up against them. They especially want all the independents that chose to protest through what they call unconventional means."

"You mean the Quantrill men."

"Yes, the Quantrill men."

Dick didn't care much for the actions of his brother-in-law Cole. Dick was of the opinion that a lot of the Youngers' troubles were because Cole's inflated ego dictated that he become known as being at the top of the rebel hierarchy. Quantrill and his bush-whackers had not done them any favors; even if Cole thought what they had done was the right thing.

Regardless of whether or not Cole's stance had been right or wrong, his side had lost. Now those drafting the new constitu-tion decided the Confederates would be forbidden to vote, hold office or be employed in any professional position. That put a big damper on what his wife's brothers could expect to do with the rest of their lives.

"All those who supported the Confederacy, whether or not they fought or aided those who fought against the Union, are now considered wartime criminals."

"We're all considered criminals for standing by our families." John spat and Bobby guessed he'd known that for a while.

"That's about the size of it."

"Are they going to try and lynch Cole and Jim then?" Bobby guessed he knew the answer to that without asking too.

"Hell, yeah," John answered. "Cole's at the top of their list."

"Well, what they're saying is that those who had the gall to be involved with the Confederate Army and the guerilla movement will be brought to trial and punished," Dick told him. "Evidently for those in power, the destruction of our homes, our families and the lives of those who opposed them isn't enough."

"You'd think taking everything we had might have satisfied them." But Bobby knew it had not and he knew that the anger between the two factions was still boiling hot.

"Well, there's a way around some of it." Dick had to give the boys *a little* hope. "A partial amnesty is being offered to those who will swear a loyalty oath."

"Over my dead body," John and Bobby said in unison.

Cole was still in California when it was all signed into law. Didn't matter. So he was once again considered an outlaw. What else was new? He knew that his enemies would continue to focus on getting rid of him should he return home to Missoura. So for the time being he would stay where he was. With Jim at the prison camp in Illinois, (he'd heard that from one of Shelby's men) his mother and the children would have to be at the mercy of the new government without him. Without combat in the area, they'd likely be all right.

Bobby and John watched the carpetbaggers march into Missoura.

"Don't listen to them. They don't care about any of us," John spat. "They only care about how much money they can make off everybody."

The hard-hearted opportunists quickly devised ways to place a stranglehold on those who sought only to rebuild. It didn't matter all that much to the Younger family. They had little left to surrender. They had paid their price.

While they looked to their mother for direction, Bursheba's children knew that where they went from here was mostly up to them. Bobby wasn't the only one worried about his mother; his older sisters were too. She had been through so much. You just had to look at her to see she was worn-out and so tired.

"Ma, the running's over. We'll go home now."

John stood before Bursheba. In his opinion he was now the man of the house. Despite the fact that they had no house, no real home, anymore. His brothers-in-law had been supportive and all but with Cole in California and Jim in prison in Illinois, he was now the eldest son. He and Bobby had been talking; they both felt it was time to return to their home in Harrison-ville.

"Oh, John," Bursheba sighed.

Her boy was only fourteen. He had been brave and had stepped up to the responsibilities that had been forced on him in the absence of his older brothers. With Bobby at his side he had handled everything that a young boy should not be made to handle. She'd like nothing better than to take her children home but without their father there was no home to which they could return.

"We can't go back to Harrisonville."

"Sure we can, Ma."

John knew that the bad times his mother had faced had weakened her. She wasn't the same as she had been before the War but she had always been there for her children and now her children had to be there for her.

"Our house took some damage but it's still there."

"*I* can't go back to Harrisonville," Bursheba whispered. Tears came to her eyes. "Not after all that's happened."

She didn't know how to just pick up and return to the life they had led before the War, before Henry had been so ruthlessly murdered. She looked at the baffled faces of her children.

"I can't," she apologized.

"But Ma..."

John didn't understand. The War was over. It was time to return to their home, their *lives.*

"John, you have to understand." Sally put her arm around Bursheba as she wept. "Mother can't bear to be there without Father. Not yet."

"But our house...Pa's business..."

"There's nothing left of your Pa's business." Anne Younger's husband Curg Jones stood with his arm around the shoulders of his wife. "The livery and the dry goods were cleaned out. Anything that was left was sold by your Uncle Frank so y'all would have some money to set up someplace else."

Bobby glared as he looked out the window. The news of the destruction of all his father had worked so hard to build was just one thing more to hold against the Yankees. He had naturally assumed that they would go back to Harrisonville and start over. It was the only real home he knew. His father had promised them his "legacy". It looked like that had been taken from them along with their father's life.

So now what? What was the next step? Did anybody know? He looked at Curg Jones. He was a kind man, had always been good to them. He'd been a member of the Younger family for ten years now. He knew their pain. He'd seen his own small farm all but destroyed. He understood that there was a lot to be done to rebuild all their lives.

"What do you suppose we should do then, Curg?"

"Your ma can stay with you young folks at the other Strother house. It's still standin'. There's no tenant farmer there no more. That'll give Cole and Jim a chance to get back and then y'all can decide what you want to do on a permanent basis."

"We don't need Cole and Jim to decide what we're gonna do." John was insulted. "We've been doin' without them for a long time now."

Curg glanced at his wife. He should have known better than to bring Cole into the equation. John was just as mule-headed as his older brother. He obviously wasn't going to take kindly to any mention of Cole.

"John, Mother just needs some time." Anne walked over to John and put a hand on his shoulder. "You've been taking good care of her and you'll continue to take good care of her. She just needs some time."

"The Strother house should be alright," Bobby considered. He wanted to go home to Harrisonville just as much as John but it was becoming obvious to him that the decision had already been made by those older than them. They needed to take care of their mother. Pa would've wanted them to do whatever she needed them to do and not think of what they wanted before doing what was best for her.

John shook off his sister's arm. He knew she was right.

"All right. That's what we'll do," he groused. "But it doesn't have nothin' to do with Cole. He's not the Big Man around this family anymore."

He looked at his younger brother, who nodded in agreement. "Bobby and I are taking care of things now."

Setting up a temporary household in Strother was what Bursheba decided but that wasn't the end of the family's harassment from those who had once declared themselves their enemy. The Militia visited the house on a regular basis, questioning if Cole had been around. They were anxious to arrest him. They said that he would, of course, get a fair trial.

His family knew differently.

They tried to go about their own business but there was just as much tension now as there had been during the War. No longer having the protection of Quantrill's men left Bursheba in a constant state of agitation. Even if those men had not been able to keep their houses from being destroyed, she knew they had, at least, kept her children from harm. And now she feared that Cole would come home and be taken to jail. Or worse, he would be lynched like so many others had been. And she had no idea how Jim would be treated once he was released and sent home. When would it all end? And how?

As for Jim, days were grim in the Alton prison. He was worried sick about his mother. He had no way to know if his family was safe. He trusted his brothers and sisters to do their best but he hated not knowing where they were and how they fared.

He realized now that the only way he was going to be allowed to get home to his family was by setting aside his ethics and issues and taking the oath of loyalty to the Federal government. He didn't believe the government was acting, or would act, in the best interest of his family but there was nothing he could do about that. Swearing to his loyalty was a hard pill to swallow but he would do whatever needed to be done. Taking the Oath to support the very people who had tried to destroy his family would likely leave a wound on his soul that would never heal but there was no other option for him.

Out in California, Cole was beginning to feel that he might be viewed as a coward if he were to stay away from home much longer. And he wasn't no goddamn coward. He too wondered what his mother and siblings faced in the course of Lee's surrender. He knew for a fact only one thing: he would *not* surrender and he would *not* swear to an oath in which he did not believe. He would always fight for what he thought was right. Nothing was going to change there. He'd just have to live with the consequences.

It took Cole awhile to get back to Missouri. He'd been gone nearly six months. The trip from California was a long one but he was home by Christmas. His family had missed him but he could also sense they were uncomfortable with him in their presence. His being with them put them in danger all over again. He stayed only a few hours.

"Cole, there's nothing for you here right now other than risk." Bursheba touched her son's cheek. 'As happy as I am to see you, it's dangerous for you to be here. Please go to Howard County and stay with my brother Thomas. You'll be safer there."

With Jim back at home and the knowledge that his youngest brothers by now knew how to take care of their mother and just about everything else, Cole had little choice but to agree.

CHAPTER 18

1866

Life on the Strother farm wasn't much better than the life the Younger family had been living the past year. The boys knew they didn't have the manpower to sow any sizeable money crops so they settled instead for planting enough vegetables to feed their own family. They might have done okay, at least for the time being, if it wasn't for the shadow Cole continued to cast over their lives.

Cole had returned a few times to check on things but the powers that be were still looking for him. Lynching him as the rebel leader he was known to be wasn't out of the question. The Militia checked in every so often just to let the family know that Cole hadn't been forgotten.

"Oh, the long tailed filly and the big black horse, doo-da, doo-da," Bob sang at the top of his voice.

John sat on a rail of the small corral as Bob rooted in the ground of his little crop garden looking for something worth picking. John was pretending to ignore the off-key singing but Bob could see out of the corner of his eye that was becoming more challenging, as John's body started to jerk.

"Come to a mud hole and they all cut across, Oh, de doo-da day…"

"Okay! Shut. Your. Piehole!" John finally demanded.

"I win," Bob simply declared.

John knocked his hand against his ear. Now tall and lean, John had grown into a handsome young man. His shock of dark hair and his riveting blue eyes was already catching the attention of the ladies, which was something John was frequently pointing out to his younger brother.

Bob stood and brushed his hands together.

"Aw, there's nothin' here worth eatin'."

He also was well on his way to the six feet of height he would grow into. His hair was sandy and brushed against his collar; his eyes a pale yet intense blue. He would have been embarrassed to hear that of all the good-looking men in his family, he was the most attractive.

"It's not you, Bobby," John consoled. "You can't wring water out of a rock."

That much was true. They had eaten all that he had planted. There was only so much to go around.

"Yeah."

John motioned for Bob to look to the west.

"Look," he smirked. "Here comes the Big Man."

Bob watched as Cole's horse drew near. He let out a breath. Cole's presence wasn't just risky to the family but it was always good for a big ole argument between Cole and John. John resented the fact that Cole treated him like a child. And Bob felt he was right to be ticked by that. While Cole had been off fighting with the guerillas, John and Bob had been at home fighting their own battle. They had risen to the challenge and kept their family from being completely shoved under by Cole's enemies. They weren't children anymore. Neither in years or experience. Cole patted their heads like they were little boys and told them they had "done good". To hell with that. They were more important to the survival of their family than Cole ever was. They may not have been old enough to fight but they had been through some brutal times of their own. Bob had little to say in Cole's defense when John ranted that Cole could up and go to hell and take his bullshit with him.

"Ignore him, John."

"Ignore the great war hero Cole Younger?" John snorted. "However does one do that?"

Cole rode up to where they were working and slid off his horse.

"Boys," he greeted. He handed his reins to Bob and tousled his hair. Bob backed away.

"Asshole," John smirked, leaning on his hoe.

"What did you say?" Cole looked at John. The boy had a bad attitude. He'd always been a smartass but he was getting out of hand. Cole was the head of this family and he demanded respect as such.

"Stow my horse," he instructed Bob after narrowing his eyes at John.

Bob started to do as he was told but stopped. It was time for him to take his own stand against the way Cole had been treating them. Cole may be the oldest brother now but he wasn't their Pa.

"Stow your own horse, Cole." He threw the reins back. "I'm not your stable boy."

Cole stared at his youngest brother. What the hell was the matter with these two? Didn't they realize the sacrifices he had made for this family? His face reddened. With all he had been through he didn't need *this* shit.

"Do as you're told, boy," he demanded.

Bob knew Cole's temper and the dangers of crossing him but he'd had enough.

"I'm not *a boy*, Cole." He looked Cole square in the eyes, ready to take whatever was thrown back. "No more than you are. And I don't have to do what you tell me."

John grinned.

Cole raised his hand.

Bob didn't flinch.

"You gonna hit him now, Cole?" John taunted. "You gonna hit your own brother now?"

"Mind your own business, John. This is between me and Cole."

Cole continued to stare at Bob. Although his instinct was to kick his butt for his disrespect, his brother's words gave him pause. Bobby had grown up. He had been gone a few years and Bobby was no longer a little boy. John and Bobby weren't that old in years yet, but damn, they had been through a lot. He hadn't given them the credit they had earned.

In an act that went against the very nature of everything that Cole believed, he did the unthinkable. In his own way, he apologized.

"You're right, Bobby. You're not my stable boy."

Bob nodded. Out of the corner of his eye he could see the look of astonishment on John's face. He looked like his eyes were gonna pop out of his head.

Cole leaned over and picked up his reins. He looked over to where John and Bob had been digging.

"Any luck?" he questioned. The issue would now be dropped.

"Some," Bob shrugged.

"Anything I can do?" Cole stunned them again.

John thought he was going to faint dead away. The Big Man was actually offering to pitch in.

"We're handling it," he dismissed.

"I'm going to go say howdy to Ma. Y'all let me know if there's anything I can do."

With that Cole walked his horse toward the barn. John and Bob watched him go.

John turned to Bob.

"Hot damn, Bobby Younger!" he chortled.

Bob was still a little shaky inside but he knew that standing up to Cole was not only what he should have done, but overdue.

"It was time," he dismissed. "Let's see what else we can find."

He turned back to the task at hand while John shook his head in disbelief, grinning.

Her children and her faithful friend Suze tried their best to raise Bursheba's spirits but the War had taken its toll. The life the mother of fourteen had known - those halcyon days of the solid success of her husband, the popularity of her children, the wonderful times around the dinner table, the respect, the security – were now all in the past. She could never, in her wildest nightmares, have anticipated the life of grief, instability and fear that she now faced on a daily basis.

How she longed for her life as it had been just a few short years ago; before her eldest boy had been taken, before that despicable Captain Walley had challenged Cole and then murdered her Henry, before her family had been destroyed by the War, that horrible and devastating war. Where there had been socials and parties held by close and friendly neighbors and friends, there was now little interaction while those same people tried to re-establish the lives that had been shattered and many times irrevocably ruined. Every morning when Bursheba woke, she felt that it took every morsel of strength just to face the day.

In January, amidst a cold and early winter, Bursheba surprised her children by insisting that John and Bob take her north to the county seat of Independence to buy what few supplies they could afford.

"There's no need for you to go, Ma." John told her. "Bobby and I can handle it."

"I know you can but I have to go," she answered.

"It's not necessary, Ma," Bob seconded. "Why take up the burden of that trip? You just tell John and me what you want and we'll get whatever it is."

"Thank you, Bobby, but I'll go."

Although they tried, none of her children could talk Bursheba out of making the trip. Even Cole had no success.

"I'll go with the boys if you're concerned about their safety," he offered.

John glared at him but he understood what Cole was trying to accomplish.

"Cole," Bursheba sighed. "You know you can't be seen in a place as busy as the Independence Square. You're being there would only serve as a magnet to the Yankees looking for you."

"Then let John and Bobby go," Cole responded.

"Please boys." Bursheba gathered the words to explain. "I *need* to go. I need to do *something* for my family."

There was no sense trying to argue her out of it. Although they didn't agree, her sons knew how she felt.

Cole took John aside and John bristled as he anticipated instructions.

"Bobby and I can handle..." he began.

"I know you can," Cole snapped. He didn't feel like arguing the matter. "I just want to tell you to pick up a revolver a friend of mine left with the gunsmith for me."

John smiled.

Once they arrived in Independence it didn't take long to select what they needed and load their purchases into the wagon that John had parked in front of the sheriff's office. As John threw the last item into the back of the buckboard, Bob helped his mother climb into the front seat.

"Well, well, if it isn't old lady Younger and her two whelps."

Bob whipped his head around to see who had spoken so disrespectfully to his mother. A large man in a tattered Union jacket stood in front of the fish market holding a wrapped package.

"What's the matter? Is that chicken-livered, bushwhacking son of yours afraid to show his face around here? Or what about the other one – or is his ass still in jail with those other Rebs?"

"Shut your mouth!" John moved a few steps in the man's direction.

"Don't you be telling me to shut my mouth, you little bastard!" The man quickly advanced and slapped John hard across the face with his package.

John fell to the ground. As he struggled to his feet, Bob tossed him Cole's gun.

"Why don't you just shoot him?" Mustering bravado, Bob glared at the man. "He deserves it."

He meant it as a threat. He should have known John wasn't much for idle threats. And shit, the gun was loaded.

John pulled the revolver from its wrapper.

"The kid's got a gun, Gillcreas!" a voice from the crowd called out.

Gillcreas' hand moved quickly to his coat.

John was quicker. He pointed the gun in Gillcreas' direction and pulled the trigger.

The shot couldn't have been cleaner. It hit Gillcreas right between the eyes. The man slipped slowly to the ground.

"Dear God!" Bursheba cried as a group of men surged forward and grabbed her son. "Don't hurt him," she pled. "Please don't hurt him!"

They didn't intend to hurt him. They were more concerned about Gillcreas' hardnosed friends.

They hurried John into the sheriff's office and shut the door.

John was stunned.

"It was...I didn't mean to kill him..he was goin' for his weapon..." he stuttered.

Even for John the reaction had been extreme. He was just so tired of people treating his family like dirt. He was so tired of hearing it....

Bob stood in the street, unsure what to do. When he had told John to shoot the man it was meant to be a threat. Now the man was laying there dead and it was his fault. But he was tired of it too. He looked at his sobbing mother.

Shit.

An old woman came out of the crowd and moved to Bursheba. Bob recognized her. She was a friend of his grandmother's.

"Take your mother inside the hotel," she ordered Bob. "Help her, now."

Bob nodded. He helped his mother down and led her across the street to the lobby of the hotel. She'd be all right but what about John? What were they gonna do to him?

Bursheba sat in the lobby. A group of women stood around her offering words of comfort. Bursheba quickly pulled herself together.

"Bobby," she whispered. "Go see about John."

His mother didn't have to ask him twice. Seeing that she was safe with the women, he pushed his way out the door and made his way through the large group of people who stood around Gillcreas' body. Several more had gathered at the door of the sheriff's office.

"Let me in," he called. "I have to see my brother!"

John was seated in a straight back chair. A handful of men stood around him. Bob recognized a couple of them as friends of his grandfather's. Thank God for that. He made his way over to John.

"Don't say anything," John whispered. "Don't say *nothin'*."

Bobby nodded.

The summoned Sheriff Hodges entered his office.

"Close the door, Cyril," he directed the man closest to the door.

Two of the men remained. The others walked outside. The door was closed. Hodges looked at John and shook his head.

"What have you got yourself into boy…?"

"I thought he was going for a gun, Sheriff," John was glad that for once he didn't have to lie.

"I understand that, John, but I also understand that you aimed a gun first."

"He hit me hard in the face," John motioned to his jaw. He could already feel the bruise rising. "I don't even know who that man is and he assaulted me."

The sheriff nodded. That's what he had heard from the men who had talked to him.

"Where did you get the gun?" He knew the answer to that too but he asked the question of John.

"I brought it with…"

"It was mine," Bob interjected.

John swung around to look at Bobby and shook his head. He had told him not to say anything and here he was jumping in!

"I got it from the gunsmith. We're up here with our mother. It's not safe, you see that. If I hadn't thrown John the gun he'd be dead," Bob blurted. "I'm the one who threw him the gun."

"Bobby, shut up! I told you to not to say anything!" John hissed.

"Hold on, boys...just hold on..." Hodges raised his hands. "I'll be taking both your statements, along with statements from those who saw what happened. We'll investigate and tomorrow we'll determine where it goes from here. In the meantime," he pointed at Bob, "you go see to your mother."

He reached behind him and grabbed a grubby, well-worn pillow. "And you, go get comfortable as my overnight guest," he told John, handing him the pillow and leading him to the door of the jail. He stopped to look at the anxious faces of the young men.

"Look, I don't think you have to worry. Gillcreas was a bullying ass. Everybody knows it. Just sit tight. Likely tomorrow you'll be on your way home."

John nodded. Well, then.

Bob sure hoped so. All he could think was that they'd stepped in shit again.

In the morning, after the doctor had examined Gillcreas and the statements of people who had been present at the scene had been taken, the coroner determined that Gillcreas had been seconds away from using his slingshot. That was considered a lethal weapon, sure was. They figured Gillcreas was probably overdue in getting what he had coming for a long time. It had only been a question of who he was going to rile one notch too high.

That it was one of the Younger boys was an interesting twist of fate but not altogether that much of a surprise. The incident was ruled self-defense on John's part and he was released.

There wasn't much to say about that or any of it.

Bursheba was greatly troubled by the incident. She had no doubt that John had acted in self-defense but the fact that he had to act at all just brought it all back to that dreadful night when Cole had done much the same at Martha Mockbee's party. It was nothing less than a never-ending circle of circumstance. She could think only of removing her children from the source of it.

Money was getting short. Bursheba knew that she needed to return to Cass County to see if she couldn't somehow straighten out the mess that was Henry's estate. There wasn't a lot there anymore; most of the land had been sold off by now and what little there was left tangled in a legal web. She decided to petition the court and at the very least see what she could raise for the care of the children. In the meantime, Emma and Retta were sent to stay with Anne and Curg up in Pleasant Hill. Now it was John and Bobby who were the issue.

"You've been here for me since Henry died and I appreciate it, Frank."

Bursheba had been thinking about John and Bobby and now she stood talking to Henry's younger brother.

"I'm happy to do what I can." His brother's murder had been a low blow and Henry's widow had been through hell.

"Things aren't as chaotic down in St. Clair County as they are here."

"No, we're somewhat off the beaten path of the worst of it. Still, there's a lot to do to return things to what they used to be."

"Frank, I'd like to ask you one last favor." She hated to ask even more from her brother-in-law but she felt she had little choice.

"What's that, Bursheba?"

"I know this is a major imposition but would it be possible for you to take John and Bobby down there with you for a while? They have been caring for me and their sisters for so long. They're young and spirited and I hate the thought that they would have to continue that burden without a break from the tension, the scrutiny. Besides, I'm sure Henry would like to see them under the influence of someone positive and law-abiding. All this can't be good for their development into good and moral men."

Frank reluctantly agreed. He didn't know what to do with them but he agreed that the life they were living was no good for boys their age. Yet after John and Bobby arrived, Frank found the responsibility of caring for the two boys a challenge. He didn't have a wife to tend to their needs, as minimal as they were. What troubled him more was the fact that John was such a loose cannon. Frank was hard-pressed to think of something the boys could do to keep them both occupied and John out of trouble.

After a few days he consulted with his brother Littleton.

"I'm sorry to have to ask you, Lit, but what the hell am I going to do with them?"

"T.J. and Bruce are staying with me," Littleton replied. He already had their two half-brothers at the house.

"Wouldn't hurt to have the boys spend some time with the two of them. There isn't that much difference in their ages. John and Bob would probably enjoy spending time with their older uncles."

"Well," Littleton considered. "God knows I could use the help on the farm." He nodded. "All right. Bring them to me."

John and Bob were happy to go to St. Clair County. Truth be told, it was good to get away from all that business. Jim was helping their ma and things would be all right. At least they hoped so.

But just when Bursheba thought she had moved forward in her attempt to restore some stability in the lives of her children she was dealt yet another blow.

Jim appeared in the living room. As much as he had been through those last few days of the War, nothing could prepare him for what he now had to do. He knelt by his mother and took her hand.

"Mother, I have some news. It's not good."

"Cole?" Bursheba's hand flew to her face. The thing she had dreaded had happened.

"No, as far as I know, Cole's fine."

"Thank God..." She could weather anything except yet another one of her children....

"It's Caro."

"Oh, that sweet, dear girl. Losing the baby last month was so hard on her...is she ill? She's been so pale and tired and she's lost so much weight. I told her I'd help with her little ones...She hasn't been well since she was placed in that awful building...that prison..."

She knew she was rambling but she didn't want to hear what Jim had to say.

"Mother....she's gone. Caro died this morning."

Jim put his arms around his mother. All she could do was weep.

Jim stayed with his mother to help her in any way he could. He was intelligent and had a good mind for organization. Bursheba was relieved to have his help untangling Henry's estate. If anything could help it was Jim's thoughtful and calm presence. He comforted her in her grief and tried to make her life easier. But her accumulated mourning was a weight she found harder and harder to bear.

"You're a blessing to me, Jim," she sighed one night. "Your father would be so proud."

Cole was another matter and his situation continued to trouble his mother. Cole couldn't be seen in public in Jackson or Cass counties without the likelihood that he would be captured and pay a huge price for his insolence. The Militia was still looking for him and he had no desire to test their abilities to throw him in jail or, as he knew they were anxious to do, dangle him from a branch. Yet he was damned if the Yankees were going to run him out of Missoura. His family was here and he had too many friends among those who had aligned with Quantrill and General Shelby to just walk away. His time was taken traveling from farm to farm, home to home, enjoying the secret hospitality of those who were grateful for his wartime actions on their behalf. He loved to entertain with colorful stories about his military activities and adventures and he found an eager audience. Other than the fact that he couldn't go home – as if he had a home to return to - Cole was in his element.

St. Clair County was just unsettled enough that Cole felt somewhat comfortable showing up there on a fairly regular basis to visit with his brothers and uncles. John didn't have much use for Cole's posturing, but when it came down to it, he was glad his older brother had made it through the War in one piece. But that didn't mean that Cole was in charge. It was he, John decided, that needed to be the one to show Bobby, who now insisted he be called Bob, the ropes. Bob, as always, could learn a lot about a lot of things from him. As long as Cole wasn't telling him what to do and how to do it, John decided he could be civil to his older brother.

Bob felt the same way. It wasn't difficult for him to do; Bob didn't have much to say. He was content to listen to the others exchange stories of incidents and encounters. But as far as he was concerned he didn't want to remember all that had happened to him and to his family. He couldn't help wishing that it was all just a really bad dream. But he knew it wasn't. It wasn't right that their home had been taken from them. They had done whatever they had been told to do whether they agreed with it or not. Now they were left with nothing. They couldn't even be together under one roof. Bob liked his uncles and was appreciative of Littleton taking him and John in but Littleton's home was not their own. They didn't have a real home anymore and might not ever again.

Whenever that thought popped up in his head, he had to let it go. It was so painful that he couldn't even bear to ponder it.

CHAPTER 19

The day's work had been long, the supper meal filling and the conversation one of who was getting on, who was trying and who was throwing in and moving out. The fate of their neighbors was out of their hands. They could only do what needed to be done for themselves.

The worst of the winter had yet to come but the air was cold and crisp with the promise of flurries. Cole had shown up at Littleton's place and Bruce, John and Bob were sitting in the barn with him shooting the breeze.

"What do you hear of the boys, Cole?" Bruce was asking. "Most of 'em staying in Missoura?"

Bruce was well-acquainted with many of the other guerillas. He had helped them all he could.

"Nobody's anxious to call it quits after all we went through," Cole shrugged. "We fought long and hard for what's ours and we're not ready to just throw up our hands and let 'em have it all because they think they won."

Bruce and Bob nodded. John threw in a "Damn right!"

"I assume Frank James is one of those who thinks the issue isn't settled?" Bruce asked. Frank's reputation was known through Western Missouri and Bruce wondered what the future held for him.

"That's right." Cole smiled. "Not by a long shot."

He scratched the back of his neck.

"Get a load of this. You've heard about Buck's little brother Jesse? The one they call Dingus?"

"Rode with Anderson." Bruce had heard a couple of tall stories about Jesse James but he took those tales with a grain of salt.

"Yeah, did some damage too," Cole chuckled.

"Why do they call him Dingus?" Bob wondered.

"Long story," Cole dismissed.

"I know it," John laughed. "He blew the end of his finger off cleaning his gun and said 'That's the gall-dingus...'"

"As I was sayin'.." Cole interrupted. It was one thing for "the boys" to call Frank's little brother by that name. The kid thought he was some kind of grand warrior. But truth be told, he had at least stood up and done a pretty fair job of it. "Well *Jesse* got himself an idea. He's saying he's gonna raise a group of the boys and emancipate all those Yankee dollars from the Liberty bank. Stick it to 'em one more time."

"Rob a bank?" John couldn't believe what he was hearing. He grinned. "Hot damn!"

"Yeah, ain't that somethin'?" Cole brushed a fleck of lint off his sleeve. "He wants me and Buck to be a part of it."

"No shit!" John was beside himself. "Ya gonna do it? Can I come?"

'We're thinking about it and no, you can't come." Cole rolled his eyes. If they were going to try and pull off something like that, all they needed was to have his trigger-happy little brother with them.

"Why the hell not?" John was indignant. He could hold his own with any of "the boys".

Cole shook his head. He should have known John would want to be in on it. He should never have brought up the subject. Why the hell did he bring it up in front of John?

Bob was still trying to get over his amazement that an attempt to rob a bank was even being discussed. Cole had told them that the War wasn't over and with news like this, that now seemed to be cold hard fact.

Cole knew he had to choose his words carefully. His relationship with John had been a little better and he didn't want to put them at odds again.

"Lookit, John," he started to explain.

"I'm not a kid, Cole," John glared. "There's no reason I can't be part of this."

"No, you're not a kid," Cole conceded. "But if they're gonna try and pull this off they need experienced men. Dingus is talking about doing it in full daylight so it's damn clear who's behind it. They need people who have already pulled off a raid."

"Whoa," Bruce exclaimed. "In the light of day. Has that ever even been done before?"

"If they're gonna to do it in daylight, aren't they gonna be recognized?" Bob wondered if in their eagerness to strike back at the Yankees and carpetbaggers they all hated so much, they had really thought things all the way through.

"Of course precautions against that would be taken, Bobby." Cole sighed. "They're not fools."

"Just askin'," Bob shrugged. Maybe they weren't fool enough to not be careful they would be recognized but robbing a bank in daylight seemed not only dangerous but damn, they were robbing a bank. That was gonna aggravate a whole slew of people.

John knew Cole was right about them needing an experienced group. As much as it pained him, he knew pulling off a bank robbery would have to be carefully planned by a group of men who were used to riding together and working with each other. It didn't make him happy that Cole had dismissed him out of hand but that's just the way it was. But, hot damn. Robbing a bank. Robbing a bank in broad daylight. He'd love to be a part of that. But if he couldn't be part of it he at least wanted to hear all about it. In detail.

"What's the plan then, Cole?"

"I don't know yet." Cole was relieved that John wasn't pressing the point of going along. "Whatever the plan is, it's gotta be a good one."

"If y'all pull it off, I'm in on the next one." John decided to put in his bid early. Providing, that is, that they would be successful.

"Yeah, you're in on the next one," Cole chuckled. There weren't any plans for there to be a next one but let the kid dream.

"And I wanna hear all about it," John continued. "Don't be keepin' any of this from us. We want to hear how it all goes down."

"That'd make for an interesting story." Bob was anxious to hear a story from Cole that wasn't about the War. He'd heard enough of them.

"Yeah, sure," Cole waved his hand. "*If* it goes down. Apparently Dingus is always comin' up with ideas. This may be just another of his fantasies."

But it wasn't. Jesse James was now putting his "fantasy" into motion.

When Jesse floated his idea of "grabbing some of those devious gains of the carpetbaggers and those loyal to the Federal government, who are now using their so-called victory as an excuse to take advantage of their fellow man", he had not been surprised at the number of boys who wanted to come onboard his little scheme. They wanted the money – God knew they could use it – but more than half of the attraction was the opportunity to let their enemies know that they had not given up the fight.

It was true that no one had ever attempted the robbery of a bank in broad daylight. That was the part that Jesse liked best. If he and the men who rode with him were to make their point, it needed to be very clear who was involved. Yes, they might wear masks to avoid any individual identification but the plan was to rage into town as the fearless and united rebels they had been and were still. Jesse had no doubt that their identity would be obvious and their stance on anything having to do with surrender more than clear. The most important thing to Jesse, as well as all of the other boys, was revenge.

And that was that.

The robbery was set for the thirteenth of February at two in the afternoon. Jesse would later say, his bright blue eyes blinking and blazing, that he believed it to be a sign that what they were doing was graced by God when the number of men who participated also played out to the number thirteen (with him, their merciless leader, the head of the body); that the numeral was associated with retribution and wrath and would make those Union sympathizers shake in their boots when they realized it.

Of course Jesse asked his brother along. Frank was the most dependable and fearless man he knew. Frank had suggested that his friend Cole Younger throw in and that was fine with Jesse. Younger had a fierce reputation among the guerrillas. The more the merrier.

But after everything was in place, there was a major set-back for Jesse. He had been seriously wounded during the War – ironically while taking part in a false surrender, damn it - and his recuperation was taking much longer than he anticipated. He had developed his plan over the winter while recovering at his aunt's farm under the compassionate care of his cousin Zee. He was convinced that he would be back on his feet by the time the robbery drew near. Yet when that day arrived, Jesse found that he wasn't strong enough to ride. Not the way he would need to ride, anyway. He didn't want his limitations causing danger to the other men, no matter how much he wanted to be there. When the thirteen men gathered in Kearney to carry out his little scheme, Jesse James was not well enough to be among them.

They rode into the town of Liberty with fierce determination that wintry afternoon. Everything had to be timed carefully to execute Jesse's plan to empty the Clay County Savings Association. Dressed in blue overcoats, an obvious spit in the face to those they had chosen to defy, Cole and Frank cordially removed more than $60,000 worth of currency and bonds from the bank and hit the street.

As the men mounted their horses outside, the cashiers discovered that the door of the vault into which they had been shoved was not locked.

"They've robbed the bank!" they shouted as they ran to the window. "The bank's been robbed!"

The people on the square stopped in their tracks. Could what they were hearing be true? Or was it some kind of prank?

Two students of nearby William Jewel College were walking opposite the bank.

"What's this?" young George Wymore muttered to his companion as he started running toward the cashiers.

"Don't move!" one of the riders shouted to the young men as he scrambled onto his saddle. For good measure he fired a warning shot at the young man, but his aim was off.

The bullet hit Wymore squarely in the back.

The man who shot him was the only one who saw Wymore go down.

The robbers sped out of town, screaming and whooping their all-too-familiar Rebel Yell.

"Who shot that fella, Cole?" John asked Cole later. "Did he mean to do it or was he just a bad shot?"

John was impressed they'd pulled it off. The Big Man and his pals had pulled it off. That someone had been shot, likely a Yankee, was just a minor setback in John's opinion. Though, of course, that was unfortunate for the fella who had been killed.

"There are some things better left unsaid," Cole said as he shook his head.

The guerrilla code of silence would hold. The killer of George Wymore was not to be revealed.

Bob figured that it was maybe all right that Cole and his buddies had taken the money. He knew where that money had come from: the hard-working farmers of Missoura. He didn't like it that a boy had been killed though. A boy just a little bit older than him; a boy who hadn't done anything wrong. That cast the robbery in a different light. Soldier to soldier, man to man, that was one thing. But when it came down to people who were just going about their business getting killed, well, it was just more of the same that he and his family had suffered during the War. That kind of business needed to come to an end, regardless of whether it was Yankees or Rebs. He wished they had just taken the money without anybody getting hurt. That would have made it a real victory.

Cole handed John a fistful of bills.

"No need to tell anybody where these came from. Use them only when you need them. I'm going east on some business."

"What business?" Bob looked down at the bills in John's hand.

"Got me some government bonds to cash," Cole smiled. "Then we're going to make some plans." He nodded. "For the family."

Bob would have to give that more thought.

The impact of the robbery was all that Jesse, Frank and Cole had hoped it would be. For any of those opponents who believed that the guerilla movement had ended with the War, it was now clear that they were obviously wrong, very wrong.

CHAPTER 20

John Jarrett had been one of those present in Liberty and the money from that little venture was burning a hole in his pocket.

"I've been thinking, Cole."

Jarrett and Cole had been visiting some friends and were now on their way to the hidey-hole where Jarrett was housing his family.

"There's no way these Yankees are gonna let up on us. At least as far as I can see."

"Maybe it'll be all right once things calm down a bit. They're on notice now."

Cole knew better than that but he wanted to at least try to stay a little optimistic. Regardless of whose hand held the authority, he still considered Missoura his home.

"I know you don't believe that horseshit," Jarrett laughed.

"Guess I'm just a wishful thinker."

"I've been giving it a lot of thought. Here's what we do."

"What's that, John?" Cole thought it a bit presumptuous of Jarrett to be including him in whatever scheme he was hatching up now, but that was Jarrett.

"I'm thinking we take this money we rightly earned and invest it in some cattle."

"Cattle? How are we going to raise cattle?" Where in the hell had he come up with this one? It was ridiculous to even consider it.

"Not here, not in Missoura." Jarrett looked at Cole. "You've seen Arkansas, and Texas when we were down there with Shelby. Beautiful land."

Arkansas had its appeal but Cole wouldn't necessarily describe Texas as beautiful, not like Missoura was beautiful. There was something appealing about all that open range though. You could see for miles.

"We can ranch it there. And make a good profit."

All right, he had Cole's interest. He was listening.

"The way I see it, we'll have ourselves a means to support our family. And it's a hell of a lot safer down there than it is up here. A lot of the boys have moved down there."

"You have a point there. But I can't leave my mother to fend for herself up here again if I were to try and set something up down there. She's got the boys but..."

Jarrett looked at Cole like he was a half-wit. "You take your mama with you. *All* of you go."

"All of us..." Cole mused.

"Hell, yeah. You can provide 'em with a new start. A *safer* new start. How can you not consider that?"

Cole did consider that and he began to think Jarrett's idea was a good one. Establishing themselves in some other state might be the very thing they needed to do. The heat would be off him and, in turn, off his mother and those still at home. Starting up a cattle operation was beginning to sound like a damn good way to move forward.

"Missoura is our home, not Texas."

Bob didn't like the idea at all. With everything they had gone through to stay in Western Missoura, Cole was suggesting they give it up just so he could move around more freely? Bob couldn't believe his brother could be so selfish and short-sighted. Well, yes he could. It was Cole. Cole always came first. He might have talked himself into the idea that picking up and moving down to Texas would be good for the family but the long and short of it was that it would be good for Cole.

"I like the idea. Texas..." John mused. He quickly dismissed Bob's opinion. He'd heard a lot about Texas from the guerrillas who had been down there. It was an outlying land, just teeming with opportunity. "Think of the possibilities, Bobby. Think of all that freedom."

"Ma won't want to go down there," Bob reasoned. "It's a long way off. It would be hard for her to travel that far. And it's gotta be a different kind of life for people down there – not like Missoura, with the farmers and all."

His brothers looked back at him with blank faces.

"She doesn't know anybody there. Missoura is her home." Bob shook his head. "That's a half-baked idea."

"Don't you think Ma would like to be some place where she's safe and she doesn't have bad memories? Don't you think she'd rather have a home like that?"

Oh, Cole was good. He knew just the right card to play.

"What do you say, Jim?"

"Maybe it'd be a good thing." Jim shrugged. "Cole's right that Texas doesn't hold the bad memories that Missoura does."

Jim would do whatever his mother needed to move forward.

"Ma's not well..." Bob didn't understand why his brothers couldn't see how impractical such a move was.

"She'll get better without all this....bullcrap, Bobby!" John believed that, he really did. "Let's get her the hell away from all this shit."

"If y'all are so dead set on it, I say it's up to her." Bob blew out a breath. "I say it's up to Ma."

Whether she believed the promise in Cole's description of a new life or because she simply didn't have anything more to give Missouri, Bursheba agreed to go.

But before he could move the family down to Texas, Cole needed more information. He and Jarrett purchased a small herd of cattle and traveled down south, all the way to Carroll Parrish in Louisiana. The Texas plan would take maybe a year to bring to fruition but one way or another Cole would get his mother down there and away from her heartbreak. This cattle thing *would* work.

But to make it work out the way he envisioned, well, they needed more money.

CHAPTER 21
1867

New Year's Day was special; it was good, if only for a moment. They were celebrating an event that brought them something they hadn't experienced in a long time: genuine joy. Sally had met a Mexican War veteran from Kentucky named Jephthah Duncan. Though he was twenty-six years her senior, Jeph was a kind man and he offered Sally the security that had been critically missing from her life. Her sisters threw Sally and Jeph a wedding that delighted them all and allowed them all to see that little glitter of hope, of true happiness.

If only their mother could have enjoyed the festive occasion more. Bursheba was happy for her daughter but the wedding only reminded her of the life that should have been theirs and would forever be tarnished by dark and sorrowful events.

"Your father, Dick and Caroline should be here," Bursheba told the smiling bride.

Jim tried to throw starlight on a burning ember of sorrow.

"But we're thankful Sally found Jeph, aren't we Mother? Look how happy she is. It's a *good* day for our family. For the first day in a long time, it's a *good* day."

When the Alexander Mitchell and Company Bank in Lexing-ton was robbed in October, people were once again surprised. Maybe they shouldn't have been; if there was one thing the guer-rillas had demonstrated during the War, it was that they were a tenacious lot.

Jesse had been anxious for the opportunity to take an active part in a robbery. He didn't feel it was fair that he had come up with the idea and had then been waylaid by the injury the Yan-kees had already made him suffer. Sure, he had been given a cut from the Liberty caper but listening to Frank and Cole tell him about the robbery was not the same as being there and experi-encing it firsthand.

"I don't think we should be pressing our luck, Jesse," Frank had advised.

"Well surely my own brother won't deny me a taste," Jesse had smiled.

When Cole came around after being in Louisiana and men-tioned that he wouldn't mind having another opportunity to finance his family's move down to Texas, Frank figured he'd indulge his little brother.

Cole didn't bother to tell John. The kid would only want to play.

The only hitch in the robbery was when it came time to demand the $100,000 that Jesse had heard was being kept in the vault. The cashier didn't have the key and the robbers had been forced to be satisfied with the $2,011.50 they took away.

"Damn Dingus," Cole complained to Frank. "I know he's your brother but his miscalculation cost us. For the little money we each got, we might not have bothered."

"Yeah, he overestimated a bit," Frank chuckled.

"More than a bit."

"All right, a whole lot."

Oh well, the event wasn't without its fun. On the way out of town, the bandits had been chased half-heartedly by a posse led by their old friends and fellow guerillas Dave and John Poole, who had made it clear to those within earshot that they would give fair chase and that no one else need bother. Har har.

When the Hughes and Wasson Bank of Richmond was robbed in May, *Cole* was one of those who was surprised. Had Buck left him out because he had spoken against Jesse? That didn't sound like something Buck would allow. He had loyalty to Jesse sure, but Cole was his friend.

Yet when Cole heard the particulars of what had happened, he didn't think Frank was involved at all. Although the twelve robbers had made off with about $3,500, there had been a gun battle and when it was all over three men lay dead in the street. That was sloppy work. Dingus was impulsive and Cole didn't think for a second that this sort of mess was above Jesse. Buck was another matter. He was too damn cool under fire.

"Those sons-of-bitches stole my idea!" Jesse complained when *he* heard about the robbery. He was outraged. "They've taken the fun out of it!"

CHAPTER 22

Cole had promised his mother than he would raise the money for their relocation through his new cattle enterprise. Bursheba was pleased that John Jarrett was involved with that. It was time that Mr. Jarrett involved himself with some honest work; she'd heard the rumors (although she didn't think for a moment that Cole was involved in any of that business). Yet as she considered Josie's husband might be settling into some level of family responsibility, her heart ached that her younger children were being denied a home. Living with their sisters and uncles was not something she had foreseen. If they were going to prepare to move to Texas and live as a family there, Bursheba wanted them to realize that her hopes and dreams for their future had not been abandoned. She decided that although she didn't feel she could gather them together in Cass County - it was still too painful there - they would come together again in Strother.

Bob squatted on his knees as he surveyed the row he had just completed hoeing on his own. It was straight. All right; it was straight. A smile spread across his face. It wasn't a big deal for a farmer to hoe a straight row but this was his first of a size and he was proud of it.

Bob loved living in St. Clair and much of the reason why was right before him. His Uncle Littleton had a good size farm going now and Bob was intent on learning everything he could about it. He wanted to be involved in the planning, the preparation, the planting...all of it. He couldn't get enough. Once he put his hands in that rich Missoura soil he knew. He knew this was what he wanted to be doing.

He remembered that day. He was waiting for his Uncle T.J. because they were going to plow. He was looking over the fields when he bent over and took a big handful of soil.

A strange feeling came over him. His vision grew dim and his mind seemed to flood with the dreadful sounds of men fighting. Fighting over this soil, this land. He shivered and the sounds faded away. But not the feeling. In that moment he thought he finally knew what his pa had tried to tell him all those years ago about Missoura land being a living legacy. He finally understood.

He couldn't get enough of it. His uncles and the hands teased him that he was going to put them all out of work. When they praised his efforts he felt more satisfied than proud. He loved farming, that was all there was to it. When His Uncle Littleton had rewarded his hard work by giving him this small patch to start up on his own, he was over the moon.

He also liked the fact that he could finally just breathe. When he took some time for himself, he could fish and hunt without worrying about the sudden appearance of a Militia unit just waiting to ruin his day. Sometimes he would go over to Monagaw Springs, a little community that was tucked into the hills. People came from all over to stay at the hotel there and enjoy what were supposed to be the healing powers of the minerals in the water. Mr. and Mrs. Snuffer, friends of his family for so long, had him to dinner a lot and he liked spending time with them and their boys. And if he wasn't chowin' down at Snuffers', he was getting stuffed with food at Suze's sister Hannah's place. He guessed that some people had a need to be kind to a boy who was apart from his mother. He missed his mother but his life was better than it had been in a long time.

"Hell, no. Not up there again."

138

Jim had ridden down to tell the boys about Bursheba's plan. John wasn't for it.

"There's nothing for me there."

Jim was used to John's negativity. His protest didn't matter. They would do what their mother wanted. They owed her that much.

"John, it's what Ma wants and that's how it's going to be."

"Well, *I* don't want it. I like it here and I'm staying here."

Here it was again. The older brother treating him like a child and telling him what to do. He expected that from Cole, but not from Jim.

Bob's heart sank. It had been foolish to think that he could stay on the farm. That wasn't really his home, no matter how much he loved it. Now he had to walk away from all that he enjoyed here. More than anything he wanted to stay in St. Clair but that didn't matter. He wasn't about to turn his back on his mother.

"You just get on your horse and go on back to Jackson County, Jim. We're staying here." John was adamant. He'd put the life they had up there behind him. Or at least he'd tried to.

"Oh, shut up, John." Bob had heard enough. "We'll do what Ma wants us to do and you know it. She's our mother. There's no way you're gonna ruin this for her. At least she's trying to take some action. She hasn't done that in a long time. Let's just get our stuff together and get on the road."

For once John didn't say a word more; but he wasn't happy.

As it turned out, John was right this time. There was little left in Strother for him or the Younger family. 1868 didn't look like it would be any better than the year before. It had not been a healthy return for Bursheba. She woke from nightmares nearly every night and she dwelled on the past so much that her children were afraid she was losing her mind.

Cole was concerned enough to risk a trip to see his mother and assess for himself the state of the family.

"So what's goin' on, boys?" he asked.

"Ain't nothin' goin' on, Cole. That's the problem," John complained. "I'm so damn sick of this place. It's nothing but gloom and doom. And I feel like a boy again. The girls shush me whenever I talk above a whisper and tell me to go outside. I'm a damn man now. I shouldn't have to put up with this shit."

"They're just being protective of Ma," Bob sighed.

He was unhappy too. The little crop garden he had put in didn't take up much of his time and there was little for John and him to do. Their little sisters were at an age where they were self-sufficient. Without land to farm or a family to defend there seemed no purpose to their lives. Their older brothers had their adventures – heck, Cole was *still* having them – and they wanted their own. It was just too damn quiet in Strother. It made them almost wish the Militia would show up so they would have something to *do*.

For once Cole was understanding. He was a young man himself and these two had been saddled with the care and concern of their mother and sisters for a number of years now.

"I'm sorry this burden has fallen on you, boys. I know it's been hard."

"Been boring is what it's been." Once John got on a rant he was loath to let it go. "Same thing, day in and day out."

"I'm about where we need to be to make the move down to Texas. Another handful of money and we should be able to be on our way."

John and Bob understood Cole's meaning. He and Frank and Frank's little brother were going to hit another bank.

"You said you were gonna let me go along on the second one, Cole. You didn't."

John had been annoyed when he heard about the bank in Lexington. He'd understood he'd be included the next time they went out.

"Yeah, well, John, it was kinda spur-of-the-moment."

"I take it this next one's not gonna be spur-of-the-moment?" John stared at his brother. Dammit, Cole needed to keep his word. He wanted *in*.

Cole had actually given the matter of including John some thought. The boy had been as involved in the War as much as any of the Confederates who had fought the War on the home front. He was seventeen – older now than Cole had been when Walley's actions first caused him to take to the bush. John had proven that he was responsible, despite his being arrogant and impulsive. Hell, he wasn't any worse than Jesse James that way. Maybe it was time to give John his shot.

"No, it's not." Cole took a deep breath. Once he agreed to this, there would be no going back for John. "All right."

"All right what?" John narrowed his eyes.

"All right, you can come."

"Eeeehaw!!!" John threw his hat up in the air. "Hell, yeah!!"

"They'll be some conditions though." Oh Sweet Jesus. Cole hoped he wasn't making a mistake.

"Yeah, sure. As long as I go." John couldn't believe it. He was gonna ride with Cole and Frank James.

"You do what I tell you, to the letter."

John nodded.

"And don't even think you're getting near the bank. You're not that experienced. You'll wait for us outside of town."

John was disappointed that he wouldn't actually be a part of the robbery but he was grateful for the opportunity to go at all. He didn't complain. "All right," he agreed.

"But he'll be breaking the law by having anything to do with it." Bob sat dumbfounded. Cole was actually going to take John along to rob a bank?

"Yeah, so what?" John rolled his eyes. Didn't Bobby understand what was happening here? He was going to ride with the gueril025! He was going to be recognized as a man. "I'm gonna be *in* on it, Bobby. It's *my* chance to stick it to 'em."

Cole blew out another breath. How would their pa feel about what he was about to do, dragging his little brother into a situation like this. Well, there was no use thinking of that. Times had changed since their pa was with them. Times had changed like no one could have imagined, especially their pa.

"What about Bobby, Cole, can Bobby come?" John looked at Bob. He'd probably like to be a part of it too.

Bob's mouth all but dropped open. He had grown accustomed to the idea of what Cole and the others were doing. That first robbery had shocked him. Before the War no members of the Younger family purposely broke the law. But he too knew that times had changed and none of them now were above doing whatever they needed to do. Robbing the bank at Liberty may have been an extreme measure but it wasn't nearly as bad as some of the things the Yankees had done during the War.

And Cole was, after all, continuing that line of work so that he could buy cattle and get them all down to Texas and into a new life. As much as Bob hated leaving Missoura, he had come to accept that they needed to get on down there and get their ma away from all this. It was the only chance she had to put everything behind her. So he guessed that what Cole and his pals were doing was justified. But he'd never thought to be included himself. That was one thought he'd *never* had.

"Not this time." Lordy, Cole didn't want to have to handle *both* of them during a robbery. He gripped Bob's shoulder. "You understand, don't you Bobby?"

Bob nodded, relieved that there would be no more discussion about it.

Quickly dismissing the notion of Bob accompanying them, John turned to Cole.

"So what's the plan?" he asked as he rubbed his hands together.

CHAPTER 23

Jesse had come up with another scheme and at first Frank questioned whether he wanted to be a part of it this time. He hesitated only briefly – aw, what the hell. He had started to think of his future and he, like his friend Bud Younger, could surely use the money to make a fresh start.

Cole was more apprehensive of Jesse now. Jesse was known to come up with embellishments on robbery that made Cole uneasy. Cole didn't want any more innocent people killed. He decided to take John and Jarrett to Russellville to check out the bank in advance.

John had pled a case all the way to Kentucky that he thought he should be more involved in the actual robbery.

"I'm fast on my feet," he declared. "And I'm a quick thinker."

"You're also quick to let fly with your temper too." Cole wasn't having it. "There's no room in this operation for that."

"What's the worst that can happen? I might have to shoot me a Yankee."

"That's what I'm talking about. We don't want no dead Yankees. We just want their money."

"Well, I didn't say I was gonna shoot one, just that's the worst could happen."

"No, John," Cole had been patient but his patience was now running out. "The worst that could happen is that you, or *me*, could get killed."

John stopped to think about that. That thought had never crossed his mind.

"Nah…" he decided.

"I swear, John." Cole threw him a dirty look. "Sometimes you remind me of that damn fool Dingus James."

"If you think Jesse James is a damn fool, why do you ride with him?" John didn't know Jesse but coming up with the idea to rob a bank in the first place had been anything but foolish, in his opinion.

"Buck keeps Dingus in check." At least so far.

"Maybe you two ought to think about replacing him with me." That sounded like a good idea to John. "I'm probably a whole lot keener. And I'm *your* brother so Frank can't crab. I could be the man who goes in to scope things out. I'd do a damn fine job…."

"Damn it, John. Shut the hell up, will you? You're making my head hurt." Cole rubbed the back of his neck.

"You two is like a minstrel show," Jarrett chuckled.

"Wasn't that fun, Coleman?" Jesse nodded a few days later, as they spurred their horses down the street and away from the bank. He winked at John. "Now that was fun!"

Jesse didn't mention, and John never knew, that Jarrett had found it necessary to shoot the bank president.

As they rode south with their booty, the Russellville robbers didn't realize that they had drawn attention in ways they would not appreciate. Jesse's remark, and the use of Cole's name, had been overheard. Although the description of the outlaws given by alleged eye-witnesses would in no way resemble the actual robbers, when a Louisville detective named D.T. Bligh was hired to try and solve the crime, he named Cole Younger and the James brothers as the culprits.

Now it stood to reason that Detective Bligh didn't pull these names out of a hat. Somebody had been telling tales out of school.

To complicate matters, Cole and Jarrett's own brother-in-law, their sister Belle's husband Dick Hall, for some damn reason had told a Kansas City reporter that it was that scoundrel Jarrett who had planned the robbery along with Ol and George Shepard. What the hell was Hall thinking? He held no friendship with Jarrett – in fact he disliked him immensely for dragging Cole, and thus the family, into illegal activities in the first place – but why did he have to go and tell the newspaper that?

As it turned out, Detective Bligh wasn't able to come up with any hard evidence that would implicate Cole, the James boys or Jarrett.

Jarrett had moved down to Louisiana with Josie and their two children but they sometimes stayed in a little house in Strother so Josie could visit her family. If Jarrett was thought to be the mastermind of the whole robbery thing, it was the thinking of those whom he robbed that he ought not be allowed to go Scot free. Add to that, he had himself quite the reputation for his time with Quantrill and what had happened at Lawrence. Jarrett had enemies that had not forgotten him.

Cole and Jim had been visiting their sister Josie and were in the Jarrett's barn when it happened.

The thunderous hoofs of a small group of men rode toward the house.

"Those men are up to no good!" Cole told Jim.

As Cole grabbed his revolver and Jim his shotgun and both ran out of the barn, a ball of flame burst from the house.

"Get the kids!" Cole yelled to Jim, as the men on horseback rode off as quickly as they had approached.

Maggie and Jeff Jarrett would always remember the bravery of their uncles as they battled their way into the house to snatch them free of the smoke and flames.

"MaaaMaaaa!" Maggie screamed. "Where's MaaaMaaaa?"

"We'll find her, Maggie, and your Pa too," Cole told the little girl as he ran with her away from the house. Jim ran with Jeff wrapped around his torso. "We'll go back and..."

The gust from the huge ball of fire pushed them all forward as the rest of the cabin erupted in furious crimson flames.

He lay in the dirt with the child's face pressed against his chest, watching the blaze. He and Jim weren't going anywhere.

There wasn't any reason to go back inside.

There were some that liked to say that Jarrett had insulted one too many Union sympathizers but others couldn't help but think that his being named in the Kentucky robbery may have played a large role in his demise. Others claimed John Jarrett wasn't in that house at all that night. Whatever the truth about Jarrett, the innocent Josie had been murdered in her sleep.

There were some who never forgave that.

With her sister's orphaned children now in her care, Anne Jones and her husband Curg decided that they had had enough. They had listened to Cole tell them about the opportunities in Texas and decided to pull up their Missoura stakes and see what a journey down south might offer them. Curg worked well with his hands and he thought he might do well with a furniture shop. They had heard good things about the area known as Sherman and that's where they would go to start their lives anew.

When Anne told her mother of their intention, Bursheba asked her daughter if she had any idea when Cole thought she herself might be able to go. Anne told her that she would like to have her mother move down there with her, despite any delays Cole might have funding a cattle operation.

When Anne told Cole that the time had come to make the move to Texas, he agreed. He had enough investment money now.

There was no need to tell their mother where the money had come from.

The news was not welcomed by seventeen-year-old Emma.

"I can't bear another move," she told her brothers. "I've been asked to marry Kitt Rose. He's taken a job in Jackson County. I'm going to marry Kitt and stay here."

Bursheba accepted that.

"And Suze would like to stay up here too, near me."

Bursheba accepted that too. Although she regretted leaving behind the daughters who would move on with their lives in Missouri, she herself just wanted to leave Missouri behind.

In the fall of 1868 Cole, Jim, John, Bob and Retta accompanied their mother to their new home in the Lone Star State.

Texas.

CHAPTER 24

The trip to Sherman, Texas had been uneventful. They all were relieved at that. Bursheba's health seemed to be growing more and more precarious and had anything happened out there on the road, they didn't know if she could withstand it. So they watched for any threat, any disturbance beyond the norm. The more things changed, the more some things remained the same. Trite, but true.

Bursheba and Retta moved in with Anne and Curg. Anne was certainly better able to nurse her mother than John and Bob. With a grown daughter in residence, maybe their mother would remember old ways and gradually return to her life. There were many Missouri families living in the area now and they thought that being close to some old friends from home would be good for her.

Bursheba didn't care about that one way or another.

Cole had found a little ranch house in nearby Scyene where he and the boys could put up. It would soon be winter again and it wasn't a bad place to base. They didn't need much.

"This is no more than a shack," Bob complained. "I don't see where you get away with calling it a ranch house."

"You're too fancy, Bobby," Cole shrugged. "This is Texas. We're cattlemen now."

"We're rough men, used to rough ways," John smiled. He liked the sound of that.

"I guess we are," Bob replied. Whether he liked it or not. And he knew, just knew, that John would soon change his tune too.

Cole and Jim purchased a herd of cattle and launched their operation. Cole was good at the business end of things but the cowboy work was left to Jim, John and Bob. John and Bob didn't much care for it.

"I hate this," John complained yet again. "I'm not cut out to be a stinkin' cowpoke."

"Do you think I'm enjoying listening to you carp day after day?" Jim frowned. He liked working with the horses but the cattle work was something else again. By the end of the day he was so tired that he couldn't even enjoy his books.

"I should be working in a store," John continued. "In my own store, I don't mind telling you. I should take my cut of the money from this half-baked idea and invest it in a business."

"You don't get a cut, John," Bob smirked. "This is the *family* business now."

"Or I should take my cut and play a little poker." John chose to ignore Bob. "I'm a damn fine poker player. I could probably win me a sizable amount in a very short time."

"You could probably *lose* you a sizable amount in a very short time." Bob hated the work too but John's bellyaching was getting on his nerves. "Quit complaining. It doesn't do any good and just annoys the rest of us."

"I'm not a stinkin' cowpoke," John reemphasized. "I'm a businessman."

"And I'm a Missoura farmer with my own spread." Bob was fed up with John's attitude but it wasn't different from his own. "It doesn't matter what we think we are. Or what we'd like to be. The fact of the matter is that we're ranchers now and that's all there is to it."

He spurred his horse into the mass of cattle.

The herd scattered, making John and Jim cough from the cloud of dust that rose.

There was another incident at a Missouri bank. The way it ended up had little to do with robbery. Two men entered the Daviess County Savings Bank in Gallatin. The president was a man named John Sheets. Some said that during the War he was known as S.P. Cox and that it was Cox who had been the Yankee that shot down Bill Anderson. Was that a fact. When the men approached the counter and asked for a bill to be changed, Sheets seemed to recognize one of them. That suited them fine. Sheets was shot in the heart. And once in the head for good measure. And for extra good measure, ol' Cox's capital was thrown into a sack.

"Damn James boys," Cole admired.

Throughout the next year the Younger family adjusted to living in a state far away from their home in Missouri. The cattle business paid off well enough to afford them a comfortable living – their needs weren't many. At least they were doing something, going forward in their own way.

Bob had planted some vegetables but the ground was so dry he didn't have a lot of luck bringing much to fruition. He was disappointed but his attempt at least allowed him to get his hands in the soil. He thought again about his father talking about the importance of land. Well, there was land as far as his eyes could see. But it wasn't Missoura land. That was the land Bob craved.

As had become his pattern, John hurried through his morning chores to enable him to enjoy more entertaining pursuits. He'd head for the various settlements to find Saturday night Faro and Poker games, rot-gut whiskey and a variety of easy women. John was having the time of his life.

Those Sunday mornings when John made it to church – something his mother asked he do (she, of course, not having a clue as to what her son had been up to the night before), he slumped in his chair with the god-awfulness hang-over anyone had ever experienced. Nine times out of ten he would be out back of the church puking by the time the service was over. When Bob asked him why he had to do everything all out and suffer such disgusting consequences, John would laugh.

"Because it's there, Bobby! It's mine for the taking!"

Cole was actually pretty good at running their small cattle business. Now Jim handled the books and Cole got done what needed doing. Then he was off to socialize with his former Missoura comrades and talk about the good ole bad days.

Jim didn't participate. He'd had enough of all that. He'd been given dozens of books from a couple of Missoura families who had tried Texas but decided to move on. His nights were spent mostly in the parlor.

Bursheba was trying to adjust to her new surroundings but it wasn't easy for her. Anne and her friends included her in many of their activities but more often than not Bursheba would say she wasn't feeling well and go to sit in her bedroom chair. Once so vibrant and accommodating, Bursheba would tell Anne that she was more comfortable when she was alone. Anne, Retta and their brothers hoped she'd somehow get used to things being different and make an attempt to adapt. That's what they hoped would happen, but not how they thought it was going to be.

Sally and their sister Laura traveled down from Missouri to see if they might have any influence on their mother. It was a long trip but they all hoped that maybe she would see how important it was to them that she at least try to be happy. Yet as pleased as she was to see her daughters, it was evident that once they were gone, things would go back to the way they were before they came.

It was a mild night in the little town; Bursheba had gone to bed and Curg, Cole, Jim and John had decided to take a walk. Bob preferred to visit more with his sisters. Sally and Laura would be returning to Missouri the day after tomorrow. They sat with

Anne and Retta on the wrap-around porch, enjoying the gentle breeze and each other's company.

Sally and Bob sat on the two-seat swing, which Bob swung back and forth. Retta sat to the left of his feet.

"Bobby, it has been so good to see you." Sally took his hand and smiled. "I've missed you most of my brothers."

"I'll be sure and tell the others that," he smiled back.

"You've been so good to Mother all these years." She squeezed his hand.

He shrugged. Of course he had; she was their mother.

"Don't think we all don't appreciate it," Laura added. "We've all had our hands full with our own families and you younger children have been nothing less than wonderfully brave and so caring of Mother." Tears rose in her eyes. "Bobby and Retty, the two of you and John...Emmy too...have been through so much....so much more than you ever should have been...."

"Aw, yeah," Bob interrupted with a wave of his hand. He was uncomfortable with her praise. "We're real heroes, aren't we Rett. Facing down Yankees...."

"With our slingshots!" Retta crowed. It was a game Bob had taught her when she was little and got scared. He would remind her of the story of David and Goliath and how David had defeated the mighty giant with nothing but his slingshot. It somehow helped calm her back then. That was before the incident at the Independence Square, when the slingshot had been held not by David but by Goliath, but John thought that little turn of events was funny, after it all was straightened out of course.

Laura frowned, not sure what the joke was. When Anne shook her head, Sally understood that the subject was not one Bob and Retta wanted to discuss. She certainly had moments from their past where she felt the same way.

"You have good things, wonderful things, waiting for you in your future, both of you." Sally did feel that needed to be said. She had found happiness and someday they would too. It wouldn't erase the horror of their past but she needed them to know that there was hope, there was something good for them on their horizon.

"Bobby, Father and Dick always thought you were special," Laura told her brother. "Do you know that?"

He shook his head. Why they would think so, he couldn't guess.

"Maybe someday you'll have the opportunity to reclaim some of Father's land. I can think of nothing that would make him more proud."

Early in May, Jim was in town when he overheard a government man who was passing through say they were looking for men to take a census. Jim didn't consider tending the cattle a full-time job. He didn't like the work and thought that with another way to bring in some money, he could maybe spend his time elsewhere. He signed up.

Cole was at first outraged that Jim had taken the job.

"You're working for the goddamn government!" he'd bellowed.

When Jim smiled and told his brother that it was "an irony I find amusing", Cole had reconsidered and laughed. Maybe he'd do it too. He always liked an excuse to visit with his neighbors.

Once again Cole was right in his element.

CHAPTER 25

E ven as he longed for Missoura, Bob had reason to attempt a greater investment in Texas. He hadn't seen it coming and was astonished that it happened to him, but if he knew anything it was that things happened when you didn't expect them.

That autumn Bob turned sixteen and he was in love.

Lily caught his eye as he watched her sing in the church choir. Her golden-brown hair and amber eyes made his heart thump so loud he was afraid people could hear it. He'd look at her and his hands would go clammy and his face would feel like it was on fire. She was beautiful. She was so beautiful that it took everything he had not to stare at her and just keep on staring.

He didn't know what to do with his feelings. He had no idea even how to talk to a girl that wasn't his sister. He thought a couple of times that maybe he could ask John about it. John always had girls around him, but he didn't want to be made fun of and that would be a given with John. Bob had never even seen Jim with a girl, so he probably couldn't give him any advice. Cole? Uh uh. He didn't want to hear about it from Cole. He'd have to go this one on his own.

And that wasn't taking him far. He couldn't seem to get beyond just hanging around the church hall and smiling at Lily when she passed. He couldn't find the nerve, or the words, to speak to her and that bothered him a whole lot. What kind of a man was he that he couldn't talk to a female? That was just pathetic.

And then one day Lily surprised him.

"Hello, Bob," she smiled.

He didn't even know she knew his name. Before he had time to react, she was gone.

That was it. He was going to have to stop acting like a cow-eyed kid and take some kind of action. He would see her at the barn dance the church was putting on. That would be his opportunity and he damn well better take it.

Bob was nothing if not an observer and he had watched Cole and John dance at the church socials. Jim evidently didn't like to dance; he always stood to the side of the hall. Bob was grateful that Jim didn't mind his company. Bob didn't want to dance except with Lily and he hadn't yet gotten up the nerve ask her.

It was time. Taking a breath, Bob walked over to where Lily stood visiting with her friends. He was relieved when she said she would be happy to dance with him, again using his name.

When he held her arms he felt awkward but Lily didn't complain. Dancing her around the floor was maybe a bit clumsier than he would have liked it to be, but she had smiled at him when the dance was over. He was over the moon.

Jim noticed Bob's flushed face as he danced earlier that evening and after they got back to their ranch house he thought that maybe it was time to talk to his little brother man-to-man.

"Not that I'm a ladies man Bob, but it's only because I know you well that I could see that you might be interested in the girl you were dancing with tonight." Jim was certainly no one experienced enough with women to give any real advice but at the very least he could pass along some of the manners their father had explained to him so long ago.

"Aw, shoot, Jim." Bob was embarrassed. He didn't want to look like he was mooning over lily. "Did it show?"

"Like I said, only because I know you well." It was probably apparent to anyone who had been watching Bob, but Jim didn't think Bob needed to know that. "You handled yourself like a gentleman."

"Did I do all right? Do you think I did alright?"

"I think you did fine, Bob." Jim smiled. "Now comes the hard part when you've got to have a conversation with her."

"I don't have any idea what to even say to her."

"You just tell her she looks nice, talk about things like the weather, how nice the social was, things like that."

Bob knew he had to take those first steps, but he was going to feel dang gawky.

"You'll do fine, Bob." Jim smiled again. "You've got the Younger charm."

"I'm gonna need some of that."

That Sunday after church he summoned up all the charm within him and struck up a conversation. Lily was sweet and Bob discovered that she had a sense of humor that he hadn't expected. The two of them were soon laughing as if they'd always known each other.

As the weeks passed, it became a pattern that they would meet behind the school house on Tuesday evenings. Bob lived for those visits. By now, conversation wasn't so difficult to come by. They mostly talked about Lily's friends, the books that Lily read and Lily's dreams of leaving Texas for someplace more interesting. Bob didn't tell her that while he wasn't big on Texas, sometimes interesting wasn't a good thing. He didn't talk much. He spent most of their time together listening to what Lily was saying. He didn't feel the need to share his past life in Missoura with her. It was nice to get away from talk of that. And he was relieved and happy that Lily didn't talk about his brothers like so many people did. She seemed to accept him just for himself. That was something that Bob could get used to, yes it was.

"Thinking about your lady friend, Bobby?"

John rode up as Bob was supposed to be watching the herd. He was looking in the direction of the cattle but he never even heard John coming.

"Don't startle me like that," he frowned.

"Pay attention and you won't startle. If you had your mind on four-legged critters instead of two-legged ones you'da seen me comin'."

"I was watchin' the damn cattle…"

"Not with that moony look on your face," John smiled. "At least I hope not."

"Shut up," Bob blushed. "I wasn't mooning. It's not like that."

"Oh, it's not huh? 'Cause if your little romance was serious, that would mean you'd have to talk with her daddy."

"What for?"

"That's how it's done. If you want to start seeing a girl on a regular basis, you have to talk to her daddy and ask his permission."

"I didn't know that." Bob frowned. He hadn't been taught any of that. He hadn't been taught anything at all, past that last conversation with Jim. It was times like this that he missed his pa and Dick more than ever. He hoped he hadn't come off ill-mannered and boorish.

"You know it now." John looked at Bob slyly. "Do you even know who her daddy is?"

"No," Bob shrugged. Lily talked about her "daddy" but Bob hadn't asked for a description or an introduction.

"I thought not," John smirked. "I didn't think you knew that little thing."

"So what? Do *you* know who her father is?"

"I do."

"Well, why are you making it such a big deal?" Bob was tired of being the pawn in John's games. "Dang, the way you're acting it might as well be the preacher."

John poked his finger in the air. "There ya go!"

"The preacher?" He hadn't seen that coming. "Her pa is the preacher?"

"You sure know how to pick 'em Bobby." John grinned. "You sure know how to pick 'em."

He laughed aloud as he spurred his horse and rode into the herd.

"The preacher." Bob wiped the back of his neck with his handkerchief. "What am I supposed to do with that?"

CHAPTER 26

Bob loved spending time with Lily. He didn't like that her father being the preacher might complicate things. Yet who's to say it would? Just because John thought it might be a problem didn't mean he did. He didn't have anything to be ashamed off, he was respectable. Her being the preacher's daughter didn't change the way he felt about Lily.

He wasn't ready to open up to her about his family and the hell they had been through but he felt at ease with her. That was something he couldn't remember feeling before. He hadn't discussed her with anyone other than Jim and John, but already his sisters were honing in on the fact that *something* was going on with their youngest brother. He sure wasn't going to discuss it with them; they'd be all over it.

Lily had blushed when Bob came right out and asked her if she was the preacher's daughter.

"Well, yes I am." She took his hand. "And my daddy is very protective so let's not appear together openly. I don't want him getting involved. Our friendship is between you and me."

Bob didn't care about that one way or another. He just wanted to spend his time with Lily. So if that was what she wanted, he was fine with it. He hadn't yet asked her father for permission to court her, as John had advised, so he was relieved when she said to leave her father out of it. He'd just as soon put that off. He was content to see Lily quietly and away from home, as long as he was with her. That was all that mattered to him.

"So what's on your mind, little brother? I can tell something is. Something serious and mysterious..." John winked.

He had watched Bob as the days passed into weeks and he knew he had fallen under the spell of the preacher's daughter. It was kinda good to see his brother have a little bit of normal; they both deserved it. The two of them were out rounding up the last of the cattle and John was anxious to clean up and get into town. There'd be a poker game tonight and he had just been paid a little something. He loved skinnin' those boys. They thought that just because he was younger than most of them he didn't know how to scheme. They were proven wrong time after time but they didn't learn. He was real good at playing cards. Maybe he'd make a living traveling all over the country and skinnin' all the poor fools who thought otherwise. His glance at Bobby had taken his mind off that. Bobby had been in the clouds all day.

"C'mon. Tell your brother all about it."

"I'm thinking of asking Lily to marry me."

"What?" John burst out laughing. "You're damn crazy, Bobby! You are really damn crazy!"

Bob bristled. He had expected as much from John but he had wanted to toss the idea out to someone and John just happened to ask. He'd been thinking of it for a couple of days.

"Why is that crazy?"

"You're sixteen damn years old! You have your whole life ahead of you!"

John couldn't believe that Bobby was even thinking about that! What the hell was wrong with him? She was just a girl. Likely the first of many.

"You've got adventures to be had. Places to go. A damn life to be lived!"

"You can be married and still have a life."

"A life of *misery*...having a woman telling you what to think and do." John shook his head. "Why the hell are you even thinking this? You're too damn young. Forget that shit."

"I knew you wouldn't understand. I don't know why I even told you."

"Because you wanted me to talk some sense into you, that's why." He pulled up his reins. "Ohhh...I get it."

"What?" Bob stopped with him.

"I get why you're spoutin' that crap."

"Because I love her. And it isn't crap to me."

"Look, Bobby. You don't have to marry a woman to get in her drawers. You just have to sweet-talk her." He'd done it himself plenty of times. Of course that had been with women who were likely going to go in that direction anyway.

"Shut up! Don't talk that way about Lily. I'm not trying to get in her drawers."

John made him mad. Lily wasn't like the women John hung around in town. Bob had seen him with them. They were all cheap imitations of the type of girl Lily was.

"That's the only possible reason you would be spoutin' that crap." If that wasn't Bobby's intent he had no idea what was driving his line of thought. Nah, it had to be that. "Wonder what her pa would think of you wanting to get in her drawers."

"I'm not trying to get in her drawers!"

"Well, why the hell not?" That didn't make any sense to him either. There had always been a lot about Bobby that didn't make sense to him. Well, it was up to him to pound some sense into Bobby's head about *this*. *This* was serious shit. He changed tactics. There was no better way to rein in your lust than thinking of the girl's father. Her *preacher* father. "Did ya ever talk to her pa like I told ya to do?"

"No."

"Why not?"

"She wants to keep him out of it."

"And why is that?"

"She just wants it to be between us."

"And why is that?"

"Because that's the way she wants it!" John was always so damn confrontational.

A bell went off in John's head. This wasn't good.

"Did'ja ever think that she wants it like that because of who you are?"

"Damn it to hell, John! What are you getting' at?"

"She's probably keeping quiet about it because she doesn't want her pa knowing she's seeing a Younger."

"What do you mean?"

"If her pa knew she was seeing a Younger he might not like it."

"What does that mean? Why wouldn't he like it? Why are you talking in riddles?" This was irritating.

"There's a lot of people here who don't like the men of Quantrill, that's what I mean. They think they're rough men. Men who are beneath them."

"What's that got to do with me?"

"Oh, Bobby, Bobby. You're such a fool in love." He tsked his tongue. "Your brother is Cole Younger. One of the more note-worthy of Quantrill's men. At least to those who don't know him. Your little lady friend might be embarrassed by that and is prob-ably keeping that little fact from her old man."

John's logic wasn't making sense to him. This wasn't Mis-soura. He wasn't Cole and Cole wasn't him. Why should his brother matter to Lily or to her father?

"Cole's got little to do with me, John. Not down here. Besides Lily wouldn't let something like that bother her."

"Okay, Bobby." This boy had it bad. So bad that he wasn't using his head. "Then ask her. Ask her if it matters that Cole is your brother."

"I'll do that, John. I'll just do that."

Bob spurred his horse and left his meddlesome brother in his dust.

But as smug and annoying as he had been, John had been right. It broke Bob's heart in a million pieces but John had been right.

"He's your brother, Bob. I know he's not you but he's your brother. Try to understand..."

Bob stared at Lily. He couldn't believe what he was hearing.

"I *don't* understand."

"He was with those awful bushwhackers all those years.' Lily shuddered.

She had hoped that Bob would understand why they couldn't go public with their relationship. She knew Bob was in love with her. She liked him an awful lot but goodness, she couldn't let her father know she'd been seeing him. He thought those Quantrill men were uncouth and disreputable. He had warned his three daughters away from them or anyone who was their family. Cole Younger, as handsome and courtly as he was, was still one of them. And Cole was Bob's brother. Her father didn't approve of Cole and he would never approve of Bob, who would be guilty by association. Surely Bob could understand that. But she looked at his face and realized that he didn't.

"Cole has stayed friendly with those boorish men. It's not like that's all just a past experience of his."

"Most of those men are honorable men, Lily. They fought for their families when no one else would."

Maybe the men of Quantrill had approached battle in a way that was different, with a resentment that was not always acceptable to everybody, but for the most part they had done what they could for the ultimate welfare of their families. Sure, a lot of them weren't polished and mannerly but Cole wasn't crude and he had manners. And Cole was the one at issue here it seemed.

"My brother is not boorish."

"Bob, there's even a rumor that he had something to do with a robbery in Kentucky! He denies it of course, but that rumor..."

"Do you care about rumors, Lily?"

"Well, of course I do." Were she and Bob really so opposite that he couldn't understand a young woman's place in society?

"Then why haven't you asked me if my brother is guilty of that robbery?"

"Well, I've listened to the talk and I know he probably *is* guilty."

"Oh you do, do you. But you didn't ask. Why not?"

"Oh, Bob." She put her arm through his. "As long as we aren't seen together, it doesn't really matter. Goodness, the talking to I got for dancing with you that first time..." she giggled.

"Are you embarrassed by me Lily?" Bob was beginning to see her in a new light. "Would you be embarrassed to be seen with me because I'm Cole Younger's brother?"

Lily blushed. "What would people think, Bob? They don't know you like I do....they do talk about your brother....and they might think that you companied with those friends of your brothers...."

So she would be embarrassed.

"Many of those men are friends of mine too, Lily."

"Oh Bob, you're teasing me now." She smiled up at him. "You're not a vulgar farm boy like they are. And you couldn't possibly approve of them or their actions during the War. It's just a matter of who one keeps company with. You can't help it that Cole and Jim are your brothers."

All right, Cole he could understand there being some mixed feelings about but Jim? There wasn't a more kind and mannered man than Jim.

"But if we keep to ourselves, none of that matters. It doesn't have to be complicated. My daddy will never find out we've been keeping company and there will be no problem. No shame."

Shame? She was telling him there was shame in their relationship. Because of who his family was. The family that had been through things that no family should ever go through. The family that had banded together to survive.

"There'd be no shame," he repeated. It was he who should be ashamed for letting her charm him and encourage him to sneak around and not be seen in public with her. To deny who he was.

Now she had said cruel things about his family and expected him to continue their relationship despite his *shame* for them.

He couldn't even look at her. The only thing that would be shameful is if he were to continue to keep company with someone who thought he should be ashamed of his family.

"I'll make it easy for you, Lily. You're right. It doesn't have to be complicated at all." Now he did look at her and he didn't like what he saw anymore. "I don't want anything more to do with you."

He turned his back on her and walked away.

Bob took it badly. He thought Lily cared for him like he cared for her but she obviously didn't. If she even cared for him at all, she cared more about how his family was beneath her. That hurt. That hurt a lot. He and his brothers had their quarrels and disagreements but when times were tough they were there for each other. They were his blood. They were his *brothers* and he would never turn his back on them. That Lily didn't understand that about him left him doubting that anybody ever could.

"I hate to see him like this," Cole told Jim as they sat overlooking the herd. Bobby was a good kid. He'd gone through everything he'd gone through and Cole had never heard him complain. He'd always done what needed to be done without bitchin' and he'd become a man in the process.

"I do too." Jim didn't have the experience to counsel Bob. Even if he knew the details of what had happened with the girl, which he didn't because Bob didn't want to talk about it.

"John says the girl had a problem with Bobby's brothers and their wartime activities. What the hell is that about? What possible problem could she have with our respectably serving the Confederate Cause?"

"Leave it be, Cole. He doesn't need his older brothers digging around in his business. This is something Bob needs to work out for himself."

Even John was not immune to Bob's melancholy. As much as he was tempted to say "I told you so", he backed off. But regardless of how Bobby might be feeling about it now, the end of the relationship was for the best as far as he was concerned. There was no way that girl's father was ever going to accept Bobby and the girl obviously had the same viewpoint. She probably was drawn to Bobby in the first place because she liked the adventure of hiding him from her daddy. It was good Bobby discovered that sooner rather than later. All that foolish talk about marrying her. Hell, he was sixteen years old. The oats waiting to be sewn by him knew no bounds. Marry her? That only showed that Bobby didn't have a clue when it came to women. So yeah, it had worked out all for the best, even if Bobby's feelings were hurt. He'd get over it.

But try as he did, Bob couldn't seem to let it go. He had been hurt, yes. And he had been angry. It wasn't fair and it wasn't right. His life always seemed to be examined by his brothers' choices. Wasn't he ever going to be known as his own person or was this the way it was always going to be? It wasn't fair and it wasn't right.

Bob looked to the person from whom he had once found comfort. His mother was sorry for what had happened to him, sorry that he was hurt, but he had done the right thing by walking away from the girl. He should never be ashamed of his family. Family was everything; sometimes all there was.

"But Ma, am I ever going to be looked at as someone apart from my brothers?"

"Family is everything, Bobby. Everything."

He took that to mean that in her mind, maybe in the minds of his brothers themselves, the answer was going to be no, never. To people's way of thinking he would always be seen wrapped within the reputation of his brothers.

While Bob dealt with his hopelessness, his mother troubled over his sadness. There seemed no end to the heartbreak. Her family was broken. Henry was gone, Dick and Caroline and Josie were dead and her girls had lost their innocence. Her boys would never be free of the War. She was their mother and she couldn't make their lives easier or better. In her eyes, she was a constant reminder to them of everything that had gone wrong. She obsessed on all they had lost so much that her health became even more precarious than it had been when they left Missouri. Finally, she asked to go home. She wanted to die in the land where she and Henry had been happiest. She wanted to go home to Missouri.

They gathered at the ranch house. Anne wanted to talk about this without the presence of their mother. She told her brothers about Bursheba's request.

"That's out of the question. We're not going back there with Ma." Cole was adamant. "She won't be any happier there than she is here. This is where our life is now."

"It's what she wants, Cole." Jim couldn't stand to see his mother this way. Where she had once been animated and involved in their lives, she now was nothing but consumed by her loss. "Texas isn't her life."

"Not much of anything is her life anymore." There, thought John. It's been said. Somebody had to say it.

"Shut the hell up, John. I won't hear you talking about Ma like that." Cole's misdirected anger was palpable.

"If we're talking about Ma's life, let's be honest." It hurt John too but they had to face reality. "She only came down here because you told her we could all start over."

"And maybe we can and maybe we can't," Jim added looking at Bob. "But Texas isn't Ma's home. Whatever thread of her life is left for her is back in Missouri. With Pa."

"Well, we're alive!" Cole declared. "Pa's dead!" What the hell was wrong with Jim? Cole was never surprised when John mouthed off but why was Jim advocating a return to Missoura?

"You think she doesn't know that Cole?" Bob shook his head.

"It's best for us to stay put here. We're staying here."

John exploded, jumping to his feet. "It's always about you! What Cole wants, what Cole doesn't want. What Cole thinks is best. For God's sake, let *Ma* decide what's best for *her*!"

"Don't you talk to me like that you damn pup!"

Cole started to cross the room toward John.

Anne jumped up and stood between them. "Please, don't do this to each other! Just don't do it."

Cole and John backed down, still glaring at each other.

"It doesn't matter what we want, Cole," Retta said softly. "Mother wants to go home. How can we not take her home?"

All eyes were on Cole, but he wasn't ready to give this up.

"We've got a drive coming up. I've got two hundred head of cattle ready to go to Oklahoma and Arkansas. Even if we decide to take her up there we'll have to wait until we get back from that."

"Ma doesn't have that kind of time, Cole," Jim said quietly. "We all know that."

"I don't know any such thing, Jim. She'll pull out of this malaise. She just needs us to help her out of it."

"You know it's true, Cole." Bob felt an unusual wave of compassion toward Cole roll over him. Cole just didn't want to face the truth. "None of us want it that way, but you know it's true. Ma has given up on her life. She wants to go home. We've got no choice."

Cole couldn't bear the finality of what they were saying. Their mother would be fine. She was a strong woman. She'd pull out of this and be the woman she once was....

"I've got the cattle..."

"We can hire some of the boys to help you with them," Jim suggested. "John, Bob and I will take Ma up to Jackson County. Belle said Ma can stay with them in Strother. We can get her home safely."

"I'll tend to her, Cole. I'll tend to Mother." Retta put her arms around Cole.

"I reckon you will, Rett," he sighed. Although she was only thirteen years old, Retta had been tending to their mother's needs for years. "But I'm saying here and now, and you can mark my words, Ma isn't going home to die. She'll get stronger up there and in the fall she can come back to Texas and be happy."

Cole grabbed his hat off the table and stormed out the door.

CHAPTER 27

After the dusty, barren terrain of Texas, Bob was awed by the beautiful fields of Missoura. There was green everywhere he looked and the cottonwoods and sweet gums blew gently in a breeze that carried memories of better times. He was home. He hadn't realized how much he missed it.

Crops were once again growing in the fields. He saw the leaves of cabbage, collards and snap beans and a field ripe with sweet potatoes. He couldn't stop talking about how good a fresh slice of watermelon would taste and John finally jumped down from his horse and grabbed one out of a field just to shut him up. When they encountered a man farming a ways up the road, Jim threw him a coin and thanked him for indulging his brother. The man tipped his hat and Bob found optimism in that. Maybe things were better now. Maybe now people had returned to the way things used to be between neighbors. Maybe now everybody was just getting along, no thought of politics or which side you were on or who it was you hatred or feared. Maybe all that was finally over.

It was less than a week when Bob's hopes for change were destroyed and once again reality came crashing down.

A group of riders appeared outside Belle and Dick Hall's home. Jim and John had gone to town and Bob was helping Dick reset his front yard fence.

"Where are your wife's brothers, Hall? We seen this one and t'other. Where's Cole Younger?"

The men astride the mangy horses didn't look local. They were shabbily dressed and Bob could smell the stink from a couple of yards away.

"Well now, I don't reckon I know." Dick scratched his chin. "I haven't seen Cole Younger in an awful long time."

The man snickered. "Yeah, we figured you'd say that."

The rider next to him looked at Bob. "This one ain't the other one."

Dick shook his head from side to side. These men were ignorant. They were probably riding Western Missouri looking for Quantrill men so they could collect the bounty. "No, this one ain't the other one."

"Where's that one?" the first man questioned as if they should know exactly who it was being sought.

"If you're talking about my brother Jim, his whereabouts aren't any concern of yours." Bob wasn't about to take anything off this mangy collection of good-for-nothings. "He's sworn his oath."

"Is that right." Now the rider smiled. A big, near-toothless grin. He motioned to the other two and they maneuvered their horses away from the fence.

Bob watched the men ride slowly down the road. "They're not finished with us," he said aloud.

Dick nodded.

"Goddamn it!"

John was pacing in front of the barn. Bob and Dick had met Jim and John there when they arrived home.

"I'm not surprised they heard you boys were around." Dick had tried to tell Belle that having her brothers stay with them would bring trouble but she didn't want to hear it. She wanted her mother home.

"I should have known they'd come looking." Jim stood looking down at the ground.

"You shouldn't feel bad about that, Jim," Bob dismissed. "You swore the damn oath. They've got no quarrel with you."

Bob was angry. It was one thing for them to come around for Cole but Jim had sworn the damn oath. There was no reason to be bothering him.

"It doesn't matter. There are plenty of those who don't care about that." Jim sighed. "It's best I go back down to Texas. I don't want them coming back and upsetting Ma."

So Jim headed back to Texas and John and Bob stayed on for the time being. John was all for he and Bob going back themselves but when Bob said he didn't think their mother had long to live and that he wasn't leaving her, John decided to stay as well. If there was any trouble he wasn't going to leave Bob to deal with it alone.

That was the right decision, but one that didn't come without penalty for John.

The sun was setting and they had just finished eating supper. Bob was thinking it was a nice feeling to be with his older sister and her family. Belle and Dick had three little girls so when it came time for the evening meal there were nine at the table.

John and Bob were teasing the Hall girls by tossing their doll around and the noise as the girls hollered and yelped was so loud that at first no one heard the knock on the door.

John held the doll up over his head as he got up.

"Someone's at the door you little wenches and I'm handing over your doll," he laughed maniacally as he opened the door.

On the other side stood the three men who a few days ago had asked about Cole and Jim.

John tossed the doll over his head and the girls scrambled to retrieve it.

"What the hell do you want?" he said quietly. "Y'all don't have any business here."

"Who is it, John?" Belle called from the parlor where she was sitting with her mother and Dick.

"Nobody."

John stepped out before his mother could see the men. She would know why they were there. He shut the door behind him and walked down the path. The men followed.

"Why the hell are you here? My brothers are nowhere around."

"Says you," the tallest one smirked. "Why don't you save us all trouble and just tell us where Cole and t'other one is and we can have a little chat with them. No need to bother respectable folks." He nodded toward the house. "Or damn rebels either."

The three men laughed.

"My brother is nowhere around and I don't know where the hell Cole is either. We haven't seen him in years. Last I heard he was out in California. So you've got no business here."

"Oh, well for heaven's sake. We didn't know all that. We'll just be on our way then."

The tall man started to turn as if to leave then turned back and grabbed John around the neck. One of the others grabbed his swinging fists.

"You expect us to believe that, you sumbitch? You think we're stupid?"

"I don't think you're stupid, I know you're stupid." John struggled to get free.

"Hey! Leave him alone!" Bob yelled as he ran down the steps of the porch.

The third man violently shoved Bob head first into the porch rail. He fell down the steps in a heap.

Dick clamored out the door followed closely by Belle and Retta.

"Leave them alone!" Retta screamed as Belle bent over Bob. "Leave my brothers alone!"

"Bring him here!" the tall man directed.

There were two other men near the barn. They took hold of John and dragged him kicking toward the barn.

"We know damn well Cole Younger ain't in California, you lyin' bastard!"

One of the men at the barn threw a noose over John's head and drew it tight.

Bob pushed up and away from his sisters. He ran blindly at the men, trying to ignore the dizziness and nausea that engulfed him.

One of the men grabbed him and threw him to the ground. He fought to break free but was pinned when the second man straddled him. As he kicked and struggled, a gun was pulled and pointed at his head.

In the barn, the rope was thrown over a beam and the men hoisted John. John grabbed at the rope around his neck, kicking out at the air.

"Where's your brother, sonny?" the tall man leered.

They lowered John.

"California." John spat.

They hoisted him again, this time holding him in the air longer.

"Where was that?"

They lowered him.

"California."

They yanked him hard. He clawed at his neck.

"Let him go!" Bob fought for all he was worth, ignoring the gun.

"Should I just let him have it?" the man atop him asked the man next to him.

"Nah, not yet. We might want him after this." He kicked Bob brutally in the side.

It was all happening so fast that Dick Hall didn't know what to do first.

"Let him down!" he hollered. "You're killing him!"

"We're searching the house," one of the men informed Dick, pushing past him.

"My children are in there!" Belle screamed.

"Prob'ly with some guerilla scum, we're bettin'."

The other men lowered John again.

"Where's your brother? Why don't you just tell me now?"

John could barely speak. The pain was harsh but he was damned if he was going to give them any satisfaction.

"California," he sputtered.

They hoisted him again. This time the rope cut through the skin of his neck. He kicked until the blood rushed from his head and he went limp.

The man who had entered the house came outside. He had found no one but the children and an old woman in the house. He didn't want to waste time and miss what was going on in the barn.

"For God's sake, let the boy down!" Dick yelled.

"Aw, hell," shrugged the tall man. "He's dead. Now he can't tell us what we want to know."

They lowered John, unconscious, to the ground.

"Let's not leave out this one." They started toward Bob.

A blast cut through the air. They all stopped dead in their tracks. Dick Hall pointed his shotgun at the men on the ground with Bob.

"Leave him alone." He couldn't let them see him shake as he held fast to the weapon. "You men get on out of here or I swear to God one or two of you won't have the opportunity."

They froze. Finally the tall man gestured to the others.

"They don't know nothin'. We might as well head out."

They walked slowly to their horses.

"You be mindin' that shotgun, mister."

"Get." Dick followed them with the gun.

They mounted their horses.

"You tell Cole Younger, when he gets back from *California,* that if he steps one foot into Jackson County he's a dead man," one hollered. "Y'hear me? A dead man!"

Dick didn't put the gun down until the sounds of their horses faded.

When John was carried into the house and placed on a bed, his mother didn't say a word. John was a healthy young man and he would recover. But she wouldn't. She couldn't take one more tragedy, one more encounter. Lord help her, she had tried. She had tried to keep her children safe but she had failed. She had nothing left to give.

After her daughters helped her into bed that night, she asked for Bob.

"Is your head all right, son?"

He had a hell of a headache, that was for sure, to say nothing of the pain in his ribs. "It's all right, Ma."

He knew she had given up. He could see it. She was fading before his eyes and he was powerless to stop it. What could he tell her to make her want to keep living? There wasn't a damn thing that would give her any kind of hope.

"Bobby, I need you to tell Jim," she whispered, grabbing his hand.

"Tell Jim what Ma?"

"Tell Jim that he must do whatever he can so you children are always a family." Tears rolled down her cheeks. "Promise me you'll tell him that, Bobby."

That was a hard burden to put on Jim. He knew their mother trusted Jim to be there for them and all but that was a hard burden.

"Promise, Bobby." She gripped his hand tighter. "Promise me."

"All right, Ma. I promise. I'll tell Jim. Now you rest."

Bursheba never spoke again. A few days later when Retta entered her mother's bedroom, she knew their mother was gone.

Bursheba Fristoe Younger was put into the ground in the cemetery in the middle of town. There is a reason a grave is called a resting place. It surely was for her.

As saddened as he was that his mother was gone, Bob was relieved that she would no longer feel her pain. She had been through a lifetime of sorrow in the past ten years and there was only so much anybody could take. Tears rolled down his cheeks as he stood in front of her grave. His mother might be with Jesus now but their enemies remained here on earth. He would keep his promise to his ma to give Jim her message, but he also made a promise to himself. She likely wouldn't approve but he owed her: whatever it took, however it came, he would somehow avenge his mother's persecution. He owed her and his pa that much.

He would make things right.

CHAPTER 28

It was decided that it would be best for Retta to return to Texas to live with Ann and Curg Jones. Bob was relieved to have a reason to go back to Texas. If he stayed in Missoura right now all he would think about was that both his father and mother were in the ground.

Bob and John loaded up a buckboard with Retta's few items and headed south to Denison, where Curg had opened his furniture store. They met up with Jim after they got there. Curg was doing pretty well for himself and Ann's family loved it down there. They tried to have few thoughts about their recent lives in Missoura.

Bob figured he might as well work with Cole's cattle in Scyene for the time being but it wasn't going to be a permanent thing. He still didn't like it all that much but he just couldn't be in Missoura right now, no matter how much he loved it.

For the first time in his life Cole felt a little guilty. He wondered if his brothers held him accountable for their mother's bad health and ultimate death. He didn't ask them that. Their likely response would only make him feel worse.

The four brothers settled back into the routine of ranching. Cole kinda liked the business. It provided them all with a little money and that was welcome. He didn't want to be doing this all his life but it was okay for now. The time Jim spent with the horses suited him; the cattle not as much. John, nothing new here, gripped about the hot conditions and the dirty work. He didn't like this ranching thing one little bit. Bob didn't mind hard work, but frankly, he was just plain bored with it.

John finally talked Cole into letting him go along to Louisiana when the time for the next drive came around. If he was going to be with the damn cows, at least he'd be somewhere new. But their troubles followed them even there. Cole was accused of rigging a horse race and during the ensuing argument he shot the man. Cole didn't kill him but the news traveled back to Scyene fast enough. Talk of Cole Younger and his questionable activities seemed to once again be on everyone's lips.

Bob was sick of it. He went to stay with Anne and Curg. He'd be damned if he was going to listen to all of it all over again.

"Aw, who cares about that talk? People gotta have something to jaw about."

Cole dismissed Bob's explanation of why he wasn't in Scyene. He and John had returned from Louisiana and were having dinner at the Joneses.

"Well, I'm tired of them jawing about us. About *you*." Bob's eyes shot daggers at Cole.

Cole took another bite of potatoes. "It's not my fault they find me interesting."

"It's never your fault!" Bob banged the table. His brothers and sisters looked at him in surprise. "We've been living through things that aren't your damn fault for ten damn years!"

"Now wait a minute...." Cole's fork stopped in midair.

"Bobby!" Anne had never heard her youngest brother raise his voice like this. She was glad that she had fed the children earlier and they weren't at the table.

"I'm sorry, Annie, but it needs to be said." Bob continued to glare at Cole, daring him to say otherwise.

"You can't blame me for what the Yankees did. I wasn't going to just sit there and let them plow through our lives, plow through Pa's land…"

"Don't bring Pa into this!" Bob jumped to his feet. "Pa never wanted war! There was a reason he never took a stand. If more men had tried to work out their differences, maybe we wouldn't be sitting here having this conversation!"

"Don't you be telling me that what I did was wrong," Cole said quietly, his eyes narrowed. "I won't take that from the Yankees and I won't take it from you. Sometimes the only way to work things out is to go to war. I'd think you'd have learned that by now."

"No! Yes! I don't know! I'm tired of it! I'm tired of thinking about *The War.* I'm tired of hearing about it, having to live it over and over again! I'm tired of it being a part of every breath I take!"

Bob threw his napkin down on the table. "I'm sorry Annie, Curg."

He walked out the door, slamming it behind him.

Cole started to rise.

"Let him be, Cole," Jim nodded. "He needed to get that out. It's been festering a long time."

"He's right, you know." John reached for the meat platter as he chewed.

"Don't you start *your* shit!" Cole glared now at John.

"Just sayin'." John cut his meat. "Everywhere we go, all people want to talk about is Cole Younger. Either they want to yak about the War or they want to speculate about robberies or shootin' or whatever the hell Cole Younger has done this time." He took a bite. "Cole Younger, Cole Younger, Cole Younger."

Cole stood up. "I'm not responsible for people talking about me. If they've got nothing better to do that's just the way it is." He walked into the kitchen with his plate.

John continued eating.

"I've had enough of his bullshit too." John leaned against the fence rail as Bob paced before him.

"It's not just Cole's bullshit, John. It's all of it. We came down here to get away from all that happened in Missoura and the fact of the matter is, we can't."

"You know, Bobby, maybe it's what we make of it. We don't have to let it hang over us like some kind of black cloud, you know."

He wasn't being rough on Bob; he just needed to point that out. Some people their sister Annie for one, had made the best of the situation and gotten on with things.

"Do you think I choose to stay in the past? Why would I want to do that? It's not a choice I make when every time I turn around somebody is bringing it up in one way or another!"

'It's like Cole was saying," John shrugged. "People have to jaw about something."

Bob didn't reply.

"You gotta stop letting it eat you up, Bobby." John stood up. "There's nothin' good gonna come of that. Brush it off; let it go."

"I'd like nothing better than to let it go, John." Bob kicked a loose stone. "You, of all people, should know better than that."

A breeze blew through. John let out a long sigh. Everybody lived their life the way they did. What could he do about that? He could only live his own.

"I'm heading to Dallas."

"It's awful late for a trip like that." So the subject was changed. That was fine.

"Not tonight. Tomorrow morning. I'm leaving this cattle thing."

"What?"

"I'm gonna get me a job in a dry goods store. I know from helping out at Pa's how to do that kind of work."

"You're saying you're going to live in Dallas?"

"Yeah. Dallas has more going for it than this dusty no man's land. Dallas has poker games, whiskey, women..." he leered. "I'm much more suited to Dallas."

"You're going to live in Dallas?"

"Yes, Bobby, I'm going to live in Dallas."

"Were you gonna stay?"

"I can rent a room." He smiled. "You should come with me. Wouldn't we have fun?"

"Nah, you go ahead and go."

Bob had never even considered the possibility that he and John would take different paths but his interests weren't the same as John's. He'd leave Dallas to John. One bad apple is all that tree could bear.

CHAPTER 29

With his charm and cunning, it didn't take John long to land a job at Geary's Dry Goods. And he was doing well at it too. He was good-looking and Geary's female customers were his delight. He'd flash them his smile and before they knew it they were buying items they didn't need and didn't even want. Mr. Geary was pleased with his work; how could he not be?

What Geary wasn't pleased with was John's hangovers, which had started to become all too predictable.

"You need to lay off of that rotgut, Junior," Geary warned. "And get some better friends. That bunch you've put in with are no damn good."

"Yeah, I need to do that, Mr. Geary."

Like hell he would. Every night John would find a poker game, a bottle of whiskey and a woman. This was the life. He had no one to be accountable to other than himself here. He'd work at the store for the money to pay for his evenings but other than that he could come and go as he pleased. This was what he'd always wanted, wasn't it?

Yet as the nights became longer and the mornings more dreadful, he began to think that maybe all this was too much of a good thing.

When Jim and Bob showed up one Sunday afternoon John was glad to see them.

"You look awful," Bob observed. "Like something died in your hair and has started to rot on your face."

"Thanks, Bobby. Good to see you too."

Jim just nodded.

"What brings you two cowpokes to Dallas?"

"We thought we'd stumble around drunk and cheat at poker." Bob wiggled his eyebrows. "Isn't that your specialty?"

"Go to hell," John dismissed.

"We're thinking of taking a trip to St. Clair," Jim told him. "To the Springs."

"Oh yeah? Why's that?"

"Just want to," Bob replied.

The fact of the matter was that Bob and Jim had both had enough of the Texas dust for a while. They longed for Missoura and her green fields and flowering meadows. Anything that wasn't dirt colored.

"Wanna come?"

John thought about it for about a second. Maybe the change in location was a good idea.

Life at the Springs was as it always had been, the quiet only disrupted by the arrival of someone from somewhere else. It was nice to kick back and it was nice to see new faces among the old friends. There was actually something to talk about for a change.

With the eyes of his brothers settled on him to keep him from overindulging, John still managed to entertain himself. He made a game of scrutinizing the transient patrons to determine whether or not they were Yankees. He participated in card games and was seen on many occasions in the company of a lovely girl, sometimes even two.

That was fine for John, but Jim's idea of how to pass the day was taking long rides throughout the countryside and alongside the Osage River. St. Clair County was a beautiful place. One day he discovered a rocky plateau that looked over the tranquility of the river and further down into the colorful foothills of the Ozark Mountains. He liked to spend time sitting there to read. And to think. Jim's mind took some interesting paths.

Many times Bob would join Jim there. Bob didn't like to read all that much but he loved sitting on the cliff to look over the green trees and pasturelands of Missoura. There was no place like it in his mind. The Bobwhites and the Kildeers called out over the hills and the cottontails and squirrels rustled in the brush. It was quiet and it was peaceful. And it was Missoura. He didn't have a real home these days but if he could call anywhere that, it was Missoura.

One day John decided to join his brothers there. As Jim read and Bob lay against the rock with his eyes closed, listening to the flutter of wildlife, John decided to explore. He wound his way downhill to a cut in the rock.

"Hey! Look it here," he called.

Bob looked over the cliff to the sound of John's voice.

"We can't see you down there, idiot."

"Come on down then."

John had discovered that beneath the plateau was a shallow cave. The rock above hung over its entrance. The branches of the trees reached out to envelop it within hardwood-scented arms.

"This is nice," Bob observed. "It's like a secret cavern."

"Yeah, it'll be *our* secret cavern," John decided. "I decree that this little spot on God's green earth belongs to the Younger boys. Visits by invitation only."

Bob would have been content in St. Clair were it not for the letters he received from Retta. She missed her brothers and felt that Bob had abandoned her. She hadn't recovered from her grief of losing their mother and as good as Anne and Curg were to her she'd like nothing better than for Bobby to return.

It made Bob feel guilty but he liked it more just where he was.

Jim was quite at ease in St. Clair too. He had been spending time in Osceola in the company of Dr. McNeill's daughter, Cora.

Cora was a pretty young woman whose enthusiasm and cheerful approach to life made Jim feel alive again. He began to think that he would like to marry Cora and start a family of his own. Cora thought maybe that was a bit premature but Jim said he'd wait until she was ready. She made him the happiest he had ever been.

"We're gonna go down and see Retta," Bob now told Jim. "I guess she feels like I deserted her."

"You can't hold as true what a woman feels." John rolled his eyes.

Jim ignored him. "You do what feels right to you, Bob. I don't think you deserted her but I know she must miss you."

"It'll be good to get back to something more profitable; a better game of cards," John mused. "I've about milked these excursionists dry."

CHAPTER 30

1871

John should have stayed in Monagaw. He wasn't able to get his Dallas job back so he took a clerking position at a store in Scyene. It was all right. He half-heartedly moved through his day and did what needed to be done but more important to him was what went on after the sun went down. Then he would lounge at the saloon with a new group of friends that included some of the Quantrill and Anderson men. He had decided that this time he would let Cole's reputation work for him. Any brother of Cole Younger and all that...

Then came that night in January when passing time with those ruffians maybe wasn't turning out to be a good idea.

John had become friendly with a Missourian named Tom McDaniels. McDaniels was interested in the same things as John, mainly drinking, playing cards and wasting time. There wasn't anything more important to do, so why not?

It was a chilly evening and the usual round-up of ole boys had been hitting the whiskey a little too hard. Gibb Russell was sweeping the floor as he always did. The spillage from the drinking and jostling made it hard for the slow-witted man to keep up with his work tonight. Gibb didn't like the saloon's loud music or the unruly behavior of the young men who came in night after night but he was happy to have the employment. He put up with their nightly teasing without saying anything back at 'em; he just wanted to do his job.

The boys were getting into their wartime storytelling and John was getting bored. Sometimes that's all they wanted to talk about and the subject had been *covered* as far as John was concerned. His mind was wandering when Gibb crossed his line of vision. John smiled and picked up McDaniels' pipe.

"Hey there, Gibb!" he hollered across the floor.

Gibb stopped his sweeping.

"C'mere!"

Gibb gave him a wary look. John got up from his chair.

"All right then, I'll come to you." He crossed the floor. "Put this pipe in your mouth."

He lifted the pipe to Gibb's lips.

"No Sir, I don't smoke no pipe." Gibb ducked his head.

"You don't have to smoke it, Gibb," John smiled. "I want to show you a little trick."

"What kind a trick?"

"Just put it in your mouth and I'll show you." John poked the pipe into Gibb's mouth. "Now you stay right there."

John walked back to where he had been sitting.

"What the hell you doing with my pipe, Younger?" McDaniel asked.

"Gibb's going to help me with a little demonstration."

John had taken to wearing a holster and he now drew out his Army Colt.

"I'm gonna shoot that pipe right out of ol' Gibb's mouth. You hold still now Gibb."

"No, Sir!" Gibb yelled as John fired two shells into the floor near his feet.

As the pipe fell out of Gibb's mouth, he dropped his broom and covered his head. John smiled as his friends roared with laughter.

"Get a little closer, Younger! You didn't come nowhere near that pipe!" one of them hollered.

"C'mon Gibb. Put that pipe between your pearly whites. I won't hit cha." John raised his gun.

But when he saw the look of terror on Gibb's face he lowered it. This was just a joke. He wasn't tryin' to hurt the man.

"C'mon, Younger! You can do better than that. That pipe's plenty big and Gibb's a good-sized target," another yelled.

Gibb stood stock still, his face drained of all color.

"Nah, I don't want to ruin McDaniel's pipe." John put his gun back in his holster and sat down. The others laughed.

"To hell with my pipe, you'da been more likely to ruin Ol' Gibb!" McDaniel snickered.

"Hey Gibb, Younger was trying to shoot you dead!" Abe Lee hollered to Gibb. "I'd go tell the sheriff if I was you."

They all laughed and resumed their drinking.

Still shaking, Gibb picked up his broom and started sweeping behind the bar. He kept his eyes on John and his friends until they were long out the door.

John and McDaniel were eating their breakfast at the hotel the next day when Deputy Charlie Nichols approached them with his friend Jim McMahon. Nichols had served under General Jo Shelby during the War and was a friend of Cole's.

"Well, John. We're going to have to arrest you," Nichols announced.

"Arrest me?" John stopped eating. "What the hell for?"

"Well, Gibb Russell says you tried to kill him."

"I didn't try to kill Gibb Russell, Nichols," John laughed. "We were just having some fun."

"That may be so but if Gibb says you tried to kill him, I've got no choice but to arrest you."

"All right." John nodded his head. He wondered who set this up. This wasn't amusing. "Can I finish my breakfast first?"

Nichols considered. It was Cole's brother, after all, and Cole was a man of his word.

"Well, I guess that'd be all right. When you're finished eating you come on over to the dry goods store. It's damn cold out. We'll be warming ourselves by the stove."

The two men walked out.

"Do you believe that?" John stared at their backs.

"Gibb must have taken Abe Lee's advice," McDaniels laughed. "Maybe he's not as dumb as he looks."

"This isn't funny, McDaniels." John frowned. "Nichols is going to arrest me for God 'sake, joke or not."

"Aw, that's his job but you'll talk your way out of it." McDaniels shrugged. "You always do."

"Maybe I should just go get my horse and head out of town for a while, let things cool," John considered. This really wasn't amusing, not one little bit. He'd been in a sheriff's jail once before and he sure as hell didn't like it.

"You do that and you'll have more of a mess."

"Yeah, don't need more of a mess. And I gave my word. I'll talk to Gibb and apologize. It'll be all right. I'll tell Nichols I'm going to talk to Gibb."

"I'll go with you. This is entertaining."

"Glad to be of service," John growled.

When they walked out the front door John stopped hard in his tracks.

"Look at this!"

Nate Harper, who sometimes worked for the Sheriff, was standing by John's horse.

"What are you doing with my horse, Nate?"

"Guess Nichols thought you might be taking off before he got a chance to talk to you, Younger," Harper smiled. That wasn't the truth but it made for good drama.

"What? He put a guard on my horse?"

John was outraged. Nichols knew him, he knew Cole, he knew his family. This was insulting!

John strode across the street to the dry goods store. He burst into the store, McDaniels right behind him.

"Why the hell did you put a man on my horse?" he yelled at Nichols. "My word isn't good enough for you?"

"Calm down, Younger," McMahon suggested.

"Calm down? This man knows me. He knows my word is good and he put a damn guard on my horse!"

Nichols knew John Younger and he knew that he was impulsive. He hadn't in fact put a guard on Younger's horse but if Younger thought that was the case maybe that was in Nichols' favor.

"Nothing personal."

"Nothing personal? You son of a bitch! You know I'm good for my word! What kind of a man are you?"

This was getting out of hand. John Younger had a temper but he was shouting at the law. Instinctively McMahon's hand went to his gun.

Thinking McMahon was going to draw against him, John drew his own gun at the same time.

"What are you doing?" John yelled in confusion as he fired.

His shot hit McMahon squarely in the chest.

Nichols was surprised at the sudden gunplay and shot at John, nicking his arm.

"Lookout, John!" McDaniels drew his gun and shot Nichols.

The mess had just gotten worse.

James McMahon fell dead by the stove. Nichols lay wounded next to him.

John and McDaniels ran out the door, jumped on their horses and rode the hell out of town.

Within a few short days Nichols too was dead. The first lawman to be killed in Dallas County.

As for John? Well, Cole had nothing on him anymore.

John was now a wanted man too.

"You goddamn fool!" Cole was angry, although not surprised. John's quick temper was bound to get him into trouble one day. He'd seen that coming for a looong time.

"The man insulted my honor, Cole!" John was pacing, holding his injured arm. "It moved too fast! It's not like I planned it!"

"You've got to get your ass out of Texas." Cole shook his head. "Now."

John nodded. Well, yeah. Anybody with a lick of sense would know that. Things had been going so well and now this. It was always some damn thing. Yet this time it wasn't the Yankees to blame. It was his own lack of judgment. Well, shit. Anybody could make a mistake.

Cole had figured John knew enough not to go to Missoura. He was wrong. John didn't know where to go so he headed to St. Clair, where he at least had friends. But after John arrived back in Monagaw, Jim told him that may not have been a smart move.

"If any law from Texas is going to make the effort to pursue you, Missoura is probably the first place they'll look." Jim was disgusted that John had gotten himself into this predicament.

"I can go over to Little Rock." John didn't know *what* the hell to do. "Nobody knows me in Arkansas, anyway."

So that's where he headed. It was as good a choice as any. He found a job in another dry goods store but the next day he discovered that the store was owned by Wade Blayne, the man who had once managed Henry's Harrisonville livery. So much for nobody knowing him.

He was in Kansas City by April. His sister Sally said he could stay with her family but he better not act up. Okay, it wouldn't hurt to lay low for a while.

The members of his family down in Texas didn't know where John was but they knew he would land on his feet somewhere.

That's what the brothers Younger knew how to do.

CHAPTER 31

On June 3, most of those who lived in the Iowa town of Corydon were gathered at the courthouse square to listen to a speech by Henry Clay Dean. They didn't know quite what to expect but it was bound to be spirited. Dean was one of those so-called Copperheads, a vocal group who were anti-war and who blamed abolitionists for the War Between the States. He was in town to talk about the proposed railroad. That was something that could affect them all and their eyes and ears were squarely on Dean – he had their complete attention.

While Dean was holding the townspeople captive with his colorful oratory, four men slipped into the bank and stole near to $10,000.

"It would have gone off without anyone suspecting us if it wasn't for Dingus's ego!" Cole later ranted to Frank.

Cole and Frank had enlisted their friend Clell Miller for this one and it was supposed to be like taking candy from a baby. Which it had been. It was what came after that had Cole worked up.

"Why in hell would that idiot stop at the assembly to tell 'em someone robbed the bank! That the clerk is tied up and someone might want to set him free?"

"Just having fun," Frank shrugged. No one could get Cole riled up like Jesse and it amused Frank. "I like the part where Dean thought it was a ploy to disrupt his meeting. That was rich."

"Goddamn Dingus!"

The Corydon banker didn't think it was funny either and he was a man of influence. He went ahead and influenced William A. Pinkerton of the Pinkerton Detective Agency of Chicago to become personally involved. Pinkerton sent a couple of his men to Iowa, and although the robbers were long gone by the time they arrived, a detective named Westfall tracked them into north-western Missouri. That was fine but no one really knew what they looked like. There wasn't much you could do with that.

Leave it to Jesse to stir the pot. He wrote a letter to the *Kansas City Times* stating that any talk that he and Frank had been involved was "a falsehood as ever was uttered from human lips".

When John heard about the robbery he was pretty sure that Cole was involved. Now people might show up at the Kelley's looking for his brother again. He immediately set off back to Monagaw.

Jim was still living in St. Clair County and Cole would likely head down that way too.

It became a real family reunion when Bob showed up.

The boys' uncle T.J. was at the Springs. He had just been married and was ready to leave on his honeymoon trip to Los Angeles.

"California's a land of promise," he told his nephews. "There's a lot going on there. It'll be exciting."

"You ought to take John with you," Cole glowered at his brother. "He likes excitement."

"Actually, you might give it some thought, John." T.J. nodded. "I have a friend named Philip Ruiz who has a hardware and saddle shop in Los Angeles. I could recommend you for a job, if you like."

That sounded good to John. He was ready for someplace new.

The day after they saw John off to California, Cole, Jim and Bob sat having supper at the Monagaw Hotel.

"I tell ya, it's a hoot to ride away with all that Yankee money."

Cole had been bragging about the robberies but Bob was only half-listening. He'd heard the stories before but he couldn't help wondering if the experience was as enjoyable as Cole said it was. There was a lot of danger involved in it. Yet just about anything at all would be more appealing than the dull life *he* was living.

"Do you even care that what you're doing is reflecting poorly on your family?" Jim was disgusted with the whole thing. "It only draws further negativity."

"Aw, Jim. You have no sense of adventure," Cole dismissed.

"Yeah, what's the matter with you, Jim?" Bob rolled his eyes. "What a sheltered life you've led."

The last thing that Jim wanted to be talking about was Cole's "adventures". And he had been deeply troubled by John's situation in Texas. He was relieved when T.J. took his brother to California. Hopefully he would stay out of trouble out there.

Jim was also concerned about Bob. The boy had no direction in life. Jim had talked to Cole about that and Cole said he agreed.

"I've been thinking about your situation, Bobby." Cole, as usual, didn't give any credit to the fact that Jim was the one who had initially broached the subject.

"What situation is that, Cole? I don't have a situation."

"Yeah, well, that's the point." Cole glanced at Jim. Cole was the oldest brother and he would handle this. "You can't just be wandering from here to Texas and back all the time."

"It doesn't bother me."

But it did. Bob didn't enjoy his nomadic life. He liked being around family but he was well aware that he didn't have any home base or anything to take up his time. He didn't need Cole to tell him that. He wanted to farm, but he didn't have that kind of money. Or any place to do it, really. During his childhood he had lived day to day, not even knowing if the next day would be there for him. Now the days passed slowly and so did the months. There wasn't much of anything there; not much to life at all.

"Well, maybe it doesn't bother you but as I said, I've been thinking." Cole lit a cigar and took a long puff.

Bob was always amused by the fact that Cole thought smoking a cigar made him look like a gentleman. To Bob he just looked like a country boy with a cigar.

"You're a smart boy."

"That so? Then maybe I ought to start up a business enterprise. A bank maybe." Bob didn't like Cole thinking about his future any more than he liked Cole telling him what to do. "But I'll need your word that you and the James boys won't ride off with what's mine."

"Ha Ha." Cole blew out a stream of smoke. Bobby had become cynical since that business in Texas. He had an edge to him now. "You know our family has ties to Virginia. Granddad was born there."

"Yeah, Cole I know." Bob had been less than a year old when their grandfather Charlie Younger had died. All Bob knew of him were the stories about how he was a colorful ole cuss and how he had a slew of children from his two wives, his mistress and his mulatto slave. Busy man, ole Charlie. Bob thought that his pa was actually embarrassed by his grandfather more than anything else. "So?"

"Well, there's a real fine college there. William and Mary. It's expensive but I'm a bit flush right now." He smiled.

Jim watched Bob's face. He thought Bob furthering his education was a very good idea. Bob was smart and it had always bothered Jim that, because of the War, Bob was not well-schooled.

Bob reacted differently. He thought Cole was out of his mind.

"Oh that's rich, even for you. I'm not a candidate for college. My school days stopped the minute war was declared."

Jim looked at Bob. He could tell his brother was embarrassed by that.

"It's true that you didn't have the benefit of a formal education, Bob, but you're very intelligent. There's no reason you can't enroll in William and Mary and expand your knowledge."

Bob had never even considered furthering his education. As far as he was concerned the time for that had come and passed. He shook his head.

"No, y'all are crazy. You must have me mixed up with someone else."

"You like being a cattleman, Bobby? It's either this or that."

"Don't give me an ultimatum, Cole," Bob bristled. "You haven't earned that right."

Jim rolled his eyes at Cole. If he thought that tactic would work he didn't know Bob at all.

"I'm heading over that way to check out some cattle," Cole lied. "I'll take you there, if you like."

"Oh, now you're going to escort me to school like I was a little child? Will you wipe my ass when it needs it too?"

Cole looked again at Jim. Jim gave a slight shake of his head.

"You're right. How's this then? I'll give you the money to take care of the matter yourself. I thought I'd have a look at Florida. I've been hearing it's quite a place. I'll ride with you to Virginia and you can take it from there."

Bob considered. It wasn't like he had anything better to do with his life. Maybe if he was better educated he'd be in a better situation to buy some land and run a farm. Yeah, that was his real dream. He didn't know how much formal education he'd need to do that; most of the farmers he knew weren't educated and it didn't seem to matter.

"I'd rather swing on the harvest moon," he snickered. His brothers didn't share the joke. "Okay, okay, I'll think about it."

"I'm going to leave on Tuesday. Make up your mind by then."

When they left on Tuesday Bob hadn't fully committed to going to school at William and Mary. At least not in his own mind. He figured he'd have time to think about it while they traveled.

After his brothers left Jim realized that, like Bob, he didn't have a job or a calling. He considered himself well-educated by his own independent efforts, but if he was going to convince Cora to take their relationship seriously he'd better put some money away. There was really nothing for him in the way of work in St. Clair. Business owners there were just starting to get back on their feet. Jim had always liked working with horses, although not with cattle, and he thought he might find some work in Dallas. He shouldn't have any trouble there. John was the one the law had the problem with, not him. He felt fairly certain that his own reputation was just fine.

So Jim returned to Texas and found work on a ranch managed by a man named J.D. Prichard. He found time spent with the horses satisfying and he saved his money so that he would soon be able to return to St. Clair and ask Cora to marry him. Now *that* was a goal.

By the time Cole left Bob in Virginia, Bob had made up his mind. There was no way in hell he was going to try to be a student and end up embarrassing himself. He didn't tell Cole that. He'd take the money Cole offered him; it wasn't as if that money was hard-earned or even Cole's own. He decided he'd see a bit of the Old South himself. This was his opportunity to be on his own, accountable to no one. Doing whatever he felt like doing as a man, not a boy. No one would know him and no one would care who his family was or what lay in his past.

He spent a few weeks in Virginia and the Carolinas. It was nice land and all but he didn't feel comfortable without any personal connection or anything to do. He'd rather be home in Missoura.

He needed to come up with a plan before Cole's money ran out. He decided on his story and made his way down to Florida to where Cole said he'd be.

"What are you doing here?" Cole greeted him. "You're supposed to be at William and Mary. You can't be done with it already."

"It's not working out, Cole."

"What do you mean it's not working out? How hard can it be?"

"I'm just not like the others there, Cole. They thought I was just another ignorant farm boy."

"That's ridiculous!" That made Cole mad. The Younger family was well-respected. He couldn't even imagine people thinking any one of them was ignorant.

"Well, it was some of that, but mostly I had to leave because of you." It wouldn't hurt to play to Cole's ego.

"Because of me?" Cole didn't understand.

"They kept asking me if I was the brother of the notorious Missouri outlaw Cole Younger. They never even gave me a chance to be my own man."

This time Bob was going to use Cole's reputation and their previous issues to further his own interest. And it worked. Cole was just puffed up enough to think that his slick reputation had reached as far east as Virginia and he was flattered.

Cole suggested that rather than return to Missoura by himself, Bob should spend some time in Florida. Yet the only thing different with being in Cole's company in Florida was that he had a new audience for his storytelling and rehashing of the past. Bob was ready to move on within days. So he needed a new plan.

He had encountered an old childhood friend when he had been down in Texas the last time. Dru Garrett was an interesting companion and Bob had enjoyed his company. Dru was now working on the docks of the Mississippi in New Orleans and Bob thought maybe he'd give that a try. He would at least know someone there and it was good decent work.

And Dru's company, almost anyone's company, would certainly be better than Cole's.

CHAPTER 32
1872

B ob was pleased that he was able to find a job with the Gulf Shipping Company in New Orleans. His days were spent lifting and loading goods onto to the seagoing ships that off-loaded at the harbor and then turned around to return to other ports. The work was hard and the pay low but it beat herding cattle.

He'd been loosening his back and was now leaning against a post outside one of the saloons. He'd just been paid and he'd agreed to meet Dru there. He didn't drink all that often. He was there to save up his money, not spend it. Still, it didn't hurt to imbibe once in a while; he'd earned it.

Right now he was enjoying watching all the people passing by. New Orleans had its share of characters. He figured there was one of each kind you could imagine. He was looking at an ugly, old man, dressed to the tees and walking with a gold-tipped cane, strutting along with a woman young enough to be his granddaughter and pretty as all get-out. Only he got the feeling it wasn't his granddaughter by the way the old goat was leering down the front of the girl's dress, where her breasts were about to pop right out and catch the breeze. Ah well, to each their own... He couldn't judge others. He'd found that easy women took to him like ants to apple pie and while he hadn't spent a whole lotta money on them, there were a few he hadn't turned away. There was nothing wrong with that; he was only human.

Now who was this fella walking up to him? There were a lot of men who worked on the docks and it was hard to remember them all. He nodded.

The man looked him over.

"I've been trying to place you and I've finally figured it out."

"Oh, yeah?" Bob clenched. He hoped to hell that the man was not going to say what he anticipated.

"I know of your brother."

Here it came. Why had he even hoped that it wouldn't, sooner or later.

"That so."

"Hard man. Doesn't take any shit off anybody."

Bob just stood there, thinking how he wanted to respond. Should he just agree and walk away or just shrug it off like Cole didn't matter and was nothing to him.

"But fair. Oh, hey…" The man stuck out his hand. "I'm Bill Tomlin. And you must be Caleb, right?"

"No…" Caleb? Where did he get that? "I'm Bob."

"You're not Caleb Horton, brother of George Horton, supervises for Pennland?

You're kidding me, Bob thought. It wasn't Cole at all.

"No Sir," he smiled and shook his head. "I'm not George Horton's brother."

"Well don't I feel like a fool," Tomlin smiled. "Sorry for bothering you, Bob." He tipped his hat and continued on his way.

Maybe sometimes it *isn't* all about Cole, Bob thought.

There was another robbery. Why the hell not? This time it was in Kentucky. Three men walked into the Bank of Columbia on April 29th while the fourth stood outside as guard. The cashier didn't like the looks of the strangers. Or the guns that were quickly trained on him.

"Bank robbers!" he shouted.

"Damn," a surprised Jesse James responded, shooting him in the heart.

Two customers jumped out the open window and a third barreled through the door, pushing past a man who looked suspiciously like Clell Miller.

"What the hell?" Cole yelled to Jesse. "Why'd you shoot him?"

"Reflex," Jesse shrugged as he scooped up the loose bills on the counter.

"Forget it, boys," advised Frank as he moved quickly to the door. "Let's just get the hell out of here."

They took out only $600 for that little venture. Cole complained to Frank that Jesse was too excitable. He hadn't signed on to be shooting people. He just wanted their money.

"Yeah, I know," Frank agreed. "But he's my brother."

Down in Texas, Jim received a letter from John. John relayed the interesting news that Phillip Ruiz thought so highly of John's work that he had suggested a partnership in the saddle business. That was a big step and John wondered if Jim might come out to Los Angeles to assess the situation with him. Knowing that Jim had his best interests at heart, John wrote that he was trying to be responsible. Better late than never.

By the time Jim arrived from the long journey west, Ruiz's true intent had been revealed and it wasn't anything John wanted to hear. Ruiz wanted John to marry his daughter.

"Help me out of this," John begged his brother. "No way am I getting' married!"

Jim offered to tend the horses of Ruiz's customers while he was there. It would give him time to think of some way for John to shake loose from his situation without offending those involved.

During one late night conversation, Jim mentioned to John that if he had a dream of how he would like to see his life play out it would be to live on a ranch in Dallas, where he could raise and train cavalry mounts for the U.S. Army.

"The Federal Army?" John was aghast.

Jim shrugged. He loved working with horses and the Cavalry paid good money. The irony was not lost on Jim. Just the same as when he had been involved with the census, he thought making money off the government would in some way be justice. John could be a part of it. Jim had even written about it to Cole.

Jim seemed to have forgotten that John hated hard work, and being a rancher was as far off the mark for John as being a pig farmer. He also seemed to have forgotten John hated the Federal Army.

"Have you lost your mind?! Let's just get the hell out of here and go home to Missoura."

John made his apologies to Phillip Ruiz but he needed to return to his family in Missoura. He and Jim had plans for a horse enterprise. Ruiz was sorry to see him go and once again attempted to entice him with an offer of half his business if he would marry his daughter.

"Mr. Ruiz, Carmelita can do far better than me," John declined. The thought of being tied down made him shudder. Being polite about it or not, it was time for him to flat out *leave.*

John and Jim headed up the El Camino Real to San Francisco. It took them twelve days to get there and after two full days and nights of John's drunken debauchery, Jim was ready to put an end to it and move on. They boarded a train and traveled into the Black Hills of the Dakotas. Encounters with Indians and muleskinners only made their description of their journey that much more interesting when they arrived back at Monagaw.

While eating breakfast at the hotel, Jim was interested to read an article in the Kansas City newspaper. Evidently the money box at the Kansas City Exposition had been snatched. When the cashier tried to wrestle it away from the robber, the robber shot at him and his bullet struck a little girl. The child would be all right but there was wild speculation that the bandit was Jesse James. That didn't seem right to Jim but then he didn't really know Jesse James. Who knew what he might do?

The newspaper's editor, John Newman Edwards, was a staunch supporter of the Confederacy and all who served that noble cause, that aborted mission to declare free-thinking and ethical independence. Those kind of phrases rolled off Edwards' tongue the same as his belief that the United States of America was the land of promise and paradisiac opportunity. But the organized troops and guerillas who served *The Cause,* now *they* had his utmost respect. It was no secret that Edwards admired the audacity of those who had robbed the Yankee banks. Can you imagine the intellect and righteous indignation that was required? It was meant to be a complement when Edwards wrote that if Jesse James was indeed involved, one had to view this latest robbery, in broad daylight and in front of so many people, so daring that the people of Kansas City were bound to admire it.

Jesse, on the other hand, felt that if he was going to be called out like that, he had better provide an alibi. He wrote a letter to the editor that he had heard that a Mr. Chiles was telling people that he had seen Jesse, Cole and John Younger on the road to the Exposition that very morning and the robbers were no doubt those men. Jesse said that was impossible. He hadn't seen Mr. Chiles for three months.

When Jim showed Jesse's rebuttal to John, John kinda liked it.

"Wonder why he mentioned me?" he questioned. "Maybe its wishful thinking. Maybe he wants me to ride with them again."

Jim had nothing to say to that.

Bob was feeling like a duck out of water in New Orleans. He wasn't used to living in a city and this one was crammed with people. Everybody was either in a hurry or lazing around. There were a lot of men especially; the docks were a big draw.

"Sometimes I can't understand what they're saying," Bob remarked to Dru one day as they sat eating supper. "The Cajuns, the Creoles, the Negroes, the French, the Southerners....It all mixes in my ears and I feel like I've forgotten the English language."

Dru laughed. "That's part of the charm of New Orleans."

"Maybe it's charming but it's still damn hard to understand."

"This is quite a place, isn't it? Look at all that's going on here. The new Cotton Exchange is a big deal. The commerce is going to grow like there's no tomorrow. And we're part of it."

"Yeah, I know. I'm not saying I don't like it here. I'm just saying it's nothing I'm familiar with."

"That why you pass so much time in Audubon Park?" Dru smiled.

"Maybe it is. I do like it there. The idea that they had to create a green area amidst all the dirt and buildings is nothing I ever expected to see. Home is nothing *but* green."

"Umm, I miss that green," Dru nodded.

"The people here have their work cut out for them to make this someplace desirable to put down roots. Now with the levee breach at Bonnet Carre, they're gonna have to do something with all of that. What a mess."

"Yeah, flooding takes a big toll."

Bob looked down at the newspaper on the table and tapped it with his finger.

"They're still talking about the death of Oscar Dunn. Pretty interesting that they elected a Negro Governor. Good for them. But people are saying he might have been killed rather than died in his sleep."

"People tend to speculate, that's for sure. They probably think about taking out a politician from time to time themselves." Dru chuckled.

"I guess that's likely true," Bob smiled.

"Besides, people have a hard time letting go of things. They're still talking about ol' Spoons Butler and his Order Number 28."

"Don't get me started on that," Bob glared, thinking of his sister Sally. "That son-of-a-bitch saying that if a woman talks back to a Federal soldier she's a whore…"

"A 'woman of town plying her avocation', please."

"Was making that up the best that bastard could do to get back at Confederates?"

"Takes all kinds. He's a vengeful man."

"Yeah." Bob took a drink of his coffee. "Strange things going on these days, but probably no stranger than years past."

"It's enough to make you start looking for the return of the Almighty." He stretched. "Well, at least we're in a place that has nightlife and entertainment to divert our attention."

"New Orleans does have that going for it."

"If we had more time away from breaking our backs, we could enjoy some of it."

"Isn't that the truth." He looked out the window and sighed. That really didn't interest him much, anyway.

Jim had tried to drum up interest among his brothers for the horse venture. They weren't interested at all, and, in fact, damn insulted.

"Raise horses for the Yankees?" Cole roared. "That's beyond comprehension even from you, Jim!"

"I'm pleased you hold me is such high regard, Cole."

Jim was hurt by that remark. He knew he was different from his brothers in many ways but that didn't mean he couldn't have a worthy idea. Yet more than that, he was disappointed. The opportunity he had imagined probably couldn't come to fruition without someone other than him being involved. He didn't really have any friends. He'd hardly lived in one place long enough for that. What he did have was his love for Cora. Cora claimed that she was in love with Jim too but her father questioned them getting married. Jim didn't have a profession or seemingly any money with which to support her. Maybe he shouldn't abandon the cavalry deal. If he had to go it alone, so be it.

Jim headed back to Texas. While he pondered his options he took a job with Dallas Marshall Tom Flynn. That was one way to avert attention from the claims that Cole was a bank robber and the family was no good. At least that was Jim's thinking.

He was wrong.

It wasn't true and it wasn't fair, but when there was a robbery in Dallas in February of '73 Jim and another deputy named JJ Hollander were indicted for it. There was nothing to even remotely connect Jim to the crime. There was that old dog nipping at his heels. The Younger name was the first on everyone's mind when it came to all things robbery. Jim knew it would be foolish to even try to clear his name. He headed back to Monagaw, well ahead of the law.

Now what?

CHAPTER 33

They were sitting on Younger Lookout, as it was now being called. It was comfortable, a place they could be themselves.

"If you needed money so bad, Jim, you should've come to me. I could find you a place with me and the James boys."

Jim looked away. Did Cole know him so little to think that his participation in a robbery was even a possibility?

No, that wasn't the case. It troubled Cole greatly that the straightforward Jim had been accused of involvement in something that anyone who knew Jim would know was out of the question. Jim was miserable about it and all Cole could think to do was make light of it.

"Although I kinda like your impersonating a lawman beforehand. That was a smart move."

"It's not funny, Cole. Any of it." Jim put his head in his hands. "I've lost all my options and now people think I'm a criminal. I'll never have any money to persuade Cora's father to let us get married and she probably won't have me now anyway."

"I'll give you some money." Cole was always magnanimous with the money from the Yankee banks.

"I'm not taking your money."

"You can pay it back when you get settled then."

"You know I don't approve of what you and the James boys are doing."

"It's not as if it isn't money the Yankees have taken from us," John threw in. "Try counting up all the money that people around here don't have any more and the Yankees do."

Cole had tried explaining to John that it was the *act* of taking the money not the money itself. John said he understood that but it was still money.

"You can justify it all you want. I don't want anything to do with it."

Jim knew that the least of his concerns right now was money. Wait until Cora's father heard that he was accused of robbery. Jim could only hope that Dr. McNeill knew Jim's character well enough to know that wasn't something he'd do.

"I don't think you get that robbing these banks is making a political statement, Jim." Cole mused. "You've seen only too well now that we're accused whether we're involved in anything illegal or not."

"And you don't think that's because most of the time you *are* involved in something illegal?" Jim sighed. "There's no one going to hire me anymore."

"You're welcome to come next time."

"No thank you." Jim got up. "I'm going to take a walk."

Cole and John watched Jim climb down the plateau.

"I feel bad for him." Cole shook his head. "It wasn't right to accuse him of that."

"He might as well have gone with you to Kentucky. Or wherever the hell you were last time." John threw a rock and watched it as it sailed off into the distance,

"He's welcome anytime."

"What about me, Cole?"

"What about you?"

"What about me going with you again next time? I would make a valuable addition to the group of you on a full-time basis."

"I remember when you were a kid," Cole smiled. "You were always trying to get Pa or me to take you places."

"Yeah, and I was always being left behind. I don't want to be left behind anymore."

"Are you serious?"

"Dead serious."

"I don't know…"

"Yes, you do. It would even things up if you had one of your own brothers with you like Frank has Jesse."

Cole considered that.

"This may seem like a game to you John, but its serious business. You never know what's going to happen during one of these. They don't always go exactly to plan. A man can get killed."

"Who can you trust with your life more than your brother?"

"Frank James is someone I trust with my life."

"But he's not your brother. His first loyalty is always gonna be to Jesse." John knew that was a valid point. "And I'm already wanted by the law."

"That's down in Texas."

"What difference does it make where? The law's the law. I want to join up as a bonafide member. Give me one good reason why not."

Cole realized that John was right. It would feel good not to be outnumbered by the James boys. Having one of his own would work out all right. And John did have that trouble down in Texas. It wouldn't be like Cole was dragging him into a life of crime.

"There'd be one big problem as far as I'm concerned."

"What's that?"

"You never want to take direction. Something like this, you've got to do as you're told. Without any lip."

"I can do that."

"Can you?"

"Sign me up."

As it turned out, Cole and the James boys would be a bit short-handed anyway. Clell Miller was arrested in Clay County and named as one of the bank robbers at Corydon. He was returned to Iowa to stand trial where several Missouri men showed up to swear Miller had been with them, far away from Iowa, for goodness sake. The judge had no option but to release Miller. There simply wasn't any evidence. Although it was suggested that Frank and Jesse James and Cole Younger might have been involved in the robbery, they couldn't be formally charged either. There was nothing to place them there.

Ol' Bill Pinkerton didn't like the outcome of Miller's trial. He didn't like it one little bit.

Unlike Cole, John thought Jesse James was all right. He had grit. Thinking in ways that others didn't was something John admired. That one time when John had gone along to Kentucky, Jesse and Frank had hardly given him the time of day. But he was a kid then and that was before he killed a man and became a wanted man. Jesse and Frank would look at him differently now.

John had always been encouraged to believe, fueled by the anecdotes of Cole, that Jesse was egotistical and foolish. Well he may be egotistical John thought, but he's far from foolish. In fact, Jesse reminded John of himself. Jesse seemed to know exactly what he wanted out of life. Revenge. John could certainly get behind that idea.

Another thing John liked about Jesse was that Jesse loved to spin a tale. Not the Cole type of tale but the type of tale that had you on the edge of your seat with attention. John was entertained by Jesse's stories and observations. That first evening John was welcomed into the fold, Jesse told the story about a popular Bushwhacker named Sam Hildebrand. Hildebrand was said to have been responsible for at least twenty murders after the War. When he was arrested for one of them, Hildebrand even tried to kill the arresting marshal. Alas, old Hildebrand was shot in the head for his effort. Yeah, Jesse liked to spin a tale.

On May 27th two men entered the Ste. Genevieve Savings Bank and relieved the cashier of $4,000.

On their way out of town Jesse grinned at John.

"Hurrah for Hildebrand!" he hollered.

While Bob was still down in New Orleans working day after day on the dirty and stinking docks, John was enjoying himself as the latest member of the band of bank robbers now known as the James-Younger Gang.

As far as John was concerned, well, he'd waited for this moment all his life.

CHAPTER 34

Bob and Dru Garrett were sitting in Rosie's. The room was dark and reeked of whiskey and sweat. The piano player wasn't very good but that didn't stop him from playing to beat the band.

It was true that there was a lot going on in New Orleans. The city flourished with trade and commerce. The streets were congested with people and the rhythmic daily life and nighttime revelry were sometimes overwhelming. It was nothing like the languorous community of St. Clair County, that was for sure.

Bob was exhausted. Every day he was up at the crack of dawn. Then down at the docks lifting and pushing until late in the evening when he felt like he couldn't lift or push one bundle more. It hadn't taken him long to determine that working the docks was as bad as working cattle. Maybe worse. Yeah, definitely worse.

"What's on your mind, Bob?" Dru had noticed that his friend was particularly quiet tonight.

"Somebody should give that piano pounder some lessons."

"That's it?" Dru smiled.

Bob shrugged. "I hate this work."

"Don't we all," Dru chuckled.

"No, I mean it Dru. I hate this work. I don't want to do it anymore."

"Yeah?"

Dru could see almost from the start that Bob wasn't really cut out for the docks. He was good at what he did and gave an honest day's work but his heart wasn't in it.

"They think highly of you, you know."

"That's fine, but I don't see where I want to be working this hard for somebody else's profit for the rest of my life."

"Most everything's for somebody else's profit."

"Good for them, but if I'm gonna work this hard, I want to be doing it for my own satisfaction, my own reward."

"What do you mean? What would satisfy you?"

"I've been giving this a lot of thought. I was raised to value the land. My father always made it a point to tell us that it was important to respect the soil and all it produced. I think that if I have any choice about what I'm going to be doing for the rest of my life, I'd like to die a farmer."

"Whoa, it's a little too early to be thinking about dying."

"You know what I mean." He looked around. "New Orleans might be an exciting place for some but I like a place where you can see green for miles and miles, with lots of trees."

He closed his eyes, thinking of another place, a better time.

"Crops in the fields other than cotton. Crops you can pick and taste the glory of right then and there."

He looked at Dru.

"I belong in Missoura, not New Orleans."

"Takes money to farm."

"I know that."

"Where're you going to get it? You sure haven't been able to save up much of your wages from this job. Not with the little we get paid."

Bob nodded. "That's not a lie."

"Are you serious, Bob? You want to quit the job?"

"Yeah, I think I am. I think I do."

"And go back to Missoura?"

The idea of returning to Missoura must have been running around in his mind but he hadn't fully considered it until just this minute.

"I think I will."

"And farm. But then we're back to the money."

"I could probably get some kind of a job in Kansas City first. Like you said, I'm a good worker. I could save up."

"Well, if that's what you want, you should do it." Dru took a sip of his drink. "I miss ole Missoura myself."

"Come on with me. You're a good worker yourself. You can get something there that won't break your back by the time you're twenty-one."

"You make a point but I don't think I'm cut out for farming." He took another drink. "I think I'll stay on here for the time being. But good luck to you."

When Bob reached St. Clair County, the first place he stopped was out at the home of Theodrick and Sally Snuffer. The boys had always been welcome there. Although they were nowhere close to being his ma and pa, Bob felt a certain sense of home with the Snuffers.

"How was it in New Orleans, Bob?" Theodrick asked as they sat on the porch drinking coffee. It was good to see Bobby Younger. He was a fine young man.

"It was all right I guess," Bob shrugged. "Just not for me."

"Heard you were working on the docks."

"Yeah. I didn't feel suited to it though."

"You're done with it then?"

"Guess so."

"What are your plans?"

"I thought I might see about getting a clerking job up in Kansas City. I want to save some money." He looked out at Mr. Snuffer's field. "I want to buy some land and farm it."

"You do, do you."

Theodrick had always wondered if any of the Younger boys would ever return to their roots. But he'd given up on that idea, since all they seemed to be busy doing these days was getting into some kind of trouble. But not Bobby. As far as he knew, Bobby had been steering clear of all that.

"Well, good for you."

Bob was surprised that Mr. Snuffer accepted what he'd said without questions or giving him reasons why he couldn't do it. He was so used to being dismissed that he was touched that the older man, a man he respected, had enough confidence in him that he hadn't felt the need to respond that way.

"More coffee Bobby?" Sally asked as she refilled her husband's cup. She too was happy to see the boy. Although they were complete opposites, Bobby and John were always her favorites of the young people.

"Thanks, Mrs. Snuffer."

Theodrick took a drink from his cup. "You do know that Cole and John are at the Springs?"

Bob was surprised. Last he heard Cole was in Texas and John was in California. "They are?"

"Been around a week or two."

Bob was glad to hear that.

When he didn't find Cole and John at the hotel, he instinctively knew that they'd likely be at the cave.

It startled the hell out of him when he made his way up the path and heard the click of multiple gun hammers being pulled back.

"Who goes?"

He stopped dead in his tracks.

"It's me. Bob."

There was a rustle in the trees, then Cole's head emerged.

"I'll be damned!" He dropped down on the path and gave Bob a bear hug. "Bobby! I'll be damned."

"What's that? Did I hear that trespasser say he was Bob? Why, our little brother is in New Orleans. It must be an imposter."

John appeared with a grin on his face. He lifted Bob off the ground. "Somebody's been doin' some manual labor," he laughed as he patted his back.

"I didn't know you two were here until Mr. Snuffer told me this morning." Bob smiled. He missed his brothers. He hadn't realized how much.

John hit his arm.

"You never know where we might be." He grinned at Cole.

Cole rolled his eyes. John had been out on one of their little missions and he thought he was a regular guerilla fighter.

"C'mon have a cup of coffee. We've got some on the fire." Cole motioned Bob around to the front of the cave.

Bob stopped when he saw two men inside. If he'd met them before, he couldn't place them.

"Bob, you remember Frank James. And this is Frank's brother Jesse."

The James brothers remained seated. Bob walked over to shake Frank's hand.

"Sir," he acknowledged respectfully. Frank was a decade older than Bob, maybe more, and seeing as he was in the War and all it seemed appropriate.

Cole beamed at his little brother's manners.

"I reckon you should call me Frank, Bob." Frank smiled.

"Jesse was with Anderson's boys," Cole added.

"I know. I've heard a lot about…"

"Jesse," Jesse finished. He shook Bob's hand and winked. "Don't believe what you read in the newspapers."

"No, sir."

Bob was more thinking about Jesse's reputation with Anderson. And of course there were Cole's stories about what a cocky little bastard Jesse was and how one day his temper and goddamn impulsiveness was going to land him somewhere he didn't want to be. Cole never realized that their father used to say the same thing about Cole, only more politely.

Bob took a seat and for the next hour listened as Cole and the James brothers talked about themselves, their service to the Confederacy during the War and the Damn Yankees. Every once in a while John would drop in his two cents.

Bob had heard Cole's viewpoint on the subject often enough but he found that Jesse, even though he was voicing the same anti-Union sentiment as Cole, put a new shine on it. He was animated and witty yet it was quite clear that he full-out hated those who had opposed him. Jesse told stories of fierce hand-to-hand combat, but then he would throw in one about a hilarious incident of brotherhood, spite and pranks. Bob listened as if a captive. He had never met anybody like Jesse James.

"Well, I don't think it's any goddamn secret that those sons-of-bitches won't rest until they've run every Confederate out of Missoura."

Frank James hadn't said much. His opinion of the Unionists was very clear in his one sentence.

"Carpetbaggers are tighter than a schoolmarm's quim with the bankers," opinioned Cole. "They control the money. Farmers don't stand a chance to rebuild or start up anything new. That's a stone hard fact."

"All the more reason..." Jesse smiled, his sentence purposely uncompleted.

"Yeah, those goddamn carpetbaggers are in with the railroads now too." Cole spat. "They've got their fingers in everybody's pie."

"Jesse was telling us about what the Reno brothers pulled off back east, Bobby." John nodded. "Back in '66 they robbed the Ohio and Mississippi Railroad. Isn't that something? They detached the express cart and not a shot was fired. Then they did it again and they kept on doing it."

"And then Pinkertons got on their tails and they got themselves lynched." Frank looked at Jesse.

"They were careless, Frank. We won't be."

Bob looked from Frank to Jesse. Were they talking about what he thought they were talking about? Right here in front of him and John?

"Yeah, we won't be," John added.

"Remember what I said about keepin' your mouth shut, John," Cole warned.

"What are you talking about John?" Bob looked at John, stunned by his statement. We?

"If I'm in, I have a right to have my say." John was still back at Cole's remark. He was a member of the gang now. He had a right to voice his opinion.

"If we want your say we'll ask you," Cole dismissed.

John started to protest but Bob interrupted.

"What are y'all talking about? You're going to rob a train?" He looked at John. "And you're in on it?"

"We're talking about it." Cole stared hard at John. "We haven't decided."

Jesse chuckled. "Well, look at your face, Bob. I haven't seen that expression on someone's face since ol' Jim Lane saw that black flag coming into Lawrence."

Bob looked around the cave at each of them. Frank James was looking at him in an odd, cold way. Cole was still frowning at John, who continued to glare at Cole.

"You know, Cole," Jesse continued. "Bob here is a big, strapping young man. We could use more hands. We ought to think about including him this time."

Bob was speechless. He could only stare.

Bob was relieved when the James brothers left without further discussion, at least in his presence, of a train robbery. He'd just happened to show up in Monagaw and already had walked into a hornet's nest.

Cole walked Frank and Jesse out to where they had hidden their horses. John lounged against a rock.

"So how come you left New Orleans?"

"Wasn't for me. How come you left California? They run you out?" It was good to get back to talk that was more normal.

"Long story. Having to do with fair maidens and honest labor."

"How long have you been back here?"

"Not too long." John chucked a rock down into the river. "So what did you think of the James boys?"

Bob looked at his brother and blew out a long breath. "What the hell was all that?"

"I'm with the gang now. Went with them last time. A bank. Over in Saint Genevieve."

Bob just accepted Cole's involvement with robbing banks because of his wartime activities and well, Cole was Cole. Always up for an adventure. He should have known John well enough to know that it was just a matter of time before he threw all-in with it.

"How was it?"

"Pretty damn exciting."

"How much did you get?"

"$500."

"Damn, John."

"Yeah…" he grinned. "Guess now you have *two* brothers who rob banks for a living."

John seemed unconcerned with the fact that robbing banks was not only against the law but also crossed the line of the ethics and morals they had been taught by their parents. He obviously didn't care about all that anymore.

"It doesn't bother you, robbing a bank? Taking other people's money?"

"Yankee money? Not at all."

"What about people seeing you do it?"

"I didn't know anybody over there. They have no idea who I am."

"What if someone described you?"

"A description of me would fit hundreds of Missoura men."

"They seem to know Cole and the James boys."

"Well, that's the problem of Cole and the James boys, isn't it." He laughed. "Besides, hell, they even accused me by name of robbing the Kansas City Exposition. It *should* have been me but I wasn't there."

John sounded kind of excited that he had been singled out as a suspect. He was buying into the whole thing. There were times when there was no reasoning with John and this was one of them. Things had changed in their world. Bob himself wasn't even sure what was ethical, moral or right anymore.

"Are you going to do it again?"

"Hell, yeah. Only next time it's gonna be the railroad."

First banks, now a railroad. Bob didn't even know what to say to that.

John considered his brother. Bobby had been as much a victim of the Yankees as he had. Maybe he'd like his own revenge.

"You should join us, Bobby."

"I'm not a train robber."

"Not yet you aren't but you could be. There's a lot of Yankee money to be had." He shrugged. "Sure beats working with cattle."

Anything beat working with cattle. Except maybe working on the docks.

"'Bout time you made your own statement against those Bluebellies. God knows they've got it comin'."

That was true enough. Look at his life. It might be satisfying to throw back some of what he had been through. They deserved it for sure. And he *had* pledged revenge at one time; no, several times.

Yet when it got down to it, he didn't much care about the Yankees anymore. That was part of the past he'd tried to put aside. He cared about the future now. He wanted that farm. He could make it work if he had the opportunity. Had the money. It would take a while to save it up from a clerking job, he knew that. But robbery? He'd never even entertained that idea.

"You think about it Bobby. I'm sure Cole and the James boys would be happy to have you ride with 'em. Jesse suggested it, after all. And I know I would. It'd be real good, and real *right*, to have you with us. You think about it."

Bob blew out a breath. He'd think about it. How could he not?

He couldn't sleep that night. He tried to empty his mind of thoughts but it wasn't working. He kept returning to John's words. "'Bout time you made your own statement against those Bluebellies. God knows they got it comin'."

He dug into his pocket. The button from his father's waistcoat was there. He carried it from the moment John had given it to him all those years ago. He hardly needed a reminder, like John intended it to be, but he carried it none the less. His father had always been very clear: we are all responsible for our own actions. We make of life what we choose. He had been raised in a Christian home to care about others and be a good person. But that was a long time ago. His father, that good man who chose to stay neutral back in '61 and not judge his neighbors, had been betrayed by that line of thinking. And his father had not seen what he had seen or been through what he had been through. He wondered what his pa would think if he were alive today. If he knew what his wife and children had been put through, maybe he wouldn't be as charitable.

His pa didn't support the Quantrill boys. He thought they were brutal vigilantes. That was a true enough sentiment. He'd have been as shocked as any Kansans at what had happened in Lawrence. But he'd also be shocked at what the Federal government and State Militia had done to innocent, hard-working people. He'd have tried to see all the sides to it but he wouldn't have been able to ignore the fact that those who supported the Union had destroyed his family.

As Bob thought back over the years he began to tally the wrongs against the Younger family, beginning with the bullying and revenge of Irvin Walley which had ended in no less than putting his father in the cold, hard ground. He saw the burning houses and the loss of what his pa held dear. He remembered the humiliation his sisters been made to bear. And the tauntings, the brutality, John's *hanging* for God's sake. On and on and on. There was plenty to be angry about and resentful of. But worst of all was the constant hounding and persecution that eventually had caused their mother, a woman who had tried to make it through violent and troubled times with every breath she took, to finally reach the point where she just couldn't take it anymore.

Now here he was. There was no home, there was no peace. Missoura had drawn him back to where he felt he belonged, but there was no sign that anything would ever be any different than what it was right now. Yeah, they've "got it comin'" but was that what he wanted to do with his life? Let the Yankees have yet another hold over him?

If he were to join up with Cole and John there would probably be no going back. He'd be in it and sooner or later everybody would know that. Look at John. He had only participated that one time and he had been mentioned in the newspaper as a suspect in another situation he'd had nothing to do with. And Jim. Jim hadn't participated in anything at all and yet he was seen as someone outside of the law too. Bob knew there would be a certain satisfaction at striking back against those who had made his life a living hell but he wondered if it would be worth the price.

Then he remembered his brother Dick telling him all those years ago that there was nothing more important than family. To never forget that. And this was how his brothers were choosing to avenge that family.

He was still thinking about that when the sun rose.

CHAPTER 35

Bob sat on a rock looking over the river as Jesse James drew a diagram in the dirt inside the cave. Cole and Frank discussed possibilities and John took in every word.

Whatever it was they were planning, he'd leave them to it. John kept motioning him over but he still hadn't decided if he was interested in committing to the robbery so he remained sitting where he was. The sure but leisurely movement of the river was in contrast to all the thoughts bellowing through his mind.

There was a rustle on the path to the cave and Bob watched as each of the four men drew their weapon.

"Hey, it's Jim" a voice called.

The weapons were put back in their holsters.

Bob stood up to greet his brother. Jim walked over and hugged him.

"It's so good to see you, Bob," he smiled.

"You too, Jim."

Jim looked back into the cave. He seemed surprised to see Frank and Jesse. He tapped his hat. "Boys."

Jesse stopped speaking and smiled. "How ya doin', Jim?"

"I'm doin' fine, Jesse."

Jesse rose and stretched. "I don't know about you fellas but I'm hungry. What do you say we go down to the hotel and have some supper?"

"Why don't you and Frank head over?" Cole got up. "I'll see you down there in a while." It was obvious that Cole wanted some time alone with his brothers.

"It's been a long time since we've all been together," Cole remarked after Frank and Jesse left.

"It has," Jim agreed.

"Used to be we couldn't get out of each other's hair and now..." Cole shrugged. "You boys want coffee? There's still some left."

He lifted a kettle off the fire and poured into a cup. He handed the cup to Jim. Bob and John shook their heads.

"Buck and Dingus are impressed with you boys," Cole nodded.

"Well, we're pretty impressive boys," John smiled.

Jim and Bob said nothing.

"This next one is going to be a pretty good deal." Cole sipped from his cup. "The three of us thought it might be even better if we brought you three in on it."

"I'm already in," John quickly announced. Why did he keep having to say so?

"What are you talking about?" Jim didn't understand.

"Buck and I just got back from Omaha. There's a huge shipment of gold coming to Iowa from Cheyenne next week on the Chicago, Rock Island and Pacific Railroad."

"Gold..." John whistled.

Jim stared at Cole. "And why does that concern us?"

"Tempt not a desperate man," Cole nodded. "That's Shakespeare." Cole didn't mention that he'd heard that quotation from Frank James. "We're going to take it. All of it."

"You're going to rob a train now?" Jim shook his head. "Is that what you're saying?"

"Sure is." Cole looked around at his brothers. "And I think it's a damn good idea if we all do it together. A little statement from the Younger boys."

"We?" Jim was flabbergasted. Cole couldn't be suggesting that he, John and Bob participate.

"We, Jim. You, John, Bobby and me. It's about time we show the Yankees what Younger unity is." He smiled again. "And what better way than their pocketbooks?"

"I don't want any part of your scheme, Cole." Jim's usually quiet voice rose. "And what are you thinking involving John and Bob in something like that?"

"I've already robbed a couple of banks, Jim," John informed him.

"You what?"

"I robbed a couple of banks. With Cole and the James boys."

Jim looked aghast at John. Then at Cole.

"You took him with you?"

"He wanted to go," Cole shrugged. "Sounded like a good idea. Turned out all right."

Jim rubbed his hand over his face. "And now it sounds like a good idea to you to include Bob and me."

"I think it's a *very* good idea." Cole looked at Bob. "What do you say Bobby?"

Bob didn't answer. What *did* he say?

"I don't understand, Cole." Jim wasn't through. "What you and the James boys do is your business. But why would you endanger your own brothers?"

"I'm not endangering them," Cole frowned. "I'm allowing them the opportunity to make a stand against the Yankees. We may have fought them, Jim but these boys went through hell because of the goddamn Yankees. They deserve a shot at evening the score a little."

Now Jim was angry.

"Don't *you* tell me what they went through. I probably know better than you what they went through."

"Now don't you be getting up on your high horse," Cole glared at him. "We all did what we had to do."

"Now, boys." John raised his hands in front of him. "We should be thinking about striking back at the Yankees, not each other."

Bob couldn't help it. He snickered.

They all frowned at him.

"Sorry." John's remark was ridiculous to him.

"Look Jim, if you don't want to participate, that's your decision," Cole continued. "And these two can make up their own minds. They're men now. If they want in, I say they can come in. If not, that's all right too."

"*As I said*, I'm in." John nodded. "How about you, Bobby?"

Bob still didn't know what to say. It was a huge commitment. "I'd have to know more about the plan."

Cole snorted. "If the plan is good enough for me and the James boys it's good enough for you, junior." He reached down and picked up a pebble and nonchalantly flicked it over the cliff. He stared at Bob.

"I guess you don't understand that it's an honor to be asked. If you're going to come into it high falutin', never mind."

"I just meant I have to think about it."

Cole rose. "Well, think about it quickly." He started toward the path. "There're things to be done."

"I'm hungry." John rose and began to follow Cole. He looked back at Jim and Bob. "You boys should come. Those Yankees owe you."

Jim watched them go. "I can't believe Cole would draw John into it. Just when I think he can't surprise me anymore, he does." He sat down heavily on a rock.

"He believes in what he's doing, I guess."

"Maybe so but that doesn't make what he's doing right."

"Is there anything anymore that is right, Jim? Things stopped being right a long time ago."

Jim considered. His little brother was a man now. And he was a man who had been personally and greatly affected by the War and the opinions and demands of others.

"I guess that's true enough Bob, but stealing money isn't something we were raised to do."

"But it's not really their money, is it?" Bob reasoned. "The banks and now the railroads are operating on the money the carpetbaggers bring them and the money they cheat Confederate farmers out of. If it weren't for them we'd be able to buy back some of Pa's land and Ma would have had some peace after going through the pits of hell."

"A lot of things would be different if there hadn't been a war. But the fact of the matter is that there *was* a war and the Confederacy lost."

"But what did the start of the War have to do with us, Jim? Back in the beginning, before the Yankees started hounding us and making our lives miserable, we didn't even have a side. Pa wasn't aligned with the Confederates and neither were you."

"But Cole was."

"Cole was sixteen years old. How did that speak to the rest of us and Ma and Pa? They just used that Cole was in the bush to judge and condemn the rest of us. That wasn't fair."

"Little about the War was fair. It never is. " Jim looked off over the river. "Cole put a target on our backs. But he was right to do what he felt needed to be done, I guess. The truth of the matter was that there were horrible things done to people on both sides."

"Maybe so but I can't recall a single instance that I harmed anybody. Why should I have to pay for what others did?"

Bob walked over to stand beside Jim. He looked down at the Osage, meandering out through the fields and hills. He loved this river. He loved the tall, green trees that were now swaying in the light breeze. He loved the smell of crops growing in the fields, no matter how small the planting. He loved Missoura.

"It makes me angry, Jim. It makes me angry all that they took from us. And all they keep taking. We're always going to be marked as some sort of renegades. No matter where we go or what we do – or don't do."

Jim let out a long breath. That was exactly what had just happened to him.

"I'm afraid you're right, Bob." He looked at his brother. "But does that mean we retaliate against our enemies by stealing their money? That still feels like crossing a line."

"I don't know, Jim. All I know is that I'm so damn sick of it all. And I'm sick of doing nothing about it."

He walked over to the fire and kicked dirt on it. The embers died.

"What can it hurt, Jim? Our reputations? Those are already ruined."

Jim didn't comment. He knew Bob was right. Rightly or wrongly the Younger name was permanently tarnished.

"I want to farm. It's what I've always wanted to do. But I can't because our family land is no longer ours and I can't afford to buy anything else."

"I didn't know you wanted to farm."

"Well it doesn't matter what I want if I don't have the money to make it happen."

The Kingfishers rustled in the bushes below. Other than their warbles it was quiet and still.

"Let's go with them, Jim." Bob nodded. "We deserve justice as much as anyone else. Let's get back some of what is ours."

The next morning while his brothers slept in, Jim went to visit Cora. She held his arm as they walked through a little common area not far from the center of town. Osceola was small but several people were bustling about even at this hour.

Jim motioned to a bench and they sat.

"Cora, do you love me?" he asked abruptly. "I need to know. I need to know if it's in your mind to marry me."

"Well, Jim...goodness...I..."

"Please just tell me. Because I love you and I want to marry you."

"I do love you, Jim," she said quietly.

"Do you want to marry me?"

"I don't know if I'm ready to marry..."

"Does my family's name come into your consideration? Are you embarrassed by me or my family in any way?

She blushed.

"Your father doesn't approve of me, does he?"

"My father knows you're a wonderful man, Jim. He likes you very much."

"Does he like me enough to grant me your hand, Cora?"

"He *is* troubled by what happened in Texas but he believes you when you tell him that you weren't involved."

"What about my brother? What about Cole?"

She looked down. "No, he isn't enamored of Cole and his activities."

"Does it color his thinking about me? About me and you?"

"I'd be lying to you if I said it didn't, Jim."

He nodded.

"We won't be getting married, will we Cora?"

She couldn't look into his eyes. "I don't know, Jim. Perhaps not."

"I understand." He stood. "I'll walk you home now."

"Jim, I know you are a good and decent man. I don't judge you by what your brother does."

"I appreciate that, Cora."

He didn't say anything else.

Jim walked into the dining room of the Monagaw Springs Hotel. His brothers were there having their breakfast.

"Look at what the cat dragged in." Cole looked at his brother's face. "What's wrong?"

Jim just shook his head and sat down.

"I don't want to talk about it."

Cole shrugged and continued eating. Bob looked at Jim with concern but Jim again shook his head.

"So when are we meeting with Frank and Jesse again, Cole?" John asked casually.

"Later this morning."

"And when will it be, this event?"

"We'll talk later." Cole looked around the room. There were no other diners present but you couldn't be careless talking about such things in a public place. He looked at Bob. "Are you in or not?"

Bob took a deep breath. It was now or never.

"I'm in."

John let out a cackle and slapped Bob on the arm. "Good for you, Bobby Younger!"

Bob wondered if he'd live to regret this moment.

Cole looked now at Jim. "And you?"

Jim looked down. What did he have to lose now?

"No one will get hurt?"

Cole sighed. "No one will get hurt, Jim."

"All right. I'll tend your horses."

Now it was Cole's turn to grin.

"Well, it looks like the Younger brothers are going to have themselves a little adventure!"

CHAPTER 36

"We appreciate the pie, Ma'am." Jesse smiled at the grey-haired woman who handed two large slices to him and John.

"It sure smells good," John remarked.

The hospitality of Adair, Iowa was pretty damn fine. They had asked this woman where they might get a bite to eat and she invited them onto her porch to have some of the pie she had just put on the window sill to cool.

'Well, I hope you enjoy it."

The two young men were pleasant. Not at all like most of the rough trade that passed through on railroad business. Her husband was the foreman here at the section house and she should know.

"Nothing beats a fine piece of pie when you've been traveling as much as we have." Jesse looked around. "Bet your husband can't wait to get some of this when he's done working."

"He's finished his work for the day but he's inside napping." She raised her finger to her lips. "He smelled that pie baking and he sat down to wait for his supper. Before I knew it he was fast asleep sitting there in his chair. I didn't have the heart to wake him."

"Well, our's the luck," Jesse smiled. "We might just eat his piece too."

The woman giggled.

Several miles out of town, Frank slipped inside the shed housing the handcar. He quickly scooped up a spike-bar and hammer and slipped back out again. He joined Cole, Bob and Jim about a mile and a half up the track.

"Pry off that fish-plate, Bob," Cole instructed. "That one connecting those two rails."

Bob worked quickly. When he was done, Cole and Frank pulled out the spikes. Cole tied a rope on the west end of the disconnected north rail then he passed it under the south rail.

"We'll carry this yonder," he instructed.

They scrambled up a bank with the rope.

"We'll just lay low here." Cole looked down the tracks. "Where the hell are Dingus and John?"

"Probably having themselves something to eat," Frank shrugged.

"They were supposed to be quick about it," Cole groused. "They weren't supposed to be taking a meal. The intent wasn't to feed their bellies; it was to make sure the foreman wasn't wandering around here."

"Well, I was just speculating. They're probably getting a feel for the activity around here. You know how those two like to gab." Frank scratched his face. "Relax Bud. They'll be along."

After Jesse and John finally joined the others, they waited over the bank on a curve in the tracks. Jim held the horses in a nearby grove. It was evening now and the men of the town were eating their supper.

"So this is Turkey Creek." Frank looked around. "I don't see any turkeys. Shame. A turkey dinner would be pleasant tonight."

"That it would," Cole agreed.

Bob was anxious. He glanced at Frank and noticed that he, on the other hand, was cool as a cucumber. Of course he was. He had been through some prickly situations. This was nothing to him. Or to Cole. Bob always just thought of Cole as his brother, as the one who liked to relive battles and glory himself up, but when all was said and done Cole was experienced and good at what he did. Now he had extended his knowledge to robbing trains. Bob needed to trust that Cole knew what he was doing.

He glanced at Jesse, who was looking into the distance, humming. He didn't know quite what to think about Jesse. Jesse had been through it too but he seemed to Bob to be a bit twitchy. He had kind of a peculiar look in his eyes sometimes. Then it would pass as quickly as it appeared. Who was he to judge? Maybe they were all a little crazy for trying to pull this off.

Bob's thoughts were interrupted by Jesse's voice.

"There it is!"

The five men raised sackcloth over their faces while the train clattered along the tracks in approach.

"Alright!" Cole yelled. "Heave!"

As the train bore down near the curve in the tracks, the five men jerked on the disconnected rail.

The engine hit the gap and slammed and screeched as it lost its track. With a massive lurch and a flagrant shudder, it toppled over on its side in the ditch paralleling the bank.

Bob stared at the engine. That wasn't how he understood this was supposed to go down. There were men inside there.

As passengers yelled and the engine emitted a dark smoke, Jesse and Frank jumped into the express car.

"Open the safe!" Frank barked to the guard as he waved him over. "We're here for the gold."

The guard didn't know what to do. The gun pointed at his head by Jesse only confused him more.

"There's no gold!" he told them.

"We know there's gold coming in from Cheyenne on this train! Be quick about it! Open the damn safe!" Jesse ordered

"There's no gold!" the guard repeated. "The shipment was delayed!"

"Open the safe! The next thing you're going to hear me say is damn, I had to kill him." Jesse pushed the perplexed man to the safe.

The guard fumbled with his key but finally got the door opened.

"Take it!"

There was about $2,000 in currency inside.

"That's all there is! The gold isn't coming in until next week!"

Bob had started over to the engine when he heard moaning. They couldn't just leave these men to die. Cole pushed him back, shaking his head that what was done was done and they had other priorities.

Cole rushed over to the open door as Frank and Jesse quickly stuffed the money into their wheat sack.

"Let's hurry it up, boys. There's two men down. The fireman might be able to pull through but the engineer has had it."

Frank and Jesse jumped down.

"I'm not leaving with just this," Jesse declared. "This will barely buy us a stiff drink."

He jumped up the step and into the passenger car.

"What the hell are you doing?" Cole called.

Jesse raised his revolver into the air. The women passengers screamed.

"Settle down in here!" he demanded. "Nobody will get hurt if you do as we say."

"What the hell is he doing?" Cole looked at Frank.

Frank shook his head. "Damn it."

"Just stay in your seats," Jesse directed. "I want whatever currency you've got on you put into this here sack. Be quick about it and we'll be on our way. Give me any grief and you'll end up like that engineer out there on the ground."

Frank jumped up into the car and trained his gun on the passengers. Cole whistled to Jim to bring the horses. This was going to be tight.

Jesse passed through the car. The frightened passengers instinctively held up their hands. The men scrambled to drop currency and coin into the sack. When Jesse had collected what he could, he stood in the doorway.

"Now just stay in your seats and everything will be all right." He touched the brim of his hat. "It's been a pleasure doing business with you."

Frank jumped down and Jesse followed just as Jim came around with their horses.

As they mounted, Bob looked back at the smoldering engine where he knew a man was dead because of something he had a hand in. As he prepared to join the others as they took to the woods, his eyes caught Jim's. If Bob didn't know better he'd have sworn there was heartbreak in them.

"Eeehawww!" Jesse, Frank, Cole and John yelled. It was to be clear that they were Rebels. That was, after all, their purpose for being here, wasn't it?

Jim remained quiet.

Bob rode for all he was worth.

They rode hard for fifteen miles. Cole finally pulled them over to rest in a thick grouping of Mulberry trees near a creek where their horses could be watered.

Jesse couldn't wait to see how much his little jaunt through the passenger car had garnered.

"There's about $1,000. Not bad. Good idea on my part to shake more loose."

"You took money from citizens, Dingus! Some of them might have been *Confederate* citizens."

Cole couldn't believe Jesse's gall. That was exactly why Cole had a problem with him. You never knew what he was going to do.

"Well, if they were, we just gave them some unique entertainment. Didn't cost them much either." Jesse continued counting the money. "It's seven, eight hundred for each of us, and a couple hundred for our junior members here. Not what we hoped but better than nothing."

"Seven, eight hundred isn't worth our time and effort," Cole complained.

"Yeah, but like Jesse said, it's better than nothing." Frank shrugged.

"I'll take a couple hundred," John grinned. "That's a lot of money to some of us."

It was a *whole* lot of money to Bob.

"It should have been a hell of a lot more." Cole was not happy. "I can't believe our bad luck that they delayed the gold shipment."

"Do you all hear yourselves?" Jim remarked quietly. "Bickering over the money?"

"Just saying," Cole snorted. "Should've been more."

"A man was killed." Jim looked at each of them. "Does that mean nothing to you? An innocent man was killed and you're bickering over money?"

Bob was already thinking about the man who had been killed. And the other one who had been hurt.

"Well, that was unfortunate," Jesse dismissed. "But he did work for the railroad which means he was part of it."

Jim shook his head. He looked at Cole.

"Does that mean nothing to you?" he repeated.

Cole looked away. "Like Jesse said, that was unfortunate."

"These also shall be unclean unto you among the creeping things that creep upon the earth; the weasel and the mouse and the tortoise after his kind. And the ferret, and the chameleon, and the lizard and the snail and the mole."

Jesse could find a quotation from the Bible for everything, even if he had to stretch to make it fit. Cole made a face and shook his head.

"Those fellows that work for the railroad get paid money by the railroad," Jesse now said. "They're all part of it. Look at it this way, Jim. It's too bad the man had to die and maybe God saw to it that we got far less than we thought we'd get because of it. We'll have to be more careful next time. Lesson learned."

"Next time it'll go better," John mumbled.

Jesse picked up a handful of money and offered it to Jim.

Jim looked at the money in disgust. "You keep it, Jesse. God probably wants you to have my share in honor of that meaningful illustration you just quoted. I don't want any part of it."

"Now Jim…" Cole was embarrassed that his brother was making such a fuss. Jim had to know going in that sometimes things didn't go exactly as planned. Of course they felt badly that a man had been killed but there was nothing they could do about that now.

"I'm heading back on my own. You men have a safe return."

Jim mounted his horse and rode into the night.

Bob thought about Jim's words all the way back to Monagaw.

By the time the news of the train robbery filtered down to Missouri there was already talk of the involvement of Cole and the James brothers. Who started the rumor was hard to say.

Jim's stance on the event had an effect on Cole. He thought it was one thing to stay silent when he was accused of a bank robbery where the end result was relieving Yankees and carpetbaggers of their money, but when their folly had resulted in the death of an innocent man he felt some guilt. But not enough guilt to take the blame for it.

Cole wrote a letter to his brother-in-law Curg Jones, which Curg would pass along to his friend at the *Pleasant Hill Review*. Cole denied involvement in the Iowa affair and named six witnesses – two of them ladies and one of them the Reverend Mr. Smith – who would be happy to tell anyone involved that he and John were in Monagaw Springs at the time and had been attending church there regularly. If Cole was off a few days, well, who would remember? And as mad as Cole had been when Jesse involved John in his written alibi about the Kansas City Exhibition, Cole thought that this time it wouldn't hurt John if he threw his name in the denial for good measure. Bob and Jim had never been named before so there was no need for Cole to offer up an alibi for them.

Jesse wrote his own letter in December stating he was in Deer Lodge, Montana.

Whether either Cole or Jesse was believed was up to whoever was doing the reading.

Bob was troubled by the death of a man which the ill-thought plans had caused in Iowa. He never meant, or expected, anyone to get hurt, or worse, killed. He had trusted that Cole and the James brothers knew what they were doing, that their experience during the War had somehow qualified them to plan a derailment of a train which would be successful and cause no one harm. He realized now that he had chosen not to think about the details of the plan in an effort to avoid responsibility. Fact was, since he had been there and had taken some of the money Jesse had grabbed, he *was* partly responsible.

He needed to do something to make himself feel less guilty so he took a hundred of the two hundred dollars he'd been given and rode over to Pleasanton, Kansas where he anonymously mailed it to Engineer Rafferty's widow.

By the time he returned to Monagaw, he regretted not sending it all.

The fact of the matter was that he needed the money. That was why he had participated in the robbery in the first place. So he shut it all out of his mind and turned to the issue at hand: his farm. Because with the $100 he had left he now had moved that much closer to his dream. He'd ask his uncles and various family friends about the different crops that might be successful and what equipment he would need to start-up an operation.

This time the reputation of his brothers was an asset – the folks of St. Claire were happy to discuss something positive with one of the Younger boys.

CHAPTER 37

It seemed like the right place to be when they were back in Monagaw. They had friends there; people they could trust. They'd stay put until some time passed between where they were now and what had gone down in Iowa.

Cole seemed to have shelved his cattle business. It was getting old hat. He said he was tired of the work. Why should he eat dust and bake under the sun like a hog on a spit if he didn't have to? He was happy being in one place for a while.

John was too. He enjoyed the transient visitors who came to the hotel. He participated in the various card games; games which were a lot more civilized than those he played in Texas but what the hell. He slept a lot during the day and told his brothers that he had earned that right after all he had been through the past ten years. They rolled their eyes but didn't see any point in pursuing an opposing viewpoint. If he wanted to get liquored up and spend his time in the sack dead to the world because of it, well, John was going to do what John was going to do.

Jim continued to see Cora but he didn't further pursue the idea of their marriage. He felt that was now out of the picture. He had not told her about his participation in the Iowa robbery nor did he feel he could. If she knew, she would lose all respect for him and he couldn't bear that thought. He loved her and he would just learn to be content to spend time with her with no hopes for a future together with her as his wife.

Bob passed his time with Owen Snuffer and some of the friends he had made during his earlier years in St. Clair. He spent time with John, enjoying his company when John wasn't drunk or hung-over. John taught him a couple of new card games but it annoyed him that John continued to cheat, just like he had when they were children. Sometimes the two of them would go to the dances that were thrown at the Monagaw Hotel. Bob met a few girls who were pretty and bright but he wasn't looking to get involved with any of them. Look at what happened the last time. So he just danced with them when he felt like it and chatted with them about their homes and their lives away from the Springs. He didn't talk about it but most of his time was spent planning his farm as he sat on top of the cave looking out over the Osage.

Whenever the thought of Engineer Rafferty entered his mind he found something else to think about.

Even if the four Younger men were finding other thoughts to occupy their minds, the people in Iowa were not. Within an hour of the train robbery a man named Levi Clay walked to the nearby town of Casey and sent a telegraph to railroad officials in Des Moines and Omaha. The subsequent posse tracked the robbers to Missouri but then lost the trail. The Pinkertons were notified and they began their own investigation. They even offered a reward. If they had to up the stakes, well that was just good business.

Within a few weeks of the robbery, Marshall Cobb of Appleton City raised a posse of a couple of men and headed for Monagaw. Cobb had only recently been appointed and he figured it wouldn't hurt to hear what those in the community had to say about Cole Younger and his possible involvement in the Iowa incident.

They tied their horses to a grouping of trees just outside of Monagaw Springs so that they could sit and plan exactly what they would say if they met up with any Youngers.

They were startled when Cole and John appeared out of the trees on horseback.

"Put your hands over your heads," Cole demanded.

The men did as they were told.

"Now give us your weapons."

The men complied.

Cole smiled. "How would you boys like some coffee and a bite to eat? Walk on up the hill. The hotel's not far."

When they arrived at the hotel Cole and John re-holstered their guns. They sat with the men while they ate breakfast, chatting away as if they were old friends. When they finished, they led the men outside.

"I'm sorry but we're not going to be giving back your weapons."

Cole stood in front of the men while John leaned against the porch railing.

"You boys know the War is over. We're all supposed to be making peace with each other. You really should think twice about hunting down your neighbors for the purpose of collecting Pinkerton money. In fact, you should be ashamed of yourselves. You've seen here today that we don't mean anybody harm."

He looked at each of the men before him.

"That's all, men. You can go now. And you should go down on your marrow bones and ask God to forgive you, because the Younger boys, they do."

As the men trudged back to their horses and rode down the road, John couldn't contain it. He laughed himself silly.

It was already winter. They had been enjoying the carefree atmosphere of the Springs and the months had passed at a pace they all could live with, even if they weren't doing much of anything.

Bob noticed that Jim was avoiding Cole for the most part. That really wasn't anything new but Bob felt it had its recent roots in what had happened in Iowa. Jim didn't say anything to Bob about the robbery and Bob was thankful he didn't. That way he wouldn't have to think about what went wrong. Even John didn't talk about it. Bob figured John felt the same way.

They went to the Snuffers for Christmas dinner. It was nice to be together but it made them miss their mother and father. Their sisters were scattered all over creation and they knew, for certain now, that the family would never all be in the same place for a meal again. That was too bad, and it saddened them, but that was the reality of it. They had also been enjoying made-to-order meals from Aunt Hannah, who was very fond of "Suze's boys". At least they had some folks here who cared about them.

Around the time of the New Year, Jesse and Frank showed up at the Springs. Cole suggested heading over to the cave, where they could talk freely. Bob hesitated about keeping company with Jesse and Frank but he was curious about why they were there. He decided to go along and hear what they had to say.

Jim frowned at Cole when Cole suggested he come along.

"No, thanks," he replied. "I don't want anything to do with the James boys."

"Well, you know how Jim is," Cole later explained to Frank and Jesse. "He's not one for groups."

"His loss," Jesse dismissed. "I've got a good plan."

"Well, last time you said the same," Cole countered.

"That was last time. Like I said at the time, it was a learning experience. This plan is different. We're not going to derail the train. We're going to stop it before it reaches the station."

"Yeah, that's the thing to do," John agreed.

Cole threw John a look.

"That was pretty bad, that man getting killed..." Bob didn't think the man's death should be dismissed so quickly. "He didn't cause us any harm."

Jesse looked at him. "We don't know that he wouldn't have if he'd been given the opportunity. But we can't dwell on it, Bob. We're going to do something that's never been done in the state of Missoura. Here's what I have in mind..."

Cole was more comfortable with Jesse's current plan and John was ready to rob another train, didn't matter to him what the plan was at all.

Bob considered whether he wanted to be involved this time or not but when it came down to it, he wanted the money. They would be more careful this time, he knew they would. He talked himself into the idea that the engineer's death had been a mistake that wouldn't be repeated. It was just one of those times when things didn't go as you'd wished they had. You did things differently and moved on. At least that was what he talked himself into.

After Jesse was finished explaining his plan and everyone had agreed to it, he took something out of his coat pocket.

"I thought you boys would like to see this," he grinned. He flashed a lengthy article in the *St. Louis Dispatch* written by John Newman Edwards titled "A Terrible Quintet".

"Edwards says he came to these conclusions after talking with Buck and me and a few of your friends."

"Our friends?" Cole frowned. "Who?"

"He doesn't say. That's not important."

Jesse began to read the article with as much fervor as he quoted the Bible. Edwards defended the James and Younger brothers by detailing alibis for every robbery in which they had been said to be involved. He provided information about who they were as individuals and how they had gallantly served the Confederate, a cause they had been driven to support by the constant and complete harassment of their families. They fought for the common man and now they were being belittled by accusations that they had committed bank and train robberies.

"Flowery hogwash," Frank dismissed.

But Jesse and Cole liked it. John was preening, he was so happy to have been included. Jim would be not be happy he was mentioned. Bob was damn happy to be left out.

Frank advised the others to forget about Edward's fairy tales and focus on the upcoming robbery. That was what mattered to him and it should be what mattered to all of them.

CHAPTER 38

This time Jesse chose the Iron Mountain Railroad as the target. He asked Clell Miller to come along again too. Clell was a reliable man, wouldn't hurt to have him.

"But that will mean less money for each of us," John complained.

"Shut your pie-hole, John," Cole ordered. "You're lucky to be along yourself."

The six of them rode cross-state to the area near the station house at Gad's Hill, some one hundred miles south of St. Louis. It wasn't a big station but a promising one according to their information. It served as a center for the cordwood and charcoal business of the Pekin Coal Company. A lot of money should be going through.

"It's ripe for the pickin'," said Jesse. "This is gonna be fun."

"Cole, can Bob and I talk to you for a minute?" John asked.

Bob looked at John and threw out his hands. What was this about? He hadn't expressed a need to talk to Cole privately.

They walked to the edge of the trees.

"What now?" Cole sighed.

"I'd like to take a more active role this time out."

John didn't think he was being a pain in the ass by asking. He'd earned it.

Cole looked off into the woods. He wouldn't let John know that he had already talked about that with Buck and Dingus. It wouldn't pay to have the kid get even cockier than he was already.

"What makes you think I can put that kind of responsibility in your hands?"

"I've earned it, you know I have." John jutted his chin. To him getting more responsibility was a given.

"And how's that?"

"What do you mean? I've done everything you've told me to do and I've kept my mouth shut. You brought me on because you thought I'd be good at this and I am."

He was annoyed that he had to plead his case.

"Yeah, fine." Cole looked back at John. "But you watch your damn ps and qs, little brother. You won't get a second chance."

John nodded.

Bob wasn't surprised that John asked for more to do but he was a little surprised that Cole agreed. Good for John, if that's what he wanted. But, shit. Maybe Cole would want him to do more too and he wasn't ready for that.

"I'll be happy to be the look-out," he told Cole. "If that sets with y'all."

If something went wrong this time he wouldn't be directly involved. At least that's what he talked himself into believing.

"There's a less money for playing that part," Cole advised. He felt obligated to tell Bob that but he was also rather relieved that Bob wanted to take that position. There was less to go wrong that way.

"That's fine." Bob felt that way too.

As evening fell, Cole, John, Clell, Jesse and Frank walked into the station with their guns drawn. Bob stayed back with the horses.

A group of men were sitting around a table shooting the breeze. Clell and Cole quickly checked them for weapons. Only one of the locals had a revolver and it was quickly confiscated. Clell held the men under guard while the others went outside.

"You men will do all right if you just stay right where you are," Clell advised.

Outside, Cole placed a signal flag on the track. The engineer would be compelled to stop the train, thinking there were people who wanted to board. And he would be right. Just those boarding, were not going to be who he expected.

Right on schedule the train came to a grinding halt in front of the station.

Conductor C.A. Alford stuck his head out the window. He was surprised when he was greeted by John's cocked revolver.

"You'll just step down now and keep your mouth closed," John directed. He nodded to the engineer. "You too."

John was thrilled to have an actual speaking role in this homespun drama.

Cole, Jesse and Frank jumped aboard. Cole headed for the express safe. Baggage Master Louis Constant watched as he loaded the contents into a wheat sack.

"I appreciate it," Cole nodded, speaking through the mask over his nose and mouth. He led Constant to John, who motioned him inside the station with the others.

Jesse and Frank were now in the passenger car. Cole waited for them at the steps. He hoped Jesse didn't do something crazy again.

"I'd like to ask you the kind favor of showing us your hands," Jesse directed.

The frightened passengers lifted their arms in the air.

"I figure this is the easiest way to identify you working men. We don't want *your* money. You earned it same as us. Those of you with the fancy watches and heavy billfolds can just put those items right here in this sack."

Jesse walked toward the back of the car as he examined hands and collected his booty.

Two well-dressed men sat at the rear of the compartment. Jesse stopped to look at them. They stared back, annoyed.

"What's your name?" Jesse asked the first.

"John F. Lincoln," was the response.

"Mr. Lincoln, what's your occupation?"

"I am the Superintendent of the St. Paul & Sioux City Railroad," the man bravely responded. Although he couldn't see the grin on Jesse's face through the mask, he could see it in his eyes.

"And you?" Jesse directed his gun at the other man.

"John Merriam."

"And what is it you do, Mr. Merriam?"

"I'm a banker," he sighed. "Merchant's Bank of St. Paul."

"I'd like you two gentlemen to step down off the train," Jesse directed.

"Now see here," Lincoln exclaimed. He handed Jesse his billfold as Merriam surrendered his own, in addition to his gold watch. "We've given you what you want…"

"Off the train," Jesse repeated. "We'll determine what it is we want."

Cole made way for the two men. His gun and that of Jesse's remained trained on them. Frank's revolver – and his eyes – remained on those in the compartment. Cole looked uneasily at Jesse. He had no idea what Dingus was doing now.

Lincoln and Merriam stood at the side of the car.

Jesse circled. Whistling a little tune as he considered them.

"Take off your clothes," he ordered.

"What?" Lincoln was perplexed.

"Take off your clothes," Jesse repeated. "Down to your skivvies."

"I'll do no such thing!" Lincoln retorted as Merriam looked askance.

"All right." Jesse aimed his gun at Lincoln's head. "If that's your choice. You'll die with your clothes on then. But if I were you, I'd take my clothes off and live to talk about it." He cocked the hammer.

Kennedy and Merriam shrugged out of their coats.

"This is an outrage," Merriam sputtered as he continued with his waistcoat.

"No, what's an outrage is what your bank, and what your railroad," Jesse nodded to each of the men. "...are doing to the farmers of Missoura and those who fought for the glorious Confederacy."

When the two men hesitated at the removal of their next garment, Jesse smiled. "Keep going, won't cha please..."

They pulled their shirts out of the waistbands of their trousers. They didn't like the way the bandit's eyes blinked. He was damn crazy.

"Watch these scoundrels, will you?" Jesse asked Cole as he walked down to where the engineer was waiting with John.

Jesse handed the man a piece of paper. "This ought to help you out."

When he heard Cole's whistle, Bob came forward with the horses. He didn't know what was going on with the two men who stood there in their underwear but it didn't look like anyone had been hurt and that was a relief.

As the six men disappeared into the woods, the engineer looked at what the robber had handed him. Written was a fairly accurate description of what had just taken place with only the amount of the booty left blank and, of course, there was no mention of the two men who stood embarrassed before him.

If Jesse was going to get his name in the newspaper, he'd provide the information.

He was tired of them getting it wrong.

"We want those bastards caught."

Lincoln and Merriam didn't waste any time.

"We'll get some men on it immediately," the local sheriff promised.

"To hell with that. Call in the Pinkertons."

It didn't take long for *that* news to spread.

"We need to leave St. Clair for the time being," Cole told them as he warmed himself by the fire they had built in the cave.

"It'll make us less of a target. Those Pinkertons have a lot of influence and they're a well-heeled outfit. They'll probably send some of their men down here."

"I thought they were based in Chicago?"

John had a hard time believing that someone would come all the way to Monagaw Springs looking for them when the robbery had been way over in the eastern part of the state.

"Like I said, they've got deep pockets and they've got a lot of men working for them." Cole took a sip of his coffee. "I'm going to amble over to Hot Springs, leave Missoura for a while. You should come with me, Bob. You said you were interested in land, you could look there."

Bob frowned. He didn't recall discussing that subject with Cole.

"I'm only interested in Missoura land."

"Why limit yourself? It wouldn't hurt to look."

"Cole's right, Bobby," John agreed. "It'll give you a feel for what Missoura land is gonna cost you."

Bob shrugged. He didn't care a whit about the land in Arkansas but if the Pinkertons were going to be looking for them here, he might as well be somewhere else right now.

More interesting to him at the moment was John. Bob was trying to remember when it was that John had started to become Cole's ally. Most of their life John hadn't had one good thing to say about Cole. Since he started robbing trains with him, Cole suddenly knew best what they should be thinking, what they should do?

John seemed to sense Bob's curiosity.

"I'll go too," he offered, as if that made it more his own idea. "How 'bout you, Jim?"

"I have no need to go. I wasn't involved in that foolishness. The Pinkertons aren't looking for me." Jim was still peeved about the robbery and he didn't much want to keep company with his brothers right now.

"They might be, from the Iowa thing," John pointed out.

Jim glared at him. "I'm happy to stay here."

"Well, fine. Then the three of us will go." Cole threw another branch on the fire.

But when the morning came, John was feeling like death warmed over. He thought it was some kind of ague. Jim thought it was some kind of too much liquor the night before.

"Y'all go on ahead," John mumbled into his pillow when Cole and Bob showed up. "I'll meet you there when I'm feeling better."

There wasn't any hesitation on the other end of it. The Pinkertons were anxious to make a name for themselves in Missouri and this business with outlaws provided them that opportunity. The law-abiding people of that state were uncomfortable with the fact that masked men were popping out of the woods and stealing money from not only the banks but decent people who just happened to be riding a train. Bill Pinkerton assured the men who had come to him with their problem that his detectives would track down and capture the outlaws. The Pinkertons Agency would execute a quick end to their reign of terror.

His first action was to send a couple of men into Clay County. That was the home of Jesse and Frank James, after all. Everything he had been able to determine led right back to those two.

When agent John Whicher arrived there he met D.J. Atkins, the president of the Commercial Bank of Liberty. This was going to be a piece of cake. How hard could it be in this two-nag smudge on the road?

"I'm going to arrest the James brothers, right there in their home territory," Whicher smirked.

"How do you plan to accomplish that?"

Whicher was full of himself as far as Atkins was concerned; one of those city-bred cocky braggarts who liked to throw their weight around.

"I'm going to pose as a hand for hire and gain the confidence of the family. Once I'm imbedded into their lives, I'll surprise them."

Atkins couldn't believe how naïve the detective was.

"They'll kill you if they even suspect you're not who you say you are," he warned.

"Oh, it'll work. My plan is bullet-proof. It'll work out just fine," Whicher responded with a smile.

The next day Whicher set out for the James farm in Kearney.

His body was found the following morning beside the road in Independence. There were holes through his head and his heart.

Unfortunately for Whicher, he was wrong about the bullet-proof part of his plan.

CHAPTER 39

B ob liked the area around Hot Springs but not enough to farm it. There was something he really liked though and that was the information the farmers freely offered him. None of them had a stick up their butt as to who he was or why he was asking. He just told them he was looking at Arkansas farm land and he asked them what counsel they might have for him. Every day he'd rise early and head out for a visit with one or two friendly and seasoned farmers. The more he learned, the more he knew that farming was what he wanted.

Cole wasn't as ambitious. He liked sitting around Flynn's saloon and talking to the other patrons. He drank whiskey in moderation and occasionally sat in on some card games. He was just passing time.

That didn't really interest Bob. Besides, he didn't want to spend his money. That was for his farm.

John recovered just fine but he decided that he really didn't want to travel all the way to Hot Springs.

"Not just now," he told Jim. "I'm getting a little tired of Cole's company. I'll just stay here for now and lay low. Get my thoughts together."

To his way of thinking, he was just in the place to do that. Everyone in the area knew not to say anything about the

Younger's cave. Even if the Pinkertons came all the way down there they wouldn't be given any information. Monagaw was where their friends were and those friends were loyal. There wasn't much to do but that was okay for right now. There usually was something happening at the hotel in the evening. In the daytime he'd sleep in or amble on over to the Snuffers or Aunt Hannah's, where he knew he could get a good meal along with the company of people he actually cared about. Yeah, he'd stay here for now. It was the closest thing to a home he had.

John and Jim were sitting in the cave. John had recently realized that he hadn't put much into his relationship with his older brother. He'd always figured that Jim would rather spend his time to himself, reading, and thinking, whatever it was that he did. Jim had been that way for as long as John knew him. They'd never really had anything that they liked to do together and nothing much to talk about. Now that they were both adults maybe they could find some kind of common ground, although John couldn't imagine what that might be.

"There's a dance at the hotel tomorrow night," he mentioned.

"I know. I'm meeting Cora there."

"I'll come along with you."

There were always a handful of out-of-town young ladies who came to the Springs with their families and John more often than not enjoyed dances and conversations with many of them. This way he could kill two birds with one stone. He'd made an overture to Jim and beyond that, he might get lucky.

They'd heard about the dance that night but Pinkerton detectives Louis Lull and James Wright were tired. Earlier that week the two frustrated men had checked into the Commercial Hotel in Osceola. They had been all over Western Missouri looking for Cole Younger and his brothers and they had come up empty.

"If the Youngers are in the area, no one is talking about it," Wright complained.

Lull didn't want to hear any of that. He was determined that he would somehow track down Cole Younger. He knew he faced a sly and resourceful enemy. Lull had served with the Union Army and was well aware of Younger's wartime exploits. News of the guerilla actions had been a hot topic of conversation during the War, even in Chicago where Lull returned after the War and served as a captain on the police force. Now here he was in the wilds of Missouri looking for someone who in no way wanted to be found.

"Younger was one of the most effective of the Bushwhackers," Lull told Wright. "Our work is cut out for us."

"It surely is."

Lull wasn't particularly enamored of Jim Wright, the detective from St. Louis. Wright was supposed to be good at what he did but he hadn't added much to the mix. The reason Wright had been hired in the first place was that he had served in the Confederate Army with some men who knew Cole Younger.

"If you were a Reb during the War, why do you want to join an effort to take down one of Missouri's Confederate heroes?" Lull had asked before agreeing to take on Wright.

"I've got a grudge to bear against Younger," Wright replied.

"What's that?"

"It's personal but don't worry. I'll do what I can to see Cole Younger behind bars, where he belongs."

Lull had come to the conclusion that the only thing personal about Wright's pursuit of Younger was the notoriety Younger's capture might bring him. It didn't really matter, as long as Wright helped him find the outlaw. He hoped Wright wasn't taking him on a wild goose chase bringing him here. Younger was savvy. He'd know the Pinkertons were in the field looking for him.

Lull hired a man named Ed Daniels once the search reached St. Clair County. Daniels was a local man who claimed to know how to flush out the Youngers but so far he wasn't offering anything that Lull himself couldn't do just as well. Daniels was working as a "sometimes" deputy with Osceola sheriff James Johnson and he'd lived in St. Clair quite a long time. Daniels assured Lull

In the Shadow

that sooner or later the Younger boys would mosey back to the area to visit their friends and relatives.

"It's just a matter of time," Daniels nodded.

Lull knew that his presence as a stranger would cause suspicion. He needed to do whatever he could to pass himself off as some kind of businessman who was visiting the area with good purpose. He sat in the lobby of the hotel, thinking about his options. Then, like so many things do, the answer dropped in his lap.

"Widow Sims is selling her cattle," one of the old-timers sitting there was telling his friend. "Just can't handle them anymore."

"Snuffer is close by and he's been helping her but he's got his own place, his own concerns."

Lull had heard rumors that some of the Youngers were driving cattle. Daniels told him that the Youngers sometimes visited the home of Theodrick Snuffer. Could it be that easy?

"Let's visit this Snuffer and inquire about Mrs. Sims' cows," Lull instructed Wright and Daniels.

"C'mon, John." Jim had come to the hotel to collect his brother. "We need to be heading over to Snuffers' for dinner."

"I'm not really up to it, Jim," John groaned. "Have a nice meal."

"What is it this time?"

"Maybe one too many dances…"

"Maybe one too many women. Get up."

"Maybe too much food…."

"Too much rot-gut is more like it." Jim pulled John's foot. "It doesn't matter. We're not going to disappoint Mrs. Snuffer or put her to any inconvenience because you've overindulged *again.*"

"Why do I let you have such unbridled power over me, Jim?" John struggled to his feet. "And look how you've let it go to your head."

Jim snorted. "The only thing unbridled is you."

"How's everything going, Jim?" Theodrick asked. He liked Jim. He had a good head on his shoulders. He was quiet but if you got him to talk he had intelligent things to say.

"Not too much going on, Mr. Snuffer," Jim replied.

Snuffer nodded. The Younger boys had too much time on their hands. None of them held down a job. He didn't even know what Jim did with his time. John, on the other hand...

"What did you do last night, John?" he asked with a twinkle in his eye. John was always good for a story. He was lazy and often times up to no good but he had a sense of humor the older man enjoyed.

"I danced with every single female over the age of five and under the age of ninety, Theodrick." John lifted his coffee cup in salute. "Even the ugly ones."

"Good for you," Snuffer smiled.

"I was the Belle of the Ball."

They all laughed.

John was reaching over for another biscuit when they heard the sound of horses outside. Mrs. Suffer looked out the curtained window.

"Strangers."

John and Jim pushed back their chairs and rose.

"The attic," Snuffer directed.

John picked up his shotgun and threw Jim his revolver. They headed to the rear of the room and boosted themselves up. Now what was this?

Lull and Wright got off their horses and approached the house. Daniels stayed behind where he wouldn't be seen. Lull didn't want to tip their hand. There weren't any horses in sight but that didn't mean they weren't in the barn.

"Afternoon," he greeted, touching the brim of his hat. "We understand Mrs. Simms has some cattle for sale."

Snuffer nodded in greeting. "Well, you'd have to ask Mrs. Simms about that. She's down the road about a mile and a half. Back where you came from."

"Guess we didn't listen well enough." Lull casually looked at Wright and back at Snuffer. "Appreciate the information. You wouldn't know of anyone else that might be interested in selling some cattle, would you?"

"No, I guess I don't."

"We'll be on our way then."

The two men mounted their horses and continued down the road.

When the strangers were out of sight, Snuffer called to Jim and John. They dropped down, still holding their weapons. John peeked out the window.

"That was an interesting encounter." Snuffer scratched his chin. "Said they were looking for old lady Sim's place. Were interested in the cattle she's selling."

"You don't think they were looking to buy cattle," Jim surmised.

"Maybe they were and maybe they weren't, but when I told them how they could find her they went in the opposite direction."

"I knew it!" John snarled. "They're snooping around. They're looking for us."

"Could be," Snuffer agreed. "They were pretty well-armed for cattlemen."

"C'mon Jim. Let's go see where they're headed."

"There's no need to do that, John." Jim shook his head. "We don't need to go looking for trouble. They'll give up when they don't find us and head off somewhere else."

"I'm not the one looking for trouble. I want to know who they are and what they're doing here."

"If they're posse or Pinkertons we don't want to reveal ourselves."

"If they're posse or Pinkertons, I want them the hell out of our territory. C'mon Jim. Let's at least find out who they are." John was already out the door.

Jim hesitated.

"Better go with him, Jim," Snuffer advised. "You know how he is."

Jim sighed.

"Yes, I know how he is."

John and Jim got their horses out of the barn and rode down the Chalk Level road in the direction of the strangers. The two men had been joined by a third and were easily spotted about three-quarters of a mile ahead.

Lull and Daniels were involved in conversation when Wright looked back to make a comment and saw Jim and John approaching. Without a word, he turned his horse and took off at break-neck speed across the field.

"Hey! Hey, you! Stop right there!" John directed.

Wright looked back over his shoulder and kept going.

"I said stop!"

John raised his revolver and shot in the man's direction. The bullet took off Wright's hat but by that time he was too far in the distance to be further influenced.

Lull and Daniels drew their guns but hesitated. What the hell was Wright doing?

John and Jim rode closer.

"I'd suggest you drop those weapons on the ground, gentle-men."

Jim trained his gun on Lull and Daniels. He was as cool as he had been in the heat of battle all those years ago. If these men were posse or Pinkerton, he and John couldn't afford to waste time to treat them any more politely.

The men complied.

Ol Davis and Speed McDonald watched from the field where they were working the land of Ol's father John. If the Youngers had their guns drawn there was probably going to be trouble.

John hopped down off his horse and scooped up the two guns. He looked admiringly at one of them.

"My, my. This is a .45 caliber Trantor. Isn't that made in Eng-land, Jim?"

"I believe it is."

The two strangers said nothing.

"This is a fine piece." John put it in his pocket. "Thank you for your gift," he nodded at Lull. "I'll enjoy it."

"Who are you two and what are you doing around here?" Jim asked.

"I'm Allen and he's Daniels," Lull replied. He wasn't about to state his real name. The Youngers might have heard of him from his time in Chicago. "We're from Osceola."

"Is that right," Jim looked at John. If these men were from Osceola they would probably have seen them there at one time or another. "What are you doing out here?"

"Just rambling around."

Lull tried to maintain calm. There was a good chance that these men were a couple of the Younger brothers. That coward Wright seemed to have known them and why else would he have taken off like that? And one of them was apparently named Jim.

"Just rambling around," John repeated. He raised his double-barreled shotgun so that it pointed at Lull's chest and smiled. "Are you boys detectives? C'mon, you can tell us. We're all friends here."

"No, we're not detectives." Lull looked at Daniels, who had lost all color.

"Why so heavily armed? Seems to be a lot of firepower for two boys just rambling around," John smirked.

Lull decided that maybe if he were more aggressive the men would not be as suspicious.

"We've got the right to be armed any way we please. What's it to you?"

"I'd say since I'm the one holding this little turkey shooter, what's it to me is whatever I want it to be." John was beginning to lose his humor.

"Look, we're just looking for some cattle to buy." Daniels thought the conversation had gone on long enough. He knew full well that he was looking at two of the Younger brothers. No, it wasn't Cole Younger but they were Youngers all right. He and Lull should just continue their guise and get the hell out of here.

They could skedaddle now and plan something for later. "We heard that Snuff...I mean the widow Sims..."

That was all John and Jim had to hear.

And Lull knew it. He started to reach into his coat as John swung his shotgun toward Daniels.

At the same time Lull's fingers touched his hidden Smith & Wesson pistol. In one swift movement he removed the gun and fired.

In that one swift movement, the bullet tore through John's neck.

Reeling in shock, John fired at Lull just as Lull's horse lurched forward. The shot hit Lull in the arm and shoulder.

Jim's horse stumbled back as Jim fired at Lull. He missed.

Lull somehow remained on his horse and took off down the road, riding as fast as he could.

Daniels, who was surprised himself by Lull's action, rode after him.

This time Jim's aim was true. Daniels fell to the ground.

Lull had no idea where he was headed as he pounded toward a grove of trees. He only knew that his life depended on getting out of range as fast as he could. He looked back to see if he was being followed and as he did, a low-hanging branch knocked him from his saddle. He hit the brush hard.

John had somehow pulled himself onto his horse and he was enraged. Blood gushed from his neck and streamed down his shirtfront. He took no mind of any of that; his eyes were wide in fury as he rode to where Lull laid on the ground.

Lull's gun had fallen from his hand. He pushed his feet into the dirt and moved backward but he had nowhere to go. As his back hit the trunk of a tree he looked up at John. He knew better than to ask for mercy.

"You son-of-a-bitchin' bastard! You goddamned Pinkerton!"

John lurched on his horse as he fired. One round missed but the other hit Lull squarely in the chest.

John turned his horse to look back for his brother. He saw Jim rolling Daniels' body over as a haze enveloped his senses.

Good, he thought, that's good. Jim is all right and the other man is dead.

As he struggled to stay in his saddle he slowly moved his horse forward.

"John!" Jim yelled. Good God, he was soaked in gore.

John's horse bumped the fence and he swayed in his saddle. He raised his head and his eyes locked on Jim's.

"Goddamn Yankees," he whispered.

John dropped from his horse, his body landing on the other side of the fence.

Jim ran to his brother, with Speed McDonald and Ol Davis right behind him. He lifted John's body up onto his lap. No, this wasn't happening. *This wasn't happening!*

"It'll be all right, it'll be all right," he all but chanted as he unhooked John's gun belt. "I'll take this....then they won't think...I'll just...."

His guerilla instincts were taking over where his mind would not go.

Jim's hand slid over the watch John wore in his waistcoat pocket. It had been their father's and had been given to John because he'd just come out and asked for it.

"I'll hold on to this so you don't lose it....you know how you're always losing things..."

Ol watched Jim's face. How could Jim not see that John was dead? If he knew it, Jim must be able to see that. Jim knew more about death than he did. He had to know his brother was dead....

Jim threw John's pistol to Ol.

"Take John's horse and go tell Mr. Snuffer what happened," he directed the boy. "Speed, stay with John."

He got up and ran toward his horse.

"Take care of John!" he yelled as he kicked his horse in the direction Wright had fled.

John Davis heard the commotion and grabbed his shotgun. When his son ran up with the news that there had been a gunfight, he was already on his way down the road. He didn't have to guess that one or more of the Youngers were involved.

"They shot John Younger, Pa!" Ol's eyes were large as saucers. "I'm pretty sure he's dead!"

"I'm on my way, son. You go tell Mr. Snuffer and John McFerrin to meet me there. And son, don't say anything about John being dead."

Davis ran down the road and saw Speed McDonald kneeling by a body.

"It's John Younger, Mr. Davis," Speed informed him. "He's gone."

Davis walked over to the body in the road. Whoever had been foolish enough to mess with the Younger boys was dead too.

"I think there's another one, Mr. Davis. Over in that copse of trees."

Davis cautiously approached the orchard. He saw a man propped against a tree covered in blood and slowly walked over to him.

Lull turned his head and looked at Davis. He slowly raised his hand.

"I'm unarmed," his voice was little more than a whisper. "I hope I've fallen into good hands."

He had. Although not exactly sympathetic hands.

"You just hang on. I've got men coming."

When Theodrick Snuffer and John McFerrin saw John's body they both fought back strong emotions. They were fond of John. John was very much a part of each of their extended family.

"My place is closest, Mr. Snuffer," McFerrin said, tears rolling down his face. "Let's take John there."

"That's what we'll do, John," Snuffer agreed.

Davis looked at where Daniels body lay. "And the other man too."

John McFerrin stiffened. He didn't know who was responsible for the death of John Younger. If it was the man lying there dead, he could just stay there and rot as far as he was concerned.

"I know." Davis put his hand on McFerrin's shoulder. "But it's the Christian thing to do."

They carried John and Daniels inside the McFerrin cabin. It had taken some effort to move the injured Lull and he was the last to arrive. They began to carry Lull into the house.

Aunt Hannah, her cheeks wet with tears, stepped out the front door. Speed McDonald had already told her his account of what happened and who was to blame.

Her husband nodded. Yes, this was the other one. The other stranger, who had come from somewhere else to hunt John down like an animal. Didn't matter why. Only mattered that John was dead.

"Let's get him inside," John Davis suggested.

"No, Mr. Davis." Hannah crossed her arms. "I'm not havin' the man who killed John Younger in my house. You can place him on the porch."

When it was determined that Lull could be moved, they decided to take him to the Roscoe House. There he was placed in the care of Cora's father, Dr. McNeill. Small world sometimes. It was a tossup whether Lull would live or die.

Wright had ridden northwest and stopped along the way to buy a hat from one of the farmers he passed. He figured with a hat back on his head the Youngers wouldn't recognize him. He told Sheriff Johnson that Detective Lull and Ed Daniels had been captured by two of the Youngers. He'd heard gunshots as he rode to get help.

Johnson and his deputy quickly organized a group of men to head out to Roscoe to see what happened. By the time they reached that settlement, Wright was long gone, never to be seen in St. Clair County again.

CHAPTER 40

J im sat in the candlelight staring at his brother's body.

It had happened so fast. They were laughing about John being the Belle of the Ball and now he was laying there cold dead.

Jim was so numb he couldn't even cry.

"Why'd you have to go after them?" he whispered. "We should have stayed at the Snuffers. We didn't need to go after them. They probably would have just gone away."

But John was nothing if he wasn't predictable that way. He never backed down from a challenge. His way was to confront rather than walk away. Jim had known from the time John was a little boy that a day such as today was probably inevitable.

"Your willfulness did you in, brother."

The posse had come and gone. They didn't see Jim but Jim didn't expect Ol Davis and Speed McFerrin to lie for him. They had seen everything. They knew he was the one who had killed the man they laid next to his brother. He didn't want to bring any trouble to the McFerrins; he cared about them too much. So he'd be on his way.

And now he had to tell Cole and Bob and their sisters that John was dead. God help him.

He didn't hear Theodrick Snuffer approach. Snuffer had been sitting on the porch allowing Jim time to be with his brother and his thoughts.

"Anything I can do for you, Jim?" he asked.

"Yes, there is Mr. Snuffer," Jim looked up. "It's not wise for me to stay here too long. I'd like to ask you a tremendous favor."

"Anything that I can do, son." Snuffer put his hand on Jim's shoulder.

"I'm concerned about John's body being disturbed. You never know what people who don't know him might do."

He didn't have to say the word "Pinkerton". Snuffer knew who he was talking about.

"Would you bury my brother? Will you bury John in a place and in a way that only we will know where he is?"

"Yes, Jim. I can do that."

In the dead of night, Snuffer and Speed McDonald put John's body into the wagon and took him over to the Yeater Cemetery. They couldn't place a marker so they laid John at an angle. His grave would be recognized only by the people who knew it was there. They put out the word that the body had been taken up to Jackson County so John could be laid with his brother, in an unnamed place. Nobody who wasn't told needed to know the truth of it.

The next day a coroner's jury determined that John Younger had been killed by Louis Lull and Ed Daniels had been killed by Jim Younger. That wasn't hard to figure out. What did raise eyebrows was why Lull had made it his mission to hunt down these two men in their own territory; a territory of friends.

Lull hung on for a while. His wife and mother came down from Chicago to nurse him but his condition only went from bad to worse. They said he died that night. They placed his body on the train in Clinton to carry it back to Illinois. At least that's what they said.

Many of the folks in St. Clair believed otherwise. They thought it was a fake for the benefit of the Younger boys. The Pinkertons didn't want John to be avenged. Some said the body box was empty and Lull himself was secreted in another car.

When Dr. McNeill was asked about it, he only replied "You must learn to keep the game in your lead."

Whatever that meant.

In the end, it didn't matter one way or another. Lull was dead by the time he arrived in Chicago. He wouldn't be looking for the Younger boys any more. Not in this lifetime.

Jim may have survived the incident but he was now quickly sinking into his own dark thoughts. He should have protected John better. Yes, John was a hot-head and yes, he was bound for serious trouble at some point but Jim was his older brother and he should have protected him better. He shouldn't have just gone off with John the way he did. John was curious, he was always curious, but Jim had a strong feeling they should just let it go. In the end he hadn't put up much of a protest. He accompanied his brother into a dangerous situation for no reason other than John wanted to see for himself who the two strangers were.

And why hadn't Jim instinctively known that the detective had a concealed weapon? Jim was the one who had been in battle. You never let your enemy get the upper hand, never. He should have demanded that the Pinkerton open his coat. John was on the ground for Godsake. Even with his shotgun pointed at the man he didn't have the advantage. Jim just sat on his horse useless while a Pinkerton detective drew a hidden gun on his brother and killed him.

It was his fault. It was all his fault. How was he going to tell the others what he had allowed to happen? Cole would be furious and Bob would be devastated.

Jim himself was just plain sick.

"You ought to stop and smell the roses, Bobby."

They were sitting at a table in the Hot Springs Hotel having breakfast. Cole looked at his little brother over the rim of his coffee cup. Only Bob wasn't his little brother anymore. When had he turned into a man?

"What?" Bob answered, scooping more biscuit and gravy into his mouth.

"You're shoveling that food in your mouth like it's your last meal."

"I'm hungry," Bob mumbled. "I was busy and I forgot to eat last night."

"Well, I can't stand to look at you rooting in that plate like a hog in slop." Cole rose and picked up a newspaper that was lying on the table next to them.

"Don't look then." He was hungry damn it. Big deal. "Haven't you ever been..."

His words trailed off. All the color had drained out of Cole's face. "What's wrong?"

Cole raised his eyes from the newspaper and stared at him, his expression blank. He seemed unable to speak.

"What is it? Cole, what's wrong?"

Cole held out the newspaper. His hand shook.

Bob looked at the newspaper and looked back at Cole. What the hell was so wrong that it had rendered Cole Younger speechless? He reached over and took the paper. He quickly scanned the front page and started to ask Cole to explain what he was upset about.

Then he saw it.

John Younger killed in gun battle with Pinkerton detectives in St. Clair County, Missouri.

Bob stared at it. This was one of those false stories, right? This was just one of those false stories that they were writing all the time about Jesse and his friends to bait them, right?

Yet the look on Cole's face told him that Cole maybe didn't think that was the case. Still...

"This is just one of those stories, Cole. One of those fake stories."

Cole still didn't speak, his eyes brimming with tears, his chest heaving. He blew out a breath and took a step backward, all but knocking over the table.

"We've got to find him."

"Yeah, we'll find him and he'll have a good laugh at this one. John loves to have his name in the paper, true or false."

"Jim, Bobby." Cole took the newspaper from his hand and folded it. He put it in his coat pocket. "We've got to find Jim."

"Well John's coming here to Arkansas, remember?"

"You're right." Cole ran his hands through his hair. He wasn't going to get through to Bobby without something more than what they were seeing in the newspaper. And who the hell knew? Maybe it *was* a pack of lies. "They might be on the way here."

"It's been almost two weeks....they should be here, or close... by now.... " Bob looked at the table. Hell, no. He wasn't going to take that newspaper story at face value.

Cole considered. Bobby was probably safer here then he would be out on the road. God knew what the Pinkertons were up to.

"All right, look. I'm gonna ride out the north road a'ways. You stay up a'ways on the west road, in case they come in that way. I'll check in with you over there."

Bob nodded.

"Stay safe, Bobby. Stay aware."

Bob bought another newspaper and rode out of town up to a thick copse of trees that stood beside a creek. He got off his horse and sat on a log facing the road that his brothers might come down when they arrived. It might not be right away but they'd eventually get here.

He read the story as if it were about something as remote as an account of California pioneers. The people at the newspaper were trying hard to make the story believable. They even mentioned John Davis and Dr. O'Neill. But it was just another

275

story; another made-up flight of fancy. John wouldn't be careless enough to allow someone to trick him like they were reporting here. Neither would Jim. Shit, Jim had fought as a guerilla. Jim would know to be smart even if John went off on one of his stupid, careless, escapades...Jim would talk sense into him....Jim would stop him...

What was he thinking...nobody stopped John if he didn't want to be stopped....he did whatever the hell he wanted to... always had....

No, no, no....He squeezed his eyes shut and laced his hands behind his neck. He began to slowly rock as the image came pounding into his brain.

He could see it...he could see John smiling that big ole grin as he stood toe to toe with the Pinkertons.

"They'll never outsmart us, Bobby. We're a whole lot smarter than any damn Yankees..."

John's voice thundered in his ears from all those years ago. When John told him that a war was coming, he hadn't been afraid.

"We'll shoot 'em and kill 'em first."

He could still hear John's icy rage after their pa was murdered.

"You have to finish it, Cole."

His robbing a bank, then a train.

"I don't want to be left behind anymore. I'm a damn man now. I shouldn't have to put up with this shit."

And his placing a target, a big ole target, on his own back.

"I'm gonna be in on it, Bobby. It's my chance to stick it to 'em. They'll never outsmart us, Bobby..."

But they had.

The story wasn't a fake.

He could feel it now. He could feel the world without John in it. His brother, his ally, his best friend. The one he sometimes fought with; the one he never could quite fully understand. The only one who knew exactly what he had been through and how it had scarred him.

The one person who came closest to knowing what it felt like to be him.

C H A P T E R   4 1

Cole met Jim on the road. Jim was evasive when Cole asked him what had taken him so long to come to Arkansas and tell his brothers what had happened. For once Cole didn't press it. It didn't change anything. John was still dead.

Jim and Cole returned to Hot Springs, to where Bob was waiting. In great pain, Jim related to Bob what had happened on the Chalk Level Road.

"I'm sorry, Bob."

He didn't know what else to say.

As the hours passed, the brothers continued to sit in silence. There was little else any of them could say.

Cole tried to think it through. He was the one who brought John into it. He knew John was reckless yet he'd allowed it, even encouraged it by his bragging. John used to call him "Big Man". Well, he had acted the role of big man and allowed his younger brother into a situation where he would draw attention and once again be vulnerable to their enemies.

But John had wanted it, even enjoyed it. He had wanted to be a part of something bigger from the time he was a boy. He had practically been pulled from the teat by uncertainty and danger and surely that had made him who he was. It wasn't Cole's fault John had been careless. Cole had warned him against that. Cole wasn't responsible for what happened in Roscoe. He even wanted to think that if anybody was, it was Jim. Jim should have disarmed the two detectives. He should have known better. He should have had John's back. It wasn't Cole's fault; he wasn't even there. No, that wasn't right. He couldn't blame Jim for John being impetuous. He couldn't even blame John. He didn't have any experience in those matters. In the end, no one was really to blame. It was just one of those circumstances of fate.

He had to get away from this. This burden of responsibility. This burden of...brothers. Jim and Bob likely felt the same way.

"I'm going down to Florida."

Jim looked at Cole absently. "Why there?"

"There's a cattle venture I need to look into." Cole knew his brothers wouldn't believe that but he didn't really care.

"My relationship with Cora will be over," Jim thought out loud. "I can't go back to Missoura."

He couldn't even face her. She was undoubtedly shocked and humiliated by what had happened. He wouldn't cause her anymore embarrassment.

"You can go with me," Cole offered half-heartedly. "If you want."

Jim shook his head. "No. I've been thinking I'll head back to California. Not Los Angeles but they have a lot of ranch land out there."

"Uncle Coleman has that big spread in San Jose." Cole looked out the window. "And Buck and Dingus have an uncle in Paso Robles, midway down, he has a sizable ranch. You should look him up."

"Maybe I will."

Neither of them had any enthusiasm. What difference would it make where they ended up?

Bob remained silent. How his brothers could make plans of any kind right now was beyond him but there it was. Cole was heading in one direction and Jim in the other. Where did that leave him? Without John there was no middle ground. He knew he could go with either of them if he asked but he didn't really want to be with either of them right now. He felt too empty to go along with the charade. He was a grown man. He didn't need to be coddled by his older brothers.

"What about you, Bobby?" Cole seemed to remember he was there. "You can't go back to St. Clair," he warned. "Not right now. It's not safe."

Bob looked at Cole. Cole, who was still telling him how to act and what to do. Maybe it wasn't safe but that was where he needed to be. He needed to face John's death head on. Cole would never understand that. He hadn't been there for either their pa or their ma's death. That wasn't Cole's fault but Cole couldn't understand how he felt. It would be a waste of time to even try to explain. Why even have that conversation.

"I think I'll head to Denison."

Cole was relieved. He wanted to be on his own and he thought Jim did too. At least for now.

"That'd be best. Be with family."

Be with family. Bob was with family right now and that wasn't much consolation. But that didn't need to be said either. He would let his brothers have their time alone and he would allow them to think he was going to Texas. He didn't want to listen to advice he didn't want to hear. He would have his time as well.

As always, they would each deal with their pain by withdrawing into the isolation of their own little worlds.

CHAPTER 42

Bob asked Theodrick Snuffer to take him to John's grave. He now stood over it alone. He could no more imagine John under the earth...almost expected him to pop out from behind a tree and say "gotcha". That was just wishful thinking. The reality of it was staring him in the face.

Looking at the ground didn't bring him any closer to grasping the fact that he was never going to see John again. Never going to laugh with him again; never going to disagree and bicker with him again. Life was strange. At least his life was.

"You always wanted justice, John. I wonder if you felt that you got that."

John liked striking back at the Yankees with the bank and train robberies, Bob was sure of that, but was that really justice? For all that they and their family had been put through? It didn't seem like much to him, but maybe it was all the justice they would ever have. But the list of enemies didn't decrease, it only grew longer. Now they could add the Pinkerton Detective Agency to the growing register. The grievances went round and round. Bob doubted they would ever end. One just replaced the other.

So here he was. Being at John's grave didn't accomplish anything to put his mind at rest. It didn't make him feel anything beyond the numb that already enveloped him. He had felt loss before. Dick... Pa... Caroline... Josie... his Ma. But he had John there to share his grief and his anger. Now he'd lost John and his two living brothers wanted to get as far away from him as they could.

He had told them he'd go to Texas but Missoura was home. It was home to those who'd gone before and it was now home to John, whether John wanted it or not. Well, *he* wanted it. It was home to him. As much horror and grief as he had seen here, it was still home to him.

He decided that he would visit the grave of his mother in Jackson County. There was a time, a very long time ago, that she could make him feel like his troubles weren't all that bad.

"There will be a brighter tomorrow," she'd say.

When had that started to feel like a lie?

On the way to his mother, he stopped where his father and his brother Dick lie buried. He heard their voices in his memory but it seemed a lifetime ago. By the time he left his mother's grave he had started to feel some emotion but it was just more bitterness, not consolation. It was clear that he would find no comfort at the graves of those he loved.

As much as he loved Missoura it made him unbearably sad right now. He probably should go back to Texas like he told Cole and Jim he was going to do. At least for now. How many times had he said that over the years?

He was lost in his thoughts on the way south out of the little town when his horse began to limp. He looked at the hoof and found that the shoe was loose. Damn it.

As he looked around for a smooth rock to pound the shoe back in place he noticed where he was, just a little bit north from Dru Garrett's people. They had been tenant farmers on some of his pa's land and had ended up buying it when his uncle needed to sell off whatever they had left to sell. He could stop there, borrow a tool and fix it properly. It might do him good to see some people from his past that were still *alive*.

He walked his horse up the road. After he tethered it to a nearby tree he looked down. He had taken to wearing a holster. It was less cumbersome than the shotgun he usually carried across his saddle. Whether or not he was known by name, he was now a wanted man and he needed the protection. But it wasn't good manners to enter a home with a gun on your hip. He unbuckled his belt and put it across his saddle horn.

As he started toward the house he saw the parlor curtain rustle. Good, someone was home. He climbed the steps of the little farmhouse and knocked on the door. No answer. He knocked a little louder.

The face of a boy appeared in the window. He looked about ten or so. He didn't remember Dru having a brother that young. He smiled at the boy. The boy just looked at him.

He heard a gasp behind him and turned, his hand instinctively going to the revolver that was no longer there. It stopped midway when he saw a woman. She must have come around the corner of the house. She was holding a small pail and she was looking at him suspiciously.

"Who are you?"

He couldn't help but stare. She had an explosion of red hair. She took his breath away she was so beautiful. Her eyes were a bright emerald green and they were staring back at him.

She stayed where she was. "I said, who are you?"

"Bob, my name is Bob. I'm a friend of Dru's."

"Dru who? I don't know anyone named Dru."

Bob frowned. "Isn't this the Garrett place?"

"It *was* the Garrett place. It's my place now." Her heart was pounding. Who was this man? Had she been tracked all the way to Missouri?

"Last time I was through here the place belonged to the Garrett's. Dru Garrett is a friend of mine."

He could feel her fear. Why was she afraid of him? Well, that was a stupid question. She didn't know him. People around these parts were right to be cautious. The War was over but there was still a lot of bad blood.

"What do you want?"

"My horse's shoe came loose." He motioned to his horse. "I thought I could stop here at the Garrett's and repair it."

"This isn't the Garrett's any longer."

"So you said." He understood her being on her guard but he wasn't posing a threat to her. She was coming off a little strong.

He stepped down from the porch. As he did, she stepped backwards. He stopped. His horse whinnied and she looked back at it. As though to demonstrate its rider wasn't lying, it lifted its foot.

She froze when she saw his gun belt hooked on the saddle.

"You have guns." She turned back to him.

"Yeah, it's sometimes rough out there. But you'll notice they're on my saddle." He gestured. "I'm not gonna hurt you, ma'am. I didn't know the Garretts had moved on. I'll be on my way."

She looked at him again, assessing if he was telling the truth. She realized that she was probably over-reacting. He hadn't asked her who she was or any other questions. It was true that his weapons were back on the horse. If she was going to be suspicious of everyone who came through she'd just tie herself up in knots. That was no way to live.

There was a creak as the front door to the house opened. Bob turned. The boy was leveling a shotgun at him.

"Whoa." He put his hands out in front of him. "There's no need for that."

"Jeremy!" the woman called. She took a leap of faith. "Put the shotgun down. It's all right." She looked at Bob. "This man isn't here to harm us."

The boy slowly lowered the shotgun.

Bob exhaled. "I'll be on my way," he repeated.

"I'm sorry. We're being over-cautious. I apologize. If you want to take your horse to the barn and fix the shoe, that would be fine."

He didn't want to be here anymore than she wanted him here but he quickly considered his options.

"You're sure that's not a problem?"

"No. Please…." She motioned toward the barn.

"Thanks. I'll make this quick."

He walked carefully around her and led his horse to the barn. The woman remained standing on the path.

Bob got to work repairing the shoe. She didn't have a lot of tools so he made do with what she had. He thought about the woman as he worked. Damn, she was beautiful. All that red hair and those eyes. Those very green, and very suspicious, eyes. Why had she been so nervous? He hadn't acted in any way inappropriate. And the boy with the shotgun, that was odd. He wondered if they had maybe had some previous trouble with strangers. There were some unsavory types on the road these days, that was for sure.

He turned as he heard a noise behind him. The woman stood holding a glass, the boy beside her. She smiled.

"I am sorry. I brought some water as a peace offering." She held out the glass.

He put the horse's hoof down and wiped his hands on his pants.

"You didn't have to do that." He walked over and took the glass. "Thanks."

"I'm Maggie." She stuck out her hand.

He was surprised. He'd never shaken hands with a woman before.

"Bob," he said as he shook her hand.

She put her hand on the shoulder of the boy. "This is my son Jeremy."

Bob stuck out his hand. The boy glanced at his mother and took Bob's hand.

"I appreciate you letting me use your tools." He held out the empty glass.

Maggie looked up at him. He was a handsome man. Taller than most, with a lean frame. His jaw was square and his sandy hair long enough to brush against his collar. Those pale blue eyes mesmerizing. His manners showed good breeding but he was still a stranger. She had to remember that he was a stranger and strangers posed a threat to all she held dear. Still, he didn't look like someone who would cause her trouble and it had been so long since she'd enjoyed adult conversation.

"Do I pass your inspection?" Bob asked, only half kidding.

"I'm sorry," she blushed. "I didn't mean to stare."

She decided to take the risk.

"Would you like a piece of pie? You could eat it on the porch if you like. Maybe Jeremy would like some too."

Bob was confused. Just a few minutes ago she had been suspicious of him and the boy had pointed a gun. Now she was asking him to have pie with them. He doubted he'd ever understand women. But why not linger a bit? He wanted to know more about this woman, Maggie.

"All right," he said simply.

"Wonderful," she replied enthusiastically.

She hadn't meant to sound that eager. She knew her actions must be baffling. She wouldn't have blamed him if he just made his excuses and left.

"Show our guest to the porch, Jeremy." She hurried inside to get the pie.

Bob led his horse back to the hitching post and followed Jeremy back to the front of the house. He dusted his clothes before taking the steps and sitting in one of the two chairs that were arranged neatly on the porch. The boy sat on the steps, looking at Bob's horse.

"Do you have a horse?" Bob asked. He'd only seen one horse and a buggy in the barn.

The boy shook his head no.

"Why's that?"

The boy said nothing.

"Yeah, I guess horses can be a lot of trouble."

He didn't know what else to say to the boy. It was strange how he hadn't spoken a word. Most children Bob knew never stopped chattering.

Maggie opened the door with her foot and Bob jumped up to take the plates from her. He was used to helping his sisters and it was second nature to him.

"Thank you," she said as he gave one of the plates to Jeremy. Bob remained standing. Flustered, it occurred to her that he was waiting for her to be seated first. She sat in the opposite chair.

They ate their pie, saying nothing. Bob wasn't good at small talk. She had been so wary of him that he was hesitant to ask any questions. What might have been normal seemed awkward.

"Good pie, isn't it Jeremy?" he asked, looking to start any kind of conversation.

Jeremy looked at him and nodded.

"You don't say much, do you?" The kid reminded him of himself at that age.

"Jeremy chooses not to speak," Maggie explained. "Please don't take it personally."

All right. What was going on in this household? Maggie seemed nice enough but something was surely peculiar.

"Do you call Jackson County home, Bob?" she asked.

"At one time." He looked across the road into the expanse of fields. The milo was blowing gently in the light breeze. He loved it here but it hadn't really been home for a long time. "I guess not anymore."

She didn't ask him why not.

"How long have the Garretts been gone?" He figured by asking about them he wouldn't be questioning her about how long she had been here and where she came from. That seemed to be off limits for whatever reason.

"Several months. You said you were friends with Dru Garrett. Is he their son?"

"Yeah. I'm surprised they left Jackson County." Mr. Garrett had seemed adamant about not allowing the Yankees to take his farm away from him. But he guessed that a lot of people may have changed their mind when they realized how hard it would be to just hold on to what they had left after the War.

"I believe Mrs. Garrett took ill and they decided to relocate somewhere in Louisiana."

"That makes sense. Dru is living there now, in New Orleans."

They continued to eat in silence. Bob pondered why he was sitting on a porch with a beautiful woman and her son who didn't talk. He figured it wasn't much more complicated than he wanted the human connection. This last week had been one of the most difficult of his already complicated life and he had chosen to face it alone. If he was going to interact with another person it might as well be somebody he didn't know. The shadow of John's death hung heavy over him but this woman didn't know a thing about it.

She was looking out over the fields. Her profile was breathtaking. He wondered what her story was.

"Is your husband putting in crops?"

"No husband. Jeremy and I live here by ourselves." She hadn't meant to say that. It certainly wasn't wise to let a man know that she was a woman on her own but something about him made her think she could trust him with that bit of information. That was ridiculous. She knew nothing about him.

He frowned. Probably another widow of the War. There were so many of them.

"Must be hard for you."

"We get by. Jeremy is a big help to me, aren't you Jeremy?"

The boy nodded. She smiled at him and looked again to Bob. She'd probably never see him again. Even so, it was nice to have the company, if only for a short time.

"Do you have family in the area Bob or are you just passing through?"

"Both, I guess. My two sisters and their families live in Strother. Well, it used to be Strother, now it's Lee's Summit. I have another in Pleasant Hill and another in Amoret."

"My, four sisters."

He smiled. "Got two more in Texas." He thought about Josie and Caroline and his smile faded. "Two more of them are gone now."

She could feel his pain. The War had torn apart so many families. "Any brothers?"

He just nodded.

She sensed that he didn't want to talk about them now.

He could tell by her odd accent that Maggie was not from Missoura.

"Do you have family here?"

She shook her head. "No family." She didn't want to talk about that either.

The conversation seemed to have run its course. He wanted to talk to Maggie more but he didn't know what else to say.

"Well, you've done a nice job with this house. It looks better than it did when the Garretts lived here."

She smiled. He did too. That hadn't come out right.

"I don't mean to say the Garretts didn't keep it up, I just meant that you've done a nice job with it."

"Thank you. It's home now."

"Well, I guess I'd better be on my way." He stood. "Got a ways to go."

She stood and took the plate from him.

"It was very nice to meet you, Bob."

"It was nice to meet you too, Maggie. I appreciate your letting me use your hammer and thanks for the water and the pie."

The boy was looking at him.

"Nice meetin' you, Jeremy." He stuck out his hand and Jeremy shook it.

Maggie walked him down the path to his horse. She wished he could stay longer. She didn't know this man from Adam but she had felt comfortable with him. It was the first time in a very long while that she had been comfortable with anyone.

"Please stop by the next time you're in the area, Bob. I usually have a cake or pie to share." She smiled. "Jeremy can only eat so much."

"Thanks, Maggie."

He left his holster hanging on his saddle horn after he mounted his horse. He'd put it back on when she wasn't watching him. He waved as he set off down the road.

He had spent an hour at the home of a woman named Maggie and her muted son. It was an odd experience, but a nice one. He didn't even know Maggie's last name or where she came from but he knew he wanted to see her again.

CHAPTER 43

Cole didn't stay in Florida long. The climate didn't really suit him; he wasn't one to appreciate so much sun. He returned to his friends in Texas, where there was some weather. Moving along didn't bother him. He was beginning to realize that he'd always be on the road, one place to another. He didn't know when he had committed to it but that seemed to be the choice he made.

Jim had visited his Uncle Coleman in San Jose, California but he didn't stay. His relatives enjoyed seeing him and that made him feel good, but Jim didn't want Uncle Coleman's name tarnished in any way because of him. He thanked his uncle for his hospitality and ventured south to Paso Robles where Drury James welcomed him as a hand on his La Panza ranch. That had turned out well. Jim loved it there. He had his opportunity to train work with horses. He thought he might finally have found a place to be content.

Bob visited the family in Dennison but he felt uncomfortable; it was as if his sisters couldn't look at him without seeing John too. It also didn't sit right that there really wasn't anything he could do for them anymore. He felt like a freeloader. He checked in at the ranch, which was now being run half-heartedly by some friends of Cole's. There was nothing for him there either. He was done with cattle.

It made some news around the guerilla grapevine when Jesse James finally married his longtime sweetheart, Zee Mimms. On their way to Mexico for their honeymoon they stopped in Wichita Falls at the home of Jesse and Frank's sister Susan and her husband Allen Parmer, who rode with Jesse during the War. When Bob heard Jesse was in Texas, he decided to take advantage of the opportunity to maybe get to know him a little better, away from anything having to do with robberies or accidental death.

Now they were sitting in Susan's parlor. The women were fussing in the kitchen and Jesse, Parmer and Bob were enjoying a cup of coffee. Jesse and Parmer were telling war stories but they didn't bore Bob like the stories Cole told. He guessed it was because he hadn't heard these before. Still, he wondered if the men involved with the Confederates and the guerilla movement would ever talk about anything else.

He was surprised and pleased when Jesse asked him to tell them about his time in New Orleans. He didn't have too much to say about it but he related some of the tales he had heard there and they all had a good laugh. This was new to Bob. He usually sat silent while his brothers told their stories. Nobody was ever interested in anything he had to say. It was nice to have Jesse actually listen to him and laugh at his remarks. It made him feel like he was finally one of the boys and not just the tag-along little brother. They enjoyed a delicious dinner and the men stepped outside for cigars. Bob wasn't much for cigars but he joined Jesse and Parmer.

"I sure was sorry to hear about John," Jesse repeated, shaking his head. "He was a good man. A real firecracker."

Bob nodded. He wasn't ready to talk about his brother's death yet.

"Goddamn Pinkertons," Jesse spat as his eyes grew cold in the evening light. "Goddamn those Pinkertons."

"What are you and your brothers going to do about 'em?" Parmer asked.

"I don't know," Bob answered honestly.

"They're going to hit another train, that's what they're gonna do." Jesse looked at Bob. "What do you say we hit one in John's honor?"

Bob didn't know if that would honor John but it certainly would be a step toward avenging him. He figured the best way to actually honor the family who had fallen at the hands of the Yankees, whether directly or indirectly, was to establish a farm and put those carpetbagging dollars to work for *his* best interest. So here it was, back to the money.

This time he didn't hesitate.

"Just tell me when and where."

"Well, I'm enjoying my honeymoon right now but I'll be back this way the end of November. We'll talk again then."

Bob nodded. "Well, guess I'd better be heading out. It was good to see you Jesse. Thank Mrs. Parmer for the meal," he said as he shook the men's hands.

"November, Bob," Jesse winked. "We'll have our say soon enough."

At the end of August, two omnibuses were robbed in Lexington and Waverly, Missouri in broad daylight. One of the passengers identified the perpetrators as Frank and Jesse James and Will Younger.

"Whoever pulled that robbery *wanted* them to think it was us," Cole groused. "And who the hell is *Will* Younger anyway?"

Another robbery occurred in Corinth, Mississippi on December 7. This time the culprits threatened with knives.

"Knives..." Cole scoffed. "Anybody who knows us will see right through this one." But even he had his suspicions...

When Jesse finally returned to Texas, both Bob and Cole were there. Frank was in town and so was Clell Miller. They met at the Parmer's.

"Is this goin' down the same way as the last one?" asked Clell.

"If we did it the same way as last time, they'd know what to expect." Jesse had been thinking about that.

Clell nodded. That made sense. "Where's it gonna be?"

"We're doing this one for John Younger." Jesse nodded at Bob and smiled. "Kansas. That was the start of it all."

Cole frowned. What was that exchange between Dingus and his little brother?

Frank looked down at his nails. "And I will execute vengeance in anger and fury upon the heathen, such as they have not heard."

Bob thought that quote had already been fulfilled that horrible day at Lawrence but maybe it still applied.

"Do the rumors place our take high this time?" Cole was not happy with Jesse's estimates to date.

"Oh yes they do, Coleman." Jesse smiled at Bob. "John will be properly honored."

On an early morning in December the five masked men approached the little Muncie depot on horseback. Jesse's information was so far so good when they noticed no one waiting to board the train. They put the section hands to work loading the tracks with ties. When they had done that, the men were marched to a shed where Clell put them under armed guard.

As the Kansas Pacific Railroad approached, Bob stood in the middle of the track waving a flag, signaling the train to stop. When the train ground to a halt, Jesse jumped up onto it and ordered the crewman to uncouple the baggage and express car from the passenger car. The engineer was ordered to move on. The people aboard never even knew that the stop was unscheduled.

As the train began to move down the track Cole, Frank and Jesse jumped into the express car.

"Aw, leave the baggage," Jesse suggested. "Too much time and anything of value is probably in the safe."

He shot the lock and the safe door swung open. And there it was. This time Jesse's information was right. The take for those fifteen minutes of work was well worth their efforts this time.

294

The administration of the Kansas Pacific Railroad was not happy. They offered a $5,000 reward for information about the robbers. The Governor of Kansas didn't know precisely who it was that dared rob a train in his state but it was undoubtedly Confederate guerrillas. He matched the reward in the name of the good people of Kansas. The express company offered their own $5,000 plus an additional $1,000 for any of the robbers, dead or alive.

"Damn, I should just turn myself in and collect the reward," Jesse laughed. "I'll take all the money I can get."

It was the Pinkertons who were perhaps the most unhappy. They had been on assignment as advisors to the railroads and they had been bested yet again. Their detectives looked incompetent and ineffectual; no, no, that wouldn't do. That wouldn't do at all. Meeting in Chicago, they put their heads together to come up with a plan to stop Jesse James and his gang of disrespectful ruffians.

They stopped near Olathe to divvy up their money. Jesse handed out the large portions with a big smile on his face.

"Didn't I say? Didn't I say, boys?"

"For once you were right, Dingus," Cole conceded. "This is a good haul." They were getting pretty good at this business.

"Well, stuff those greenbacks in your saddle bags and let's get the hell out of here," Frank advised. "This is no time to dally."

As the men mounted their horses to return to Texas, Bob turned to Cole.

"I'm not heading straight back," he informed his brother.

"You're not going to Monagaw," Cole firmly directed. He had no idea that Bob had already been there and gone. "That's the first place they'll look."

"I'm not going to Monagaw, Cole." He had expected Cole's response.

"Where do you think you're going then?" Cole frowned.

"I don't *think* I'm going anywhere. Where I *am* going is to visit some friends."

"Who?" Cole demanded.

His tone irritated Bob. He had expected resistance to his having plans of his own but it was still annoying.

"If it were any of your business, which it's not, I'd tell you I was going to the Garrett's place."

"In Greenwood?"

"Yes, in Greenwood. I'll only be a day or so behind you."

When Cole started to open his mouth Bob held up a hand.

"I'll be fine, Cole. I know how to navigate on my own. I've been doing it all my life."

He geed his horse and took off into the fields.

He'd write a cover note to imply that he'd earned the money working as a hired hand here and there and divvy up a share of his money to send to Retta and to Annie, to help with the care of Josie's children. Then he wanted to see Maggie again.

CHAPTER 44

As his horse neared the farmhouse he saw her in the little side-yard garden. She was bent over the frozen soil. Her mass of red curls tumbled around her face and a deep flush appeared on her cheeks because of the cold winter air. She was every bit as beautiful as he remembered, even from this distance.

He got down from his horse and walked toward her, holding his reins.

She looked up at the sound of the horse's quiet padding, her forehead wrinkled in concern. When she saw who it was, her face lit in a breathtaking smile.

His heart jumped.

"Hello, Maggie."

"Hello, Bob."

She remembered his name. He wasn't sure she would.

"I was passing through and I thought I'd stop by to see how you're getting along."

He'd keep it casual but he didn't want to create a false pretense as to why he was there.

She wiped her hands on her dress and pulled her coat tighter against the chill.

"I'm pleased you did." She walked toward him. "But I'll bet you came for that pie I promised."

"That wouldn't be bad," he grinned.

"There's a requirement this time though."

"What's that?"

She had been thinking of him since the day he left and she planned what she would do if he returned.

"You'll have to suffer through one of my meals first. I'd like you to stay for dinner."

He didn't take the time to think that through.

"That wouldn't be bad either."

Suffering through the meal was pure delight to him. Anything would have beaten the beans and camp biscuits he had been eating but Maggie had undersold her skills in the kitchen. The food was delicious. There was a meat pie and snap beans. Mashed potatoes and rhubarb. And real, honest-to-goodness biscuits. It took all he had to not gobble and groan.

"This may be the best food I've had in years," he complimented. He wiped his mouth with his napkin. "It's quite a meal for just the two of you."

Maggie's smile faded.

"We're only two but we're a family." She looked at Jeremy. "We deserve to eat family meals."

Bob frowned. There was some of that strangeness again.

"I didn't mean…"

"I'm sorry," she smiled. "I know you didn't."

"You must have paid close attention to your ma to learn to cook this good."

"I learned a lot of things from my mother. Cooking was the least of them." A wistful smile crossed her face. "I miss my mother and father."

"I know how that is," he nodded.

She could sense his pain. She instinctively felt the loss of his parents could be attributed to the War.

"Do you see much of your brothers and sisters?"

"Not much of some, too much of others."

"Well, that's an honest reply," she laughed.

He smiled. It was easier to talk with her this time.

"How did you come to know the Garretts?" It seemed like a natural question.

"I've only met them once. I heard they were looking for a tenant farmer and I came to meet them. It worked out well for all of us."

"They're good people. Guess they had enough of the politics around here."

He realized that he didn't know what Maggie's politics were. She could well be pro-Union for all he knew.

"I think we've all had enough of the politics."

He nodded. Would it be impolite to press the issue further? Probably.

She understood the way he was looking at her. The divide between people in Missouri was still palpable. He no doubt wondered which side she had been on.

"I'm from New England. I guess that's about as Yankee as you can get, but the fact of the matter is that I can't support war regardless of its intent. I've seen first-hand the damage it causes. In the end, few benefit."

He studied her face. That was the most level-headed assessment of the War that he had heard since his father spoke of it.

"I agree with that. But around this area people are reminded of it every day."

"And that makes me very sad. People have suffered greatly here. A person shouldn't be excluded by their politics and no one should suffer because of them."

She stared down at her plate and then her eyes rose to look at him.

"I'm guessing you were too young to be a soldier?"

"In the formal sense of the word but that didn't make much difference. We all had our own battles." He didn't want to talk about it anymore than that. "How long have you been here from New England?"

"We left Boston about a year ago."

"Why Missoura?"

"It was somewhere that wasn't Boston." She left that statement to hang in the air. She didn't know this man well enough to get into the whys and wherefores of her relocation. "We fell in love with Jackson County as soon as we saw it."

"It's special here." He'd let it drop.

"Yes, it is." She smiled again and rose. "Now you can have your pie. Let's have it near the fire. It's chilly tonight."

Jeremy took their plates to the kitchen. As Maggie cut the pie she told him he could be excused if he wanted. He took his plate and went to sit in the parlor, by the window.

Bob walked over to an overstuffed chair by the fireplace and sat down. As he looked around the nicely furnished little house he couldn't help but ask himself who were these people? Maggie thought in ways he'd never known a woman to think. Something bad had obviously happened to her in Boston and he wondered what it was. Since she had a son and had told him the first time he met her she didn't have a husband, she was likely a widow. And why didn't Jeremy speak? He was a polite enough boy but not talking at all was just strange. He returned to his original thought: who were these people?

Maggie came out with the pie and took the chair next to him. The parlor was pleasing, decorated in florals and rich wood. Everything about it was comfortable. She fit right in.

"Where do you live Bob?"

He had to be careful about divulging too much information. You never knew who might be asking questions about him later.

"Mostly down in the South right now."

"In the South..." He didn't mention anywhere specific. He sounded like he had his secrets too.

"I've been spending time there with some of my family. But what I really want to do is buy some land here."

He couldn't believe he'd just said that. He hardly knew her and here he was telling her about his dream. At least he didn't tell her that this very land had once been his father's. But that was a lifetime ago.

"It's a good place to farm. I wish I had more resources to put into farming."

"Yeah, I imagine it would be hard for a woman to do alone."

Maggie bristled. "I can do anything a man can do."

"That's not what I meant..." Bob cringed. "I just meant it would be hard for any one person to do without some help of some kind."

"I have Jeremy."

"Yeah, you do." He held up his hands. "I'm sorry. I'm not meaning to insult you. I'm just sticking my foot in my mouth."

"*I'm* sorry. Again. I guess I'm a bit oversensitive about it."

Bob took a deep breath and let it out. "Great pie."

Maggie smiled at his effort to diffuse the situation. "Thank you."

She hadn't meant to become confrontational. The fact was that what he said was right. She needed to put in a crop when spring came and it wasn't that far off. She had never farmed before and she didn't really know how. Her reaction to Bob's comment had been a reflection of her doubts and fears.

"Maybe you can give me some farming tips. I'm not sure what I need to be doing come spring."

He had never been asked for farming advice before. There was a lot he could tell her but he wasn't sure she really wanted to hear it. She was more likely trying to lighten the conversation herself.

His lips twitched and he looked at her slyly.

"First thing is hire yourself a strong hand, hopefully one who knows something about farming."

She burst out laughing. She liked Bob. He made her comfortable and no one had accomplished that in a very long time.

"Are you available?" she smiled.

"I guess I could be available to advise you." He didn't want to hire on as anybody's hand. He wanted to direct his efforts to his own place.

"Now I've insulted you." She was being impulsive asking that question. The fact of the matter was she liked his company and had conveniently found an excuse to ask him to stay. "I'm sorry. How many times have I said that to you in the short time we've known one another?"

"I'm not insulted, Maggie. Truth be told, I've worked as a farm hand. And ranch hand too."

"How do you make your living now?"

Whoa, that was a good question. What should he say, robbing trains? That would go over well.

"I've been helping out family members so long that I really don't have a trade. But what I want to do now is farm my own land." He set his empty plate on the little table next to him. "I'd be happy to advise you with your farm. I'm looking at land in the area anyway."

"I'd appreciate that Bob. I really would. That's very kind of you."

Jeremy knocked his boot against the wall as if to announce that he was still there. She had been so involved with their conversation she'd neglected to realize the time.

"Jeremy, you should wash up for bed now." Although he was playing with his marbles she knew he had been listening to their conversation. He was very protective of her and the presence of a stranger in their home had to be unsettling for him. She watched him get up and walk toward the back of the house.

Bob watched the boy go.

"Is there a medical reason he doesn't talk?"

"No, I wish it was that simple." She looked down at her hands. "My son suffered a horrible experience and his way of coping with that is to not speak."

"I'm sorry to hear that." He knew all about children and horrible experiences.

"Had it been something physical, he would have had all the medical help he needed from his parents."

"You're a doctor?" He'd never heard of a lady doctor.

"My husband was a doctor. I learned from him and helped with his patients."

Bob pondered that. There were so many interesting things about this woman.

"Was your husband killed in the War, if you don't mind my asking?"

"No, he wasn't. He wasn't a soldier."

She didn't seem to want to talk about it so he left it alone.

They sat in silence for a few minutes.

"This is good land here and you should be able to seed some healthy crops. I'll give it some thought and bring by some things to help you get started if you like." That would be heavy work. "I'd be happy to put it in for you."

He hadn't meant to make that offer. It just slipped out.

"Oh, that's so very kind of you but I couldn't ask for that kind of time from you! I'm sure you have other, more impor-tant things to do." She was touched. She'd only been asking for advice.

"Right at the moment I don't."

"I can't tell you how much your offer means to me.' She hadn't been the recipient of such kindness in a long time. "I'll take you up on it only if you understand that I will be working right alongside you."

He smiled. It was maybe the best offer he had ever made.

"All right. Deal." He stuck out his hand. She took it and they shook.

"It's getting late…" he noted. He saw Jeremy standing in the doorway.

"Where are you staying?"

He had figured he'd just camp out in the trees tonight but that information would seem tacky. He thought about what he should say.

Maggie understood his hesitation. His family was up in Lee's Summit and they were miles from a hotel.

"You're welcome to stay if you don't want to travel tonight. We don't have a guest room but its cozy here by the fire. I can get you some blankets and a pillow."

He was surprised by her hospitality. He didn't know the propriety of staying the night on the parlor floor of a widowed woman and her child.

"I don't mean to be presumptuous...." She was flustered. She'd hardly given the invitation any thought. It just seemed like the kind thing to offer.

"That's nice of you," he smiled. "I'd be just as comfortable in the barn, if you don't mind that."

"Of course." She was embarrassed.

"After that wonderful meal I should sleep pretty well out there." He picked up their plates and carried them to the kitchen. When he turned back, Maggie was standing.

"I really appreciate your hospitality, Maggie. This is one of the most enjoyable evenings I've had in a long time."

She saw he was not offended by her offer of the parlor floor and that he took it for the kindness in which it was offered.

"For me as well, Bob." She returned his smile.

Despite being full from the meal, he didn't sleep well. He couldn't get Maggie off his mind. He'd never met anyone like her before. She was everything a man could want in a woman. The best thing about her was probably that she took him at face value. She didn't judge him by what she knew or what she had heard about his brothers. He was just Bob to her and she accepted him on his own merit.

And there was the problem. Maybe if he'd met her before this point in his life he could have attempted a relationship with her but he was a different person now. He was a train robber. There was no way to sugarcoat that. And that fact alone meant there could be no relationship with Maggie. He had to get that little fantasy out of his head. He'd seed her farm come spring, like he said he would, but that had to be the last time he'd see her. That was disappointing but he'd deal with it, he'd just have to. He was good at dealing.

She appeared on the porch as he cinched his saddle the next morning.

"I've made breakfast," she called.

Once again he was taken by her beauty. Her smile made him smile back at her. It would be so easy.....no. He had to face the truth of it. He knew she was attracted to him but he couldn't draw her in just to have her discover who he really was and put them both in a position where they would have to say goodbye. And if he couldn't include her in his life, he didn't want to spend one minute more with her.

"Thanks, but I'd better hit the road."

Her smile faded. "It wouldn't take you long to eat. A person needs nourishment."

He'd like nothing better than to have another meal with her but he couldn't.

"I'm just not hungry but thanks."

She tried not to be hurt. She had been up at first light preparing a special breakfast. From his comments last night it seemed that wasn't something he enjoyed on a regular basis, but he was obviously in a hurry to leave and she'd just have to accept that.

He got on his horse.

"I'll come around in the spring and we'll discuss what you want planted."

"I won't hold you to that, Bob."

She was unhappy with him. What had he expected?

"It's not a problem for me, Maggie. I'm happy to help." He sat there uncomfortably. "Well, I'd better go."

"Good-bye Bob." She'd probably never see him again.

Jeremy came to the door.

"Good-bye, Maggie. Jeremy. You both take care of yourselves."

He didn't look back.

CHAPTER 45

B ob was no sooner back in Texas when some disturbing news reached them.

"Lord Almighty." Cole shook his head in disbelief.

Cole and Bob were out at the ranch sitting around the fire with some of their Missoura friends when Joe White came in with the news.

"A fire bomb, can you believe it?" White shook his head. "The Pinkertons threw a goddamn fire bomb right into the farmhouse. Tore the arm right off Frank and Jesse's mother and their little brother Archie is dead. That boy was only eight years old."

It made Bob sick. Taking the life of his brother John was one thing. John was an adult against whom the Pinkertons held a grudge and with good reason. But a little boy? He'd done nothing wrong. He'd been nowhere near any of those robberies. And Frank and Jesse's mother...as ornery as he had heard she was, she was their *mother*, for God's sake. No one deserved to be attacked in their home in the dead of night. It was Josie and Jarrett all over again, but this time the child had not made it out.

The Pinkertons had quickly taken the place of those who had been their enemies during the War. No innocent person was safe if they chose to battle back against those who wronged them. The difference was that this time, they had no one to blame but themselves.

307

As February turned into March, a heated debate played out on the pages of the *St. Louis Dispatch* and the *Chicago Tribune*. The Pinkertons had not won allies by their callous bombing of the James farm. People were beginning to tire of lives lived under siege by those still involved in the politics of the War. There was a call to grant amnesty to Jesse and Frank James and Cole and Jim Younger. Let the robberies be forgiven and hopefully that would be the end of it.

Most didn't see it that way and questioned why men who had robbed banks and trains and caused the deaths of innocent people should be let off Scot Free. This was the United States of America; hadn't the War settled that? Criminals were tried in a court of law.

It was countered that former Confederates could never get a fair trial and there was no solid evidence against those men in the first place.

And so it continued. Many people with an opinion but few who would make the effort one way or another to settle the issue.

It didn't matter to Cole, Frank and Jesse one way or the other. They hadn't asked for a pardon and they'd be damned if they'd take the matter to court. They knew they wouldn't get a fair deal and if they even sniffed around such a proposal that would be an admission of guilt. So to hell with that.

Jim was still in California. He was unhappy when he heard that his name was being dragged through the mud again. He also knew that he was now powerless to protest.

Bob read about it as it played out in the newspaper. He hadn't been named and that was something he could live with. He knew Cole would never publicly bring him into it and he felt that he could trust Frank and Jesse to leave him out of it too. Jesse liked to see his name in print but Bob dreaded the day when he might see his own there. And if he continued keeping company with those boys, it would likely be only a matter of time.

The next story that caught Bob's eye didn't have anything to do with amnesty. Dan Askew, neighbor to Frank and Jesse's mother, had been found murdered.

"I'm bettin' Askew had something to do with the bombing," Cole figured. "It's harder than ever to tell who our enemies are."

Cole took no personal responsibility for the fact that people might be striking back at actions Cole and his friends had instigated themselves. It was all just a continuation of the War to him.

"We need to talk to Buck and Dingus. If we head on up to Monagaw, I'm bettin' they show up."

Bob thought about that. He'd be drawing attention to himself if he was seen in the company of Jesse and Frank in Monagaw; but it wasn't like he hadn't been seen with them there before. He had already made that bed. The folks there were their friends anyway; their movements were always kept on the down-low.

He thought about his options. He had enough money now to buy a small parcel of Missoura land but what he had wouldn't fund the gathering of all that he'd need to get it going. Anyway, he promised himself that once he was done robbing trains, he was done with it. He didn't want to rely on that in the future. Truth was he could use some more money. If that was even an option. He had no idea what Cole and the James boys had in mind for the future. Maybe they were done robbing now. Frank had told Cole that Jesse was going to head off to Nashville and lay low for a while. So maybe participating in another train job wouldn't be something he'd be asked to do. That was okay too.

But he could sure use the money if they returned to the trains. It all came back to that. He wished he had John to talk it over with, but he didn't, did he.

When Bob and Cole met up with the James brothers the following week, Jesse confirmed that Dan Askew did indeed have something to do with the attack on the James farm. He'd been in the pocket of the Pinkertons. Jesse got red in the face just talking about Askew. Cole had told Bob that Jesse's constant blinking was a medical condition, but just talking about Pinkertons and who might or might not be associated with them got him blinking all the more.

"Askew got what he had coming to him," Jesse raged. "He got off easier than he should have."

"Seems to me dying isn't getting off easy." Frank reasoned. It had been his bullet that put the bastard in his grave.

"Well, what's done is done. We did what we needed to do and now we need to put our minds on other things." Jesse smiled. "Zee is having a baby."

Cole and Bob congratulated Jesse. Bob could only think of the complications having a child would bring to Jesse and Zee.

"I'm heading to Nashville. Zee needs some peace and quiet. I'll get her a little place and then I'll buy a racehorse and see what I can turn over with that." Jesse loved racing horses and had wanted to invest time in that for a while now.

"Speaking of horses, come take a look at the one I bought off of Tom McDaniel," Frank said to Cole. The two of them ambled off.

"Have you been feeling any heat?" Jesse asked Bob. "At least your name didn't make it into the newspapers."

"No, I haven't."

"Well, you should lie low for a while too and keep it that way."

Bob nodded. He certainly hadn't thought of doing anything without the others.

"What are your plans?"

Nobody ever asked his plans. It felt good to have someone interested in him.

"I'm looking to farm."

Jesse nodded. "Always a good deal if you can pull it off. Hard work." He threw a stick. "Got yourself a lady, Bob?"

Bob shook his head. He had tried to put Maggie as far out of his mind as he could but it wasn't working. He thought about her all the time. It was getting time to put in her crop. He was half-talking himself out of going up there to do it. He didn't know if he would have the strength of character to let her be after it was done.

"But you're thinking of one, aren't you," Jesse smiled. Bob didn't respond. "Well, you're a young man. You've got your whole life ahead of you."

It was only true he *might* have his whole life ahead of him. Dick and John had their whole life ahead of them too and now they had no life at all. And if Bob did have his whole life ahead of him, he had begun to question how he wanted to spend that life. Alone?

His mind returned to Maggie. He didn't know her anywhere near well enough but he could almost imagine a life with her. In his perfect world he had his farm and a woman to come home to. In his perfect world.

Frank and Jesse parted company with Bob and Cole that afternoon. The next day in the newspaper Bob read that some men had robbed $300 from the store of D.B. Lambert in Clinton and the Younger brothers were mentioned. Like they would stoop that low. The story died out fairly quickly. All the incident accomplished was to reinforce the idea that regardless of whether they were involved in events outside the law or not, they were going to be suspects.

Bob threw down the newspaper. To hell with them all.

He was headed up to Maggie.

CHAPTER 46

As he approached Maggie's garden this time he could see she'd been busy. The small patch of ground there had been tilled and planted in straight rows. He figured it was a good place for her to start.

Tethering his horse, he noticed Jeremy on the ground near the barn and Maggie standing by a Rock Island plow with her hands on her hips. He walked over.

"Well, looks like I got here just in time."

She turned toward his voice. One of the biggest smiles he had ever seen graced her face.

"I didn't think we'd be seeing you again."

"Why not? I said I'd come. How are you doing Jeremy?" He leaned toward Jeremy and offered his hand.

The boy shook. This time a little smile crossed over his lips.

"We were just trying to figure out if this was in acceptable condition and if it was, what we were supposed to do with it," Maggie sighed. After Bob's abrupt departure the last time she thought he'd probably not return. Yet here he was. He'd come back. Just like he said he would.

"I reckon I can help you with that." He bent over the plow. "It just needs a good cleaning."

"I'm happy you're here, Bob."

He turned his head and Maggie looked into his eyes.

"You're a man of your word."

"I'm not much, but I am that." He stood.

"Got some pie…" she teased.

"That'd go down good while we decide on your crop. You can tell me what you're thinking."

"Oh, you never have to worry about that," she smiled.

They went inside and Bob sat at the table, as directed, while Maggie went to the kitchen. Jeremy hung back.

"Pull up a seat, Jeremy. I figure your ma wants you to be a part of this and I wouldn't mind that either. Two men can get this done faster than one."

Jeremy's face couldn't mask his surprise. Bob was calling him a man. He tried to take care of his mama as best he could but there was only so much a boy could do. But Bob was calling him a man and telling him he could help. Still, he didn't know how he felt about Bob. He had come out of nowhere and that made Jeremy nervous. His mama sure took to him fast enough. He guessed he had to trust her judgment. If she thought Bob was all right, he probably was all right but he'd keep his eye on him anyway.

Bob read Jeremy's face. He'd been in that position where you don't know who to believe or who to trust. He also understood that the boy would be looking to protect his mother. That was only natural. He didn't know what Jeremy had seen that would make him go quiet like he had but the boy probably had scars similar to his own.

"Jeremy, I want you to know I'm here to help. You and your ma have things in control here but putting in your crop is going to take some experience and hard work. I can help you both with that. There's nothing in it for me. I'm just here to help y'all."

Maggie stood behind Bob in the doorway, holding the pie. She'd heard his remarks and watched Jeremy's reaction. Her son was cautious. He had every right to be. Yet Bob's words were just the right words. That he had the sensitivity to say them over-whelmed her.

He felt her presence and turned his head.

"You being city folk and all…" he smiled. He wanted to move away from serious subjects.

"We'll see how 'city folk' I am when I have dirt all over my face from helping you plow my field."

She placed the piece of pie before him and handed one to Jeremy. She sensed that Bob didn't want to discuss what he'd just said.

"Jeremy and I can take care of the plowing." He raised a hand as she started to protest. "Not sayin' you can't do it. Just that it's easier without too many in the field. You can do your share planting. There'll be plenty for each of us to do."

Maggie sat. She had to remember to not be over-sensitive. She didn't want to spend so much of her time apologizing like she had the last time he was here. She had sounded like a fool.

"I defer to you then. You being the one with the experience, because I will go on record right now that I don't know a thing about it. And it's not often that you will hear me say those words, so savor them."

He laughed. "Then here's my suggestions. I don't think you're interested in cash crops, like cotton, right?"

She shook her head.

"You want something put in that will feed the two of you. There was a drought last year and the ground is pretty dry but you should be able to get some corn, some wheat… If we keep it small we can toss in some cabbage and snap beans, some tomatoes." He took a bite of his pie. "You'll also need to get some chickens…"

"Chickens?" Birds made her uncomfortable. All livestock did, with the exception of horses.

He raised his eyebrows.

"Yeah, chickens. It's a waste of money to buy eggs and chickens when you can raise your own. Maybe a hog and a sow.…"

"Oh, no. I draw the line at hogs and sows." Maybe she was more 'city folk' than she cared to admit. The idea of slaughtering a pig made her sick to her stomach.

He smiled. "All right, no hogs or sows."

He laid out what they would plant and how it would grow. He had already checked on market prices for seed and he laid out the finances of it all as well. He'd considered the upkeep and, even though she thought she could handle things with the best of men, he'd tried to consider the effort involved with it all and not give her too much for the two of them to handle.

As the discussion drew to a close, Maggie smiled.

"I'm a farmer."

Bob let out a breath. He hoped he wasn't getting her in over her head.

"Yeah, Maggie, I guess you are."

The next day they rose before dawn and began the effort to lay out Maggie's farm. They worked hard, the three of them in sync. They plowed the field and readied it for planting. It was hot work, but by the time they were finished for the day each one of them felt their own sense of accomplishment. They had eaten their supper in relative silence as Maggie correctly assumed that Bob was just too damn tired for small talk.

Bob stuck to his commitment of not giving Maggie and Jeremy more than they could handle but at the end of each day they were exhausted. No one was offended at the lack of chat as they ate the meal Maggie had thought to make ahead in the morning and then headed off to bed. Each night Bob wondered if he could make it to the barn before he collapsed in a heap of taunt and throbbing muscles. He had worked hard before but never as hard as he had in the past few days.

Tonight he looked as if he would fall asleep right there at the table. So did Jeremy and, truth be told, Maggie could shut her eyes and sleep for a day or two herself. She stood at the stove warming stew.

Bob sat with his head propped on his hand. He'd have been happy with a couple of pieces of bread, but he didn't want to be rude. Jeremy sat across from him twirling a marble on the tablecloth.

"You did a real good job, Jeremy. Next time you'll know what to do yourself."

Jeremy looked up at him. Bob not only talked about what they could do, he had stayed there and worked alongside them to do it. He hadn't expected that. Bob had helped his mother and that put him square with Jeremy. He smiled as Maggie put the stew on the table. "Thanks, Bob."

Maggie almost dropped the bowl.

"Jeremy." He had spoken. It had been so long since she'd heard the sound of her little boy's voice.

Bob smiled. He knew this moment meant a lot to the two of them. He didn't want to take anything away from it so even though Jeremy's words had been directed at him, he didn't respond.

Jeremy smiled at his mother but said nothing more.

Maggie didn't want to make Jeremy uncomfortable, this was a huge step for him, so she didn't pursue the matter. She only beamed as she put stew in their bowls.

"I don't know about the two of you but I'm starving."

Both Bob and Jeremy nodded as they began to eat.

"Bob, I can't thank you enough. I don't even know where to start."

"You don't have to thank me again, Maggie. We all did good work together."

"That we did. And every muscle in my body knows it."

"My pa used to say that a good day's work is a day well spent."

"Your father must have been a very wise man."

"Yes, he was." And Bob knew that he would be proud of the hand he had extended to help Maggie.

"You know, with all you've done for us, you've never even told us your last name."

Bob swallowed. It had been only a matter of time until they came to this.

"It's Younger. My last name is Younger."

"I've heard that name..." Maggie wrinkled her brow.

Bob said nothing while he continued eating.

"Wasn't there a Younger who was a Confederate hero here in Missouri? I remember hearing about him when I first moved here. Is he related to you, Bob?"

"Some people consider him a hero. Others don't. He's my brother."

"I'm sorry, I don't remember his first name."

"That would be Cole."

"Oh yes. Cole Younger." She frowned again. "Wasn't Cole Younger accused…." She looked at Jeremy and back at Bob.

"That would be Cole," Bob repeated.

He had known this moment would come but he had hoped it would, by some miracle, never happen. Now his time with Maggie would come to an end. Just like he knew it would. He rose.

"If you don't mind, Maggie, I think I'll head to the barn. I'm awful tired and I'll be setting out in the morning."

Yes, it was Cole Younger that she had heard about. Heard about being suspected of numerous bank and train robberies. She looked at the set of Bob's jaw. He clearly didn't want to talk about it. Her comment had made him uncomfortable. She'd feel the same way if it was her brother being accused. She couldn't read his expression. She had no doubt that Bob was tired but she had hoped he could stay longer. Now he was uncomfortable and backing away again.

"Of course, Bob. We'll see you in the morning."

"I'll be leaving pretty early." He would walk away before he would cause Maggie to disapprove of him.

"That's all right. I'm an early riser."

This conversation wasn't over. She was developing emotions for Bob that wouldn't let it be over.

"I'll see you in the morning." If she had to stay up all night she would make sure that happened.

The next morning, as Bob saddled his horse, Maggie walked into the barn.

"I brought you some coffee but what I would really like is for you to stay and have some breakfast."

She set the cup on the fence post.

Staying for breakfast meant more conversation and he didn't want to go there. It was hard enough to leave.

"Thanks, Maggie but I'd better be on my way."

She nodded.

"Do you always just leave when the situation gets uncomfortable for you? You impress me as a man who doesn't usually run from prickly situations yet this is the second time you've chosen to walk away."

He stared at her. Leave it to Maggie to call him on it.

"No, I don't run from situations. Sometimes it's better not to let situations develop."

"I don't know how you feel, Bob, but I think this situation has already started to develop."

"Doesn't mean it should."

"It doesn't mean it shouldn't either."

He was so hard-headed and, she realized, so much like her.

"You're not obligated to me in any way. I'm the one who is obligated to you. But I'd like to talk this out Bob. Can you give me that?"

She was so beautiful standing there. He hardly knew her yet he knew it would be hard to deny her anything. That was why this needed to end now. She already had heartache of some kind. He couldn't give her more.

"Maggie, you're the most interesting woman I've ever met. And the most beautiful. You have a heart that's been broken and still you give life everything you can muster. I know that if anybody can do it, you're going to make a good life for yourself and Jeremy here in Missoura. You're a good and decent woman, Maggie. You don't need more pain. You don't need more complications."

"If knowing you will bring me pain and complications, I should at least know why. Because your brother robs banks and trains? That's his business and the business of those whom he encounters. I don't judge you because of who your brother is or what he does."

He had waited to hear those words all of his life. He had lost hope years ago of ever hearing them. He'd never expected a woman like Maggie to enter his life and say them. And now it was too late.

She crossed to him and put her hands on his face.

"Don't walk away from this Bob. You don't have to."

He looked down into her eyes. "I don't want to Maggie but I will."

"You don't want to but you will?" Her eyes blazed. "To protect me from your brother's reputation? Do you think I'm that shallow? I've been the source of gossip most of my adult life. The woman who stepped out of her place to work alongside her doctor husband. The woman who dared to think like a man might think. The woman who cared more about who people were than what social position they could provide her. The woman whose husband was murdered in front of their son because he wouldn't provide medications for the black market. Who had to leave lest her son be tracked down and killed because he witnessed the sordid and cheap way his father was removed from being a problem."

She wasn't through.

"I don't care what people think or who they gossip about. And there is no one more qualified than I am to know who to let into my life. I've seen the kind of man you are Bob. I know you're a man of character who loves his family too much to turn away from them because they have chosen a path society doesn't understand. I don't judge you by the standards the social order places on us regardless of the people of moral principle we know we are. I judge you by your own actions and your own heart. I've seen the way you've helped a stranger and been kind to a troubled young boy. I may not know much about you but I know this: you're a man of integrity, Bob. And I want to know you better. I want you to stay."

He realized that he had been holding his breath and he let it out. That was quite a speech and it about drove him to his knees.

"Honest to God, Maggie, I want nothing more. It would be so easy to stay. But it wouldn't be easy to stay without a clear conscious. Because to do that, I'd have to tell you that it's not just my brother who's robbed trains." He looked down at the ground, then back into her eyes. "I have too."

She closed her eyes.

"You see, Maggie?"

She continued to stand before him. She hadn't expected that. Yes, there was a lot to learn about Bob Younger and she'd have to think about what he'd just said. Yet she still knew in her heart that he was all she thought he was. She reached down and took his hands.

"Please walk with me. And tell me why."

They walked along the edge of the newly-planted crops. Maggie linked her arm in Bob's when he shoved his hands into his pockets. He wasn't going to get away easily.

He didn't know where to start so he started at the beginning. He didn't go into the details but she felt his pain through each incident, every tragedy his family endured. She felt the desperation, the anger, the tenacity, the love. He made no excuses, played no card of pity. He relayed the facts as he knew them and the loss he'd rather forget. Although he'd never told another living soul, he found himself revealing to Maggie the dark places his early life had taken him.

He spoke of his father, his mother, their hopes for their family and the dreams that hadn't come true. He told her of his loss of Dick and how he had never known such a kind and compassionate man, either before or after. He described the sisters who left motherless children. And he told her of John, his uncontrollable brother who had never felt satisfied, who had never learned to let go of his bitterness. And who he missed almost more than all of them.

He spoke sparingly of the shadows cast by the War, by his brothers, by all that had come before. As they walked, he gave her only an inkling of what it was like to be who he was. But she knew. For everything he told her, she knew there was that much more. She never spoke, never interrupted or plied him with platitudes. She listened.

He told her of his dream to own his own farm and how he didn't know how that could ever come to be. And when he told her why he had felt desperation so great that he would rob one train and then another, she knew that his decision was the only one he felt able to make. It was no matter that she should have felt shock and repulsion at his disclosure. She knew that it was the only way he believed he would ever get control of a young life gone so very wrong.

When he had finished, when he felt there was nothing left he wanted to say, he turned to face her.

"So you see, Maggie, walking away from you is the best I can do."

She once again put her hands on his face.

"No, Bob, it's not. Walk toward me. It may not be best for either of us but I want it and I think you do too. There's nothing I can do about your past but I know I can bring love and happiness to your future."

He searched her eyes and saw no pity, no regret. He laid his forehead against hers. And he kissed her.

"God help us then."

CHAPTER 47

He sat eating breakfast. He couldn't recall when he'd ever been so hungry. He wondered if his appetite came from yesterday's hard work or from some sort of odd need to feed the hailstorm that was raging in his mind. He didn't know what to think. He couldn't believe that he had opened up like that to Maggie. To someone he hardly knew. Yet it had felt so natural, so right. So did kissing her. The passion and the tenderness of that one kiss nearly overwhelmed him.

Evidently it overwhelmed Maggie too. She hadn't said another word. They'd walked back to the house, spent from all that had been said. When she murmured "breakfast" he had just nodded and went to wash up.

Now, as he watched her in the kitchen, he realized the appetite wasn't any of things he thought it might have been. It was for her. Her heart, her mind, her body. It was for her.

Jeremy sat staring at Bob. Something had happened between Bob and his mother, he could tell. They both had an odd look about them. Bob was so distracted he didn't even realize Jeremy was staring at him. He dropped his blue marble loudly on the table. Only then did Bob turn his head to look at him.

"Morning, Jeremy," he half-smiled, his face turning a shade darker.

"Morning."

Jeremy didn't know why he had stopped talking out loud. It just became something he didn't want to do anymore. Bob had never asked him why, had never tried to coach words out of him like others had. Maybe that was why he had begun to feel the way he did, but he guessed he was just ready to start talking again. Something was different now and he wanted to be a part of it.

Maggie brought the food to the table without looking at Bob. She knew if she did she wouldn't want to stop. Nor did she think of the profound heartbreak that Bob had experienced. She could think only of the kiss and the man who had shared it with her.

She brought in a platter of eggs and sat down.

"Are you staying, Bob?" Jeremy asked.

Bob didn't know what to say to that. He looked at Maggie.

Jeremy assumed that was a yes.

"Then what do we need to do next for the farm? What are we gonna be doing today?"

Maggie looked at her son. He had chosen not to speak for so very long, such was the horror that he had experienced. Yet now it seemed to once again come naturally to him. It might be that her boy's re-entry into society was as simple a fact as time had healed him enough to make his decision. Yet she felt it was likely more that he felt comfort with a man, with *Bob*, something that had been missing from his life for so long. Jeremy had adored Marcus. She feared he would never get over his father's death. She wondered if somehow Jeremy had innately known that Bob had been through something similar himself. Kindred spirits. The Confederate rebel and the little Yankee boy.

But Bob had robbed trains. He was an outlaw. Such a man was certainly not a good influence for her son. Yet no one had ever been kinder to Jeremy. No one had ever been more honest with her. She had never met a man with more character. It was all so confusing…

So did she want Bob to stay? Oh yes, she wanted him to stay. But whether he would was up to him.

Bob looked at Maggie's questioning face. It was a complicated situation. All his life he had been in complicated situations and he just didn't want to think about it. He wanted, for just once, to just go with he felt instead of what he thought.

"Well Jeremy, today is probably our most important day." He paused for effect. "Chickens."

Maggie shuddered.

"You and your ma could go into Lee's Summit by yourselves to buy a good starter stock but I don't think I want to miss that adventure."

He figured that if he kept aware, going into town would be all right. He'd keep a low profile and be sure not to be seen with Maggie and Jeremy. That was just the way it was going to have to be.

"Thank you, Robert." Maggie gritted her teeth and forced a smile.

"You're welcome, Ma'am." Last night when he had been thinking about Maggie, he realized that she was probably a few years older than he was but it didn't matter to him. He didn't care about any of that.

"All right, chickens!" Jeremy whooped as he ran off to wash up.

Bob stood.

Maggie took his hand and smiled up at him.

He nodded and sighed.

Then smiled.

Later that day Maggie stood watching as Bob and Jeremy repaired the coop. She cast a wary eye on the birds that were in a makeshift crate on the ground.

"Do they always flutter around like that and make so much racket?"

"Sure they do." Bob cut his eyes toward Jeremy. "They're females."

Jeremy grinned.

"Very funny." As uncomfortable as the chickens made her, she was enjoying this moment with her beautiful son and the man with whom she was falling in love. It felt so good to laugh again.

Bob was patient when Jeremy placed the chickens one by one into their new home. He explained the entire egg to chicken process to the boy. Jeremy drank it all in, just as he had Bob's explanation days earlier of sowing and reaping.

Jeremy thought about it. Life on a farm was nothing he or his mother had known about. When they'd first come to Missouri, he wondered how they would ever know what to do. His mother had been brave, he knew that, but where they lived now wasn't anything like where they'd lived before. He didn't think they could stay here. Until Bob showed up.

Maggie knew that Bob would keep on working if she didn't entice him to stop for a while. She didn't know exactly what drove him but she felt certain that he was invested in this. He was putting in all this hard work for a farm that wasn't even his own.

"You've accomplished so much today. Too much." She offered Bob water.

They were sitting on the porch steps. Jeremy had stretched out for a rest on the parlor floor and had quickly fallen asleep.

Bob wiped the sweat off his face with his sleeve as he reached to take the glass.

"I'm enjoying it."

The fact was that he didn't want to run out of things to do to get her farm up and going but it was a small farm and things were pretty much under control now. If there was no work, there would be no reason for him to stay. And he wanted to stay.

"You mentioned working as a farm and ranch hand. All this must make you think about having your own farm."

"It does."

He looked over the field. Getting his hands back into the Missoura soil only made the need stronger. Maybe it was because it had once been his pa's soil.

"I want to own the land though. I guess that's my father in me."

The prices that the carpetbaggers and banks were charging to buy land were ridiculously high, she knew. People saved for years to own their own land. She tried not to think of the way Bob got his money. She didn't even know if robbing trains paid off that well. She had already learned not to believe all she read in the newspapers. It seemed to her that if he had enough money from his train adventures that he would already have it invested in land, if that was what he wanted.

"It's important for one to own their own home if they're to develop real roots. I wish I had the money to purchase this land but in the meantime I'm going to get everything I can from this experience."

"It must be pretty different from living in Boston."

"Oh, let me count the ways," she laughed. "But it's much more satisfying. Especially so since you've helped us truly start our new life here."

He continued to look over the field. "I probably should warn you. Once you've tasted life in Missoura, there's nowhere else you'll be satisfied."

"I understand why you love it."

Maybe she did. But all that had now been complicated by her entry into his life. As much as he loved Missoura, he would now think of it in terms of his time with Maggie.

"Jeremy talking. It's good to hear."

He wanted to change the subject. He had had enough trips down memory lane for one day.

"I'm still amazed. You have no idea." She touched his arm. "You did that Bob. Your kindness reminded him who he was."

He put his hand over hers. "I think it's probably more that it was just time. He's starting his life over too. He's starting to see that maybe there's hope for him here."

She sensed that the boy in Bob wanted to think that there was always hope. Even when he had seen it dashed time after time.

"I only know the little you've told me of your brother Dick but the selflessness you described to me is very evident in Dick's youngest brother."

He felt the sting of tears in his eyes. How had she known to say something that would validate his very life? It had been his boyhood dream to become half the man Dick was. For someone to see that in him was...he didn't even have a word for it. He turned his head to look in her eyes. No, they weren't just words she thought he'd like to hear. She had already started to know him.

Jeremy stood at the door and watched the exchange. His mother was happy and he liked seeing her that way. He wanted Bob to stay. He wanted Bob to be a part of their lives.

Bob felt Jeremy's eyes on him.

"Hey, Jeremy. Ready to get back to work? We need to patch that barn or our little chicken friends will need to teach themselves how to swim. That rain yonder is almost here." He smiled. "Unless your ma would like to bring them into her bed for the night."

She hit his arm. "If that's the case, I'm going to go get a hammer and patch that roof myself."

As the sun set and the rain started to fall, it was the end of another good day. Bob kept them entertained at supper by relating the fine points of some of the pranks his brother John had pulled. Maggie laughed until tears ran down her face. He could see she identified with that side of John. Maybe a little too much. Bob was learning that a lot of what made John laugh made Maggie laugh too. Enough so that he already knew he didn't want to be on the receiving end of any of her mischief. And as she laughed, he and Jeremy laughed. He couldn't remember the last time it had been like this for him. And now it was good, *good*, to remember John.

He played a game of marbles with Jeremy. Jeremy strutted like a rooster when he won. Bob tossed a pillow at him.

"Next time, you're all mine."

"Hah!" the boy chortled. "Losers always say that."

"And winners get to dream of their victories when they go to bed, which is about now." Maggie came in from the kitchen.

Bob stood as Jeremy ran off to his bedroom.

"I'll be dreaming of driving nails." He looked out the window. "It's raining like hell out there."

"I don't want you to sleep in the barn anymore, Bob. It makes me uncomfortable."

He turned to look at her.

"Jeremy can sleep on the sofa. He likes it there. You take his bed tonight."

He shook his head. "Barn's fine."

He wasn't looking forward to the dampness of the barn but sleep in Maggie's house? Near Maggie? That wasn't a good idea.

"I'm not a loose woman for suggesting it, Bob. You've earned the right to be comfortable. Please."

Jeremy walked back into the room with a pillow.

"I was gonna tell you to take my bed tonight, Bob. I want to sleep in the barn so I can help the chickens settle in."

"It's raining hard, you know." Bob didn't know if that had been Jeremy's original idea but he thought it probably was.

"That's okay. I love sleeping outside in the rain." Even though he'd never done it, but Bob didn't know that. "Besides, I'll be in the barn. You fixed the roof yourself."

"Yeah and found a lot of other places that need patching."

"Not near the chickens." Jeremy kissed his mother. "Good night, Mama." He nodded at Bob. "Night, Bob. Can I use your bed roll?"

Bob nodded. "Go ahead."

Maggie started to protest. She questioned the safety of her boy sleeping alone in the barn.

"Jeremy…" she called to his retreating back.

"He'll be fine." The boy needed his own adventure. If it was sleeping with the chickens, that was up to him.

"Night, Mama!"

"He's growing up so quickly." She turned her attention to Bob. "So the bed is yours tonight. I want you to have a good night's rest."

The look in her eyes said otherwise.

His heart hammered in his chest. Once that step had been taken, everything would change. He wanted her. And if she wanted him, there was nothing he was going to do to stop her.

She was out of her depth. Although her words had not been in any way inappropriate, her longing for him was. She wasn't a woman who gave her body freely. She had not been with a man since Marcus and he had been the only one she had ever known. But she wanted Bob. She wanted to taste his kiss again. She wanted to feel his body against hers. She wanted to know him in every way. She undressed for bed. Knowing he was in the next room made her heart pound.

In that next room, he sat on the bed. He'd taken off his boots and now stared at the closed door across from him. He was embarrassed to have thought that Maggie might be offering herself to him. She wasn't that kind of woman. Yet he had felt that reflection of her longing in direct response to his. Was it cheap and wrong to feel this way about a decent woman? No, it couldn't be. Because there was nothing cheap and wrong about the way he was beginning to feel about Maggie. What would be wrong, would be to walk over to that closed door.

Bob wasn't the type of man who would initiate anything improper. She felt maybe she knew him well enough to know that. She slipped her white lace gown over her head. Her red hair tumbled around her shoulders as she shook it free. She would wait. She needed to wait. There was no reason to rush into this relationship. Every good relationship grew from time. That's what she had thought but that was not how she was feeling about Bob. The feelings that he stirred in her defied any conventional thought, any conservative timetable. She needed to think this through, not simply act on whatever physical yearnings she might have for him.

As was her habit with her child in the house, she crossed the room and opened the bedroom door. She saw Bob sitting on the bed staring back at her. He slowly rose, holding her with his eyes.

As he walked toward her they both knew that any opportunity for rationalization had passed.

The loneliness, the aching for more that was as deep a part of one as it was the other, would be no more.

CHAPTER 48
Spring, 1874

The first buds had appeared. Bob had irrigated the field and couldn't help but feel pride and satisfaction when the corn began to sprout leaves and the smell of new crop started to rise in the air. This was going to work. Maggie's farm was going to work.

As he walked to the barn he heard the chatter of the chickens. He smiled. It had taken Maggie only a few days before she decided that the chickens were kindred spirits and made them her personal responsibility. Maggie – the one who had shuddered when he had first told her a farm wasn't a farm without chickens. Now she doted on them like every cluck was a conversation. He had raised the stakes by suggesting a couple of cows. He knew she was committed when Maggie received the idea without any fuss or opinion.

"Oh, Bobby, I'm a farmer!" she laughed.

"My brother Cole calls me Bobby," he frowned. "I've always hated him making me feel like a boy."

"Well, would it be okay if the woman who loves you calls you Bobby sometimes? Because she loves the boy in you and she loves the man you are."

"I guess that'd be all right," he considered.

He was the happiest he had ever been. He loved Maggie more with each passing day. She made him see life through new eyes; she made him feel whole. Every time he looked at her his heart beat more sound, more fulfilled, more content. As he came to know Maggie, he came to know himself. The man he was, the man he could be. And he had Jeremy in his life too. He wasn't Jeremy's father, wasn't even old enough to be, but he could teach him things that a father would. He had found a family where everyone was on equal ground.

For the very first time, the War seemed a lifetime away. So did the robberies. He knew he should feel guilt, especially if Jeremy would somehow become aware of what he had done, but he didn't. He would always be remorseful about the engineer of that Iowa train but innocent Confederate civilians had been killed every day of the War. Although all that would be part of who he was for the rest of his life, he chose not to think of any of that.

In the beginning, Maggie had insisted that she pay for everything that went into the operation of the farm. She was the tenant, after all. As they went along she came to know how much it meant to him to pay some of the expenses and she seemed to choose, for now, not to think of where his money might have come from. Although neither of them owned the property of their farm, they each had made a financial, and emotional, life-changing investment.

Their life was stable and peaceful. What with all the noise and drama of his brothers and sisters, he couldn't remember it ever being so quiet and calm. He and Jeremy grew closer and he enjoyed that, enjoyed the boy's company. Bob was grateful that the work of the farm was there for him – he shuddered to think of what affect Maggie's cooking might have on his body otherwise. Every day they each had their chores. In the evening they would sit on the porch, Jeremy reading aloud to them while Bob sat with his arm around the woman he loved. He slept in Maggie's bed. Now it was their bed. If she had explained his presence there to Jeremy, neither of them chose to discuss that.

Although he had thought he would never feel it again, he felt peace.

Maggie had called him in to supper but he stood looking off to the west. There was an odd piece of sky out there. Low-hanging clouds he expected this time of year, but these were troubling enough that the thought of a windstorm or twister crossed his mind. The light was fading and he wanted to make sure the animals were secured. By the time he finally headed in, the cloud seemed to have turned off to the north.

It was early morning and he was washing his face in the basin when Jeremy started to yell.

"Bob! Hoppers! Millions of them! Hoppers, Bob!"

Bob looked at Maggie. What the hell?

He threw on a shirt as he walked to the front door. Jeremy was at the window. He motioned him over with flapping arms and Bob looked outside. What he saw was a cloud of gray so dark it nearly looked black. The air was thick with the chirping frenzy of thousands of locust.

The noise became so loud that he could barely hear what it was that Jeremy was saying. He heard Maggie scream when dozens of them swooped down the chimney and into the parlor.

"What do we do, Bob?" Jeremy was near hysterical.

He didn't know what they should do. He had never seen anything like this in his life.

"Maggie! Take Jeremy into the bedroom. Shut the door and get a blanket. Stuff it under the door. Get under the bedclothes if you have to."

The grasshoppers were all over everything, including him. He swatted them from his face and arms as he pushed Maggie and Jeremy out of the room. He upended the kitchen table and pulled it across the fire box so that more couldn't enter the room that way. He hesitated at the door. To open it would let more in but he had to see what in the *hell* was going on. He slipped through as quickly as he could.

He tried to look upward, to see where they were coming from or where they were headed, but there were so many of them that that was impossible. He heard the horses whinnying and the cows bellowing in the barn and ran to them. He saw that while they too were engulfed, it was nowhere near as bad as it was where he was standing. He sank to the ground, his arms over his head.

As he crouched there, trying to think about what he should be doing, the noise began to become less deafening. He peeked through his arm and the swarm, if that's what it was, seemed to be gathering and heading south. He waited a few minutes and slowly stood. As quickly as they had amassed, they were retreating.

He ran to the house. Flailing his arms, he opened the door. A rush of the insects caused him to jump back. He pulled off his shirt and waved those that remained in the house out the door. Only a dozen or so continued to hop and leap inside and one by one they joined the others outside, up and away.

"They're gone," he hollered, standing there stunned. "You can come out now."

Maggie and Jeremy cautiously emerged from the bedroom.

"Are you *sure* they're gone, Bob?" Jeremy looked around before venturing out into the parlor.

"Most of them." He walked over to where his shirt was balled on the floor. He picked it up and put it on.

"My God, Bob. What was that?" Maggie's eyes were as big as saucers.

"A hell of a lot of grasshoppers." He walked over to the window and looked out. "I've heard about that before, over in Kansas, but I never... Shit."

He went out the door. Jeremy and Maggie, still in her dressing gown, followed. Bob had drawn on his boots from where they were on the porch. He was walking toward the field.

Maggie and Jeremy stood where they were.

The crops.

What little still stood was full of holes. The rest of it ragged and torn. The grasshoppers had not been there long but they had done their work. The crop, just starting to reflect all the hard work the three of them had put into it, was pretty much gone.

Bob stood silently before it.

Maggie and Jeremy walked up beside him.

"The crop....what are we gonna do Bob?" Jeremy looked to him. Bob didn't respond.

Maggie put her arm around Jeremy's shoulder and gave it a squeeze. "Go on in and put your shoes on, Jeremy."

Her eyes remained on Bob. It was her loss too but it was his heart and soul.

"But Mama…"

"Just go do that, son. Please."

Jeremy ran toward the house.

"It never even got a chance to be something." He snapped his fingers.

"I'm so sorry." She could think of nothing else to say.

"Everything that touches me turns to shit." Okay, now he was mad.

"Bob…"

"It's true, Maggie. I don't know why I would ever think otherwise."

"Oh, Bob, you can't take a force of nature personally…"

"I can. Might as well have put my name on a goddamn map to direct them."

She had to be strong for him. He was devastated but that line of thinking couldn't consume him.

"Before you go too deep into that well of self-pity, you might want to consider that these things…these grasshoppers…surely didn't single out just our farm."

He closed his eyes and took in a deep breath. She was right. He knew better than to make this something that had only happened at this place but still…their hard work…their money… their fresh start…

She knew, without him saying so, that he realized it had little to do with him and everything to do with the unpredictable measures

337

of nature. There were some things you just couldn't control. He knew that as well as anyone. She put her arm around his waist and laid her head against him.

"We'll just have to plant again. Some ugly ole grasshoppers aren't going to get us down. We've faced enemies bigger and stronger than them."

He kissed the top of her head.

"Well, it's not like either of us doesn't know how to start over. That's probably what we do best."

They waited to make sure it was over before they put in any replacement crops. The locust had devastated the farms of hundreds of hard-working people. But most of those people didn't give up; they gathered what little money they could get their hands on and replanted, if they could. The War hadn't taken them down and the damn grasshoppers weren't going to have that satisfaction either. Those who held the money and granted the high-interest loans were happy to accommodate them. If they couldn't make it, well, that was a shame.

Bob planned the new crop down to the penny. He was thankful that he had the money from the train robbery but that was supposed to be for his own farm, his own land. Still, he'd draw from his nest-egg for Maggie's. She wanted to put in her share and he knew better than to tell her no. Between the two of them, he could make it work.

So it was back to the field. He wanted to overturn the soil again so it was almost like starting from scratch. The three of them worked together, as they had the first time, and maybe this time it wouldn't be in vain.

Bob had been so comfortably encased in his life with Maggie and Jeremy that he had hardly given his family a thought. He felt a bit guilty about that. There was no reason why he couldn't make room in his heart for all of them. He didn't want to take the time to go down to Texas though. He had exchanged letters with Retta, postmarking them from Lee's Summit with the help of Jeremy, and he knew things were going well. Cole was spending most of his time there, so he was in a better position to provide whatever his sisters might need. Bob hadn't written of Maggie. He wanted to keep that for himself just now. Retta said she missed him terribly and he knew that she did, but this time was for him. He told the others he was staying "down south" with some friends. That wasn't a lie. There would probably be hell to pay when his sisters compared notes, but he'd deal with it then.

He did miss Jim but Jim seemed to be doing very well out in California and Bob was thankful for that. Jim wrote his sisters that his life there was the most content and enjoyable that it had ever been. Jim deserved happiness, maybe more than them all.

CHAPTER 49

On a chilly February morning, Bob and Jeremy were finishing the repair of some planks near the barn door that had loosened the night before. There had been one of those small winter twisters.

"Things like this happen all the time when you have a farm." Bob pounded another nail. "You have to try to keep ahead of them but sometimes quirky things happen."

"Like the hoppers." Jeremy had not forgotten them. Not at all.

"Yeah, like the hoppers." Neither had Bob.

They both looked over when they heard the sound of hoofs plodding along the patches of snow. Bob didn't have to get closer to recognize Cole.

Cole slid down from his horse and walked over.

"How you doin' Bobby?" he smiled.

They exchanged a hug. Bob wondered how Cole knew to look for him here.

"How are you, Cole? It's been awhile."

"Yes, it has. People haven't seen hide nor hair of you."

If Cole was trying to make him feel guilty for that, Bob wasn't going to rise to the bait.

"What brings you around here?"

"Why you do, Bobby."

Cole looked at Jeremy and stuck out his hand. "How do you do, young man. I'm Bob's brother Cole."

Jeremy looked him over. He was a big man. Bob was taller but Cole had more to him. Bob had told them about Cole. Jeremy knew that many people, those who Bob considered right to have such an opinion, considered Cole a brave man who stood up for what he believed in. And that others, who Bob considered vultures and cowards, thought Cole was a butcher and a sneak. Jeremy shook Cole's hand and wondered for a second if he would ever see that hand again.

"What's your name, son?"

"Jeremy."

"Nice to meet you, Jeremy."

Bob thought Cole had an odd attitude about him.

"Jeremy, why don't you head on inside. I'll be in in a bit."

Jeremy nodded and headed toward the house.

Cole watched the boy go inside. "You've got him well-trained."

"Is this a friendly visit to your brother or do you have something else on your mind?" Bob didn't like Cole's tone.

"Well Bobby, I heard from some of the boys that you were shacked up with a fancy Yankee widow lady and her kid and I came to see if that was indeed a fact." He raised his eyebrows. "Lady might not be the appropriate term. You tell me."

Bob's fists clenched at his sides. "You watch what you're saying, Cole," he warned through gritted teeth.

"Whoa." Cole raised his hands. "I guess my information was wrong then." He nodded toward the house. "The boy is just a hand for the Garrett's? You too?" He shrugged. "Too bad. I grinned when I heard you were getting some Yankee ass."

Bob's fist shot out and clipped Cole's jaw. Hard enough that Cole stumbled against the barn.

"I don't care if you are my brother, you don't talk about Maggie that way, you hear me?"

"You better have a goddamn good reason for doing that, boy." Cole touched his jaw.

"You want to talk about this, Cole, I can do that. If you're going to come here judging and confronting me, I can do that too."

"Back off, Bobby." He looked at his brother's angry face. "I might, I *might*, be out of line. Tell me what's going on and I'll see if I am."

"I don't owe you shit, Cole, let alone an explanation of the way I choose to live my life."

"For God's sake, calm down."

"I'll calm down when you stop acting like your usual asshole self."

Cole considered if he was going to let Bob get away with that remark. He wanted to know what was going on with his little brother but he really didn't come here to argue. He didn't want to take up with Bobby where he left off with John.

"Okay, okay...my apologies if I offended." He squinted his eyes. "So is there a Yankee woman we need to be talking about?"

Bob stared at his brother. He didn't want to argue either.

"Her name's Maggie. And she's only a Yankee because she's from Boston, not because she chose that side. She knows the truth of what went on around here back then and what we all did to live with it."

"And she's all right with that?"

"She's all right with that."

"And she's a widow?"

"Her husband didn't die in the War. Wasn't any part of it except to give medical attention to those who were."

"And you're living here with her?"

"We live here together. We're tenants."

"And that's her boy?"

"Yes."

"What about the heists. She know about that?"

"Yes."

Cole raised his eyebrows. "And she's all right with that?"

"We don't talk about it."

They said nothing for a moment. Bob stared at Cole while Cole mulled over what his brother had just told him.

"Damn, Bobby." Cole finally smiled. "I've got to meet this woman."

Despite his trepidations, Cole liked Maggie. She was pretty damn appealing to the eye, even if she was some years older than Bobby, and she put together a hell of a meal. He could see both those things drawing Bobby in. But as he chatted with her over supper, he began to see the stronger attraction. She was smart, quick-witted, had a sense of humor and was crazy in love with his little brother. Cole didn't know what he had expected to find, but to see Bobby so content and at ease exceeded any expectations he had ever even remotely entertained. By God, Bobby was finally happy. And if the woman making him that way was a Yankee, well, so be it. But before he went and signed off on that, that issue needed a deeper look.

"Wonderful meal, Maggie."

They were sitting in the parlor drinking coffee next to a warm, roaring fire Bob had laid.

"Mama's a good cook." Jeremy was fascinated by Cole. He'd never met anyone quite like him.

"That she is, Jeremy." Cole couldn't get over the fact that Bob was acting as something of a father to the boy. It was obvious Jeremy thought he hung the moon.

"Why'd you pick Missoura, Maggie?"

Out of the corner of his eye Cole watched Bob furrow his brow.

"I don't really know, Cole. When we got here, it just seemed like it could be home."

"And is it? No thought of going back east?"

"No, there's nothing for us there. And there is everything for us here." She smiled at Bob.

"Bobby said that you understood about Missoura's war – how it was different here than it was other places."

"Cole…" Bob narrowed his eyes. They had already covered this ground.

"It's all right, Bob. Cole fought a long and hard battle for what he believed in. He's earned the right to ask me about that."

Cole nodded.

"As different as war might be from place to place, it's still war. I don't condone it. And I don't condone backing away from those things in which you believe. I understand that the circumstances here were dire and unacceptable. Bob has told me some of what your family has gone through and that "some of" is beyond anything a family should endure. No, I am not a proponent of slavery but that really wasn't the entire issue, was it? Some despicable actions were taken by despicable people, on both sides. And some who were involved in that chose to maintain their ethics and humanity despite it, despite having to fight tooth and nail to represent and protect their families. So yes, although I wasn't here at that time, I do understand that the War here in Missouri was a complex and brutal time."

Again Cole nodded. Maggie seemed an intelligent and fair woman.

"Do you think your husband would have seen it the same way?"

"I believe he would."

"All right, then." Cole took a drink from his cup. "Is there desert?"

Bob knew that few people stood up to Cole Younger and he was proud of Maggie not only for doing that but for what she said. It was obvious to him that Cole now saw how special she was. He didn't need Cole's approval, but the fact that Cole had made the effort and not pursued the idea of judging her based on where she was born, was good for them all. He smiled.

"The best pie you've ever tasted."

Cole spent the night and in the morning as he prepared to leave, Maggie let the two brothers have some time alone.

"So where to now, Cole?" Bob watched as Cole cinched his saddle.

"I'm going back to Texas." He looked at Bob. "The folks down there are concerned about you, Bobby. What should I tell them?"

"Whatever you like. I'm not hiding anything from the family."

"Is that so? Nobody in your Texas family has heard about this. And Em and Belle and Laura, they all know about you living here with Maggie and Jeremy?"

Bob colored. "Well, no."

"What is it you don't want the family to know, Bobby? Maggie's a wonderful woman. She has a special boy. From what I can tell she's crazy about you. And you love her."

Cole didn't smirk when he said that last part and Bob was glad for that.

"You're happy. Why wouldn't you want to share that with the people who have been through the worst of times with you?"

"I've just been keeping it for myself, Cole."

"I guess I understand that," Cole nodded. "But if Maggie's going to be a part of your future, you need to consider telling those others who are part of your past."

Bob patted the horse. "I'm glad you stopped by, Cole. Although I don't know how you found me."

"Once a scout, always a scout." Cole smiled. "I'm glad you're happy, Bobby. I really am." He clasped Bob's shoulder. "You take care of yourself."

Bob watched as Cole rode away. The idea of revealing his life with Maggie was complicated. He'd have to give that more thought.

CHAPTER 50
1876

His home with Maggie was all he'd ever hoped to have. She was beautiful, smart, she loved to laugh, and she was kind and affectionate. She excited him and had him completely at her mercy. Just the sight of her quickened his pulse and made his heart leap. They hadn't known each other long, but he loved her beyond words and her love for him was real. She understood who he was and how he came to be.

He occasionally thought about taking her to St. Clair. That beautiful and tranquil locality had so long been his refuge. Yet his need to share it with her wasn't greater than his need to keep what was theirs to himself. His home with her and Jeremy was now his sanctuary and opening up his relationship with Maggie to others somehow seemed to threaten what they had together, what he had come to treasure as his own. Maybe someday he'd take her there, but not just now.

When spring rolled around they planted again. With any luck there wouldn't be hoppers to wipe out their labor. And their little crop thrived. The next planting season Bob would expand the crop but he lamented the fact that there wasn't enough land to put in all that he wanted. He wished that he had the money to buy the farm outright and maybe several more acres on either side of it. God knew that the bank, the carpetbaggers, whoever, would make him pay top dollar and then some. Well, thoughts of that were for another time. In the meantime he would do what he could with what he had and be happy for it. Still, owning the land remained his dream now as it had most his life. Being a tenant farmer for the rest of his life, raising crops in somebody else's field, wasn't going to bring him that ultimate satisfaction. Now was good in so many ways but there was better out there for him and he would have to figure out how he would move toward the one last thing he needed to make his happiness complete. He thought of what his sister Laura had told him all those years ago in Texas. *Maybe someday you'll have the opportunity to reclaim some of Father's land. I can think of nothing that would make him more proud.* Maybe that someday was coming soon.

He was sitting at the table with Maggie, figuring how to stretch their money to increase their yield. Their false start had cost them and the money they had now was tight. He was frustrated and she knew it.

"I know you'd like to expand but I think we need to be thankful we have enough."

"I'm a little tired of having *enough*, Maggie. I'd like to figure out a way to have what I *want*."

Jeremy was outside. He didn't like it when they talked money. Bob would always say that he wanted to make the farm larger. It put Bob in a bad mood, so Jeremy had gone out in the yard to play mumbley-peg.

Now he was at the door.

"There's a fella here to see you, Bob."

The excited tone in his voice had both Bob and Maggie turning their head.

"He saw me playing mumbley and he gave me some pointers. I didn't even see him until he was standing right beside me. He's funny, too. He said it was hard to teach a pig to sing but if it was in a game of mumbley with you, you could make it dance. He went in the barn to put his horse up."

Bob stood, frowning. Who the hell was in his barn? Jeremy knew better than to let a stranger approach their house. He grabbed his holster off the wall and was out the door in four long strides. He was headed toward the barn when he saw the figure walking toward him.

"Hey, Bob!" Jesse called.

Bob stopped in his tracks. Ohhh…a smile passed over his face.

"Hey, Jesse!"

He hadn't seen Jesse in quite a while. Then he remembered Maggie and Jeremy. It was one thing for him to be with Jesse but another to expose his family like that. Still, Jesse had always been a friend to him and he certainly wasn't going to turn him away.

Jeremy was beside him now and Maggie stood on the porch.

"This is some boy, Bob." Jesse leaned over and ruffled Jeremy's hair. "He's a smart one."

Jeremy grinned.

"A smart one who knows better than to let a stranger into the barn." Bob frowned at Jeremy.

Jeremy hung his head.

"C'mon now, Bob. I'm not a stranger, I'm like family." Jesse put his arm around Jeremy and walked him to the porch.

"And this must be the beautiful lady from the east I've heard rumors of."

Bob took note of the fact that Jesse hadn't said "Yankee."

"This is Maggie." Before he could say more, Jesse was sticking out his hand.

"Pleasure ma'am. I'm Jesse."

Maggie smiled. This Jesse was charming. Not many men would pay so much attention to a boy they didn't know. The men associated with Bob seemed to be cut from a different cloth.

And then she realized who it was who was standing on their porch.

"C'mon inside," Bob invited.

As Jesse walked through the door, Maggie turned her look to him, her eyes wide.

"Jesse James?" she mouthed.

Bob nodded. Oh boy.

"It's been awhile, Bob." Jesse grinned as he looked around the comfortable home. "Looks like things have turned out for you."

Jeremy took Jesse's arm. "Sit over here, Jesse!"

Bob was surprised to see the boy's enthusiasm. Then he remembered that it was Jesse. People were drawn to him like bees to honey.

Maggie exchanged another look with Bob. Regardless of whom he was, Jesse was now a guest in their home.

"Would you like some coffee, Jesse?"

"Now that would be appreciated, Maggie."

They sat talking for the next hour, Jesse telling them all about his adventures in Nashville and bringing them up to date on his family. Zee was doing well, he said. His little boy Jesse Edwards, Bob did know that he had named the boy after their friend the great John Newman Edwards, was almost a year old already. Bob didn't know that he considered the newspaper editor *his* friend but he didn't say anything about that. Jesse told them tales and regaled Jeremy with humorous events that Bob was fairly sure hadn't happened but which made the boy and Maggie laugh just the same.

Jesse stayed for dinner and his compliments to Maggie were genuine. With Jesse's hatred of all things Yankee, Bob was surprised and relieved that Jesse took so well to Maggie. As the evening wore down, Maggie asked Jesse if he'd like to stay the night.

"I appreciate the offer Maggie, but I'll hold on to it for some other time, if you don't mind. I've got to do some traveling tonight."

If Bob had forgotten for a moment that Jesse was wanted by all kind of law enforcement and more than a few men with a huge grudge to bear against him, he remembered now. It was safer for Jesse to travel under the cloak of darkness than in broad daylight and that's what he would do.

As Jeremy and Maggie said their goodbyes, Bob looked at Maggie. From the look on his face she knew that Jesse had likely not just come by to visit but had something to discuss with Bob. She felt uneasy and hoped she was not reading into the unexpected stopover.

Jesse stood in the barn with his foot on a stump.

"I like her, Bob. Maggie is a helluva woman."

"She is."

"It's good to see you happy."

Bob knew Jesse meant that. He nodded.

"And it's good to see you got your farm."

"We're just tenants, Jesse. We don't own it."

Jesse nodded. Bob got the impression that he already knew that.

"What are your plans to change that?"

Bob blew out a breath. "Don't know."

"Well, I'm not going to chit chat and try to pull one over on you, Bob. I've got an idea and I'd like to discuss it with you. But only if you want to hear it."

Bob looked toward the house. Things were going so well but he wanted this farm to be his. And to be his, he needed money. But did he want to go down that path again? Now that he was with Maggie?

"I'm not going to commit, Jesse, but I'll listen."

They sat, Jesse on the stump and Bob on one opposite.

"I know you've never done a bank, Bob, but this idea's novel."

"You've had a few novel ideas in your time."

Jesse laughed. "I guess I have. But this one's different yet. You ever hear of Ben Butler? Do you remember him?"

"I heard a lot about him when I was living in New Orleans. They called him Spoons."

"Yeah, he got that nickname from stealing silverware from Confederate mothers." He spit on the ground.

"He also issued that Order calling out women as whores if they resisted the advances of Union officers, at least the way I interpreted it." It still made Bob angry. "Son-of-a-bitch."

"Yeah, that's him too." Jesse was well-aware of what happened to Sally Younger, even though it was never mentioned. "He's had himself quite the career since the War. He lives in Massachusetts but he's been involved in some carpetbagging in Mississippi and Louisiana with his daughter's husband."

"He has his hand in a lot of things, if you believe all the talk."

"I believe it. His son-in-law, man named Ames, lives off the sweat of the working man too. He was Governor of Mississippi at one time. Took all his goddamn carpetbagging spoils up north and developed a mill operation in Northfield, Minnesota. Most of the money in that city's bank belongs to them." He winked. "Or so they think."

Bob was already seeing where this was going.

"A lot of the people of Missoura like to hide behind the cloak of ambiguity."

Jesse liked to use decorative words and phrases. Frank said an educated man intimidated people. Jesse wasn't well-educated but he was intelligent and at the least sounded as if he was.

"They'd rather not address the kind of hold the baggers have over them. In Minnesota, they don't much care where a man gets his money." He smiled again. "I say we make them care."

"Take a bank in Minnesota?" Jesse had some interesting ideas but this one was the brashest of all. "That's pretty far north."

"Yes it is. So far north that nobody would ever even suspect we were interested in their bank."

"I sure as hell don't know anything about Minnesota. I don't know that any of us do. Isn't that a liability?"

"Well, that's the beauty of life. You can look at things either as a liability or an advantage. This situation is definitely an advantage."

"I don't know, Jesse."

"Well, Bob, you said up front you weren't committing and I don't expect you to. I'd just like you to think about it."

"What do Frank and Cole say?"

"I haven't mentioned it to them yet. I thought I'd talk to you first."

That surprised Bob. "Why's that?"

"I thought you'd like the opportunity to be in on the planning. Once those two get involved, it passes out of our control and becomes more of a democratic effort. If we have it all planned in advance *they'll* be accompanying *us*." Jesse smiled. "Just because they're the older brothers doesn't mean they're any more capable of a good plan."

Bob agreed with that. "Well, like I said Jesse. I'll need to think about it."

"That's fine, Bob." Jesse rose. "Now that I've seen what a fine little farm you've put together, I figure you might like the opportunity to raise some money and buy it, maybe make it bigger. But that's up to you." He held out his hand. "Don't say anything about our conversation to Cole, if you don't mind. If you think you want in, you and me can get together in a couple of weeks and discuss it further. I'm heading up to Clay County to see my mother and the family."

Bob shook Jesse's outstretched hand.

"I'll think about it Jesse."

When Bob went back in the house, Maggie looked at him anxiously.

"Jeremy?" Bob called. The matter of Jeremy letting Jesse into the barn without asking him needed to be addressed.

Jeremy came bounding out of his room.

"I like Jesse, Bob."

"That's fine and good but what have I told you about letting strangers near the house without my permission?"

"I'm sorry." Jeremy hung his head. "He knew your name and said he was a friend."

"That doesn't mean that he was. Next time someone comes up here that you don't know, they stay down the lane until you ask me. Is that clear?"

"Yes." Bob had never raised his voice to him and he was embarrassed. He never wanted to do anything that would upset Bob. He returned to his room.

"Is everything all right, Bob?"

"It's fine, Maggie."

"Was there a reason Jesse James stopped by?"

"He's a friend. He doesn't need a reason."

Maggie stared at him. It wasn't like Bob to be short with her. "Anything I should know about?"

"No." He latched the door. "I'm going to bed."

She watched his retreating back.

What had Jesse James stirred up?

He didn't like keeping anything from Maggie but he needed to think about this. It was a big step, back to who he was before he met her. He wasn't going to say anything to her about it unless he decided in favor of it.

This would be the greatest risk of all. Minnesota was a long way away and they didn't know the area or the terrain. There wouldn't be friends or allies if they found themselves in trouble but it wasn't like they were inexperienced or stupid men. If a problem came up they'd deal with it. Like Jesse said, you could look at the location as either a liability or an advantage. That part of the equation didn't really trouble him. It was the moral aspect that needed his consideration.

He had participated in past robberies so that he could invest in a farm. He had now done that. But it wasn't really *his* farm. The land now belonged to the Garretts. He wanted to buy this farm. Owning some of his pa's land was one of the most important things that he wanted out of his life. He was so happy with Maggie. He never knew happiness like this. The months flew by and unlike his past experiences, things only changed for the better. Yeah, he was happy but if he was able to buy the farm and it was successful, he would finally know real contentment. It would be a home for Maggie and Jeremy and for him, finally for him. There would be no more moving on. It would always be his final destination.

But the fact was that he didn't have the money to buy this or any of what had been his pa's land. That business with the grasshoppers had set him back. He needed more money. If he went along with Jesse's latest plan, he would have that money. He could buy the farm from the Garretts and the extra land that ran alongside it. He would no longer have just "enough", he would have what he wanted. What he'd always wanted.

And Maggie and Jeremy would share in it. There would be no more looking back to days past. There would be no more wishing that he had done this, that or the other. He'd have his pa's land back and he would be satisfied.

But if he were to participate, it would be with the understanding that there wouldn't be another robbery in his future. He would have what he wanted. That would be the end of it.

No, he wasn't going to tell Maggie anything about it yet. Not unless he committed to it. He'd cross that bridge when he came to it. In the meantime, there were some things Maggie just didn't need to know.

Ten days later Jesse sent word asking if Bob could meet him at the Harris Hotel in Kansas City. Once Bob met him there, Jesse told him what he had come up with. He had thought about the original plan and altered it. Rather than go into Northfield they would target the bank in Mankato, a town to the west. The town was growing fast and there were a lot of Yankee dollars there too. Plus it was further off the beaten track. It would be a quick in and out situation.

"What happened to Spoons Butler and his money?"

"Oh, I still like that idea. Maybe for another time."

"But if this location is so remote, won't getting out be more of a problem?" Bob couldn't ignore the fact that they were talking about a place a long way from Missoura and what they knew.

"I know a man named Bill Chadwell. Chadwell's from up that way and he'd like to be in on it. He can serve as our guide."

Bob agreed to talk the plan over with Cole. He would write to Cole in Texas and ask him to come up to Monagaw to talk business. They would get together with Jesse, Frank and this Chadwell fella down there.

"Looking forward to it," Jesse smiled. "I like to see a good plan come together. I'll bring Clell Miller along too."

When he thought about it after leaving Jesse, Bob knew he should have questioned Jesse further about why he changed the location of the bank. Getting back at Spoons Butler made going up to Minnesota more justified. That Order Butler dictated made him furious, no matter how many years had passed and whether or not it had anything to do with Missoura or not. He'd love to take that son-of-a-bitch's money. But Jesse had changed the location to some other town and he hadn't really said why, other than it was off the beaten path. Hell, there were a lot of places closer than Minnesota that were off the beaten path. He should have brought that up. Truth be told, he was a little intimidated by Jesse and that was embarrassing. He had no problem standing up to Cole, why couldn't he ask Jesse James a simple question? Damn it. Jesse thought enough of him that he brought the thing to him first. That was quite a vote of confidence. Jesse must have a lot of faith in him and his abilities. Well, he was just going to have to be more forceful; be more of a man about it. From now on, that's how it would be.

Bob told Maggie he had some family business in St. Clair. She found that curious, but when he didn't tell her what it was, she didn't ask about it.

Bob was surprised that when he got to Monagaw, Cole was nowhere to be found. Bob wasn't even sure that Cole had received his letter. After a few days he apologized to Jesse but he didn't feel it was what he wanted to do to discuss the robbery further without his brother. Jesse said he understood. He always liked a trip to the Springs, so he'd just kick back and enjoy the minerals.

Bob had not been back in Jackson County three days when he ran into Tuck Hill, who told him he had seen Cole in Monagaw just the other day.

Bob told Maggie he needed to go back to St. Clair.

"What's going on, Bob?" Maggie asked. "What aren't you telling me?"

"It's just business Maggie."

"I thought you and I were in the farm business. Together."

"This is family business. Nothing for you to worry about. Let me handle this, all right?"

"Bob…" She knew he wasn't being truthful with her. He was keeping something from her and she didn't know why. She'd thought they were partners. He seemed determined to shut her out of whatever was being discussed. She didn't know why and she didn't understand.

Neither did he, really.

But he did it just the same.

CHAPTER 51

Bob discussed Jesse's plan with Cole as they sat in the cave. He was comfortable here, in this rock cocoon, but it also made him miss John. A breeze passed by outside and Bob drew a deep breath of it.

"It sounds like a good strategy, Cole. We should be able to get a lot of money out of it."

"Sounds risky to me. Too far away. I don't like it."

"Every job is risky. It'll be fine."

"I don't like it."

Bob sighed. He looked out over the river.

"Of course you don't."

"What's that mean?"

"It wasn't your idea so of course you don't like it."

"You think that's what this is about?"

"Yeah, I do."

"You really think I'm saying no to this because it was Jesse's idea? I've been a part of Jesse's ideas before."

"You don't like it that he talked to me first."

"Yeah, why was that do you think?"

"I'm my own man, Cole, and Jesse knows it. I'm not just your little brother. I'm perfectly capable of planning something and carrying it out."

"Jesse's just trying to rope me into a hare-brained scheme by using you. The adventure of it means as much to him as the money."

"Go to hell, Cole," Bob glared. "Nobody uses me."

Cole studied Bob's face. Goddamn Jesse had done that very thing and Bob's need to assert himself had blinded him to it. Cole decided that worrying that bone would get nothing but animosity from Bob so he changed tactics.

"Minnesota is a long way from Missoura. We've done jobs far from home before but not that far and not in a place we know nothing about."

"Bill Chadwell is from there. He'll serve as our guide."

"Who?"

"Bill Chadwell. Jesse knows him."

"Oh, that makes it all right for me then," Cole sneered sarcastically. "Put my fate in the hands of a man I don't know who is a friend of Jesse fucking James."

"I didn't know Clell Miller until I rode with him."

"But I did. Neither you or me know this Chadwell."

Damn Jesse. Goddamn Jesse. He was trying to usurp Cole's family authority. He had no damn right to be talking to Bob first. Bob knew better than to get puffed up like this. He'd never seen him act like this before.

I sound like an ass, Bob was thinking. Age and experience told him he'd never be on an even level with Cole when it came to this. Yet he was tired of being pushed around. It always had to be Cole's idea, Cole's way. Well, Bob was a man with a family now and it was up to him to do all he could to secure their future. He didn't deserve to be treated like the little brother any more. To his way of thinking he had actually accomplished more with his life than Cole had with his. And Cole should damn well show him some respect.

"What does Maggie think of this, Bobby?" He didn't know Maggie well but he thought if she knew anything about it, she wouldn't be happy with it.

"That has nothing to do with this conversation." He wasn't going to talk to Cole about Maggie. Not having anything to do with this.

"Thought you were happy with your farm. Was that just a whim?"

"No, it is *not* a whim. I've worked hard for that farm."

"But you're not happy with your life there?"

"I'm happy with my life there and all that goes with it. I just want to own that farm, Cole. Can you understand that? I want to *own* it."

He threw a rock hard at the wall of the cave and watched it career off the side and begin its descent down to the river.

"If I do this, I can buy the farm and it will be mine. Maggie's and mine. Then that will be the end of it. I just want to take advantage of one more opportunity. With that money I'll buy the farm, expand it a little bit and live off it for the rest of my life. It'll finally be my home."

He looked back.

"Can you understand that Cole?"

Cole guessed that he did but he still didn't like the plan. Foolish decisions had been made out of money and greed. This seemed one of them.

"Come up to Kansas City and talk to Jesse at the end of the month," Bob suggested.

"I've got plans."

"All right, don't come."

"I'm planning to be up that way in a month or two. We can all talk about it then."

"We're talking about it now." Bob stared defiantly at Cole.

Cole saw John in Bob's eyes.

"You don't want to be a part of it, that's your decision," Bob shrugged. "But I'm doing this, with or without you."

Cole stared at Bob. He didn't know where this posturing was coming from and he sure didn't like it. He also didn't like that Jesse was rubbing his nose in the fact that he could influence

Cole's little brother. Jesse knew Cole didn't like him and the little bastard was getting even.

"Goddamn Jesse. I'd like to put a bullet in his brain pan."

"Nice talk about a comrade, Cole."

Cole shook his head as he looked down at the river. He tried to think how he could possibly talk his fool brother out of doing something he might live to regret.

"You know Bobby, you've inherited Pa's livery."

"What are you talking about? There's nothing left of the livery except the building and the ground its standing on."

"Well, there's your Missoura land."

"Oh sure, Cole. I'm going to waltz into Harrisonville and do business right there in the open. Better yet, I'll start up my farm in the middle of town on the square footage."

"Pa left me some land. You can have that."

Bob didn't know that. "One of the farms?"

"Yeah. I'll never use it. Everybody knows its Younger property. They'd be all over me."

"And not all over me?" What might have seemed like a shimmering possibility was quickly dashed. "You seem to have forgotten I'm a Younger too."

Cole let out a long stream of breath. He'd likely regret it but if he agreed to talk to Jesse about Minnesota, he might be delaying Bob and Jesse from actually going on to make that fool mistake.

"All right. If Frank can meet me there, I'll go with you to have this little meeting."

"Like I said, it's your decision. I've already made mine."

CHAPTER 52

Jim couldn't believe his good fortune in landing this position. It had for so long seemed out of his reach. He loved working on Drury James' La Panza ranch. He had been put in charge of the horses, just as he wanted. It was his job to see that they were well-tended and productive. He bred the mares and delivered the foals. He groomed them, he exercised them. He loved the horses and the horses loved him.

The only thing missing from his life was Cora and his family. As much as this California adventure suited him, he felt as if a big part of his life was back in Missoura. It saddened him that he likely could never go back there to live. More importantly, he was trying to come to terms with the fact that he and Cora would never be husband and wife. That was hard to do because he truly did love her. Yet he understood why she couldn't take that step and he wanted only the best for her. A life with Jim Younger would not be what was best.

He thought of his family often and wrote them long and newsy letters. It was the highlight of his day when he received letters from those left behind. He was happy today. He held a post card from Cole in his hand.

Cole's note was neither long nor newsy.

"Come home," it read. "Bob needs you."

Cole had written the name of a hotel in Kansas City and a date. Dear Lord. What was going on now? He hadn't heard from Bob since he'd been in California but he knew from Cole about Maggie, her son and the farm. He'd been a little hurt that Bob hadn't told him himself but Bob was a young man in the prime of his life and evidently he was in love and trying to run a farm. Jim forgave him. Bob had been through so much in his short lifetime; he was entitled to keep this time in his life for himself. He hoped to God it wasn't something bad Bob was going through.

He looked down at the card. Leave it to Cole to be ambiguous. He put the note in his pocket. It didn't really matter. If Bob needed him, than he would leave immediately.

Bob sat in the Harris Hotel with Cole. He hadn't known if Cole would show or not but he was glad he had. He was also relieved. The more he thought about the robbery, the more he felt that it was his only chance to accomplish his dream. He was going to commit to Jesse. He'd do it even if Cole decided against it, but having Cole along would make him a whole lot more comfortable with it. He trusted Jesse but not like he trusted his brother.

Bob was asking Cole about the family. Cole was telling him how things were going down in Texas as he sat in the corner with his hat pulled low over his eyes. Even though the hotel was filled with former Confederates they had to be careful in this neck of the woods.

"You ought to get down there and visit them, Bobby. Retta's become a young woman. I don't know where the time went."

"She wrote me that she wanted to teach school. She'd be good at that."

"She would. She has my smarts and your determination."

Bob knew it was a barb thrown at the reason they were sitting here in Kansas City. He decided to ignore it.

"What do you hear from Jim?"

Cole was looking over the room. "He likes working with Drury James' horses. Jim always did like horses." Cole's eyes lit up. "Why, you can ask him about that yourself."

Cole rose as Jim spotted them and crossed the room.

Bob looked over his shoulder. That looked like Jim making his way over...

Cole hugged Jim. "Thanks for comin'," he said in his ear.

"What the hell?" Bob jumped up smiling. He too hugged his brother.

"It's good to see you both." Jim smiled. Then he looked at Cole with raised eyebrows. "What's going on?"

Cole puffed out his cheeks.

Jim looked at Bob. Bob looked all right to him. Older and full of muscle. It didn't seem to be his health. Was neither of them going to tell him why he had been summoned from California?

"What do you mean?" Bob puzzled. "Why are you here, anyway?"

"Let's head out and take a ride." Cole threw his money down on the table and grabbed Jim's arm. This was going to get ugly. When Bobby found out that Cole had asked Jim to come back to Missoura for this meeting, there was going to be hell to pay.

They walked out to where their horses were hitched.

"What's going on, Cole?" Bob asked suspiciously.

"Let's take a ride," Cole repeated.

They rode down to the river without speaking. They tethered their horses and sat down along the bank.

"Are you all right, Bob?" Jim asked with concern.

"I'm all right, Jim." Bob nodded. "Surprised to see you is all. I thought you liked being in California. What brings you back here?"

"If you need me, I'll always come from wherever I am. I hope you know that, Bob."

"You think I need you?" Bob was confused. "Is that why you're here?"

Then it dawned on him. He jumped to his feet.

"Son of a bitch!" He looked at Cole. "Is this your doing, Cole? Did you tell Jim I *needed* him?"

"Yeah, I did," Cole glared. "I haven't been able to talk any sense into you. I thought maybe Jim could."

"Goddamn it! You had Jim come all the way from California for this? What the hell's wrong with you?"

"You want to act pig-headed and throw in with Jesse James and his idiotic idea! There's nothing wrong with me but there's sure as hell something wrong with you!" Now Cole was on his feet.

"Now hold on." Jim rose between them. "Both of you. If my being here is going to be the topic of a bad conversation, I want to know why I'm here to begin with. Cole? You're the one who posted the card."

"Bobby's got a ridiculous idea in his head, put there by that son-of-a-bitchin' Dingus, and he won't listen to reason. I know he doesn't give two hoots in hell about anything I think or I say. I figured he'd listen to you."

Jim looked at Bob. "Is this a robbery we're talking about?"

"I appreciate your coming Jim," Bob seethed. "Especially if you were led to believe I needed you. I appreciate that. Fact of the matter is that you were lied to and I regret that happened."

"I didn't lie to him!" Cole raged. "I said you needed him and in my opinion you do!"

"I don't give a rat's ass about your opinion!" Bob yelled. "If I needed Jim, I would have told him myself. I *don't* need him and he's come all this way for nothing! He's living clear across the country in California! What the hell's the matter with you?"

"You both need to cool off." Jim put up his hands. "Let's do something novel and discuss this like adults instead of pissy little children."

Bob and Cole stopped shouting and stared at Jim.

"As to the most important matter, it doesn't matter to me, Bob, whether Cole misled me or not. If he even thinks you need me I want to be here."

Cole nodded.

Jim looked at Cole. "But you didn't choose to be fair-handed with me. I was worried sick the entire way back here."

Cole sighed. Jim was right.

"I apologize for that." He glared at Bob. "But I'm still glad you're here to help me talk some sense into this fool."

Bob gritted his teeth. "I'd like to visit with you before you go back to California, Jim. Let's make arrangements for that. But I'm not going to have any further conversation with Cole."

"Bobby, goddamn it…"

"I'll give Jesse your answer." Bob started toward his horse.

"Bob…wait a minute…" Jim grabbed Bob's arm. "I've come a long way. I'm tired and it's been stressful. I think I deserve the right to ask that we sit down and discuss this – whatever this is."

Cole nodded.

Bob hated this situation. Not just Cole dragging Jim away from his life in California, a life where Jim was really happy, but refusing to treat him like an adult. That was nothing new. And Jim was right. He had come a long way for him. He'd earned the right to hear what they both had to say.

"All right, Jim. I doubt you'll find this of any interest, though."

"If it's something to do with one of my brothers, I'll always find it of interest."

Bob told Jim about Jesse's plan. Jim said nothing. He hated anything to do with robbing a bank. Or a train. Or robbing anything at all. He was surprised by Bob's enthusiasm for it. Bob usually wasn't the reckless type. Bob always thought things through.

Jim felt compelled to ask Bob why this meant so much to him. When Bob explained, Jim's heart broke. Bob was still just looking for a home, something permanent, somewhere that would last.

"I know you don't want anything to do with this, Jim, and that's fine." Bob knew that the last thing Jim wanted to do was get involved with any more robberies. "I don't expect you to. I respect your feelings on the subject."

Jim knew that was probably true. Cole, on the other hand, didn't understand his feelings or really accept them. He thought Jim was being judgmental. So be it. He was.

Bob looked at Cole. His outrage had lessened but he was still pissed off.

"And if *you* don't care to be present for this one, that's fine with me too."

Cole looked at Jim. "Can you please explain to him that this plan is ill-advised? That it's got too many unknown elements to make it safe?"

"I'm not an expert on plans like this, Cole," Jim dismissed.

"Well then at least tell him Dingus is using him to get his own way. How Dingus would know I'd reject this scheme out of hand and he decided to go to my little brother first to put on the pressure."

"He's not using me, Cole," Bob glared. "Shut the hell up with that!"

Cole and Jim exchanged looks. They both knew Bob was wrong about that but they also knew Bob was hard-headed. It seemed to be a Younger trait.

"This decision is up to you, Bob," Jim sighed. "Do you think the plan is sound?"

"Yes, Jim I do."

"And being present for that is something you're committed to doing?"

"Yes, I am. I want the money."

"Well, Bob, you're a grown man. If you want my opinion, you'll ask me for it."

Bob thought about that. He respected Jim's opinion but he also knew Jim believed robbing banks and trains to be wrong. Jim had never moved beyond the death of the conductor in Adair and that wasn't something Bob thought weak-willed but rather something that he admired in Jim.

"I think I know your opinion, Jim and I respect it. And this is just something that we disagree on."

"You're going to do this." Cole let out a long breath. "There's nothing we can say to stop it."

"No, there's not."

They stood in silence.

"Well, if you're doing this Bobby," Cole finally said. "You need someone there that is on your side, just yours. Buck is a fair man but his first loyalty is to Dingus. You need somebody who has *your* back." Cole looked at Jim. "You need your brothers. Both of them."

Jim frowned. Cole was trying to pull him into this regardless of what he thought about it. He had been adamant that he was finished robbing and he thought Cole had accepted that. Yet as he looked at Cole's worried eyes he understood that his statement had nothing to do with robbery and everything to do with looking out for the safety of their youngest brother.

"No, I don't want Jim to go along. He doesn't want to and that's the end of it." Bob turned to Jim. "You need to go back to California. Tomorrow. I'll be all right. If Cole wants to go along to keep an eye out for me, that's up to him. I don't need him either. If that's how he wants to justify going along, so be it but don't let his mother-henning drag you into this too."

"Let Jim speak for himself."

Jim looked at the two of them. His brothers. And he thought of John. He hadn't protected John and now John was no longer with them. Bob was the youngest of them all. It was his concern for Bob that had caused him to come here all the way from California. How could he turn his back on him now? Cole didn't worry easily. Jim had no doubt that Cole thought Bob needed them along in case something went wrong.

He hated the idea. He hated it. He wasn't a bank robber. That had been how Cole had chosen to live his life. Jim's 'political statement' was his good and satisfying life. What is it they say? Living well is the best revenge. Jim didn't doubt that Bob wanted the money to buy the farm but Jesse had dragged Bob into this and Bob's pride would not allow him to back out of it. If Jesse thought so little of exposing Bob to danger now, what would stop him from throwing him to the wolves if something went wrong? Cole was right. Bob needed his brothers to have his back.

"If you're determined to go Bob, Cole and I will go with you."

Bob was surprised. That wasn't the answer he thought he'd hear from Jim.

"Why do you say that? I know you don't want to go."

"Well, I've been thinking about buying my own ranch. I could use the money too," Jim lied.

Bob didn't want to think about it anymore, didn't want to talk about it anymore either. He was a grown man and had made his decision and Cole and Jim were grown men too. He wasn't responsible for what they chose to do. If they wanted to come along with him, well that was just fine.

They met with Jesse and Frank later that day. It wasn't easy all of them being in the same place. It was dangerous and Bob couldn't help but wonder why they hadn't just met at the Springs, where they usually did. The thought crossed his mind that maybe the danger was part of the appeal to the James boys. Now they sat out in the trees listening to Jesse. To no one's surprise, except maybe to Bob and Jim, as Jesse laid out the details of the plan, he added something to the mix.

"We need to get some money to finance all this. They're building a bridge over the Lamine near Otterville. The Missoura Pacific passes through on a regular basis. The train slows down and all we have to do is take advantage of the delay and jump the train."

"Another robbery wasn't part of the plan…" Bob protested.

"I know that Bob, but the more I thought about it the more I realized that we needed money to carry out the bigger plan. It's a long way up to Minnesota. We'll ride the railroad, won't that be a hoot? We can do some things to change the way we look. We've got to dress ourselves in good-looking suits so we look like wealthy men. We'll need to buy good horses along the way and we'll need money for food and board for a couple of weeks' time. If we don't finance this with someone else's money, it will eat into our profit." Jesse looked around. "We've got a sure-fire team here. We'll just pull this other thing off first and then not a penny goes out of our pockets."

"I'm not doing that."

Jim had been silent. It was one thing to agree to the Minnesota deal for the sake of his brother, but he wasn't going to add to it by throwing in another robbery. Especially not a train robbery, when he had seen first-hand how very wrong that could go.

"What do you mean?" Jesse looked at Jim.

"I'm not going to be part of another train robbery."

"Well Jim, Jesse's right." Damn Jim. Cole didn't want the others to think there wasn't unity here. "Why should we spend our own money to steal somebody else's?"

"Think of this as a dress rehearsal, Jim." Jesse smiled.

"It's a train, not a bank." He looked at Cole. "No, I'm not going to be a part of it."

Jesse sighed as Frank raised his eyebrows at Cole.

"Well, all right, Jim. If that's your decision." Jesse scratched his chin. "I suppose we can get Hobbs Kerry to stand in for you."

Bob and Cole nodded. They knew Hobbs as a friend of their Uncle Bruce's and he seemed to them like a good man. Bob didn't see any point in trying to encourage Jim to participate if he didn't want to. This was, after all, just an extra piece of business.

On July 7 they stopped the train at a location known as Rocky Cut. The watchman was taken into custody at the bridge and when the approaching train slowed down as a precaution against the construction, a red lantern held by Hobbs Kerry signaled the train to stop. Bob and Cole emptied two safes while Jesse and Frank moved through the passenger car.

"Oh, Lord spare your children! Please command these men to show mercy," a rotund man in a suit called to heaven as Jesse made his way down the aisle. "Let your blanket of loving-kindness be spread upon us, Lord!"

Jesse stopped in front of the man and frowned.

"That's annoying, you calling up to God like that. Makes me feel like a sinner. Are you a preacher?"

The man nodded.

"Well, I'd much prefer it if you would just have these good people sing a hymn. That would be pleasant. 'Shall We Gather at the River' would be appropriate."

The preacher began the hymn as Jesse looked over the passengers.

"Y'all feel free to join in while we conduct our business. There's nothing more joyful than a good old Baptist song."

Soon most of the car was singing along but they weren't any less wary when Jesse's gun indicated that they contribute to his wheat sack.

The entire affair was over in minutes, with over $15,000 going into the Minnesota fund.

The robbery drew the usual attention. Missouri Governor Hardin offered a $300 reward for any information about the train robbers; surely someone would come forward with something about the criminals with *that* little incentive.

It surprised them all when it was one of their own. Cole was further ticked at Jim for not taking part in the heist when Hobbs Kerry was arrested down in Granby. Seems Kerry had forgotten the cardinal rule of conspiracy as laid down to him by Jesse James. He started throwing money around and running his mouth.

Things were further complicated when a Sedalia farmer said Kerry had been with a group of men who had stopped at his house just before the robbery. Kerry was taken into custody. Things got even more interesting when Bruce Younger was also arrested for the crime.

"How did Bruce's name get involved in all this?" Bob puzzled to Cole. "He wasn't even there."

"Kerry wrote to him about some horses he had for sale and the letter was intercepted. They said Bruce was guilty by association but they didn't have anything on him except for the letter, which didn't have anything to do with robbery, so they let him go."

"It wasn't guilt by association," said Bob. "It was guilt by being a Younger."

"It gets better." Cole shook his head. "Kerry folded his hand. He admitted he was at Otterville and you, me, Frank, Jesse, Clell and Chadwell were with him."

Shit.

It was time to talk to Maggie.

CHAPTER 53

He walked her to the barn, away from the ears of Jeremy. "Maggie, I need to tell you something and I want you to hear me out before you say anything."

"All right, Bobby."

She had a knot in the pit of her stomach. She had been waiting for him to tell her what was going on with him. She was glad he was finally at that point but she dreaded what she was going to hear.

"I didn't want to say anything until it was set. I know you'll have your concerns."

He was having a hard time looking at her. That couldn't be a good sign.

He took a deep breath.

"Jesse presented me with an idea to get the money I need to buy the farm. It involves a bank in Minnesota. I know we've never talked about it, but I don't have a problem financing my life with Yankee money. I think you know that. The Yankees made my life such a living hell that I've had no other choice."

"We all have choices, Bobby."

"Damn it, Maggie. I asked you to hear me out."

"All right." Her heart was pounding.

"This idea of Jesse's is a good one. Cole and Jim are in on it too." He wasn't going to tell her how that came about, at least not now. "It'll get me the money to buy this land and some on either side. We can finally have a farm of our own."

"We have a farm of our own. Our life is good. We don't have to own the land for it to be ours."

"Yes, we do. *I* do. You know I've always wanted my own land. My father use to say that if you owned land, you always had a place to come home to. I need that in my life again, Maggie. I've gone too long without having it."

"Aren't Jeremy and I a place to come home to?"

"Of course, but this farm is on somebody else's land. And damn it. This was once my father's land."

She didn't know what to say. He had never told her that. How painful it must have been for him to farm this land, knowing it had once belonged to his family and had been torn from their hands along with everything else.

"This is something I need to have Maggie. Then I can put the things that have happened to me in the past sixteen years behind me. I'll never have a reason to look back."

She looked into his eyes. He was still so tormented by the past. She had hoped her love would take some of that pain away. Maybe it had, but obviously not enough so that he could completely move on. She wondered if time would ever accomplish that or if he was doomed to carry it on his shoulders as a dark and heavy mantle for the rest of his life. She knew it was important to him to own the farm and she thought she understood why, but at what cost?

"And you need to accomplish that by taking other people's money?"

"It's not other people's money, Maggie! I thought you could understand that." The old anger rose in him. "Its money put in banks, transported through the cooperation of the railroads, that carpetbaggers have stolen from hard-working people. It's no more theirs than it is the man in the moon's. They haven't earned it. *I* have. By all that my family has gone through, by all that *I've* gone through, *I* have."

"I know you believe that, Bobby. I'm trying to understand."

"You believe it, Maggie. You know you do. If you didn't believe that you wouldn't be with me. Just because we haven't talked about it doesn't mean it never happened. You know I've used money from a train robbery to throw in my share on this farm. You never asked me where I got the money because you figured it out."

She was guilty of that. She knew he believed he had come by the money through moral default. And she had silently accepted that despite her own ethical questions about it. When she gave him her heart, she gave him forgiveness for that. But she thought that was all in the past. They were so happy and the farm was prospering, despite its small size. It was good, their life was good. Now he wanted to complicate it with thorny justifications.

"Yes, Bobby, I did accept what you believed. But I thought we had moved into a new stage of our lives. The horrible things that we each endured are long past now. We have each other. With Jeremy, we have a family. We have a future. We don't need to look back anymore."

He sighed and shook his head.

"I knew if I talked to you about this, you would talk me out of it. It's hard for me to say no to you Maggie. But it was a good idea. It was important to me to buy you this farm. Buy myself this farm."

He had changed tense. He was now saying *was*. Thank God.

"We'll be happy here, Bobby. This is enough. We can raise a cash crop if you want...some cotton or soy beans...we can save our money until we have enough to buy the farm honestly..."

"Honestly." He looked away. "That hurts, Maggie. I've always considered myself an honest person."

"I didn't mean it like that. You are an honest person and I know you believe the money you have stolen belongs to you and your family. You're not like Cole, who does it for the escapade, or Jesse, who does it for the fame. It's not your way of life."

Bob nodded. At least she knew that much about him.

"You work hard on this farm. You deserve to own it. I don't deny you that. Maybe we can work together to somehow raise the money to buy it."

"It's too late for that."

This was one of the hardest things he'd ever had to say to someone.

"What do you mean?"

"We're never going to get that opportunity."

"Yes we will, Bobby, if we're patient and we plan…"

"It's too late, Maggie. I can't stay here."

"What are you saying? This is our home. I don't understand."

"We needed money for the Minnesota plan." He looked at the ground. "It's complicated and it would've been foolish to use our own money to take someone else's. We needed money to carry it out."

She felt faint. She sat down hard on a stool. What had he done? What had he gotten himself into?

"We robbed a train over near Sedalia. That's what I was doing when I said I had to meet my brothers."

"That didn't cross my mind…" she said weakly. "When you said you were meeting Cole I never thought…."

"I know. And I took advantage of that. I'm sorry."

"Why didn't you just tell me, Bobby?" She was mad, she was frustrated. "If this whole thing is something you believe in, why didn't you talk to me about it and try to make me understand?"

"I should have." He crossed to her. "I'm sorry, Maggie. I should have."

He knelt before her and took her hands. "I never meant to hurt you and now I have."

She looked into his eyes. She could see his pain and she knew he regretted what he had done. What he had failed to do. Even if she didn't think it was moral or ethical or anything she might have done, she knew his character. He believed in something that was nothing more than bitter payback but he had built it into something bigger than he; into a justified accounting for all he had lost. He was a good man; a young man of whom others had obviously taken advantage and nurtured into believing that stealing was righteous revenge.

"We'll get past this, Bobby." She put her hands on his face. "We love each other too much not to. We'll just have to find a way to put this behind us."

"We can't."

"We can't?"

She knew he was guilty and remorseful but their love was true, it was strong. She could forgive him. She had to. And she needed to help him to forgive himself.

"We can't put it behind us." He rubbed his hands over his face. "Hobbs Kerry was with us and he got arrested. He told them who had been with him. Named each and every one of us."

"Oh, Bobby…" she gasped.

"They'll be looking for me now."

"Oh my God." She paled. "What are we going to do?"

"I'll have to leave. You and Jeremy aren't a part of this…"

"No, Bobby! Whatever we have to do, we'll do it together."

She would deal with the dreadfulness of his being a wanted man later. Right now she needed to put all that aside and make him understand that even though he had chosen to get into this mess himself, they were in it together now. She wasn't going to lose him. They would somehow have to find a way to fix this.

"Maggie, walk away from this." He grabbed her hands. "You owe it to Jeremy. You owe it to yourself."

"If I owe anything to myself it's to stand by the man I love."

"Maggie…"

"What do we need to do, Bobby?"

He needed to walk away from her. Far away. If he loved her he would do at least that. But he couldn't, as embarrassing and wrong as it was, he was selfish. He was selfish because despite advising her to the contrary, if she chose to stick it out with him, he had already thought of a possible way to go forward.

"It's not going to be easy, Maggie and it's not without cost to us."

"I'm listening." She put her arms around him. "Tell me what we do, Bobby."

"I keep my plans with Jesse. We go to Minnesota and get that money."

"But…"

"It's the only way I can see, Maggie. I get my share of the money and we leave Missoura."

"Leave our farm?"

"It's not our farm." That was what had started this situation. "I can't stay in Missoura. Not now. If we have the Minnesota money, we'll have something in our pockets to set up somewhere else. Maybe California. Jim loves it there."

It was all too much to absorb. California? When Bob had put their future in jeopardy to steal money so that he could own his father's land? She wondered how he could accept that.

"Leave Missouri?"

"I don't have any choice."

He walked over to the shovel standing against the door, picked it up and threw it.

"Goddamn it! How did I get to be such a fool?" He looked back at her. "I have everything I could possibly ever want, Maggie. I have you. What made me think I needed more?"

"Bobby." Tears slid down her cheeks. She walked over and put her arms around him. "What's done is done. Now we have to figure out how to deal with it."

She didn't want him to go to Minnesota. It was so far away. Regardless of what she may or may not think of the morality of robbing a bank, it would be perilous at best. She didn't know if she could bear to have him so far away from her and facing danger. Yet the same determination that had caused this dreadful situation was now dictating that stealing relocation money from a bank in Minnesota was the only way out. She knew it would be useless to try to talk him out of it. He truly believed that this was the only way their life could move forward. There was nothing more she could say.

The way he saw it was that regardless of whether either of them liked it, he didn't have a choice. If he had it all to do over, things would be different.

But like Maggie had said; what was done, was done.

CHAPTER 54

Cole waited under the tree while Bobby said his goodbyes to Maggie. He could live to be a hundred and he would never understand any of his brothers. He never had and he never would. That's probably what the rest of the family said about *him*...so be it.

He couldn't move beyond Jesse's manipulation of Bob but he knew he needed to do just that. He couldn't carry that attitude into battle, and robbing a bank five hundred miles from Missoura had to be looked at with just the same scrutiny and execution. He was never going to feel agreeable toward Jesse again and he'd be damned if he'd ever ride with him again. Still, he couldn't lay it all on Jesse. Bob was a man and he'd let himself be talked into it. Hell, so what if none of them ever owned Missoura land? That's just the way it was. It was not the time of their pa and never would be again.

Most of all, Bob had Maggie. He'd found a woman who'd grown to love him. He'd found a woman to share his life with. Why couldn't he be content with that? *He* would be. But Bobby had to push it, had to own his own damn Missoura farm. Well, now his little brother was a wanted man just like the rest of them and Maggie and Jeremy were saddled with that now too.

Jim couldn't stand to watch the scene playing out before him. It only broke his heart.

"Please stay safe, Bobby." Maggie was fighting back her tears but she was unable to keep them from forming in her eyes. "Oh, please stay safe."

Jeremy watched from behind her, thinking of his earlier conversation with Bob.

"Listen to me, Jeremy, this is important," Bob had told him.

"I am, Bob."

"I don't know how long I'll be gone, and it's up to you to keep the farm going along while I'm away."

"Where're you going?"

Bob looked off. "I've got some business to attend to."

"What kind of business?"

"Family business." He looked back at Jeremy. "I trust you to do what needs doing. You know all that by now."

"Okay."

"If anybody should come looking for me, you tell them you don't know who I am, all right?"

"You mean lie?"

"Not so much lie as to mislead them away from you and your mother. For safety's sake, while I'm gone. 'Cause you need to take care of your mother, Jeremy, that's the most important thing. You understand?"

"I understand, Bob."

"There's nothing more important than that." Bob swallowed.

Jeremy nodded. Bob was acting strange.

Bob put his hand on Jeremy's shoulder and squeezed.

"You're a good man, Jeremy," he smiled. "I love you."

That was the first time Bob ever told him that. Jeremy already kinda knew it, but it was good to hear Bob say it.

"I love you too, Bob."

What Jeremy didn't know was that with Bob's last remark to him, Bob's mind echoed back to his brother Dick's last words to him. His love had come full circle.

"I'll stay safe, Maggie. I promise." Bob held her close and stroked her hair. "Try not to worry about me. It'll all be over and I'll be back here before you know it. I'm with good men who know what they're doing."

He kissed her. It seemed that he did little else this past day or so.

"You make our plans while I'm gone. When I get back we'll have a new life ahead of us. This time you'll call the shots."

He smiled, trying to get her to do the same. She didn't.

"I wish that time was now, Bobby."

"I know."

"My heart is going with you. You be careful with my heart."

"I love you, Maggie. I'm sorry I got us in this mess. " He kissed her again.

"Let's go, Bob," Cole called, mounting his horse.

"I love you, Bobby. God, I love you."

She and Jeremy watched them ride north. Every fiber of her being ached with love, sadness and dread.

"Is he going far, Mama?"

"Yes, Jeremy, very far."

"I wish he wasn't."

"I do too."

They watched the horses fade from view.

"Please God, bring him home to us soon. Please keep him safe and bring him home."

CHAPTER 55

B ob was trying to focus on the job ahead and not on leaving Maggie. They met up with Jesse, Frank, Clell and Chadwell just outside Clay County and were now on their way to their first stop at Council Bluffs, Iowa.

Bob hadn't given much thought to the inclusion of Bill Chadwell outside of the man's reliability. He had been surprised, though, at the presence of an eighth man.

"I want to include Charlie Pitts, Bob," Cole told him as they rode behind the others. "He's a good man. I don't know if you remember him. The last time you saw him he wasn't more than a boy and so were you. They called him Sam Welles then."

"When did I meet him?"

"Pa's funeral. Charlie was the boy that found Pa lying in that grove."

Bob blew out a breath. "That's right."

"He's a good man," Cole repeated. "Good at thinking on his feet. He's done work for me down at the ranch. Works hard and is well-liked by all the boys. Even though he was too young to serve with us, he's got a loyalty that can't be matched."

"If you trust him, so do I."

"I'm feeling better about Chadwell now that I know more about him. Buck says he'll be all right. Real name's Stiles. He got hung up in St. Louis on a horse-stealing deal he wasn't guilty of.

At least Buck doesn't think he was guilty. Decided to change his name and start over."

It was interesting to Bob that as proud as Cole was of his own name, he was now keeping company with men who felt the need to change theirs. Things were different now. He was enveloped in a world of shadow and smoke.

After they arrived in Iowa, Jim accepted the task of selling their horses. He was the one who knew the most about it and he figured that was something he could do that had little, if nothing, to do with anything illegal or unethical.

They bought tickets to ride the train up to Minneapolis. Bob had never been on a train before. He quickly understood the attraction. It was a hell of lot easier and more comfortable than traveling by horseback.

Jim and Bob sat together, away from the others.

As Jim watched Jesse make his way to a seat in the rear, he clicked his tongue in disgust.

"This is what you call irony, Bob."

When they got there, they split up so as to not appear to know each other or be seen together. Cole had suggested Bob stick with Charlie. It would give Bob a chance to get to know him. Charlie did, after all, play a role in their family history.

"I'd rather not talk about all that, Cole."

"That's all right. Charlie's respectful. He won't press you."

Cole would travel with Chadwell so that he could suss him out and he decided Jim would stay with Jesse, Frank and Clell so that the Youngers would remain a part of any changes in plans.

"The hell you say," Jim complained. "I don't want anything to do with Jesse."

"I know that Jim, but we need you in that position. You're good at listening. And Jesse is good at changing things." Cole scowled. He swore to himself that he wouldn't think about how pissed off he was at Dingus.

"This all okay with you, Bob?" It was strange as hell for him to check the plan with his little brother but that's what it had come down to.

"Yeah," was the answer. Bob didn't have any problem with Cole deciding who they should ride with. He knew more about that.

Cole would give the kid credit for letting experience trump ego.

That night Bob found himself in a saloon playing poker with Charlie. His heart wasn't in the game; he was playing only to distract himself from his thoughts of leaving Maggie. As he watched his pile of chips dwindle, he realized that his distraction wasn't benefiting him at all.

"I'm done here," he told Charlie. "Luck isn't with me tonight and it doesn't look like it's with you either."

They bowed out of the game and walked outside.

"Guess we'd better get ourselves a room." Charlie looked around. There were half a dozen hotels within eyesight here on Sibley Street.

Bob looked in his billfold. They had earmarked a sum which would be each man's allowance for the day, to include rooms and meals. Bob realized he had spent most of what was designated for the night on the poker game. He guessed Charlie had too. They both were strung tight and they hadn't paid enough attention to what they were losing. He had only been up here a day and already he had made a mistake. Paying attention to each and every detail was damn important if this whole thing was going to work. He wouldn't be that careless again.

"I think we're gonna be sleeping over on that bank, Charlie. We're broke for tonight."

"If you say so, Bob."

"Be careful not to soil your handsome new outfit," Bob smiled.

The eight of them had gone all out to buy good-looking suits of clothes and long, linen dusters. They would be posing as prosperous cattlemen and they needed to look the role.

They walked over to the bank. Bob didn't mind sleeping out-side. It was better than sleeping in a bug-infested hotel bed. It probably didn't matter. He doubted he could sleep wherever it was he laid his head that night.

The next day they traveled in their groups to St. Paul.

"I want to get my ear to the vine and see if I can pick up any-thing that will make our plan go smoother," Jesse told Bob.

Bob felt like they were just wasting time, but what did he know?

That afternoon, Cole and Chadwell checked into the Mer-chant Hotel on 3rd Street and decided to head over to Guy Salis-bury's gaming parlor; those places were always full of gossip and information. They were sitting at a table when Bob and Charlie walked in.

Bob had no intention of sitting in on the game. He wasn't about to lose any more money playing poker. He was on this adventure to raise money, not spend it. He thought he'd just casually stand opposite Cole and let him know that everything was going okay.

Cole cashed in and rose when Bob arrived at the table. He gave Bob a dirty look.

"What?" Bob mouthed.

Cole brushed past him.

"I'm not sitting in a game with you. You stink at cards."

Bob chuckled. Unlike John, he had never learned to cheat.

Out on the sidewalk they ran into Jim, Frank, Jesse and Clell.

"We're heading out to the Nicolette, if y'all want to join us. There's no better place than a whorehouse to get useful infor-mation," Jesse told them. "Care to come?"

Jim had a pained look on his face. He clearly did not want to go along. Cole ignored it. Jim's job was to stay with Jesse and represent the Youngers. He could just suck it up.

"Nah, y'all go on ahead." Bob had no interest in it either. He was with Maggie now.

"What's the next move?" he asked Cole.

"See if you and Charlie can find us a couple of good horses," Cole directed. "Pay for them."

Bob shook his head in disgust. He might be an outlaw now but he wasn't a horse thief.

Bob and Charlie checked out a couple of liveries but they were unable to find anything they liked.

"What is it with this town?" Bob wondered. "There doesn't seem to be a good horse to be had."

He was happy when they were finally able to buy a bay and a nice black mare from a man named William Judd on 4th Street.

When the group that had stayed at the Nicolette House returned to St. Paul, Jesse excused himself to go into a book-shop. He had something on his mind that he was not yet sharing with anyone other than Frank.

"Are you looking for a particular book, Jesse?" Jim asked.

"No, Jim," Jesse smiled. "I thought having a map wouldn't hurt."

As Jim and Frank waited with Chadwell, a policeman approached. "Well, how are you doing, Bill?" he asked Chadwell.

Frank frowned and took a few steps back to remove himself from the encounter, his hand on his belt.

"I'm doing well, Officer Kenny." Chadwell smiled.

"Staying out of trouble?"

"Yes sir, I am," he smiled. "Planning a trip to the Black Hills."

"I don't like this," Frank muttered to Jim. "See what this is about. I'll meet you back at the horses."

Officer Kenny nodded at Chadwell and continued on his way.

"Kinney was the one arrested me for stealing a horse a few years ago. It's not a problem," Chadwell dismissed.

When Jesse heard about it, he agreed with Frank that they best be on their way elsewhere. They took the train to Red Wing.

Cole directed Bob to stay another day in town with Chadwell while he and Charlie took a train in the opposite direction to St. Peter.

"Just to mix things up."

"What's your reasoning?" Bob asked. "If the law is keeping an eye on Chadwell, they will be looking at me too."

"It'll be all right, Bobby," Cole told him. "They don't know who you are and Chadwell needs to stay in town so that it doesn't look like he's taking the first opportunity to skedaddle."

Cole was annoyed when he later heard that Frank and Jesse immediately separated from Jim and Clell once they reached Red Wing.

Jesse's buying of the map wasn't random. He still had North-field on his mind.

He and Frank decided they needed more first-hand informa-tion and they headed to Brush Prairie, where Jesse had read in a newspaper that a farm was for sale by a man named John Mulli-gan. Jesse pretended he liked what he saw once Mulligan showed him the land. As Jesse considered whether or not he'd buy it, and Mulligan had no reason to think his leg was being pulled, he wondered about things like whether or not there was a good bank in the area. Mulligan said that was no problem; there was an excellent bank in town that catered to the local businesses. Northfield thrived with milling and lumber business and Ad Ames and Ben Butler had a lot of money tied up in Northfield mills. The bank was solid. Jesse nodded.

Cole and Charlie waited for Bob and Chadwell in St. Peter but they didn't show that morning. Bob later told Cole that Chadwell had been so busy making time with a woman during breakfast that they had a late start. The boys had all agreed to meet in Mankato, so Cole guessed he'd see Bob again there and he and Charlie continued on.

Cole and Charlie rode their new horses west and passed through the little community of Hanska, where they spent the night at the house of a man named Mads Ouren. Cole paid for their lodging and for the nice dinner Mrs. Ouren laid out.

While they were eating, Cole noticed the rifle that hung over the kitchen door.

"That's a mighty fine rifle," he remarked.

"Yes, it is," Ouren agreed. "I like it very much."

The next day Cole and Charlie rode to Madelia and stayed at the Flanders Hotel, which was owned by a man named Tom Vought. Cole and Vought hit it off and had a long conversation about driving cattle.

"At least we're having a few interesting moments along this dismal adventure," Cole told Charlie.

Bob and Chadwell finally made it to St. Peter but when they didn't see Cole and Charlie there, they checked into a hotel. The next morning they headed out to Mankato.

Bob wasn't comfortable being without his brothers. This moving around and switching partners wasn't what he signed up for. What was going on? Why didn't they just go to Mankato and get this thing *done.*

CHAPTER 56

Finally, and it felt to Bob like a year since they had left Missoura, all eight men were in Mankato. As they ate their meal and listened to town chatter, they learned that the grasshopper invasion of the year before had been disastrous for most of the farmers in the area. Bob could sure relate to that.

"If they were hit that hard, maybe there's not all that much money in the bank," Bob suggested to Jesse.

"Jesse keeps to a plan," Jesse replied.

Bob frowned. He had never heard Jesse refer to himself in the third person like that but then Bob didn't really know Jesse all that well to know what his habits were. When Bob saw the look on Cole's face, he guessed that maybe it struck Cole as a little odd too.

"Maybe he's writing his own dime novel," Bob shrugged and mumbled to Cole.

"Or it's a cover for one of his snow jobs," Cole grunted.

Bob sure hoped that wasn't the case.

The next morning Bob and Jesse walked toward the First National Bank of Mankato to check it out from the inside. There was a lot going on and it was sure noisy on the street. They passed a public meeting of the Board of Trade, which had people hollering questions, and added to the mix was the fact that a building was being constructed next door to the bank. There was all kinds of hammering and sawing. Bob wondered if all that racket would be in their favor or against them.

"Favor," Jesse answered, although Bob hadn't asked the question.

Inside the bank, Bob walked up to the cashier and asked to have a $50 bill changed. He was nervous. The cashier hardly looked at him, though, as he counted out the money.

Jesse casually looked around, noting the location of the vault.

As they crossed the street after leaving the bank, they passed a well-dressed man with an elaborate cane. Bob couldn't help but notice him. It reminded him of New Orleans. After they passed him, Bob felt the man's eyes on him and he glanced back. The man picked up something from the street. He turned around to look at them again but he seemed focused on Jesse.

"Keep walking," Jesse whispered.

"Excuse me," the man called.

Bob looked back. Jesse stared straight ahead.

"Did one of you gentlemen drop this?" The man held up a key.

Bob shook his head. "No Sir, but thanks for asking."

Bob and Jesse got on their horses and headed out to the meeting spot, where the others waited. Jesse was stiff as a board.

"Everything all right, Jesse?" Bob asked.

"That man recognized me. He knew who I was."

"Somebody must have dropped the key on the ground. He was just asking if it was one of us."

Jesse shook his head. "No, he knew who I was."

Bob didn't think that was likely. The odds of someone all the way up here in Minnesota knowing what Jesse looked like seemed slim to him. He didn't think Jesse wanted to argue that point so he let it pass.

"What did you think of the bank?"

Jesse didn't turn to look at him. "We'll talk about it later."

When they reached the others, they slid down off their horses.

"It's off," Jesse announced.

Bob's head whipped around.

"What do you mean it's off?" Cole asked. "What are you talking about?"

"We had an encounter with a man outside the bank. He recognized me," Jesse informed them matter-of-factly.

"Who'd recognize you all the way up here?" Cole looked at Bob.

Bob shook his head and shrugged. He didn't think that's the way it was.

Cole then looked at Frank.

Frank looked at his nails.

"Doesn't matter who it was or how he recognized me, Cole." Jesse spat on the ground. "He did. We'd be foolish to go back into that town."

Cole continued to look at Frank. Frank continued to look at his nails. Something wasn't right here.

No one else said a word.

"We're all the way up here now, Jesse. No one wants to go home empty-handed. What are you suggesting we should do?" Bob asked. Somebody had to ask it. Since he was supposedly one of the leaders of this venture, he felt it should be him. He wondered why Cole wasn't saying anything. He was staring at Frank and now at Jesse.

"I suggest we head back to Northfield." Jesse avoided Cole's stare. "That was the original plan, after all. Frank and I confirmed for ourselves that Butler and Ames are still heavily invested there. We stopped there on the way here. We talked to one of the locals about the roads and getting in and out of town shouldn't be a problem."

Cole returned to looking at Frank. "That so?"

Frank finally looked at Cole and nodded.

"Chadwell knows those roads anyway, don't you Bill?" Jesse continued. "It's all in our favor. We'll just return to the original plan."

"I'd like a moment with Buck." Cole rose.

Frank knew this was coming. He got up and he and Cole walked off away from the others.

"What's going on here?" Cole frowned.

"How's that, Bud?" Frank returned Cole's unyielding look.

"What's Jesse trying to pull?"

"Don't know that he's trying to pull anything."

"You're talking to me, Buck."

Frank shrugged. "If Jesse thought someone recognized him, we'd be fools to ride back into that."

"Does he really think somebody recognized him or is he using that as a ruse?"

"A ruse?"

"What's going on?" Cole repeated.

"You don't trust me now, Bud?"

Cole's gut told him Jesse, and maybe even Frank, was trying to pull something over on them but he trusted Buck James with his life.

"Of course I trust you. I'm just wondering why the plan switched to Northfield so damn fast."

"Seems like the thing to do. It was Jesse's first target, if you remember. Jesse *and Bob's*. On our way over here we stopped by there to see if what Chadwell had told us was so. If it might work. We're both of the agreement that it would."

"All right. It just seems to me that might have been the plan before Jesse thought some stranger hundreds of miles away from Missoura knew who he was. Seems a mite vain, even for Jesse."

"You saying Jesse and I changed the plan without consulting you, Bud?"

"I'm asking."

"No, we did not."

Cole said nothing.

"Does that answer satisfy you?"

"I reckon it does." How could he say different?

"All right then."

Cole and Frank returned to the others.

Jesse began discussing the new plan, the Northfield plan.

Bob just listened. What choice did he have?

Cole trusted Frank at his word but still was uncomfortable. He wanted to talk to Bob alone.

"Bobby, you still committed to this? Because this whole thing, all these changes, isn't sitting well with me."

"It didn't from the onset, Cole."

"Yeah, yeah, all that aside."

"It surprised me when Jesse thought that man knew who he was but I guess a man's got to go with his instincts."

"Jesse thinks the whole damn world knows who he is."

Bob shrugged. That was probably true.

"You see now why you need to have your brothers along? The only ones you can trust 100 percent are your own family."

"I thought you trusted Frank with your life."

"I do. But Frank's with Jesse. His brother will always be his number one."

Bob nodded. Hadn't he heard John say something like that once?

"Well, if you're going to stay with this plan, the plan you and Jesse came up with I might remind you, you need to stick close to him. God knows what else he'll imagine. Take Charlie along with you too. Jim's tired of being with Jesse and having to listen to his bullshit. And I'm pretty disgusted with him right about now so we're not a good fit. Take Charlie."

Bob figured that was good advice so he didn't argue the point. He hoped this situation wouldn't get any more complicated. He was anxious to just get the job done.

"Is this all right with you then, Bob?" Jesse asked when Cole and Bob rejoined the group.

Bob glanced at Cole, who just raised his eyebrows. Clearly this was going to be Bob's decision as far as the Younger's participation was concern.

"I reckon so, Jesse."

"Good," Jesse nodded. "Let's get on with it then."

Cole, Jim, Chadwell and Clell traveled on to Cleveland. Bob, Jesse, Frank and Charlie made it as far as Waterville before evening fell. All the travel was getting real old to Bob.

As they sat eating their dinner in the corner of the dining room of their hotel they spoke quietly. No one could hear them. Jesse explained to Bob that a change of plans wasn't necessarily a bad thing.

"It's true that this situation will be beyond what we're used to, but the *payout* will be beyond what we're used to."

"That's why we're here." Bob agreed. "And Northfield was the original plan so it's not like we're going in cold. All that matters is the money."

Listen to him. He was even beginning to talk like an outlaw. Wouldn't his mother be proud. No, best to not even have that thought. This was all beyond what his mother would ever want to hear or know. "Get the money and run", he could hear John telling him. That was maybe John's life, but it wasn't his. This would be his last one. He now knew that more than ever. This was not the way he wanted to spend the rest of his life nor was it the person he wanted to be.

"That's right," Jesse agreed. "And now that Frank and I have had a look at the town ourselves, I feel all the more confident that I was right the first time."

So now, although he had told Bob that they were the ones making the plans, Jesse was putting himself out front of this. Bob was getting a little weary of Jesse fitting things together so that his ego was served. He may have been a little awed when he first met Jesse but, like Cole and Jim, he was becoming weary of listening to him promote himself.

"Why did you make the decision to check out Northfield with Frank and not with me, Jesse? I thought we were in this together." He probably shouldn't say anything in front of Frank and Charlie but the time for confidences seemed to have passed.

Jesse's eyes darted to Frank. "Well, Bob, it was just opportunity. Frank and I were over there and we thought it wouldn't hurt to have a look." Jesse dabbed his mouth with his napkin. "And we *are* in this together, Bob. We're *all* in this together."

They continued with their meal.

"You have a problem going inside the bank, Bob?" Frank asked.

"I'm prepared for that."

He and Jesse had already discussed it. Jesse said Bob was young enough where he wouldn't be of suspicion. He'd just look like the junior member of a group of cattlemen. It seemed one or another of the boys was always pointing out his age. He guessed it just went with the territory. It was odd though. The next month he would be twenty-three years old, but right now he felt about forty. Damn, he wished this was over.

"Hey, you over there! I've been looking for you!"

They stopped talking. Jesse and Frank's hands slowly went toward their concealed guns.

A grey-haired man was coming their way. None of them said a word. If this was going to play out, that would have to be accommodated.

"You're the one Abe Hungerford said could sell me a good mare," he said to Jesse.

Jesse relaxed. This man had no idea who he was.

"I don't think so old-timer. You must have me confused with someone else."

"Ain't you John Bruegger?" The man looked at him closely.

"No, I'm afraid I'm not."

A woman crossed the room.

"You old fool, this isn't John Bruegger. You can't see didley-squat." She grabbed the man by the arm and led him away.

"Damn, Jesse, you're more popular than a stage star," Charlie grinned.

Jesse smiled and picked up his fork.

"Again? This is getting kinda strange, don't you think?" Bob was uneasy. This was the second time in two days they had found themselves in this situation. Maybe they should take it as a sign and just forget this whole thing. At least in Minnesota.

"Nothing strange about it." Jesse didn't seem to be concerned this time. "I have one of those faces."

Frank took a long sip of coffee. He looked at Jesse then at Bob.

"If you think you want to pull out Bob, now would be the time to mention it."

"No, I didn't say I wanted to pull out. Just seems the people up here are real concerned with strangers."

"People everywhere are concerned with strangers. It's no different here than it is in Missoura." Jesse knew he had to dismiss Bob's concern. It wouldn't be for the greater good to have the boy edgy. "You saw how I handled it. Just shrug it off."

That was completely contrary to the way Jesse had acted the day before but Bob decided he'd have to defer to the judgment of the others. He had little experience in this whole business and absolutely none in robbing banks. He may have postured with Cole and Jim that he was an important part of the plan but the truth was, he was just along for the ride.

Bob's brothers were not far away, having their meal at the Cushman Hotel in nearby Millersburg.

"You sure you don't want something to eat, Jim?" Cole was asking. "You're looking ashy. Food might help you."

"I'm not hungry. You go ahead." He rose. "I'm going to turn in."

Jim couldn't stand this. He just wanted it to be over so he could return to California. He didn't want to rob a bank and he didn't want Bob to rob a bank either. If that was a line of work Cole had chosen, that was his business. Bob was doing it out of desperation and anything done out of desperation never came to a good end. But the day of the robbery would arrive the next morning with the sun whether or not he was ready for it, whether or not he wanted it. He hoped to God his decision to back his brother wouldn't turn out to be the worst mistake of their lives.

CHAPTER 57
Thursday, September 7, 1876

Bob was thinking the same thing as his brother Jim. He wished it was over and they were on their way back to a place where things were familiar. This just felt all wrong. He had to have more faith in his partners, he guessed. Little of it had been going according to the plans they'd made, but there were intelligent, experienced men involved and he'd just have to trust that they knew what they were doing. He was the one who had pushed this little escapade and he was damn lucky to have those men along. He had to get over second-guessing and just throw in and be done with it. Worrying about it would only complicate an already complicated set of circumstances. Still…

The next morning the eight of them were together again, having a cup of coffee and eating biscuits in the woods outside Dundas.

"All right, let's go over this one last time," Jesse advised.

Everyone nodded.

"Cole and Clell will be at the end of the street and will give Frank, Bob and me the signal. After that, they cross the bridge that leads to the center of town. Bob and I go in the bank. Frank

403

has volunteered to go in with us. Jim, Charlie and Bill move up and wait on the bridge. If they see anything that puts them off, they'll signal. After we're in the bank, Cole and Clell will ride up to hold positions near the door of the bank. If any kind of trouble starts, they'll be right there. If that should happen, Cole will signal Jim, Charlie and Bill in to assist. If any shooting starts up, they'll fire into the air and whoop and holler to distract the people on the street. With any luck that won't happen. We get the money, back out of the bank, get on our horses and ride the hell out of town. 'The Lord giveth and the Lord taketh away.' And He puts those carpetbagging spoils right in the pockets of those who deserve them."

Jesse threw down the cigar he'd been smoking.

"Any questions?"

The others shook their heads.

"All right, then," Jesse nodded.

Bob, Jesse and Frank entered Northfield a little after one. They ate their lunch at a little establishment across the street from the bank. Well, Frank and Jesse ate. Bob was too tense.

"You ought to eat something, Bob," Jesse advised. "We don't know when we'll have the next opportunity."

Bob picked at a dinner roll. "I'm not hungry."

"Why don't you have a glass of spirits?" Jesse suggested, indicating his own. "Take the edge off."

Bob considered.

"No, I don't think so," he decided. He thought it might make him puke.

After they were done eating, they checked to see that their horses were still tied to the hitch in front of the bank. Yup, they were there. They walked over to sit on some dry goods boxes that were stacked in front of the Lee & Hitchcock store. Jesse and Frank chatted casually.

Bob looked at the scene in front of him and as he did, he thought there were too many people walking around. Wherever they had gone there had been people around, so he kept his opinion to himself. All the activity made him nervous but that was probably just his lack of experience talking. He saw Cole and Clell up by the bridge. He turned away and looked elsewhere. More of the same. There were almost as many people on the street here than there'd been in Mankato. The people of Minnesota sure seemed to have a lot of business to conduct.

As Clell and Cole waited there at the bridge, Cole leaned forward on his horse and frowned.

"There's still a good number down there on the street. You'd think all the people who'd come into town would be heading home for dinner by now."

"They're Yankees. Who knows what goes on in their minds," Clell responded. He put his pipe in his mouth and lit it.

"What are you doing?" Cole asked.

"I'm gonna smoke this here pipe throughout the proceedings. Damn Yankees don't give *me* no jitters."

At 2:00 the game began.

Jesse saw Clell put the pipe in his mouth and took that as the signal. Jesse, Frank and Bob crossed the street to enter the bank.

"What the hell are they doing?" Cole exclaimed as he watched them. "We didn't give them the signal. They have no business going into the bank with so many people milling around. Why didn't they just get on their horses and ride through?"

"They're going in, Cole."

"Well, there'll be an alarm, sure as there's a hell, so you better take that pipe out of your mouth."

Cole looked back and saw Jim and the others riding forward. He and Clell clicked to their horses and rode slowly down the street. As they did, Cole noticed a man in the company of two others walking their way.

"Look, it's the Governor himself," he remarked to Clell.

Adelbert Ames was a distinctive looking man. Cole had once seen his photograph.

Ames watched them as they rode by.

"Those are Southerners," he told his companions. "Nobody up here calls me Governor."

Bob, Jesse and Frank entered the bank. There were no customers inside so at least that was in their favor. Three men stood working. They looked up.

Jesse stepped up to the cashier's window to address the teller.

"What's your name?" Jesse asked cordially.

"Alonzo Bunker."

"Well, Mr. Bunker, it'd be a good idea if you were to throw up your hands," Jesse ordered as he drew his gun. "Now!"

Bob trained his gun on the clerk. His heart was beating fast. Damn, he hated pointing a gun at an unarmed man. He was so close he could see him sweat.

Frank had his gun pointed at the cashier. He had a little smile on his face but there was nothing friendly or engaging about it.

"We're robbing this bank," Jesse told the three men. "Don't any of you holler. We've got forty men outside."

Bob glanced at Jesse. *Forty* men outside? Who would believe that?

He waited for Jesse's nod. When it came, he, Jesse and Frank climbed over the counter.

"Who are you?" Jesse asked the man Frank was covering.

"Joseph Heywood," he announced defiantly. The robbers had no way of knowing that he was the acting cashier, in charge because his boss was in Philadelphia attending the Centennial Exposition. That didn't matter. He'd been given the responsibility and he would defend the bank as if it was his own.

"Are you the cashier?"

"No, I am not," was the reply.

"I know you are," Jesse insisted. "Now open the door damn quick or I'll blow off your head."

"I can't. I don't know the combination." Heywood glared at them. He didn't know who these men were and the gun trained on him made the point, but he would be damned if they were going to take the bank's money.

Bob looked at Heywood. Either this man was telling the truth or he was a damn fool. Either way, something bad would come next. He felt a trickle of sweat roll down his neck and his heart started to pound.

"Do you know the combination?" Jesse asked the clerk. The man shook his head no. "What about you?" he asked Bunker. He too shook his head.

Frank stepped over to the vault to have a closer look at the safe. It was possible they didn't even need to know the combination. Bankers were so goddamn arrogant that they were often just damn careless and left the vault door open.

As he approached the vault, Heywood rushed forward and tried to push Frank inside. Frank shoved the man back, but not before his hand was almost crushed by the heavy door that Heywood attempted to slam shut.

Bob grabbed the cashier and threw him down to the floor. This one was going to cause them trouble. Shit.

While Frank seethed, Jesse crouched down where the man had landed. He drew a knife from inside his coat and held it to his throat.

"Open the door," he whispered. "Or I'll cut your damn throat from ear to ear."

"Then you'll have to do it," Heywood replied, in a shaky but determined voice. "I can't open it. It has a chronometer lock."

Jesse looked at Frank. Frank shrugged.

"What's that?" Bob asked. He'd never heard of such a thing.

"It's a time lock," Heywood told him. "It can only be opened at certain times of the day."

Bob stomach began to turn. This wasn't going well. They should just cut their losses and leave. His eyes fell on some cash and coins lying on the counter. He grabbed what was closest to him and stuffed it into his pocket. He'd be damned if they came all this way to go away without *anything*. They'd been too cocky; too sure that everything would go as they'd planned, as they wanted. Well, guess what? Nothing had been going that way since they'd come up to this god-forsaken state with its curious and forward people. They kept pushing it, even when things started to sour. All signs told them they ought to just ride on back to Missoura and be done with it. Hadn't Jesse seen that?

Back outside Cole and Clell neared the door of the bank. Cole noticed it had been left ajar. He got down from his horse and pretended to adjust his saddle girth. He looked casually down the street, touching his hat when a pretty woman walked by.

"Close that door," he whispered.

Clell ambled over and shoved it closed with his foot without attracting attention. As he walked back to Cole, a man started to enter the bank. Clell grabbed his arm.

Immediately suspicious, the man looked at Clell and then at Cole. He jerked his arm away from Clell and started to run down the boardwalk.

"Get your guns!" he hollered. "They're robbing the bank!"

Bunker, who noticed that Bob's full attention was no longer on him, heard the noise outside and ran for the back door.

"Stop him!" Jesse yelled to Bob.

Bob aimed at the fleeing man. He didn't have any experience at this. He fired.

Bunker grabbed his shoulder and stumbled but was able to throw himself out the door.

"They're robbing the bank!" he yelled.

Cole and Clell were shooting warning shots up into the air but soon the street erupted in gunfire. The men who had been near to the bank and heard the alarm, grabbed whatever weapons they could get their hands on.

Cole and Clell ran for cover while shooting back against handguns, rifles and shotguns. Some people were even throwing *rocks* at them.

Cole tried to deflect the gunfire coming his way but he didn't necessarily want to hit anybody. These were citizens, as far as he could tell. Just because they happened to live in Northfield didn't necessarily make them his enemy; this wasn't war. He fired his shots into the air. Where the hell were Bob and the James boys? They needed to get the hell out of here before this turned into a bloodbath.

And now here came some damn fool stepping down from the sidewalk and ambling into the street. Was he deaf? Didn't he hear what was going on around him?

"Get out of the damn street!" Cole yelled to him.

The man continued to stumble forward, looking around in astonishment. Until he was caught in the crossfire.

"You damn fool," Cole muttered as he watched him go down. "One of your neighbors just ended your life."

A young man had stationed himself at a second story window across the street from the bank. He held an old army carbine. He considered himself a good shot and he'd be ready when the opportunity presented itself.

Clell started over to the bank to see what the delay was. Couldn't the men inside hear the ruckus? He would be too exposed if he went up to the door, so he put his foot in his stirrup and started to mount his horse.

Cole dodged fire left and right. Where the hell were they getting all these guns?

Someone from up high in a window started shooting at Clell and Clell turned to face him. Cole cringed when Clell's face was peppered with shot.

By this time Jim, Charlie and Chadwell had their horses on the street. They too fired into the air as they deflected the shots being taken at them.

Jim hadn't seen this type of battle since that last stand-off with Charlie Quantrill. This wasn't good. The noise was deafening. Smoke rose in the air all over the street. He spotted Cole but didn't see Bob.

One of the Northfield men noticed the three horses hitched to the rail in front of the bank and figured correctly that they belonged to the men inside. He took aim at the first horse and felled it. An outlaw's horse was the same as the man who rode it in circumstances like this.

Cole jumped on his horse and the man shot again. This time he missed. The next shot was critical. From seventy yards away, the man took aim and fired on Bill Chadwell as Chadwell rode his horse in a circle to drive people from the street.

Ol' Bill was dead before he hit the ground.

The man in the window was aiming at whoever passed in front of him. Jim was hit in the shoulder. Clell was his next target and his aim was spot on.

As Clell fell from his horse, Cole ran over to help him. There was nothing he could do. Clell was dead.

When Cole scrambled back up on his horse, he was hit in the thigh. They needed to get away from this madness. Those boys hadn't come out yet. Lord have mercy, were they dead too?

Inside the bank, Jesse wasn't through. He dragged Heywood over to the vault.

"Open it, goddamn it!" he shouted.

Frank was looking at the door. Jesse had to hear what was going on out there. Frank motioned that they should forget about the vault and help their allies in the street. This was going nowhere.

Jesse wouldn't accept that state of mind. He'd be damned if they would walk out of here with nothing at all to show for their efforts. He would *not* admit defeat to these goddamn Bluebellies.

When the cashier continued to play dumb, Jesse pointed his gun away from Heywood's ear and fired a shot into the floor.

"Open it!"

The door burst open and Cole yelled from beside it. "Get out here! They're killing our men!"

Bob stopped gathering the bills on the counter. To hell with the money, his brothers were in trouble. He could hear the shots.

He had never been in a gunfight but he couldn't give that any thought right now. He ran out the door and into the street, looking for Jim.

Jesse was disgusted. For once he wouldn't savor the sweet taste of success. He saw a handful of coins that Bob had missed and scooped them into his pocket.

"C'mon, forget it," he yelled back to Frank as he walked out the door. "We'll have our will another day, sonofabitchin' Yankees."

Frank started out, and then paused to look at Heywood. He hadn't believed a goddamn word the man had said. There had to be a way to get in the vault. The son-of-a-bitch was lying. And his hand still ached where the bastard had tried to push him into the vault. He needed to pay for that. Nobody treated Frank James that way. Nobody.

Frank jumped over the counter, firing at Heywood. He missed. Heywood fell hard into his chair with his back against the wall. As Heywood stared into the outlaw's eyes, Frank walked up to him, put the gun against his head and fired.

With Heywood's blood and brain matter a messy spot on the wall, it was time to take Jesse's little getting-to-know-you party out the door.

Bob couldn't believe what he was seeing in the street. Powder billowed and the noise of gunfire was greater than anything he had ever heard. He thought he saw men lying in the street but that couldn't be, could it? He tried to spot Cole or Jim but couldn't see either of them through the enveloping smoke.

He headed for where he had left his horse but stopped short when he saw it lying dead in the street. The sight of that stunned him. He saw a couple of other horses running free without riders and that must mean…. This was out of control, so out of control.

He couldn't spot his brothers. Where were *his brothers?*

He raised his gun and ran in the direction of the closest of the horses when a bullet whizzed by his shoulder. Someone was shooting at him, at *him.* He shot in the direction of the shooter as he ran down the sidewalk, hoping that they would stop.

Why didn't these people just let them turn tail and run? It wasn't like they had gotten anything out of the bank. A few dollars? They could have it.

The shots were coming from the upstairs window of the hotel. He ducked behind an outdoor staircase and shot in that direction. He wanted nothing more than for the shooting to stop.

The man in the window didn't have a clear line of vision now but he got lucky. The next ball he fired exploded into the bone of Bob's elbow.

As his arm erupted in a blaze of paralyzing fire, he caught his breath and shifted his gun to his left hand. He had a brief and vague memory of the day Dick had pointed out he was ambidextrous and told him that it was very special to be able to use either hand with equal ability. He needed to stop thinking of what Dick had said all those years ago and demonstrate that ability now. He fired again.

Cole's bridle was clipped by a shot as he spun his horse in a circle. He finally saw Bob out of the corner of his eye. Bob in trouble. Guiding his horse with one hand and knee, Cole took off for the staircase while Charlie covered him. His guerilla training and experience had come in handy on a number of occasions but none more important than this one. Cole whirled his horse to put him in position to reach down and hoist Bob up behind him. He grabbed Bob by the belt and pulled.

"Keep low!"

Shots continued to pepper the street. Cole felt one graze his side and another, his shoulder. The horn of his saddle was ripped loose. They'd be damn lucky if they both could stay atop the horse.

Bob held on to Cole with his one good arm. The other dangled uselessly.

Frank and Jesse were on their horses and when they saw the others finally mounted, they signaled to retreat.

"Let's go!" Jesse cried, but his voice was lost in the chaotic wrath as a ball clipped his thigh.

Jim waited for Cole and Bob to catch up to him. To hell with Jesse and Frank. He wasn't going anywhere without his brothers.

Cole's horse finally streaked by with its double burden.

"Go!" Jim yelled, as Charlie's horse pulled up alongside. Charlie, riding for all he was worth, took a shot in the calf.

The hoofs of their horses pounded heavy as the gunfire chased them down the road. Finally, they were able to pull away from the town of Northfield and break their horses into a dead run.

It couldn't have gone worse.

CHAPTER 58

They rode fast and hard, heading southwest. The plan had been to clip the wires as they headed out of Northfield so that communication of the robbery was impossible by that means but there wasn't time for that now. They were lucky to get out with their lives. Clell Miller and Bill Chadwell hadn't been that lucky.

Miles away, as they passed by the road to Dundas, they eased their horses down to the bank of the Cannon River. It was time to assess the damage.

Bob slid off Cole's horse. His arm hung loosely at his side, a mangled mass of blood and broken bone. As badly as it hurt, as he looked around at the others he thought that Cole was probably hurt worse.

"Cole…." He didn't know what to say.

Cole threw up his arm. "Not now," he growled.

"Clell and Bill…"

"They're dead, we're not."

The shooters weren't necessarily good shots but they had found their mark often enough to make an impact. Most of them had used firearms best suited to game. Despite the blood, Cole didn't consider his wounds to be all that serious. He'd have Frank dig the lead out of his shoulder. He was more concerned about the thigh wound. It would be hard to bear weight and he wondered how that was going to factor into their escape. He looked at Jim. Jim had a shoulder wound but it didn't look to be serious.

"I'm all right, Captain," Charlie told him when Cole looked his way. He didn't feel his calf wound was any big deal.

"Son-of-a-bitch!" Jesse was ranting as he examined the torn fabric of his pants.

Jesse had a small ragged wound at the side of his thigh but it wasn't bleeding much and it didn't look bad to Cole. He'd certainly seen worse and many of those men had lived to tell about it. Jesse was over-reacting. That was nothing new.

"For God's sake, Jesse. It's only a damn flesh wound. You've had worse." Frank hadn't been hurt at all. He crossed to Cole. "Yours don't look too bad but I bet they hurt like hell."

"Help me dig this lead out, will you?" Cole asked.

"Cole..." Jim directed his eyes to Bob, who was now sitting on the ground. Thick blood oozed from between his fingers as he clutched his arm. Raw flesh was mixed with shattered bone. Cole saw that the wound was far more serious than he had at first believed it to be. Didn't look good at all.

"Bobby, let me see that. We'll fix you up." Cole tore at his shirt, ripping a long strip off of it.

Bob struggled to stay conscious. The pain was harsh but the loss of blood was causing him to see double.

"I can't stop the bleeding..." he whispered. How could he complain when the others had been hurt worse and two of them were dead?

Jim took the cloth from Cole. "You tend to your own wounds. I'm all right. I'll help Bob."

Jim cinched the cloth tight around Bob's arm. The first thing, he knew, was to stop the bleeding. He didn't know what to do with the bone that stuck straight out from the mass of blood.

"Hang on, Bob. I'm going to try to do something with this bone and it's going to hurt."

Bob nodded. Charlie ran over to his horse and sliced the end of his rein. He brought it back to Bob.

"This might help."

"Thanks, Charlie." Bob placed it between his teeth and bit down.

Jim straightened the arm the best he could and pulled.

Bob grimaced and bit down harder on the leather. Showing any weakness now would just be pathetic.

"I think that's the best I can do for now, Bob." Jim decided to bind the arm tight against Bob's chest. "Charlie, give me some water so we can wash this out before we wrap it."

While Jim tended to Bob's wound, Frank picked the shot out of Cole's shoulder. When they had each done all they could do with their injuries, they sat on the ground to catch their breath and regroup.

"Where do we go now, Jesse?" Cole demanded. "Your guide is dead. What's your goddamn plan now?"

"Don't be blaming Jesse, Bud," Frank warned. "We're all in this together."

Cole looked at Bob. His little brother was staring at the ground. So much for his big plan with Jesse fucking James. He wanted to be angry with him, as angry as he had been with John for getting himself killed maybe, but the kid was hurt bad. He might lose that arm. But Frank was right. Now wasn't the time to come apart or cast blame. They needed to get as far away from Northfield as they could, as quick as they could. That's what they needed to focus on.

"Look yonder," Charlie interrupted. A young man was hauling a rail with his horse. It was obvious that he hadn't seen them.

"Charlie, get his horse. Bob needs a horse."

They watched from the brush as Charlie pitched a story about his wound and exchanged money. The boy stood watching Charlie make his way down to the river, leading the horse.

"He's not armed," Charlie reported. "I told him my horse faltered and I fell in the river and hurt my leg. The horse ran off. He didn't want to sell me the horse so I asked if I could take it for just awhile to get into town and get me another. Then I'd bring it back. He went for it."

"We've got to get moving," Jesse directed. Although it annoyed him that Frank had reprimanded him in front of the others, he would take back control. "Can you ride, Bob?"

"Yeah," Bob nodded. He didn't have any choice.

Jim held Bob steady as he climbed up on the horse, his good hand grasping the saddle horn. He would ride between Cole and Jim so they could keep their eyes on him.

"He's got grit," Cole whispered to Jim.

Jim nodded. "He needs that wound cleaned with some fresh water, Cole. If it isn't, infection's going to set in quickly and that could be the end of it."

"I know, Jim, I know."

They had been riding for over an hour when they spotted a farmhouse off to the west. They didn't see any activity so Cole rode up to Frank.

"Bob needs to have that wound cleaned out. He's gonna lose the arm if it isn't. We need fresh water."

"I'll take him up there," Frank indicated the house. "I'll string together a believable story."

Frank and Bob rode slowly up to the barn. There was someone coming up the side of the building but they couldn't look suspicious or jumpy.

"Howdy," Frank nodded.

The farmer nodded.

Bob said nothing.

"My brother got into a fight with a Blackleg miner back in Northfield," Frank explained. "He's been shot and we need a pail of water to clean out his wound. Could you help us out?"

The man didn't know these strangers but that looked like a hell of an injury.

"What happened to the miner?"

"Dead."

From the look of the man doing the talking, that seemed probable. "What was his name?"

"Man named Stiles." It was a nothing short of a fact that a man named Stiles was lying dead in the street back in Northfield.

"I'll get you that water."

"Appreciate it."

They continued west but they weren't covering a lot of ground. Cole led Bob's horse as Bob hung on to the saddle horn. So far, so good.

Bob felt like a fool and certainly a burden to the others. If he wasn't injured like this they might have been able to ride hard. God knew the others knew how to do that. He and Charlie had been the weak links and Charlie was doing all right. He hated that he was the one holding them back. He should have found a way to better protect himself back at that staircase.

He'd never been wounded like this. Add that to being in a bank *robbery* for the first time, being in a gunfight for the first time… His life in the last couple of days was just chock full of new experiences. None of them good. He didn't know how it had all gone so wrong.

God, he wished he was just back home with Maggie and had never thought to take any of this on. He'd insisted this happen. No one pushed him into anything that wasn't his own idea, after Jesse posed it. But never mind that, he needed to return to the here and now. He had lost a lot of blood but his arm had finally stopped bleeding. It hurt real bad but he wasn't going to moan and groan about it. Chadwell and Clell couldn't complain at all. They were lying back there on the street at Northfield, dead. Dead. Clell… he always had something amusing to say. He was always entertaining and enjoyable on these outings; a good man, he supposed. Chadwell had seemed all right; he couldn't attest to his character. He hadn't known either man for any length of time but…he couldn't think about it now. Right now he had to concentrate and hold on to the damn saddle horn.

There was a saloon outside of Shieldsville and it seemed like a good place to stop and get more water. They still wore their linen dusters so their wounds were fairly concealed. They pulled up at the water pump.

Jim got out the strips of cloth he had torn as bandages. As they pumped and drank the water, he wet the rags to use when they were back in the brush. They couldn't run the risk of interacting with anybody once word came down from Northfield.

An old man was sitting on the porch in front of the saloon watching them. He'd never seen any of these men before. They were a peculiar group.

Bob had been fighting to remain conscious for over an hour. He could fight it no more, as everything dimmed.

He fell off his horse onto the dusty road below.

The old man looked at him with wide eyes. What the hell was going on here?

Jesse was closest to where Bob fell and he grabbed him. He roughly dragged Bob back on his horse.

"We're going to hang this damn cuss," he told the old man.

"What's that?" the old man questioned.

"We caught up with him back a few miles. He's a damn horse thief," Jesse explained.

The old man nodded and continued to watch them. When the others finished drinking, he got up and walked into the saloon. Something wasn't right and he'd better bring it to the attention of the boys inside.

As they mounted their horses, a group of four men emerged.

"What's going on out here?" one of them asked. His face dropped as four guns were quickly drawn on him. He and his friends had left their own outside, as was courtesy in the area.

"You all just stay put," Cole directed. "We'll be on our way."

The four men who had been at the saloon ran for their guns as they watched the strangers ride out of town. They recruited fourteen others from Faribault to join the chase. They didn't know who those men were, but it was a sure bet they'd been up to no good.

About four miles out of town the group overtook the riders. As shots were exchanged, Charlie was thrown from his horse. He remounted but his saddle girth broke, once again sending him to the ground. There was nothing but bad luck all around. Cole was hit in the crazy bone by a spent shell as he tried to grab him. Charlie waved him off and clamored up onto Bob's horse. It was better this way anyway, he could help Bob hold on.

The men from Faribault were soon left in their dust. The impromptu posse wasn't a surprise. There was very little that could surprise them anymore.

Word of the robbery may not have reached the men at the saloon but there were men from Northfield who were already on their trail. Adelbert Ames' son J.T. was now Mayor of Northfield and he wasted no time in calling for a volunteer posse. To add to the manpower, he had telegraphed St. Paul for assistance. There was an enthusiastic response from both entities. Minnesota wasn't going to tolerate bank robbers the way other states seemed to do.

This wasn't Missouri.

CHAPTER 59

And then it started to rain. A torrential, relentless inundation of water.

"Just what we need," Jesse hollered as they rode into a heavily wooded area where they couldn't be seen. "Goddamn our luck!"

It was raining so hard now that the men pursuing them decided it wasn't worth it to go any further. It was time for supper anyway.

They pulled up in a dense grove and pitched a couple of tarps. Cole's leg had started to bleed again but he was more concerned about Bob.

"He's got a fever," Jim told him. "That arm is already in trouble."

"You don't look so good yourself," Cole pointed out.

"My shoulder's probably growing an infection but it's not so bad."

"You tend to Bobby then. I've got to wrap this leg again and put together some kind of a crutch. I can't put my weight on it but I can ride."

Jim went over to Bob and started to unwrap his arm.

"Just leave it, Jim," Bob shook his head as he wiped the sweat from his face. He didn't want anyone wasting time on him. "If it's getting infected there's nothing going to change that right now."

"We need to clean it up again. If we don't, it'll get even worse and you won't be able to ride."

"Jim..." Bob wanted to say something to his brother, he wanted to try and make some kind of sense of all of this.

"Just let me do this." Jim didn't want to hear it now. He wanted to deal in facts, not emotion, and the facts were that they had some serious injuries to take care of and that was the priority.

They would stay here for a few hours rest but they knew they needed to get on the move again. Frank stood watch and Jesse and Cole spelled him. They didn't know where they were going anyway and with the dark and the rain, the best thing to do was to regroup and start out again in the morning.

By this time more than 200 men were in the field looking for them; many of them from various law enforcement positions and others were veteran soldiers. They were doing a fairly good job of tracking the outlaws but it was the unofficial posse that was becoming a problem. They didn't know what they were doing and rather than be a help, they were little more than a bother.

By Friday morning another 300 men had joined the chase. The bank and the governor were offering large rewards for the outlaws and who wouldn't be interested in that? Seeking the thrill of the hunt and anxious to show off their abilities, a lot of these men were nothing but a thorn in the side of those who were more qualified. They only got in the way, disobeyed the instructions given them and in general made the hunt that much more complex.

It really didn't matter. They knew that eventually they'd catch up to the outlaws and it would all be over.

It had been a day and a half since the robbery and they slogged on, using the cover of the woods. The continuing rain helped shield them but that was about the only benefit of it. But cussing and carrying on wasn't going to change it so they just tried to ignore it. Fat chance.

"We're not making any progress." Jesse was talking in a low voice to Frank. "Bob's slowing us down."

"Well, there's nothing we can do about that. We'll just do the best we can."

Cole, who wasn't supposed to hear that exchange, appreciated Frank's reply.

"We've got to get across the river," Cole hollered to Frank. "The rain isn't going to make it easy but if we don't cross, we're going to be going in a circle, making no ground at all."

Sheriff Ara Barton out of Faribault had put together a good group of men. He placed picket lines on the various routes the robbers could take: the roads, the bridges and anyplace where they might be able to ford the river. Yet the rain made any tracking nearly impossible. Any evidence of the outlaws having been in a specific area was soon washed away.

Later that day they came upon a small group of makeshift posse.

"They don't know what they're doing," Cole quickly assessed.

"Any sign of them?" Frank called out to the strangers as the others, save Jesse, hung back.

"No, we haven't seen them."

"Well, good luck to you then. We'll find them one way or another," Jesse guaranteed.

The posse continued on its way.

In the clearing was a farmhouse.

"Let's see if we can get some information that might make this easier," Jesse suggested.

While the others remained hidden in the trees, Jesse and Frank rode up to the house. A woman answered their knock.

"Hello, ma'am," Jesse smiled.

"And who might you young men be?" she replied. One had to be cautious about strangers.

"Ma'am, we've got a problem." Jesse sighed. "We're traveling through and we stayed the night in the woods up there. While we were sleeping, two black mules that we had with us somehow loosed their tethers and wandered away. We're wondering if there is any marshy area up ahead by the river where they might have bogged down."

"Well," she pointed. "They might be yonder, over there by the crossing."

The Cannon River was high and getting higher as the water bombarded the ground and everything on it. Frank tried to cross the river but his effort only made it evident that it was a risky move so they continued down the Cordova Road.

They soon spotted a few men who were sitting under a shelter. Again Frank and Jesse approached.

"Hey there," Jesse called. "We're looking for those Northfield robbers. Have you seen them?"

"Nah, we haven't seen them. We've been trying to work on the road but it's raining so damn hard that we had to stop."

"What's the best way to reach the other bank of the river?"

"There's a bridge just a ways down there."

But as they approached the bridge they saw a posse waiting there. They retraced their steps and started to go around the lake when they came face-to-face with the rest of the group.

"Captain Rodgers!" one of them yelled. "There they are!"

Shots rang out and the outlaws spurred their horses into the lake. They made it to the other side, where they were once again enveloped by woods.

Bob was hanging on. He'd rather have been anyplace else in the world but at least he wasn't lying face down in the mud. The last cleaning of the wound seemed to have had helped some. He was still in pain and his fever was there but he'd somehow gained a little strength. At least that's what he told himself.

"We need fresh horses, Buck," Cole called. "These are just as exhausted as the men who are riding them."

They were watching a farmer lead two nice mares into a barn.

"I hate to ask you to do the honors again but I'm fairly lame unless I'm in the saddle." Cole hated that he wasn't completely in control of his own fate. This was something he'd never experienced before.

Frank nodded. "Jesse and I will go get them."

As soon as the man entered his house, Jesse and Frank slipped into the barn, where they exchanged the two horses for their own.

A little further down the road they saw a boy leading two horses toward a barn. Finally they were seeing some luck.

"We'll have those horses, boy," Frank directed. "You hop up on mine. You can keep him after you lead us across the river."

When that task was accomplished they continued on.

"Do you think we'll be able to get some food soon, Captain?" Charlie asked Cole.

"We need to do that, Charlie. Everybody's hungry."

They saw two boys in a field with a pair of plowing horses. The horses were soon unhitched and under Jim and Charlie. When they came across yet another farm, Jesse and Frank rode up to the house and asked if they might buy some food.

"Good that we can put that twenty-six dollars and seventy cents to some use," Cole remarked as he watched food being handed to Frank and Jesse.

"What's that, Captain?"

"That was what was *earned* back in Northfield. Bob was able to grab it off the counter."

"Twenty-six dollars and seventy cents?" Jim shook his head. "All that, all *this,* for twenty-six dollars and seventy cents."

Bob hung his head. Not only was this the biggest mistake of his life, it was just plain stupid.

After they had eaten some bread and jam, a little chicken and some applesauce, they noticed some trees in the middle of the small lake in front of them. It mirrored like a mirage. They had been out in the elements so long it might have been just that.

"Wouldn't hurt to put some water between us and the posse," Cole suggested.

"Sounds like a good idea," Frank agreed.

As their horses hit the water, a huge commotion erupted behind them. It looked like a hundred men…and they were coming right at them.

Cole and Frank led the way, spurring their horses into the water as they made their way to the island.

The posse figured the outlaws would keep going. They were probably on the other side now.

They were wrong.

"Let's wait here a bit longer," Frank directed.

In the morning they released three of the horses and tied the other three to a tree.

"They won't think we've given up our horses," Cole figured. "They'll wait for us to swim them off this island."

That's exactly what the posse thought. It wasn't until they made their own way off the island that the civilian posse figured out what happened.

By that time the popular consensus was to just pack it in. The outlaws were too far gone.

Bob felt like maybe they had a chance after all. Cole and the others were experienced enough to make that call and it worked. They'd figure out how to get out of this mess. That's what he had counted on before they had even left Missoura, their skills. They'd find a way….

The next day they were relieved to find an abandoned farm where they could sleep indoors, redress their wounds and somehow pull themselves together.

"Are we making any progress at all?" Bob asked Cole. It didn't seem like it to him. He didn't feel as optimistic today as he did yesterday.

"How should I know? Other than we're west of Northfield, I don't have any idea where the hell we are."

"So much for Chadwell leading the way." Jim was recovered enough that he was beginning to get angry. He wasn't so much angry at Bob as he was Jesse for dragging Bob into this. He knew Bob was a grown man and held a degree of responsibility but he was new to all this. Jesse wasn't and it was Jesse who had called the shots.

Cole glared at Jesse. "Yeah, so much for Chadwell."

"Don't you be blaming me for that Cole," Jesse bristled. "I wasn't out there in that street."

"No, you sure as hell weren't."

"Are you trying to say all that was my fault? If you are, let's hear it square."

"You couldn't just admit defeat there in that bank could you, Dingus?" Cole was angry. He'd done a good job keeping it to himself but this point had been gnawing on him. Bob had told him what happened, when he asked. Bob felt he deserved to know, as unflattering as it might have been. "You couldn't just walk away when it would've been the sensible thing to do."

"Bud, we're not going to start blaming one another." Frank didn't want to hear this shit. Cole may have been right but Jesse was his brother. "We've got enough to contend with without that."

Cole continued to glare at Jesse as he picked up his gun to clean it. Maybe not now, but the matter would be a conversation he would have with Jesse another day, another place. He'd drop it for now, but that would be one goddamn "conversation" he and Jesse James would have later.

The following morning they walked along, skirting the woods as they once again looked for horses. They heard a rustling and hoped it was either a horse or, at the least, game. They were hungry.

So was the man picking raspberries. He was reaching to take a handful when he heard the click of a number of gun hammers. He stood stock still.

"Stay right where you are," Jesse growled.

"Yes, Sir. I will," the man replied. Holy Cow, what had he walked into?

"What're we gonna do with him?" Charlie asked. "He'll be able to tell the posse we've been around. He'll lead 'em to us."

"We can kill him. Then he won't be leading anybody," Frank mused.

The man's eyes grew wide.

"He's done nothing to us." Cole wasn't about to kill a man in cold blood. "We can tie him to a tree."

"If you tie him to a tree way back in here, he might die of exposure before he's found." Jim couldn't see harming one more person. It was their problem, not this man's.

"What's your name?" Cole asked.

"Jeff Dunning."

"Tell you what, Dunning," Cole proposed. "If you'll tell us where we can find some chickens without attracting a fuss, and if you keep your mouth shut about seeing us here, we'll let you go." He grabbed the farmhand by the shirtfront. "But if you tell a soul, we'll know. And that will be the last thing you tell anyone, you understand me?"

Dunning nodded. "I won't say anything. You have my word."

"I say we just kill him now and be over with it." Frank didn't think there was much chance of this man keeping his word. Not when there were so many looking for them.

Cole shook his head. They'd just have to disagree on this one. Cole didn't want one more dead body attributed to him or his brothers unless it was a matter of life or death.

Dunning directed them to a nearby henhouse. Once they grabbed a handful of the birds they couldn't wait to enter the depths of the woods, light a small fire and cook them.

The few scrawny chickens were a feast.

Jeff Dunning made it about three hours before caving in and telling the man who employed him about the men in the woods.

They trudged on through the rain. That was the only thing they could do. They crossed the Blue Earth River at a railroad bridge, and then found another spot to hole up.

"We've got to come up with some kind of a plan, boys. This is going nowhere."

Cole looked at Frank and Jesse. The others were less experienced and didn't know much about surviving in the bush. Jim may have been with Charlie Quantrill but not for long and Quantrill and Jim had, after all, allowed themselves to be captured. Cole didn't hold that against Jim but he didn't want Jim making decisions for him in this regard. Charlie Pitts was basically just a ranch hand and Bob...well, he had no experience with this whatsoever. He was smart enough but the kid was fighting his own battle against the infection in his arm. He wasn't in any position to weigh in.

"We need horses again. Something other than field nags." Frank had been thinking of a way out of this but it wasn't yet time to share it with the others.

"Frank and I will go out and see what we can find. You men get some rest." Jesse looked them over. They were a sorry lot.

"All right." Cole attempted a thin smile. "We're not going anywhere."

After they left, Jim looked at Cole.

"Do you think they'll be back?"

"What do you mean?"

"If they find good horses, what's to keep them from just heading out on their own? They know we're a liability. We're too banged up to move quickly, but on their own they could make good time."

"Jim, you have to understand something." Cole wasn't annoyed at the comment. Jim had struggled like the rest of them this last week. He never complained, he did just what he needed to do. But there were some things he didn't know, hadn't been in the heat of battle to realize. "I know Frank James isn't my brother but just like I'd trust either you or Bob with my life, if it came to that, I'd trust Buck. He's a man of his word."

"A man of his word but a man who shot a cashier back at that bank for no good reason. In cold blood."

"We don't know that for certain. Bob said he heard a shot but he left the bank before that happened."

"And Frank was the last to leave."

"Like I said, we don't know what happened in there after Bob left."

"And why is that, Cole? You never even asked Frank about it as far as I know."

"It doesn't really matter right now, does it?"

Bob started to say something, but what was there to say? He didn't want to hear them argue. Arguing only spent energy and what little energy they could muster needed to be devoted to somehow getting the hell out of this predicament.

"It always matters when a man's life has been taken," Jim told Cole.

"Are you going to harp on that damn conductor again, Jim?" Cole had had enough. "For God's sake, give it a rest."

Jim got up and walked away.

"Will they be back, Cole?" Bob asked.

"They'll be back, Bobby."

Bob would just have to take Cole's word on that. Here he was, somewhere in Minnesota, broken and desperate, with his brothers and three men he really didn't even know. His arm was acting up again and it hurt. He didn't feel as good – or as confident - as he had the night before. If he were home, Maggie could fix him up and everything would work out fine.

But if he was home with Maggie, he wouldn't be here.

It was almost morning when Frank and Jesse led two horses back into the woods. Cole nodded at Jim.

"We were able to snatch these two a little while ago," Jesse told them.

"They're pretty good mounts." Frank sat down on a rock.

"We've been thinking…" Jesse started.

Here it comes, thought Jim.

Bob looked from Jesse to Frank and back to Jesse.

"If we only have two horses, maybe you and Bob should take them, Cole. The rest of us can keep goin' on foot until we can find a few more but you two trying to muck through all this brush is doing you in. You with your leg, Bob with his one arm and his fever and all."

"I've got a better idea." Bob had been thinking about this too. "You men take the horses. We've seen it'll be just a matter of time before you find more. Leave me here. I'm just costing you time. I don't want to be in that position. I'll be all right until I'm stronger. By the time the posse calls it quits, I'll be ready to make my way home."

Everyone just stared at him.

Finally Cole rolled his eyes.

"Yeah, sure, Bobby. We're going to leave you on your own here in these stinking woods in the rain and go on home. When we get there we'll raise us a toast to your kind heart and humble sacrifice."

"He's just offering what any one of us would." Jim looked down at Bob. "And just like you would, Bob, if the situation was different and it was one of us in trouble, there's no way in hell we're going to go along with that."

Cole snorted. His little brother was acting dumber than he looked right about now. He turned to face Jesse and Frank.

"I appreciate the offer boys, but I have one of my own. We should split up. You take the horses. The two of you can travel faster and your chances of making it out will be better. Besides, if there's any posse left out there, they will most likely follow the horses. That'll give the rest of us time to lose 'em. Then we'll find our way out of this great state of Minnesota. I think I can speak for Bob and Jim on this." He raised his eyebrows.

"Charlie?" Cole asked.

"I'll do whatever you think best, Captain. I'll stay on with you."

Jim wanted nothing more than to get Bob some medical attention but Cole was right. There were only two horses and there was no way that he and his brothers were going to split up.

"I'll go along with that," he agreed.

Bob had made his offer and it had been rejected.

"I don't feel I've got the right to a vote here. You men do what you think is best."

Frank looked at Cole. "You sure that's the way you want it?"

Cole nodded. "Yeah, Buck, it makes the most sense."

"I wish it was different, Bud."

"I know, Buck, but this is how it is."

Jesse walked over to Bob. He put a hand on his shoulder.

"Don't be blaming yourself for all this, Bob. This isn't the fault of either you or me. Sometimes things just turn bad. Proverbs says that "the lot is cast into the lap but its every decision is from the Lord". I guess the Lord didn't want us to have the money this time but he spared our lives and we'll all make out all right."

Bob had nothing to say to that. Jesse would always come out all right because he could talk himself out of anything bad he encountered... or created.

Jesse and Frank got back on the horses. They saluted and were off into the woods, unburdened and headed for someplace that wasn't Minnesota.

CHAPTER 60

A nd on they plodded...
Jim and Charlie spotted a watermelon and they pulled it from the field, along with several ears of corn that were already going to seed. They grabbed a small turkey from a nearby farm. It was risky to light up a fire and cook the meat so they'd start with the watermelon and see where it went after that.

They came across the rails of the Sioux City Railroad and hid down below the bank. Being this close to the track meant they had to be particularly vigilant but they were so hungry, and it was halfway dry, and they decided to chance it.

Bob couldn't remember when he'd had watermelon that tasted this good. It took him back to that watermelon he'd eaten when they'd moved back to Missoura from Texas. That was then. A lifetime ago, it seemed. This one could have been the worst of the crop but it wouldn't have made any difference. It was food.

They had just finished off the melon when they heard voices off in the distance above them. They weren't going to take any chances. They scrambled up the bank and back into the woods.

They had been right to clamber out of their hiding place. A posse appeared within the hour and found what they had left behind.

A couple hours later, once more embraced by the trees, they stopped to get their bearings.

"Where are we now, Captain?" Charlie asked.

"I don't know, Charlie," Cole replied.

Bob was doing better now, stumbling over the broken brush. Whatever pain he was in was of no matter to him now. He was still somewhat feverish but he needed to do his part. He didn't know what that might be, other than trudging on to somewhere, someplace else. Wherever it was they were, they were heading into swampy areas that were swollen from the constant rain. They stopped for the night when they came to another woodsy area.

Huddled into their coats as they all sat there on the ground, they had little to say to one another.

"We'll head out early before the sun is up," Cole finally said. "That way we can take that road we saw. It'll be easier to walk and there shouldn't be any folks up and about if we start out real early."

Cole was running out of ideas. They needed to find some horses. Today. They couldn't make their way back to Missoura on foot. If they would just come across a sizable town. Maybe they could catch a train. He and Bob didn't have much money left but Jim did and they somehow might be able to pull that off. The chances of it working were thin but any plan was better than no plan at all. But there was nothing around them but prairie, sloughs and the occasional farm. The chance to settle on a plan like that, regardless of how far-flung it might be, didn't look likely.

The sun was just beginning to rise above the horizon after they found their way around another lake. There were lakes everywhere in Minnesota and it seemed like they were seeing them all.

"Hold up," Cole whispered. The others followed his eyes. It was dark still but they could see a boy milking a cow in a barn.

"Morning," Cole called. "Just keep walking and head into those woods," he directed under his breath.

As the men disappeared, the boy, his name was Oscar Sorbel, ran to tell his father what he had just seen.

"I think they might be the Northfield robbers, Papa. There were four of them."

"Well, six of them rode out of Northfield according to the newspaper," his father replied. "They're probably just travelers. Finish those cows."

"That boy didn't seem suspicious, Cole." Jim didn't know what it was they should be doing, but they were all so hungry. "Maybe Charlie and I can go back and ask him if we could buy some bread."

Cole sighed. The watermelon hadn't done much to fuel their bodies. Any interaction with one of the locals would be dangerous, yet if they didn't take a chance and try to get some food in them, they wouldn't be able to continue on.

"All right," he agreed.

The boy watched as the men approached him. This time there were only two. They sure were scruffy, even though they were wearing those expensive coats. They didn't look like anyone from around here.

"Say young man," Jim greeted him. "We had to fork over our horses to a group of men who were looking for some bank robbers. We've been traveling by foot until we can buy some fresh mounts. We're hungry and we thought maybe your mother might have some bread we could buy."

"I'll ask." The boy ran to the farmhouse.

He was soon back with two loaves fresh out of the oven.

Charlie thought the aroma liked to make him faint.

Jim handed the boy some money and thanked him.

The two men once again disappeared into the woods.

"I bet they *are* the robbers," the boy insisted as he and his father watched them walk down the road.

"You might be right." The older man scratched his chin. "Ride into Madelia and tell Sheriff Glispin about them."

The boy took off, riding as fast as his horse could carry him.

"Ma's going to have to forgive our lack of manners," Cole mumbled through a wad of bread.

Bob didn't want to think of his mother; only the food he was stuffing into his mouth.

When the boy arrived in Madelia he found Sheriff Jim Glispin in the company of Mr. Vought and described his encounter with the strangers.

"You know, last month I had a conversation with a cattleman who was passing through the area," remembered Vought. "He stayed at my hotel. He was asking about the terrain and the roads in and out of Madelia. I've been thinking since I heard of the Northfield bank robbery that he might have been one of the men involved. When I read the description of the robbers, one of them just might have been that fella."

"Well, this is something that definitely should be checked out," Glispin agreed. "Let's you and me head out to Sorbel's."

As they went to get their horses, they saw Will Murphy talking to a lady in front of the dry goods store. Murphy had served as a Union Captain during the War. He would be useful.

"I'll ask Murphy to get some men together and meet us out there."

Glispin and Vought rode toward the Sorbel farm, but they slowed at Hanska Lake when they saw movement.

"There," Glispin indicated. "They're trying to cross the slough."

Jim, Bob and Charlie lumbered through the slime and mire of the spongy slough. Cole, using the cane he had made out of a tree branch, was having a particularly hard time.

"We need to be rid of this mud…" Bob thought it was pointless to try to make any time trying to snake their way through this muck.

"Hey!" Glispin called. "You men halt right there!"

"Run!" Cole ordered.

They ran as fast as they were able, Cole tossing the branch aside to run unabated on his injured leg.

Bob called on all the energy he could muster.

He knew that this time they were running for their lives.

Murphy arrived with four others. Glispin quietly directed them to divide into two groups and walk their horses silently around the slough.

They weren't able to see much of anything but they knew the outlaws couldn't be far. A man couldn't move fast here, that was a sure thing.

They spotted them about a quarter of a mile from where they first saw them, deep in the brush.

"You men can't get away from us," Glispin called. "Surrender!"

"Keep moving!" Cole ordered.

One of the posse began firing. Cole and Jim returned the fire and ran into a thicket where they could check the load of their guns. They looked back at those who pursued them and saw seven heavily armed men backed up by maybe another nine or ten who had just arrived.

"Captain, they outnumber us." Charlie knew a bad situation when he saw one. "We can't outrun armed men on horseback in this mud. Maybe we should surrender and be done with it."

Cole looked at him. Charlie didn't have experience with these things but he had been brave and had stood right alongside him through all of it. He could have chosen to go with Frank and Jesse but his loyalty to Cole and the Youngers tied him to the situation they were now facing.

But Cole Younger did not surrender. He never had and he never would.

"Charlie, this is where Cole Younger dies."

Bob was horrified. He never thought he would *ever* hear Cole admit defeat. Yet there it was. They were trapped to death in circumstances of their own making.

Bob tried to reload his own gun, using his left hand. His full participation was important if they were to make a stand. Yet none of this seemed real to him. He was now in a position where he would have to square off against strangers in an attempt to save the lives of his brothers...and his own.

Although he should have been focused on the task at hand, his mind drifted to Maggie. He heard her laughter when he sang "Do Da" at the top of his lungs. He shared the pride she had of Jeremy, the boy who he loved as if he was his own. He felt her arms around him, holding him close in the stillness of the night. He loved her with his heart and with his soul.

Now he was about to shame her by dying as a criminal at the hands of a posse of men with whom he had no direct quarrel.

His thoughts were interrupted by the sound of Cole yelling in his ear.

"Bob, take the right side with Jim! Charlie you and me will take the left."

They were likely facing their deaths, but Cole would be goddamned if he would go down without a fight.

"Murphy, you're the man with experience here." Glispin's intent was to somehow take the robbers prisoner. He didn't want to kill anybody. He'd let these men have their day in court. "How do you propose we take these men alive?"

"Shoot low, men," Murphy ordered the initial group. "But don't shoot unless they do. We'll ask them to surrender and Sheriff Glispin will try to take them in alive."

He motioned to the others, who watched from the distance. "You other men stay back."

The seven men slowly followed the bank of the river. The brush was so thick that it was hard to navigate. They swiped at the branches and pushed through. It wasn't pleasant but you had to admit it was kind of exciting. This was a new experience and it sure would be something to tell their grandchildren about.

One of them looked under the brush and saw that they were drawing away from the river. He brought that fact to the attention of Sheriff Glispin and Glispin signaled them to stop.

No one ever knew what inspired Charlie to jump up and fire right then, but that's what he did. They couldn't even see the posse from where they were at that moment.

Bob watched in horror and surprise as three or four shots found their target and Charlie's body was lifted into the air. It fell harshly to the ground.

"Fire, boys!" Cole yelled.

Bob couldn't see those who were shooting at him but that didn't really matter. He fired into the brush hoping that, if anything, he might be able to do something to keep the posse from killing them too.

A volley of gunfire was returned.

Cole's gun was shot out of his hand but he was experienced at this. He picked up Charlie's and resumed firing.

Jim had just emptied his gun when a rifle ball hit him high in the jaw, taking out several of his teeth. He fell to the ground.

As Cole glanced back to his brother, he was hit by a ball himself. This one grazed his face and lodged over his right eye, knocking him over. He too fell to the ground, his eyes closed. He didn't stir.

The gunfire stopped. The air was still. Nobody moved.

Bob looked at his brothers laying there on the ground. Charlie was dead. If this didn't stop right now, the three of them would join him. There was only one thing to do.

"I surrender!" he called. "They're all down but me!"

"Hold your fire, men!" Glispin ordered.

Bob grabbed the white handkerchief that he had been using to buffer his wound from his shirt sleeve. He staggered up the bank holding it high in his left hand. He figured this was how surrender worked.

The posse trained their guns on him. Glispin didn't know the extent of the injuries of the other two or if they were even alive but at least one of them was going to be brought in. He'd done his job.

A shot rang out from behind and Glispin's head whipped around.

Buckshot hit Bob in the chest.

"I was surrendering," he said out loud, stunned. "Somebody shot me while I was surrendering."

He sank to his knees.

"Hold your fire!" Glispin again called to the men. "I'll shoot the next man who fires his weapon!"

Bob sat hard on the ground. So maybe they had taken him out too.

The seven men, led by Glispin, slowly advanced. When they reached Bob, one of them offered him a hand up and he stumbled to his feet.

Behind him, Jim slowly rose to a sitting position. His head was swimming and his eyes were slow to focus. As he blinked in the light he saw they were surrounded by strangers. So this was it, then.

Cole began to regain consciousness. He didn't know what was happening; only that men with guns were walking toward him. He started to get to his feet, swinging his fists at the men closest to him.

"Cole, it's over." Bob broke free to quickly put his uninjured arm around his brother. "Give it up or they'll hang us for sure."

CHAPTER 61

Bob watched them carry out the body of Charlie Pitts. Charlie had been nothing but a friend to the Younger family and it wasn't right that he should meet with such a tawdry end. It was funny how your life changed right in front of your eyes. One minute you were playing poker and sleeping comfortably on a bank in a faraway city with a friend and the next you were looking at that friend lying face down dead in the mud. Yet in the end, Charlie had wanted the unlawful adventure and somebody else's money same as the rest of them and, like the rest of them, his death was maybe his just reward.

Bob, Cole and Jim were helped up into a wagon so they could be transported to Medelia. Each one of them knew this was the beginning of what was bound to become the worst day of their lives.

At least the men herding them were civil. Cole recognized Vought as he helped Bob.

"Landlord," he nodded.

Bob was almost relieved it was all over. He was more than thankful that Cole and Jim were still alive. His quest for easy money, for more of the good thing he already had and hadn't been satisfied with, had almost ended them all.

For what that was worth. He suspected they would soon be dangling from the branch of a tree. At least they'd go out together. Dick had said, all those years ago, that there was nothing more important than family. He sure didn't see his last three brothers, held together in a shameful bond, exiting the world this way.

It was his fault, every last bit of it. Had he not been so stubborn and greedy and bought into what Jesse was offering, Cole would not have been sucked into this nightmare and Jim would not have felt obligated to come along. Jim's being there at all was only because he wanted to keep his little brother safe and now here they were, as unsafe as they could possibly be. It was his damn fault. He'd always thought of himself as a victim of circumstances and mean-spirited strangers. He'd been unable to control or change any of the things that had happened to him when he was a boy but now he was a man. He had made a very bad, very wrong decision. This time he wasn't a victim. He had no one to blame but himself.

He looked at Jim. Jim was bleeding so badly that he held his face over the side of the wagon so the blood wouldn't spill onto his lap. The posse hadn't even field-dressed his wound. Maybe they weren't as kindly as he wanted to believe.

A man with his wife and children passed them as they traveled down the road on rickety wheels. Cole remembered visiting the man's store in St. James with Charlie. He acknowledged the shopkeeper with a nod of his head. When the woman up front saw Jim's condition, she asked that they stop long enough for her to give him a handkerchief to hold over his jaw. If anyone deserved compassion, it was Jim.

Cole had more than a dozen wounds, some old, some fresh and bleeding. The exposure they each suffered was almost as uncomfortable as any damage the bullets and balls had caused. Their feet were just about pulp.

Where it had once played a major role in all of this, Bob's wounded arm seemed the least of their injuries. At least as far as Bob was concerned.

"Jim, I'm sorry," Bob whispered. He could barely look at his brother. "This is all my fault."

Jim said nothing. He just looked out to the road, trying to ignore the men alongside, in front and in back of the wagon. His silence was worse to Bob than anything he might have replied.

"Be quiet," Cole murmured. "This isn't the time."

"I'm sorry, Cole."

Cole just shook his head.

The streets were lined with people who cheered when the wagon came into view as they entered the little town of Medelia. The Northfield robbers had been captured and it was the men of their town who had accomplished what others could not. They were proud.

Bob was humiliated.

Not Cole. It had taken hundreds of men to take him down. He struggled to his feet and tipped his hat in salute to the crowd.

They were taken to Mr. Vought's hotel. Cole's visit this time was nothing like it had been the time before. They weren't guests anymore and wouldn't be treated as such. Mads Ouren greeted Cole on their way into the hotel.

"I saw that nice rifle of yours out in the field against us," Cole remarked. "But you didn't shoot it. Somebody else had it."

"I'm glad it wasn't me," Ouren answered.

That response somehow gave Bob a semblance of hope.

Cole and Jim were escorted to a room at one end of the second floor while Bob was placed at the opposite end, alone. Glispin placed guards on each one of them, even though they were in no condition to attempt an escape. As far as Glispen was concerned, these men had managed to somehow evade the largest manhunt in the history of the United States for almost two weeks and he wanted to be sure that their running was finally at an end. There would be no escape while they were in his custody.

Bob lay in bed looking up at the ceiling. It was fitting he was separated from his brothers. He didn't deserve to be in their presence. How was he going to ever look them in the eye again?

Not that it mattered. They were all going to be dead soon anyway. He wondered how this was going to play out. Would they be hanged? These didn't seem like the kind of people to do that, not without a trial, but men had been hung for less.

In the end, it would do no good to think about any of it. It was what it was. If there was a way he could take the punishment for Jim and Cole, he'd gladly do that. Why not just put to death the man who had craved money so much that he had risked the lives of his brothers. He'd never thought that money would mean that much to him but that's what his need to own, to *possess*, had come to. Cole and Jim would say that he wasn't responsible, that they each had made their own decision, but the reasons why they had chosen to make those decisions were because of him. Because of his need to own that land. How foolish and how selfish he had been. Owning it was only something *he* wanted. Maggie was perfectly content with things the way they were. She said their hard work made it theirs whether or not the deed was in their name.

If he should have learned one thing in his life, it was that Missoura land was never possessed. His father had the papers that said he owned all that land, yet in the end it hadn't mattered. It was all so much burnt cinders and ravaged fields that should have been rich with crop but the Yankees had seen to it that it all withered and died. Even when he had brought their little patch of dirt back to life, the grasshoppers had chosen to destroy it all.

How had he missed the lesson that what you had at any given moment should be enough to see you through? Maggie had accepted that. She was content to have a home with him and she didn't need more. What they had together was special and honest and good. It should have been enough for any man but it hadn't been enough for him. God knows he had more in that last year than he had ever hoped to have in his entire life, but even that hadn't been enough. What the hell had he been thinking? Why did he risk the best thing he had ever known?

He missed her. He missed Maggie so much. Now he would never see her again.

And without Maggie he didn't care if he lived or died.

446

There was commotion outside his door but he didn't pay any attention to it. They were all at the mercy of an entertained crowd of strangers. Like just so much of a carnival attraction. Come see the bank robbers. See how far they've fallen from the arrogant sons-of-bitches who walked into that Northfield bank and demanded someone else's money.

A man walked into his room.

"I'm Dr. Overholt," he introduced himself. "I'll take a look at those wounds."

"You can leave 'em." Bob had almost grown used to the pain of his arm. The chest wound might be worse than he thought but that wasn't necessarily a bad thing right now. He deserved it.

"No, son. I can't do that." Overholt looked at Bob's arm. "You've got a good infection going there but it's not as bad as it probably should be. I'll do what I can, but I don't expect it will ever be the same."

Nothing would ever be the same.

"The chest wound isn't too bad. Your lung may have been nicked a little. Are you having trouble breathing?"

He shook his head. Just take the lung if you want, he thought. I don't care right now if I breathe or not.

"Let's patch you up."

He shrugged. Let's let me die.

Afterward, Overholt helped him wash up and put on some fresh clothes that had been donated by someone in town. As he dressed he could hear the crowd outside the hotel. It sounded like it was growing in number. It reminded him of the noise the grasshoppers made when they ate his field.

A man named George Bradford was sitting in a chair by the door. He remained there throughout the night. Bob said nothing to him. He wanted to sleep. He wanted to sleep and never wake up.

He awoke in the morning to voices. He shook himself awake and looked around. For a minute there he thought he was home in his own bed and Maggie was coming toward him. No, that wasn't the case. Bradford was handing him a tray of food.

"I bet you're hungry."

"Thanks." He was starving. Someone had gone to the trouble to fix a breakfast of eggs, meat and biscuits. He devoured it.

Someone entered the room and Bob remembered the man who had been in charge out there in the slough.

"I'm Sheriff Glispin." He looked Bob over. "You're looking a bit better with those wounds dressed."

Bob nodded.

"My apologies for the foolish action of the man in the field who shot you after you surrendered. He's been dealt with."

"No need." It didn't make any difference. "How are the others?"

"Cole Younger is doing all right."

So Cole had told them who he was. They had agreed after the Hobbs Kerry incident that if it came to it, they could admit who they were but wouldn't say anything as to the identities of any of the others.

"The other man has a pretty dreadful wound. Doc Cooley had to cauterize it a couple of times. I think the bleeding has stopped but like I said, it's a dreadful wound." He paused. "You want to give me the name of that man?"

"No." That would be up to Jim.

"All right." Glispin pulled up a chair. "I need to take your statement, son."

"Five dollars, Sheriff." Bradford was holding Bob's billfold. "Just like Cole Younger. The other man had $150 in his."

"What's your name, son? Who are you?"

He told Glispin his name but that was as far as he was willing to go in identifying who robbed the bank beside himself.

"Were you in the bank, Bob?"

"Yes."

"Did you kill Cashier Heywood?"

"No, I did not."

"Who did?"

448

"Somebody else, but not us."

"Did you see your brother Cole kill Nicholas Gustavson?"

"I don't know who that is."

"The man who was shot down in the street."

"My brother didn't shoot down a man in the street. That man was caught in the crossfire."

"Did you see that happen?"

"No. But if my brother said that's what happened, I believe him."

"Who was with you in the bank, Bob?"

"That's all I have to say about it, Sheriff."

"All right, then." Glispin stood.

"Sheriff?" Bob wanted it said. "I appreciate the kind way we've been treated."

Glispin nodded.

"I expected we'd be lynched by now."

CHAPTER 62

Some reporters were allowed in to talk to the outlaws later that day. Their excitement wasn't any less than the people who read their newspapers. This was big news and each one of them was reaching for an exclusive angle.

Jim was told of a rumor that he was the notorious Cal Carter of Texas, whoever that was. With great effort he told them his name. Then he turned his face to the wall.

Cole, on the other hand, didn't mind the interest of the press. He recounted the stories told in Edward's "Terrible Quintet" and added some of his own.

"It was the circumstances of the War and all we lost that brought us to Minnesota," he explained. Even though that had long ceased to be Cole's reason for robbing banks and trains, the press ate it up with a spoon.

Bob had never been the subject of a newspaper article and he didn't like being one now. He knew the reporters were just doing their job though and he figured that any goodwill he showed them might help out his brothers down the line. He wasn't about to tell them the truth of why he was lying in a bed way up here in Minnesota but he'd answer a few questions.

"Why did you rob the bank, Bob?"

"We tried a desperate game," he shrugged. Why not tell them what they wanted to hear? "And lost.

Then he thought of John and how he would react to questions such as these. He'd enjoy talking to these people. He'd toy with them and make it interesting.

"But we're rough men, use to rough ways." He tried not to smile. John would have his two cents after all. "And we'll abide by the consequences."

"Who shot the cashier, Bob?"

"It wasn't us."

"Why was he shot?"

"It was an act of impulse. One that we all regret."

"Do you like baseball, Bob?"

"What?" What the hell did baseball have to do with any of this?

"Baseball. People here in Minnesota are quite taken with it."

"Oh, yeah, I saw the St. Paul Red Caps when they were leaving the Merchant Hotel." What was the point here?

"Have you seen the articles in the *Pioneer Press?*"

One of the reporters handed him a copy of the newspaper. He glanced at it. It didn't matter what they wrote, they weren't ever going to have the real story.

"I heard hundreds of papers have been printed. I'm glad somebody's making money off the botched affair," he grimaced. "I'm out five hundred dollars."

To say nothing of his happiness and the life he'd been building with Maggie.

He didn't want to talk anymore.

When Cole's time with the reporters was up, Sheriff Glispin returned. The newspapers seemed to be gathering more information than he and his deputies. Still, one burning question needed to be answered.

"Who were the other men, Cole? Police Chief McDonough out of St. Paul has been working with the Pinkertons. We know the two left dead in Northfield were Clell Miller and Bill Stiles."

Cole, for once, said nothing.

452

"He thinks the two who ran off were Jesse and Frank James. Did they leave you and your brothers there to die, Cole?"

Even Cole had finally had enough.

"I'll give you a statement in the morning."

When morning came, Cole handed Glispin a note. On it he had written *Be true to your friends, if the heavens fall.*

That was all he had to say on the matter.

They were to have been taken to the county seat of Faribault that day but Doctor Cooley didn't feel Jim's wound was under control and he didn't think Jim should make that journey just yet. They delayed the transfer but only until the next morning, when they were placed in the custody of Sheriff Ara Barton.

Charlie Pitt's body was loaded into the baggage car when they were taken onboard the St. Paul and Sioux City Railroad. Here they were on a train again. Bob thought the irony of it was just; trains, banks, they'd robbed both. Their sins were tied together with all of that now.

He looked around the car as he sat between his brothers.

"Do you think we can take it, Bob?" Cole whispered and smiled.

Bob didn't find his remark funny at all.

Hundreds of people had gathered the day before when they heard that the notorious outlaw Younger brothers were going to be stopping at the station in St. Paul. Those folks were disappointed that the transfer had been delayed. When the train bearing the Northfield robbers finally did arrive, there were less people, but even so there were still a helluva lot of them.

"I wonder what they'll do with ol' Charlie," Cole mused as he watched Charlie's body being taken off the train in a wooden box. "He was a fine and loyal friend."

So loyal, Bob thought, that he had given his life for something that meant almost nothing to him.

The people who had not been present in St. Paul for their arrival came in great number to Faribault. They didn't want to miss a thing, although they didn't know what it was they were supposed to be seeing. The crowd was too dense for many to even have a look at those miserable thieves. Yet some of them did get a glance and they would have something to talk about for their effort.

As they were taken to the Faribault jail, Cole once again bowed to them. Bob thought maybe Cole should have tried performing on the stage. Things might've turned out better for him.

Now they'd be put in their cages. They were assigned separate cells; Sheriff Barton didn't want to give them the opportunity to plan a break-out. They wouldn't be together this time. Cole didn't mind one way or the other. Jim was in so much pain it didn't much matter to him where he was.

Bob was taken to his cell; a small dreary box with two other men inside. As he tried to adjust his 6'2" frame, he felt like he couldn't breathe. The only way he could get comfortable was to put his feet on the grate.

"This one's a bit bold, isn't he?" he heard one of the jailors remark when he noticed Bob's position.

So be it if that's what they wanted to think. It was bad enough he had to share a cell with two strangers. They tried to talk to him about the robbery and his exciting life of crime, but he was sorry; he was tired and had nothing left to say.

This was interesting. Cole wasn't required to stay in his cell. He sat on a chair in front of it instead. Bob guessed they liked Cole's stories, undoubtedly made more colorful when he was not sitting in a metal box like a chicken in a crate.

That evening one of the deputies brought him a newspaper. "I thought you'd like to see this, Bob."

It was an article in the St. Paul *Pioneer Press*. What he read about himself made him sick to his stomach.

"He is a man fully six feet high, well built, sandy complexion, and has a pleasant face. We should pick him out of any crowd as a kind-hearted man whom we should expect would grant a favor readily. He conversed freely and answered most of the questions put to him without apparent reserve."

Wouldn't Maggie be proud.

At home in Missouri, Maggie was nothing other than worried sick. Bob should have been back days ago. He had said he might be gone a couple of weeks but she had a horrible intuition that something had gone very wrong.

"When's Bob coming back, Mama?" Jeremy asked every day. "Shouldn't he be back by now?"

"Maybe tomorrow, Jeremy," she'd reply. God, please bring him home to me tomorrow.

The next day Bob looked out the tiny window and saw a long line of people gathered. Well, it looked like they were going to hang them after all. So be it.

He wondered if he might be allowed to send Maggie a letter. There was so much to say and yet so little that made any sense. He thought about it. There was really nothing to say to her other than he was sorry. He would be humiliated to put that tired remark even in a letter. She deserved to just be left alone.

"When is it?" he asked the man who brought him a plate of food.

"When is what?"

"The hanging. I figure that's what all those people are out there for."

He passed on the plate. His stomach was in knots; he couldn't eat anything. So much for enjoying one last meal.

"There's no hanging. All those people are lining up to come through the jail and have a look at you fellows."

"Have a *look* at us?" Those people were going to file in one by one and stare at them?

"You're famous. They want to see you for themselves. Have something to tell their grandchildren."

Good God. No. As much as he deserved every bad thing that was happening to him, having people look in on them like they were carnival freaks was too much to ask.

"Could you get Sheriff Barton for me?"

"What can I do for you, Bob?" Sheriff Barton peered into the cell.

"Sheriff, I know my brother Cole is probably just fine with those people coming through but do Jim and I have to allow it?"

"I can see where it might make you uncomfortable, Bob."

"Please don't put Jim through that. If it's something I have to face, all right. I don't want to, but I understand that I've got no say in the matter. But please don't make Jim go through that."

Glispin considered. "I guess Cole can keep them entertained enough."

Entertained. This adventure had gone from an expensive lark to something he couldn't even comprehend.

Oh yeah, Cole was an entertainer. Over 400 people filed past him that day. He answered their questions, as pertained to him at least, and told them woeful stories of how his family was mistreated and how their decision to rob the Northfield Bank - his first and only crime – had been one of desperation.

Bob heard him holding court down the hall. It made him realize that Cole maybe would have gone to Northfield even if Bob hadn't put his back to the wall about it.

CHAPTER 63

James McDonough arrived in the company of C.B. Hunn, the superintendent of the United States Express Company. Hobbs Kerry had done a good job describing the individual gang members who had robbed the train at Otterville and McDonough wanted to confirm that these were indeed the Younger brothers. Didn't seem to Bob to be too much of a challenge there; he and Cole had already told them that.

Jim hadn't been in on the robbery Kerry had confessed to and some of those who held him still murmured about him maybe being Cal Carter. Anybody who was aware of the Youngers as robbery suspects at all should know that two of them were named Cole and Jim. It wasn't like they hadn't been mentioned in the newspapers before this. Evidently this Carter was a big deal. Not to Bob; he'd never heard of him. Ah well, they wanted to believe what they wanted to believe. So Jim shook his head in denial and Cole offered to bet them $500 that Jim was telling them the truth.

Jim had things on his mind other than being identified as another man. The bullet was still embedded in front of his left ear and he was in quite a bit of pain. He thought he would rather die than go through this circus. All he could think about was that he hadn't influenced John back in St. Clair and he hadn't influenced Bob either. He hadn't attempted to stop either one of them from making a deadly decision. He was nothing short of a failure as a brother.

The doctor continued to monitor Bob's arm. It had been set and sewn back in Madelia and was still in a sling. He had a bit of a wheeze now and then from the chest injury but he figured he was doing all right physically. What was strange was that women were sending in nuts and candy to be delivered to him. Women he didn't know or care to know. When the *Pioneer Press* dubbed him "The Knight of the Bush", he was done talking to the newspapers for good.

Bob listened as Sheriff Barton told Cole that Mayor Ames of Northfield wanted to speak with him. This was one conversation he wanted to hear.

"You're finally exactly where you belong, Younger." Ames stood in front of Cole sneering.

"That may be so Ames, but your father and Butler belong right here beside me." Cole wasn't about to take shit from anyone named Ames.

Ames glared at him. He'd read those interviews in the newspaper and he actually had come into this thinking Younger would be contrite. That obviously wasn't the case.

"Nicholas Gustavson is dead, but I guess you already know that."

"I only know what I'm told."

"You didn't need to be given that piece of information. You already know it to be true, since you're the one who killed him."

"I did not kill that man. You find one witness who says otherwise."

"There are dozens of witnesses."

"Then you already know the truth. That man was caught in the crossfire."

"The crossfire of a gun shot by you."

"You can say that if it makes you feel better than believing that someone in your town killed one of their own by their lack of ability with a gun. But you know it's not true."

"Why should I take your word? You're nothing but an inconsequential brigand and a damned Confederate bushwhacker."

"Go to hell, Ames. You come from a family of stinkin', thieving carpetbaggers."

"You, your brothers and your friends are nothing but common traitors and thugs. The Younger name stands for nothing but disgrace. You likely learned disrespect and insolence at your mother's teat."

"Don't you speak about my mother, you piece of shit!"

"From what I understand she was a turncoat too."

Cole seethed. He wanted to beat the crap out of this son-of-a-bitch. He wanted to hurt him. He wanted to hurt him bad. He knew he was being baited and he was helpless to meet Ames' accusations and epitaphs on a man-to-man basis. Ames was lucky for that.

"Get this man out of here, Sheriff Barton," Cole directed, never breaking eye contact with Ames. "He's stinkin' up the joint."

"I think you better leave, Mr. Ames," Barton agreed.

Ames left, smiling, as Cole watched with a look that could kill. He kicked the side of his cell. These bars were the only thing holding him back from tearing that bastard limb from limb.

"Let it go, Cole," Bob called. "We know the truth."

Barton stood in the front room of the jail. He'd had no choice but to let Ames have access to Younger but he didn't like the man. He had come in entitled, and although some would say he had a right to do that, Barton didn't feel that taunting a man with no recourse was warranted or honorable.

"Is that true that you have witnesses?" Barton asked Ames.

"The coroner's jury ruled that a stray bullet fired by an unknown party caused the idiot's death. Younger is facing a murder charge."

"You son-of-a-bitch! You have proof to the contrary!" Cole yelled. He may have robbed that bank but he hadn't killed one person during that crime.

He couldn't say the same for his friend Frank James, but that was information these people were never going to get.

The lights burned day and night and Bob had lost all sense of time. It wasn't until after they were transferred from the jail that Bob realized that he didn't even know why the other two men in the cell with him were even there. It didn't make any difference. They were criminals, same as him. He hadn't wasted time thinking about anything other than Maggie and his regret that he had let her down. Let her down, hell. When she found out what had happened to him she would be destroyed.

Although he paid little attention to what was going on outside his small cell, he couldn't help but notice that there had been an increase in the guard.

"Doin' all right in there, Bob?"

Sheriff Barton had treated them all fairly. Bob didn't know why he thought that but, without saying anything, Barton seemed to be of the opinion that none of them had been the one to kill Heywood.

"I guess I am, Sheriff. Is it my imagination or are there more men on guard?"

"You're not imagining it. We've received threats that your friends are going to try to break you out of here."

"I don't know what friends those would be." Unless they were guerilla friends of Cole's, which might well be the case. But they sure wouldn't announce it, if that was their plan.

"Well, whoever they are, we need to be cautious about it."

"I'm not going anywhere." That was the truth.

"You've got some visitors coming by today."

Maggie? Did she know? Had she come to him?

"There's a Detective Bligh from West Virginia. Wants to talk about a bank robbery there."

"I don't know anything about that," he sighed. And he didn't.

"And two other men who want to have a word. A Minnesota state legislator named Merriam. And a railroad man named Lincoln. "

Barton crossed to the door where two well-dressed men had just entered. He shook their hands and ushered them inside.

John Merriam stepped up to Cole's cell.

"Seems to me we might've met before," Cole greeted him. The man looked familiar but he couldn't place him.

"Well, I guess we have," Merriam smiled, tightly. "I'm John Merriam. I was a passenger on the train you robbed at Gad's Hill, Missouri back in '74. I believe it was your brother Bob who was there with you and several others."

"I don't know what you're talking about, Mr. Merriam," Cole smiled. "Bob and I were in St. Clair County when that robbery took place."

In his mind's eye, Cole saw Merriam standing there beside the train in his long-johns.

John Lincoln, Superintendent of the St. Paul and Sioux City Railroad was standing before Bob, asking about that same robbery.

"I think you were there with your brother, Cole."

"Cole and I were in Arkansas then," Bob denied. His first lie through all of this. It didn't feel good.

The next day, as Barton and his men feared that any of the hundreds of people milling about outside the jail could be some of the Youngers' allies come to liberate them, there was another request.

"Bob, we need to take photographs of you and your brothers," Barton told him.

"What for?"

"It's part of the process," Barton explained. "We were waiting until you boys healed a little bit, but it needs to be done."

He looked into Jim's cell. "Do you think that would be all right, Jim?"

Jim said nothing. He hadn't communicated with any of them in days. He just lay on his cot, staring at the ceiling.

On September 26th Justice John B. Quinn arrived at the jail in the company of Judge Samuel Lord. They were there with the official warrants charging the three men with robbery and murder. They would take them to trial, if that was the way they chose it to be.

"Can I speak with my brothers for a minute, Sheriff?" Cole asked, after they left. "I need to talk about our situation."

Barton considered the heavy guard and the fact that Bob's arm was still bound. Cole had never made any attempt to move beyond the jail into the outer rooms. He figured there was little risk of the three of them being out of their cells together.

"I'll lock the jail door and you can talk freely, but when I tell you to re-enter your cells, you will do so immediately. Are we in agreement?"

"Yes," Cole and Bob agreed. Jim said nothing.

When Barton left, Cole and Bob moved into Jim's cell. They knew Jim wouldn't come to them.

"An attorney from Medelia told me that he would represent us," Cole told his brothers. "I think he's a good man. He'll give us a good defense."

"What's there to defend?" Bob asked. "We've already said we did it."

"Robbed the bank, yeah, but we didn't kill that cashier or that man in the street. If you'd bother to read these warrants, they say we did."

Bob hadn't read his copy. He glanced at it now. He would take his penalty for robbing the bank, but he hadn't killed anyone and he wasn't going to let anyone say he did.

"If you think he's all right, then fine," he told Cole. "It's not like we have any choice."

That night brought foolishness and death. Some friends of a guard played a trick on him and the guard wound up dead.

Barton apologized, but he had no choice but to put Cole and Bob in irons.

"You've got to do what you think best, Sheriff."

Bob didn't blame him. That was what you did with people who had broken the law.

It was already October. At the end of the month Bob would turn twenty-three. Time was only slowing down for him. He wanted desperately to send a note to Maggie but if he did, she'd be drawn right into this mess. He had made enough bad judgments. That was one he wouldn't make. He knew there was a slim to none chance that whatever he wrote wouldn't be examined by whoever's hands it fell into. She'd probably read all about it all by now anyway. Maybe she was on her way back to Boston with Jeremy. He wouldn't blame her for getting as far away from Missoura and memories of him as she could.

The next visitors surprised them.

"Boys, your sister and brother-in-law are here."

"What?"

Had he heard correctly?

"Retta! Dick." Cole saw them first. He knew his family would stand by him. They knew what he did and they didn't judge him wrong for doing it. Although he had never asked them that directly. But they were his family so he could assume that, couldn't he?

Bob was at the end of the row of cells and couldn't see them at first. He heard them moving toward him, Retta and Dick. He'd never thought he'd see his little sister again.

"Oh, Cole!" Retta sobbed.

He could hear her in front of Jim's cell now. "Oh, Jim!"

"Bobby!" She now stood before him. "Oh, Bobby!"

"Rett." He tried to smile but couldn't.

"I prayed they were wrong." She grabbed his outstretched left hand and brought it to her tear-stained face. "I prayed the newspapers were exaggerating, like they always do."

"I'm sorry, Rett." He squeezed her hand.

There were so many people he needed to apologize to. His innocent little sister was one of the more important of them. He couldn't look at her sweet face without stabbing pains of regret and shame.

"Go to Jim, Rett," he whispered. "He needs you most."

"I don't know what to say, Bob." Dick Hall stepped up to the bars, shaking his head.

"There's nothing to say."

He heard Barton open the door of Jim's cell. Retta might be able to reach Jim when no one else could. Thank God for her.

She held Jim; tears streaming down both their faces.

"You're all hurt." She touched Jim's face tenderly.

Bob realized it had been so long since he had seen her. Retta was a grown woman now, not the little girl he had tried to protect so long ago. Bob had sent her some money a few months ago so that she could attend the Baptist School in St. Joseph. She wanted to be a teacher. He wanted for her whatever it was that she wanted, whatever made her happy. She had the same childhood as him. But unlike him, she was doing something good with her life.

Retta stepped in front of his cell and he pulled her close.

"Maggie?" he whispered in her ear. In his last letter to Retta, he had finally told her.

She shook her head. "I couldn't bear to see her until we were sure it was you."

He understood.

"Cole, are you all right?" Retta moved to her eldest brother.

"I'm all right, Rett." Cole took her hands and drew near to her face. "We're worried about Jim."

Jim had already returned to his cell to sit on the cot. What was he supposed to do? He wasn't able to even talk to them, at least not that they could fully understand.

After about twenty minutes Sheriff Barton returned.

"I'm sorry, that's all the time I can give you."

"That's all Sheriff?" Cole frowned. "We've talked to the damn reporters longer."

That was true. "All right, ten minutes more."

Retta wanted to know all about their injuries. There was little else to talk about. She never once asked if they were guilty of the robbery. Bob guessed she just didn't want to hear them say it.

Dick Hall, on the other hand, wasn't one to beat around the bush.

"Are these charges true?" he asked as he looked over the Warrants.

"We've admitted to the robbery, but we didn't kill those men, Dick." Cole tried not to look at Retta.

"We'll need to hire a good attorney then." Hall considered himself a take charge man and he would do whatever needed to be done.

Retta was looking at Bob with tears in her eyes.

"Why, Bobby?"

The question rocked him and her need to ask it broke his heart. He could only shake his head. Saying why was something he couldn't bring himself to tell her. Owning up to being someone who robbed a bank was all he could muster.

"I'm sorry, Rett."

"Would you be still about that, Bobby?" Cole was tired of hearing it. What was done was done. "We know you're sorry, now we need to move along to facing these charges. Quit your whining."

Bob turned away. He didn't really care what Cole said or thought anymore.

Retta grabbed his arm and drew him back.

"What should I do about Maggie, Bobby? What do you want me to tell her?"

Finally he was going to have the opportunity to tell Maggie what was in his heart.

"Tell her I wish to God I had listened to her. Tell her I love her with all my heart. Tell her I was foolish and selfish to think I needed to own that land when all I ever really needed was her. Tell her I'll go to the grave I deserve regretting that decision."

465

"Don't talk like that, Bobby!" Retta sobbed. "We'll get you an attorney and this will all be worked out!"

"I don't think it will be worked out, baby sister." He kissed the top of her head. "You were always the special one, Rett, the one who always thought that things *could* be worked out. I guess we both know that isn't usually the case."

He tilted her head so he could look at her again.

"I need you to tell Maggie one more thing."

She nodded. Whatever he needed, she would give him.

"Tell her I want her to forget about me now. I don't want her coming here; I don't want her getting involved in any of this. If she has any love left for me at all, I want her to stay down there on the farm with Jeremy and remember what we once had. But that's the end of it now."

Retta and Dick returned the following day but Bob didn't feel much like talking anymore. He listened while Retta told them again about how concerned the family was. She and Dick would go back to Missoura now, but they would return the following month to help with the defense.

Jim's wound slowly started to heal. At least as much as it ever would. He began talking if someone addressed him, but he still spent most of his time staring at the ceiling. To his way of thinking, any efforts to get them out of this would be futile. Cole just needed to accept that. He was concerned about Bob. If they weren't sentenced to death, they would be spending a long time in prison and Bob was young to be throwing those years away. But Jim's concern didn't make the problem go away. So he said nothing about his feelings to either of them.

Cole suggested that Tom Rutledge should serve as their attorney. Jim and Bob agreed; Rutledge seemed as good as any. He brought in two local men named Buckham and Bachelder to assist him.

"I need a strong argument if I'm going to have any chance here," Rutledge told them, looking at Bob. "Something that might weigh things in your favor. We need to show them you're contrite and cooperating."

He paused.

"Who killed the cashier, Bob?

"I'm sorry, Tom. I can't give you that. Please don't ask me again." Frank James may have been very wrong in taking that action, but Bob wasn't going to implicate Jesse and Frank. They'd all made a pact and he was going to honor it. The attorneys would just have to take his word for it that it wasn't him who killed Mr. Heywood.

A week later, they sat once again with Retta and Dick Hall. They had returned after raising money from each of their sisters to pay for Rutledge's expenses.

"Minnesota law has a clause that might benefit you." Rutledge had initially been drawn to the notoriety of the case; it was an opportunity to raise his professional profile in the community. The three brothers had already said they were guilty of the robbery. He wasn't surprised to see that they had also been charged in connection with the murder of Heywood, but he didn't understand why the murder of Gustavson was part of the indictments. The coroner's jury had found any potential evidence of who had caused Gustavson's death to be inconclusive. The man probably was just caught in the crossfire.

As to Cashier Heywood, the only one here who might be guilty of his murder was Bob Younger. There were no witnesses and Cole and Jim were out in the street, never having entered the bank at all. Rutledge didn't know Bob Younger but he didn't think the young man was guilty of cold-blooded murder. His involvement in Heywood's death would be for someone else to prove.

"If you plead not guilty, your case will go to a jury trial," he was now explaining. "But if you're found guilty, you will hang."

Retta gasped. "You can't let that happen, Mr. Rutledge!"

Rutledge held up a hand. "There's where the clause might benefit you. If you plead guilty, you cannot be sentenced to death. You will be sentenced to life in prison and although I can't guarantee it, you will probably only serve ten years or so before they release you on parole."

"I'm not pleading guilty to murder, Rutledge." Cole shook his head. He'd be damned if that was going to happen. Those Yankees had set him up when they knew damn well that he had not killed that man on the street.

"Tom?" Bob was the only one who could do this. "If I plead to Heywood's murder will they drop it against Jim and Cole?"

"I've already asked Judge Lord and the answer to that is no."

Rutledge brought out the indictments.

"I know you've read these, but let's review the charges. All three of you are charged with robbery of the First National Bank of Minnesota at Northfield. You've already said that you are guilty of that. You're charged as *accessories* to the murder of J. L. Heywood. Even if you say that it was you who killed Mr. Heywood, Bob, it doesn't change the charges for Cole and Jim."

Rutledge leaned forward in his chair.

"There's also a charge of attacking A.E. Bunker with intent to do bodily harm. Even though you've told me that was you, Bob, it doesn't really affect the other, more serious charges."

"But Jim and Cole were nowhere near Heywood *or* Bunker." There had to be away out of this, at least for Jim.

"Doesn't matter. At least not legally. Then there's the final charge. Coleman Younger as principal and Robert and James Younger as accessories for the murder of Nicholas Gustavson while participating in the robbery of the bank."

"But the coroner's jury ruled he was likely caught in the cross-fire. Which I know for a damn fact he was!" Cole could not understand their persistence with this charge.

"Doesn't matter," Rutledge sighed. "They get around that inconvenience by adding 'while participating in the robbery of the bank'. That's all they need."

Bob sighed. They had them nailed.

CHAPTER 64
November 18, 1877

The courthouse and the area around it was filled with so many people that walking through the crowd was nearly impossible. Especially when they were shackled one to the other like they were. Many in the crowd jeered and Bob felt they had that right but he wouldn't let them see how he felt about it. His actions might be one thing but his emotions weren't theirs to judge.

Cole tried to charm them, as he always did. He didn't smile; that wouldn't have been appropriate. So he remained solemn and nodded occasionally.

"We're as popular as stage actors," he murmured under his breath. "Or whores. I don't know which."

Neither Bob nor Jim found anything funny about any of this, regardless of Cole's attempt to put a small amount of humor into the dismal proceedings.

Although it was November, the air inside the courtroom was stifling. There were too many people. It seemed everyone wanted to be a part of the historic event that would finally put an end to the infamous James-Younger Gang.

Bob saw his father's face in each male he happened to look upon. It made him shutter. He wondered how, in the end, his father and Dick would have judged them. He'd been thinking about that for a long time and he guessed he knew the answer. No, he *knew* the answer.

The Rice County District Court was called to order. Those who had been fortunate to have obtained a seat were ordered by Sheriff Barton to take it. Despite the notoriety of this case, the rules of the court would be followed as usual.

The prosecuting attorney, a man named Baxter, called for the indictments to be read as each of them was charged with their alleged crimes. Tom Rutledge informed the court that each man was in the courthouse and ready to participate. Baxter suggested that the shackles and wrist irons be removed for the duration of the hearing. He didn't want anyone to think that these prisoners were being treated any differently from any of the others who had appeared before the court. One criminal, no matter his name, was the same as the next.

Jim seemed comforted by the fact that Retta was in the courtroom, again in the company of Dick Hall. Bob was thankful that Jim found at least some solace in that. Bob couldn't look at Retta though. His mind was overwhelmed with the shame of standing before this judge, guilty of selfish greed.

One by one they were called to deliver their plea.

"Guilty," said Cole, shaking his head. Did that mean he couldn't believe that he had done something so wrong or that he couldn't believe that he had been caught?

"Guilty." Jim's voice could barely be heard.

Bob looked at Judge Lord and admitted his guilt, for all to hear, for all to know.

Each man was asked if he had anything to say in regard to the charges or their impending sentencing.

"No," they replied as a group. Let the chips fall.

"I will deliver my sentence then." Judge Lord looked at the three men before him. "You Coleman Younger, you James

Younger, you Robert Younger, will be confined to the state prison to the end of your natural lives."

That was what Cole expected to hear but from all Rutledge told them, they'd only be behind bars for ten years. That would take a large bite out of his life but he would get by. He looked at Jim and wondered if he would, if he could.

Jim turned to Retta and put his arm around her. He was only relieved that this chapter had come to its conclusion.

Bob had nothing to say. It was over. He was a guilty man, convicted of crimes that may have been severe in the eyes of the law but were far more agonizing to him as crimes against the woman he loved.

He felt a hand on his arm and turned, expecting to finally look on the tear-filled face of his sister.

Only it wasn't Retta.

It was Maggie.

"Bobby," she whispered for only him to hear. "I love you."

He couldn't respond. He felt tears well in his eyes. He could only shut them tight and turn away.

Somehow, she still loved him. God in Heaven, he'd thrown their life away and she still loved him.

Sheriff Barton walked them back to their cells. Bob wasn't aware of anything he thought or did from the moment he saw Maggie. He moved in a daze.

"They'll be transporting you boys to the state prison the day after tomorrow," Sheriff Barton told them.

"Where is that?" Cole wondered.

"Stillwater. A pretty little town northeast on the St. Croix River."

"Something tells me we won't be seeing much of the town, or anything that's pretty," Cole replied. That said, he'd try to keep positive. This was a hell of a deal and being negative about any of it wasn't going to serve any of them well.

"I'm sure you boys want to see your family." Barton had been impressed with the compassion and intelligence of the Younger relatives. He was used to dealing with the lowlifes whose families had long ago abandoned them to their ill-disciplined ways and their lives of crime. "Your brother-in-law and your sisters are here."

"Our sisters?" Cole had seen Retta in the courtroom but he hadn't noticed the presence of any of his other sisters.

"Retta's here with Josie, I believe she said her name was."

What the hell? Josie was gone, murdered along with Jarrett by the cowards who thought it was justice to set fire to a man's home in the middle of the night with his family inside. Cole looked at Bob. Who was posing as their sister Josie?

When he saw the look on Bob's face, he knew. It had to be Maggie.

"I'll give you some privacy. It'll be a long time before you'll see them again."

Nobody knew that better than Bob. That Maggie had come all this way to be by his side overwhelmed him. Yet he had asked her to move on in her life. He trusted that Retta had given her that message. What more was there to say to her?

Barton left the room and stepped aside to let the others in. He closed and locked the door after they were inside.

"Jim," Retta threw her arms around her brother.

"It'll be all right, Retta." Jim returned her embrace. There was nothing he could say but that. They knew where they were going and there was nothing to do except what they were told.

Bob stared at the floor. He felt Maggie's presence but he still couldn't look at her. He hurt so badly and there was nothing that could be said or done that would overcome his humiliation.

"Bobby, look at me."

She knew he didn't want her there, but that was just his shame and regret speaking. She needed him to know that she forgave him. She needed to have him know she still loved him, that she would wait for him as long as it took for him to return home.

He couldn't raise his eyes. He sensed his brothers, Retta and Dick move away to give them privacy. He didn't need privacy. What he needed was a large, deep hole so he could fall into it and be swallowed up. Maybe that was what prison would be like. That was fine with him.

"Everyone makes mistakes." She put her arms around him. He would expect nothing less from her but for her to be direct and speak the truth as she saw it. She would give him that, but she would also let him know what was in her heart.

"You made a big one." She touched his face. She couldn't believe she was touching his face. "But it doesn't change the fact that I love you with my heart, my soul. I love you so very much, Bobby."

As much as he ached to put his arms around her, to hold her to him, he couldn't do that. He needed to somehow muster the strength to convince her to let him just go to prison and pay for that big mistake and let her get on with her own life.

"I know how hard this is for you…" she began.

"No, Maggie. You don't."

He finally looked at her. He wanted to do nothing but look at her but he couldn't give in to his emotions. This was going to kill him but he had to make his play. He needed to be rough, needed to be direct and truthful. That was the only way he could think to convince her to continue on without him.

"Oh, Bobby. It happened and yes, it was wrong. But you did it out of love. It was what you felt you had to do. So we could go to California, so we could start over. It's what you needed to do for me…for Jeremy…"

"If I'd been thinking of you and Jeremy instead of myself, I would have just taken you to California and not delayed it by coming up here and robbing a bank. I'd be there right now instead of looking at ten years trapped in the cage of some Yankee prison."

"You have to just accept what happened, do what needs to be done and then put it behind you…"

"Put it behind me? How can I do that, Maggie? I'm going to be reminded of how selfish and bull-headed I was every day for the rest of my life. How I ruined the lives of so many people. People I said I cared about. People I said I loved. My brothers. You Maggie, you and Jeremy. The ones I loved most in this world and the ones I said I'd protect and take care of. I can never put that behind me. I don't deserve the right to put that behind me."

"Then you'll just serve your sentence. It isn't so bad that you can't come out of prison with your debt paid."

"My debt paid to who? Society? I don't give a goddamn about society. I only care about the people whose lives I've destroyed. I can never pay my debt to any of you."

"I know how badly you're hurting Bobby but…"

"I don't want your pity, dammit, I want your anger. I ruined your life, Maggie! I let you think you were safe with me, that you could build a future with me. And I threw everything we had away! None of it was true."

"Bobby…"

"What about Jeremy? How did you explain to that boy how the man he looked up to, the one who stood in for the father he'd lost, the *honorable* father he'd lost, had robbed a bank and was responsible for the death of five people? What did you tell him? He was just doing it for us, Jeremy? He was just doing it so we could take us a nice little trip out to California?" He shook his head. "How is that boy ever going to trust anybody again? How is he ever going to give his heart again? He'll probably go back to not talking. Yet another little gift I've given you both."

"That's not the way it is, Bobby. I've told him what happened and why. I told him that even people we love and respect sometimes make big mistakes and face serious consequences. But I also told him that when we love someone as deeply as we love you, we just have to help them through it."

"I don't deserve your help and I don't want it. Leave it be, Maggie. Say goodbye to me right here and now. Find yourself a decent man who knows enough not to hurt you. Who knows the value of love and knows the value of a family. I'm not that man, Maggie. You deserve better."

Maggie's eyes searched his face. Everything he was saying may be valid, but mainly in his own mind. He was going to be confined to prison for a long time, but a life in a cell wouldn't punish him any more than his own self-hatred. She didn't know how to reach him.

"Maybe I do deserve better Bobby, but what I deserve and what I want is something only I can decide. I told you long ago that no one knows better what is best for me than I do."

When he turned from her it was more than she could bear.

"You go ahead!" Her eyes blazed with anger as tears flowed down her cheeks. "You go ahead and walk away from me, from our family. Sit in a damn cell and feel sorry for yourself, if that makes you feel better. Think of nothing except what you did, how it affected you. Don't think of how I waited every day to hear news of what had happened to you. How I didn't care if you had been caught as long as you hadn't been killed. Because I couldn't go on living if you were not in this world anymore, Bobby."

She took his hand and brought it to her lips. "Maybe you'll be in a cell, in a place where they don't love or care about you, but my heart will always be with you. Wherever you are. I love you and you are a part of me. You will always be a part of me. Regardless of what you've done or how you feel. There's nothing you can say, nothing you can do to change that. I will love you until the day I die."

The others had been trying to let them have their time, but it was impossible to ignore what was taking place. They tried to talk over it but the pain in Bob and Maggie's voices cut through to their own hearts.

"Don't be a fool, Bobby," Cole whispered under his breath. "Don't be a goddamned fool."

"Don't cry, Maggie. I can't stand to see you cry." He wiped her tears away with his thumb. He put his arms around her and drew her tightly to him. "There's nothing we can say that will change the way it is."

The door opened and Sheriff Barton entered the room.

"There're some men here from the state prison to talk to you boys, go over things. That's all the time I can give your family today."

The others shielded Maggie and Bob from Barton's direct view. She was supposed to be his sister. Even if it was his long-dead sister.

Maggie looked up into Bob's eyes.

"I love you, Bobby. *I love you.*"

He couldn't bring himself to say it. Those words would only damage her further.

"Go home to Jeremy, Maggie. Have a better life."

He leaned down and softly kissed her lips. That kiss would have to hold him forever.

"Good-bye, Maggie."

CHAPTER 65

They boarded the train bound for St. Paul and Bob couldn't get Maggie's face out of his mind. Not when he had watched every emotion pass over it: concern, frustration, love and heart-break. He knew it would be the most difficult thing he would ever do but he would try not to think of her. He didn't know how he was going to do that but he knew he had to if he was going to get through this at all. He had asked the same of her. There was no other way. That was all there was to it.

"Here we are in St. Paul again, boys." Cole looked around as they transferred to a wagon for the trip to Stillwater. "Guess we shouldn't have left."

"I didn't even know St. Paul existed a year ago." Bob mused.

"Wish to hell you never heard of it."

If only they could turn back time.

They saw small groups of people gathered alongside the road as they traveled.

"You're getting what you deserve, you damn Rebel cusses!" someone yelled. Others whooped their approval of that remark.

"God speed, boys! Better luck!" a man called out. They clapped for him too.

"Ya see?" Cole nodded. "It's a complicated issue."

477

Whatever you want to think, Cole. To Bob, the comments only served to underline that they were now, and for God knew how many years, in a place foreign to them which was certainly not Missoura.

When they at last reached Stillwater, they saw the high and imposing walls of the prison. The complex backed to the banks of the St. Croix but a clear view of that river was maybe something they'd never see.

They were led inside where they would assume their new identities.

"You'll be known here as Convict #901," the clerk told Bob.

This would now be his world, his community, his reality. Convict #901.

"There's only one way we're going to get through this, boys," Cole had instructed earlier. "When those iron doors shut behind us, we submit to the prison discipline with the same unquestioning obedience that I exacted during my military service. That will reflect on us best when it comes time to be paroled."

The thought of Cole Younger being obedient to anyone other than Cole Younger was as unimaginable to Bob as it was to Cole himself.

"We're going to search you boys now," they were informed.

"If we were armed in any way, we wouldn't be standing here..." Cole muttered.

Bob shook his head. More posturing from Cole, even in the face of his defeat. He had a fleeting thought himself about what would happen if they tried to escape. But all of that was just a waste of thought and it didn't matter.

They gave up their belongings, which at this point consisted of little more than somebody else's clothes. Cole's watch and ring had been given to Frank and Jesse back when they went their separate ways, so none of them really had any personal affects to surrender.

They were allowed baths, which were welcomed, but when they stepped out they had to put on the black-and-white striped uniform of a prisoner. To top that off they had their heads shaved nearly bald. How fashionable, Bob thought.

They were read the rules by which they would abide for the duration of their incarceration. The list seemed endless but to the point: they would walk with their eyes ahead, there would be no talking unless spoken to, particularly during meals, nor would they have any interaction with other prisoners. They would do only that which they were instructed to do.

That was fine with Bob. He didn't want to follow his own instruction anymore.

For some kind of experiment in criminal identification from France called the Bertillon System, measurements were taken of their head, ears, trunk, arms, fingers and feet. Bob didn't know what the hell that was all about. They were fingerprinted and given physicals. Bob couldn't remember ever being so thoroughly inspected, even by his mother. Or so thoroughly humiliated.

As Bob finally stepped into his tiny cell, he was overwhelmed at the thought that this would be his home for a very long time. He looked around. So this was it then. It was damp. He shivered. The only furniture was a bed. A water jar and a slop jar had been provided for his "convenience". On the bed was linen, a couple of towels and cups, a spoon, some soap, a comb, a mirror and a Bible. What more did anyone need? His own greediness raised up to slap him in the face yet again.

He made his bed, but sleep didn't come that first night. The walls were so close. He felt like he was suffocating.

They met with Warden Reed to receive their work assignments the next morning. Reed wanted to keep a close eye on them and thought it best to place them at one basement station, where they would make tubs and buckets. He didn't know if their friends were making plans to break them out but they might as well realize right now that wasn't going to be allowed to happen.

Those first few days they tried to adapt to their daily routine: up at the crack of dawn, breakfast, work, supper, bed.

It drove Cole crazy. He couldn't talk to anybody.

Jim couldn't care less about that. He was resigned to the changes, to the way his life was now going to be led.

Bob went through the motions. He ate, he worked, he read the Bible. If that was what his life had been reduced to, well, so be it.

Here he was and this was what it would be.

The first few months passed fairly quickly. Bob thought it actually felt good to have time to himself after all those weeks of being at the beck and call of strangers who wanted their attention, their words, their deepest thoughts. Nobody at Stillwater wanted anything from them other than submission and a day's work. He figured he knew how to deliver on that, although his arm hadn't healed properly and that was a problem. Try as he might, he couldn't straighten it. Sometimes it was painful and interfered with his work but he felt fortunate to have the arm at all. Look at Jim. His jaw was ruined. He had to soften all his food. He couldn't even chew; he had to eat pap, same as a baby.

Cole, even though he had the most injuries of them all, seemed to be doing just fine. Oh, he had the occasional headache; probably caused by that last bullet at Hanska Slough. He'd live with it; it could certainly be worse. The hell of it for him, the thing that drove him up the wall, was that he had to keep his stories, his explanations, his rationalizations, *his history*, to himself.

One day during the fourth month they were called to the Warden's office.

"I'm impressed with you men," Warden Reed told them. "You seem to have adjusted well and you've not given us any trouble."

Bob found that amusing. What had they expected, that they would instigate a rebellion? Get all the other prisoners to rise up? Against what? He kept his silly thoughts to himself.

"I'm going to elevate you to second grade," the Warden was saying. "We'll see how you do."

"What does second grade mean for us?" Cole couldn't help himself. He wanted to engage in at least some kind of conversation.

"Well, let's see. You can turn in those uniforms you're wearing for checkered ones. And grow your hair to a length that can be combed. How does that suit you?" Reed smiled.

"I can't wait," Cole replied. If that was Reed's idea of a joke, it wasn't amusing. His hair was already getting pretty thin.

"You'll have privileges. You can eat in the dining room with other second grades. You can write two letters a month and see visitors once a month, which includes visits with one another."

Jim was content by himself but Cole missed the company of his brothers. Bob thought it might be nice to spend some time with them both, although he didn't know what they would talk about. Writing letters would be welcomed by Cole and Jim, as they both longed for contact with those at home. Bob didn't think telling Retta about the gloomy condition up here at Stillwater was worth the paper to write it on. He wasn't going to write Maggie either, so that benefit didn't matter to him.

"You're being assigned new jobs. You'll move to the thresher factory, Cole. You'll be making sieves now. Jim, you're making belts. Bob, I've talked to the doctor and he thinks it would be good for your arm if you're put to work painting."

Painting would be good for his arm? He could barely lift it.

"Oh, and for your entertainment, you will be allowed to take advantage of our library."

Jim could cry.

So they got on with their sentence as Second Grades, which wasn't all bad. Books were as important to Jim almost as much as the air he breathed. He spent most of his time away from his job devouring literature and books on theology and metaphysics. Cole figured he'd never really had time for books before this and he turned his attention to reading historical biography and some of the classics. He liked a good story, always had. Bob had never been a reader of books, but he found periodicals interesting. He leafed through books on medicine, just because it reminded him of Maggie.

He'd been foolish, once again, to think that he could ever get her out of his mind.

Bob didn't think it was wise to talk to Cole about it, but when he read that a train robbery had taken place at Blue Cut, Missoura, he knew Jesse was back at it. It didn't surprise him that Jesse hadn't learned a lesson at their expense. Jesse would always think he was a cut above and that bad things only happened to other people.

Shortly after Bob read the report of the robbery, they were called to the Warden's office. Bob wasn't surprised.

"I've been asked to talk to you about Jesse James." Reed watched their reactions. None of them seemed even remotely interested in the topic.

"I don't know anything about Jesse James, Warden." Cole offered. "I knew him during the War, but I haven't seen him in many years. Jim and Bob don't even know him."

"I didn't expect you to tell me he was one of your friends, Cole. This is something else. There's a story in Missouri that Jesse James was killed by a former Confederate guerilla named George Shepard."

Hogwash.

"Do you believe that could be true, Cole?"

"I believe it's true if George Shepard says it's true."

So much for that.

As the time passed, even though she didn't hear from him, Maggie wrote letters to Bob without signing her name. She knew he didn't want her identity to be known, although she didn't agree with that. She told him that she and Jeremy continued living on the farm and that they loved him still.

Reading the letters only made him long for her even more.

"Please, Bobby, write to her," Retta wrote. "You're breaking her heart."

As far as he was concerned, how could you break a heart that had already been broken?

One day he received an envelope with unfamiliar handwriting. He opened it to find a letter from Jeremy. It'd been almost a year and Jeremy was a young man now. Bob hadn't been there to see that happen.

"Dear Bob," he wrote. *"Mother told me what happened and why you are where you are. I'm sorry about that. I wish you hadn't gone to Minnesota. We would've been happy in California, I think. Mother is so unhappy now and I blame you for that. Still, I know you did what you thought you had to do and I want you to know I've forgiven you. But I don't know how you can just shut us out of your life. People don't do that to people they love. Maybe you don't love us anymore, I don't know. You taught me to be a man and take responsibility. It seems to me you're not doing that in regard to Mother. I wish you would. Jeremy."*

He felt like a dagger was embedded in his heart. Leave it to the boy to tell it honestly and direct. But even that letter, that plea, couldn't move him to open that door. He had nothing more to say.

CHAPTER 66

The days passed and turned into months, then years – three years, four. The time moved slowly but at least it moved. There was little to think about and nothing to look forward to. In the end, it was just time; numbers on a clock.

Maggie continued to write letters. She told Bob of planting new crop and harvesting when it was time to do so. She followed their initial plan to the letter and he was so proud of her efforts. But he didn't tell her so. He didn't tell her anything at all. He had kept to his oath not to interact with her. It pained him to do it, God knew, but he still believed it to be the best thing he could do for her.

Every once in a while Cole would ask.

"Have you written to Maggie yet?"

"No I haven't, Cole. Don't ask me about that."

"I know you're bull-headed, brother, but I never knew you to be cruel like this."

"Mind your own business."

In his mind, it would be cruel to saddle her with a long-distance convict lover who hadn't had the decency to marry her in the first place because all along he knew their relationship was wrong. No, this was the right thing to do. If she wanted to write to him and tell him she loved him still, tell him about her activities, well, he couldn't stop her. But that would be as far as it would go.

There were reports of robbery. A stage at Mammoth Cave, Kentucky; a paymaster at Muscle Shoals, Alabama. Bob wondered if Jesse and Frank were involved or if they had finally learned their lesson.

Apparently they felt there was no lesson to be learned. In July of '81, five men boarded the passenger and express cars of the Chicago, Rock Island and Pacific Railroad at Winston, Missouri. Bob read that a conductor named Westfall had been shot in cold blood. Jesse always said that if he ever found the man who carried that train of Pinkertons that delivered death to the doorstep of his little brother, well, that would be all she wrote. Looks like Jesse might have finally had his vengeance.

Retta arranged a personal audience for their Uncle Littleton with Governor Pillsbury of Minnesota. Littleton had come armed with affidavits from several influential Missourians stating that they thought the boys had served long enough, but the governor didn't feel there was anything he could do for them at this point. Bob was disappointed but really not surprised. They would be here for the long haul; their attorney had told them it would likely be ten years and that's probably what it would be.

Bob *was* surprised to read that on March 31, 1882 a man named Dick Liddil, who apparently was part of Jesse's new group of thieves, turned State's Witness against the men who had participated in the robbery at Winston. Bob brought it to Cole's attention by suggesting that he read the newspaper that particular day.

They had barely digested this latest development in the life and times of Jesse James when something even more startling was reported. The newspapers were saying that Jesse had been murdered by one of his own.

"Do you think it's true?" Bob asked Cole during their monthly visit.

"From what I've read, they seem to have a lot of information that wouldn't be otherwise available."

Cole wasn't really surprised. He figured Dingus would one day push his luck too far. As to his death at the hands of one of those who rode with him? That wasn't a surprise either. Cole himself had wanted to put one in the back of his head on occasion.

"Do you know those men, the Ford Brothers?"

"Nope. Probably just a pair of low-lifes wanting to be noticed."

"It's hard to believe that Jesse wouldn't be more cautious than that."

"Jesse's been looking to find himself in a bind since the day he was born."

"Still, by one of his own men. I wouldn't have expected that."

"What a twisted web we weave," said Cole, one of the spiders.

Jim looked at Cole. Bob likely wouldn't approve of him saying what was going through his mind. That didn't matter.

"Good riddance. At least now we're free of him."

When Bob thought about it later, he felt some sorrow. He thought of Jesse as a friend. He wondered if Jesse had thought the same of him. Maybe Cole had been right that Jesse just used him. He guessed he'd never really know. Jesse had really only flitted in and out of his life those last years. He'd had greater interests than being friends with Bob. He wondered if Jesse had any real friends. With that big target on his back, he pretty much stuck to his family and those that rode with him. And there it was. To be killed by a man you trusted, that was cold.

Jesse was something, though. He remembered the way Jesse told a story, the way he laughed out loud when something amused him. The way he loved seeing his name in the newspaper. Hell, they even wrote dime novels about him. He remembered Jesse's indignation against those he thought had wronged him and how the man justified every action he took, right or wrong. He could lie, he could steal, he could take a man's life with no more than a casual thought. In the eyes of most, he was a bad man and that was an accurate description. Bob guessed he had been like just so many that had fallen under his spell in a lot of ways. Well, yeah, Jesse was unlike anyone he had ever known.

Of course they had to once again deny knowing Jesse, let alone why they thought he might have been murdered. Why did it matter? The James Gang, the James-Younger Gang or whatever it was the newspapers cared to call it, was now a footnote to history. It was over.

The bigger news at the prison was the fire that broke out in the wood burning shop. Apparently someone had set it on purpose. Most of the prisoners found it entertaining. At least they did until two weeks later when various spots around the prison simultaneously caught fire while they were all in their cells. The arsonist wasn't such a comedian anymore.

Now over 350 prisoners were waiting to be chained together to stand in the subzero weather, waiting for the National Guard to come in to oversee their removal and relocation from the burning buildings. Everyone had been fairly calm but the excitement level was on the rise. No one wanted to be trapped, trampled or have burning pieces of the buildings fall on them. Now people were yelling and pushing.

Cole, Jim and Bob stood waiting their turn to exit. This was a hell of a note. Everywhere they looked they saw flames.

"They're going to leave us here to freeze or burn!" someone yelled.

More pushing and yelling.

"Calm down!" Cole ordered. He was ignored.

Head Guard George Dodd ran by. It seemed everyone who wasn't shackled was running. Away from the prisoners, not toward them.

Cole grabbed the guard's sleeve.

"Anything we can do to help, Mr. Dodd?" He figured it didn't hurt to ask.

"What is he doing?" Bob whispered to Jim. "They probably think all this has something to do with us."

"Well, it doesn't," Jim shrugged.

Dodd stopped to consider Younger's offer. And he made a decision, a decision that would be shrouded in controversy for a long time to come. He walked back to Cole.

"Yes, there is something you can do," Dodd consented. "My wife is the matron of the female prisoners. Those women need to be escorted somewhere they will be safe. I'll ask you three men to do that. I've got my hands more than full."

Damn. Bob hadn't expected that response.

"Take them to the Deputy Warden's house outside the compound, just around the corner. Don't let any of the prisoners anywhere near them. I'll let the guard on the gate know you're helping me." He grabbed one of the guards who were running down the hall with weapons.

Bob never expected Dodd to actually enlist the help of convicts, let alone the three of them. Cole would later say that he figured it was probably their reputation as model prisoners that had persuaded Dodd to ask for their help at a time when he really needed it. Bob figured he probably also reckoned that none of the prisoners would mess with the Younger Brothers. He'd be right about that.

"I'm trusting you men." Dodd handed Cole a revolver, Jim an axe and Bob an iron bar. "Don't let me down."

The fact that they did as they were assigned, and returned the weapons when it was all over, was a great relief to those in charge when they later heard the story. Of course this was after those in charge were able to remove their jaws from the ground at the audacity of their Head Guard.

"I can't believe he gave us weapons." Bob shook his head. They were sitting in their temporary quarters at the Washington County Jail.

489

"The important thing is that we gave them back." Cole didn't understand what motivated Dodd, but he was thrilled for the opportunity. "Our actions will serve us damn well at the end of ten years when our parole comes up."

That remained to be seen, but the immediate affect was somewhat beneficial. Cole was assigned to work in the library and Jim was put in charge of the mail. Jim and Cole liked their new assignments, even if it did seem like their jobs had been reversed, seeing how Jim loved books and Cole loved to visit.

Bob's new job was to bind medical books. He found that far from interesting and wondered if he'd ever be assigned something that might appeal to *him*. Aw, what the hell. He wasn't here for the fun of it.

That October Frank James surrendered to Missouri Governor Thomas Crittenden. Now Frank was being treated as some sort of luminary. They had even outfitted a jail cell for him, with simple furniture, a rug and such.

"How'd he pull that off?" Bob wondered.

"Edwards," smiled Cole, referring to Jesse's old pal the newspaper editor. "Edwards orchestrated the whole thing. Frank's trial will be the grand spectacle Dingus didn't live to see...or participate in."

By the time it all played out, Frank James would pay no debt to society, serve no prison time. Not one person stepped forward to testify against him. They couldn't prove a thing.

"Leave it to ol' Buck," Cole chuckled. "He's a wily one."

Bob thought about it, probably too much. It figured. The man who shot Cashier Heywood in cold blood and had indirectly been responsible for their life sentences, had found a way to manipulate the law and those who served it. Bob should have been happy that one of their own was going to go free, but it angered him that the one to walk away from all of it was probably the worst of the lot.

More weeks passed, months, time. There seemed to be nothing but time. The only way to know the date was to read it in the newspaper.

"We're going to give you different jobs," the Warden was telling them. "Cole, you're going to be put to work in the infirmary."

Cole liked that. He'd have the opportunity to chat and visit. He missed that more than anything.

"Jim, you're a literate man. You'll be in charge of the library."

Jim was delighted. He could think of nothing better than to lose himself among the books he loved.

"Bob, I've been thinking of you too," Reed nodded. "You don't have any experience with it, but you might find it interesting to work as an accounting clerk. You're a young man and it will serve you well to learn a trade, so that when you leave here you're in a better position to find employment."

Bob considered farming his trade but he doubted he'd have the heart to ever do that again. He was happy to move on from the uncomfortable physical jobs he had been assigned since he'd been there. The factory areas of the prison were damp and he had taken to catching colds that he seemed never able to completely shake. Working with numbers wasn't his favorite thing. He remembered crabbing about it to Maggie. Yet he figured tedious work was better than doing something unpleasant. He'd do anything to move the time along. Quit grumbling, he told himself. You've certainly had worse things in your life.

CHAPTER 67

It was approaching the tenth year of their incarceration. It had seemed so long ago that they had been free men, living the lives of drifters they'd lived for so many years. They had become so institutionalized that freedom to make their own decisions seemed like a fruitless dream. To even think they might be close to returning to the outside world was almost overwhelming, let alone what plans they might have for their futures. If Cole and Jim had such a plan, they weren't discussing it. Bob didn't allow himself the luxury of even thinking it. But first things first: the Warden wasn't just going to appear one day with the key in his hand. It was now time to mount a drive for their parole.

"Retta has been nothing but supportive and I know she wants to be involved in this thing, but she's still just a young woman."

Retta had said she would do everything within her power to gain their parole. Bob didn't know, because none of them told him, that Maggie was working right alongside Retta.

"What does she know about putting pressure on people? I know you want to get this ball rolling but is that really the way to do it?"

"Retta is thirty years old, Bobby.." Cole reminded him.

"My God..." The time....and he was a few years older than Rett...

"I don't see where we have any pressure to put at all." Jim interrupted his thoughts. As much as it would be nice to be free of this place, Jim wasn't looking forward to this procedure. It made him uncomfortable to ask people to speak on his behalf. He'd be more satisfied if his time served would speak for itself.

Bob knew it would be a waste of time to attempt to take any leadership position in this. Cole would be in charge like he always was. Besides, it was Bob's attempt at leadership that had gotten them into this situation in the first place.

"I've been thinking that Aunt Frances Twyman would be a good choice to head a parole drive," Cole mused. "She's a woman of standing, what with her being the daughter of Judge Fristoe."

"We're the *grandsons* of Judge Fristoe. Don't see where that fact has any influence over anything at all when it comes to us."

Cole knew Bob was going to be a problem. The older he got, the more cynical he became. Just because he had decided to cut Maggie out of his life and had nothing to return to didn't mean they all were going to roll over and play dead. Cole would never have made that decision. Maggie loved his brother, probably more than he deserved. If Cole had someone like that in his life, he would never let it go. He didn't understand Bob's reasoning but Bob just flat out refused to discuss the matter with him.

"If you'd let me finish..." It was hard enough that they had to think this thing through. He didn't need a sour attitude. "Aunt Frances has already written to me that she is willing to introduce some people and see if she can get them to speak for us before the parole board. Uncle Lydall is a prominent doctor there in Jackson County. They know a lot of important people."

"That's very kind of her, Cole, but why would important people want to get behind the parole of three bank robbers serving a life sentence for murder?"

"Damn it, Bobby! Jim and I are trying to figure out what we can do to get the hell out of this place. If you want to rot here, that's your business, but stop being a goddamn pain in the ass!"

Cole was right. If the parole board was even going to think about letting them out of this place, they were going to need all the help they could get and they needed to work together.

"I apologize, Cole. I'm sorry. It's just that I've tried all these years to not think about this and now it's the time to do nothing *but* think about it. I guess I'm just afraid the result won't be the one we want."

"Yeah, I know how you feel, but we have to think positive." Cole had to remember that regardless of whose fault it was that they were in this mess, it was Bob who had maybe lost the most. "You remember Rutledge saying that most men serve ten years on a life sentence. We have to go with that line of thought."

Bob nodded. That was what they had been told and they had to believe it. They had to believe something positive. He felt a chill and started to cough. He'd had this damn cold for over a month now and he felt terrible.

"What's with that cough?" Cole noticed Bob looked peaked. Of course they all did. They never saw any sun.

Bob took a drink of water. "Just a cold, it comes and goes. Sorry I'm grouchy. I just feel like crap today."

Jim looked at his brother. "You know Bob, maybe your problem is that you've shut yourself off from hope too long."

Jim wasn't one to tell other people how to feel or what to think, but he had watched Bob choose to go this alone. It didn't have to be that way for him.

"I remember when you were a boy. No matter what the family was put through, you always had hope."

"I want to have hope, Jim, believe me. I just can't seem to find it."

"Write to Maggie, Bob." There, Jim had put in his two cents. It wasn't something he usually did, but it needed to be said. "If we're fortunate enough to leave this place after ten years, you're still a young man. You can still have a life. You have a woman who loves you, Bob. There lies your hope."

Bob couldn't remember the last time Jim had given anyone advice. Jim was a smart man, probably the smartest man Bob knew. And he was right. There was no hope without Maggie.

"I can't let her get involved in a parole drive, Jim. I don't want people at home to know she's associated with someone like me. Starting over, if I was to get out of here, would be one thing but I don't want her being known for trying to get her….I don't even known what you'd call our relationship…get her *man* out of prison. And I don't want that put on Jeremy."

"Maggie doesn't care about any of that, Bob." Cole knew Jim was right. "I heard what she said to you all those years ago. And the woman writes to you all the time. Jim sees the letters come through."

So they had discussed this behind his back. That should make him angry, but it somehow just made him know that they cared about him. As alone as he may feel, that wasn't really the way it was. He was the reason the two men beside him were in this penitentiary. Yet neither one of them had ever gone out of his way to blame him for it or make him feel guilty. He had done all that on his own. They had stuck by him by making that trip north and he knew they would stick by him whichever way this parole thing turned out.

Maybe they were right. It was time to stop defining himself by his last great mistake and look to the future. He wanted Maggie back in his life. The future was being paroled out of this place and returning home.

The future was Maggie.

CHAPTER 68

Maggie clutched his letter to her throbbing heart. He had written to her. After all this time, these long, long years, he had written to her. She understood his decision, his need, to keep her out of his predicament but she didn't agree with it. Whether he chose to accept it or not, she was emotionally involved in everything that had happened to him, everything that mattered to him, since long before the day he left for Minnesota.

She had written to him ceaselessly and stayed in close touch with Retta since the days he first entered the prison doors. There was rarely any news from Stillwater, but what there was Retta passed along. She thought of him constantly, every day. He had been beside her far less time than they now had been apart, yet her feelings for him hadn't changed, not at all. It had been almost ten years now. The years may have passed but she didn't love him any less.

She and Jeremy had stayed on the farm. Jeremy was now nearly as old as Bob had been when she'd last seen him. Jeremy was a blessing to her. He knew how much pain she was in yet he always tried to find the positive in life. She knew that he too missed Bob. He was angry with Bob's decision to rob a bank but she knew that more than anything he wanted Bob to return to the farm. She'd watched as Jeremy learned to love the land as much as Bob had. Their thriving crop was small but the seed of it was still Bob's. When he came back to her it would be there for him. Just as she would be there for him. No matter how long it took.

Dear Maggie, he had written. He had been so careful about revealing her identity and her place in his life that she didn't think she would ever read those words. Retta had told her that Jim had cleverly tucked the letter in Retta's sleeve when she had last been there to visit. No one knew of it.

You probably cannot believe you're reading a letter from me after all this time. You have never left my mind. I have done little these past nine years but think of you. I hope you can understand why I have not written. I cannot for the life of me understand why you still love me. If I were to respond to your letters with my own, I would have nothing to offer but to share the desolation of this place. That would accomplish nothing but to bring you more sadness.

Your letters keep me informed of your life and that of Jeremy's. It sounds like he has turned into a fine man. That doesn't surprise me, as he has a wonderful, loving mother.

They say that most men serving life sentences are paroled after ten years. It is almost that time and Retta tells me things are afoot to try and make that happen. I do not know if it will happen Maggie, but if it does, maybe I can return to you and we can start a new life. A life like the one we planned before I acted like a selfish fool and threw it all away. Try not to set your hopes too high. Who knows if what is usual for other people is usual for us, but I hope for the day that I can return to you a free man. A man who loves you with all his heart.

Bob

He loved her still. Oh, God, he loved her still and he wanted their life to be together again. He *would* return to her. The thought that he wouldn't was impossible for her to imagine. Prison was supposed to be about repentance and rehabilitation. If any one person in that entire Stillwater Penitentiary had repented, it was Bob Younger. Now was the time to set him free and send him back to the people who loved him. She and Retta would do what needed to be done to bring Bob and his brothers home.

Before that could happen, the parole board needed to be convinced that Cole, Jim and Bob Younger were worthy of being set free and returning to lives spent more productively. Their prison records were exceptional, no one could argue with that. They had accepted their punishment and had since done every-thing they could to demonstrate their rehabilitated character.

"We need to ask some men to speak on our behalf," Cole reminded his brothers. "Those who know us as the men of integ-rity that we are. Men who just made a wrong decision."

All three of them were thinking that the moment in North-field wasn't the only wrong decision they'd made, but why go into that?

"Finding men who really believe that and want to come for-ward might be difficult, Cole." Jim had been thinking about how to approach the parole request and he wasn't coming up with anything that he thought was a good idea. At least Cole *had* an idea.

"Well, I met a man named Wal Bronaugh. Served the Con-federacy."

"How'd you meet someone like that up here?" Bob ques-tioned.

"Frank James had him look me up."

Anything having to do with Frank James didn't sound like a good idea to Jim and Bob.

Cole chuckled. "Bronaugh told me that the Warden said they look upon Missourians here with a great deal of suspicion, but he let him meet with me."

"How does this concern us?" Jim wanted to know.

"Well, Bronaugh said he wants to put together a parole drive. He's a good man, a smart man. I think we should let him do it."

Cole was the most vocal about any plans to ask for parole, but Bob thought maybe he was the most invested. Cole and Jim both liked their jobs and both had recently taken up woodworking. Cole was making beautiful walking sticks and Jim was carving delicate boxes and picture frames. With his bum arm, Bob had all he could handle with his clerking job. He didn't have any such hobbies. Jim had settled in and he seemed almost comfortable being there. He had even taken up playing the violin and he was good at it. And Cole, well, Cole could land on his feet anywhere and he'd make do with whatever happened. Although Bob was sure his brothers wanted to be released, he figured both of them were making the best out of their situation. That was fine, but the only thing he could think about now was leaving. So if this Bronaugh thought he could help, they might as well give him a shot.

"Why the hell not?" he shrugged. "We don't have anything left to lose."

It tuned out that Wal Bronaugh was a man of his word. He had served in the regular Confederate Army but he had great respect for the guerrilla movement. Being a Western Missourian, he thought highly of Frank James and Cole Younger, although he had never met either.

When Bronaugh finally met Frank, Frank talked to him about Cole's parole. Frank thought Wal was intelligent and savvy; he'd be the perfect candidate to help out Frank's old friend.

"I'd be happy to help in any way I can," Wal told him. "But I'm getting married and about to go on my honeymoon."

"Where do you plan to go?" Frank asked.

"I haven't decided."

"I hear its real pretty up in Minnesota. Lots of lakes, I hear."

"I've never been there."

"You might consider that area for your honeymoon. I've heard there's a pretty little village by the St. Croix River up near the Stillwater prison."

Wal understood what Frank was suggesting. How could he say no to Frank James? Or Cole Younger, for that matter.

When Wal finally had an audience with Cole, he was surprised to note that he had already met him. During the battle of Lone Jack, Wal and a friend had become separated from their unit. They met a picket who told them not to go into the little town, as it was now occupied by Yankees. They talked with that picket for nearly an hour. Now Wal was staring him in the face again.

"I had no idea that picket was you, Captain Younger." Wal shook his head in disbelief. "You likely saved my life that day."

"Well. Us meeting again under these circumstances is providence, isn't it, Wal?"

Wal was sold. He offered to do whatever it took.

"The first thing I'd like you to do is meet with my aunt in Independence. She knows some powerful people. She'll help you get what you need."

Cole was gratified that he still had pull with those who had been involved with the Confederacy. Surely his service to that great cause would garner him some respect and assistance when he was in need. His vision of the possibility of parole, of finally getting out of this situation, became sharper.

By letter of introduction, Aunt Frances arranged for Wal to meet her old friend William Marshall. Marshall had served as governor of Minnesota and Aunt Frances was thrilled when he agreed to speak on behalf of her nephews. In a move Bob could hardly believe, Marshall brought former Missouri governor Thomas Crittenden onboard the effort as well.

"Tom Crittenden? Wasn't he the man who arranged for Bob Ford to kill Jesse?" Bob asked Cole. Some of this didn't make any sense to him. Or was it that it was just too good to be true?

"Yeah, ain't that a hoot?" Cole grinned. "He thinks we've served enough time and says we aren't a danger to Missoura anymore. I'm tellin' ya, Bobby, we've got this ten-years-served parole in the bag."

Will Marshall wrote a long and detailed article that was published in the St. Paul *Pioneer Press*. He wrote of Cole's many heroic deeds while serving in the Confederate Army and detailed how the brothers were from one of the most respected families in Western Missouri. He noted that none of the Youngers had killed the unfortunate cashier Heywood. They were simply guilty of robbing a bank and being associated with some very bad people.

"Like Byron's Greece," Marshall wrote, *"it were long to tell and sad to trace, their fall from splendor to disgrace."* The Youngers had already served beyond the amount of time most convicted bank robbers served before being paroled and they should now be allowed to return to Missouri and serve the society which they had wronged.

Not to be outdone by Marshall, Cole himself wrote to the newspaper. He humbly recounted his days as an officer and a gentleman who was known for his acts of kindness and fair play in regard to his enemies.

Jim figured it was all just more of the same from Cole and he didn't think Cole's letter would carry much weight. Although Jim was certainly articulate, he had no desire to sling "literature" about himself or his family in a public forum. That didn't mean that Jim was going to stifle his viewpoint. He had done that far too many times throughout his life. Rather than write letters to the editor, he had chosen to write witty little essays, which he accompanied with droll drawings and unequivocal opinions. It was published as a little newspaper and circulated within the prison. Although he didn't care what the other prisoners thought of his musings, Jim found it satisfied him that his words had been published.

Bob figured anything worthwhile he had to say had already been said.

Bob's life was passing him by and there was nothing he could do about that. He had made his bed. The tenth year of their incarceration had finally arrived, but now he was hearing that those serving sentences like theirs were being considered eligible for parole at seven years. If that was the case, that period had long passed. He didn't know which rumors to believe anymore. Cole and Jim felt the same.

Unbeknownst to any of them, there was a new element coming into play and it did not bode well. The Younger's fiercest enemy to date would figure heavily into any appeal when former banker William R. Merriam was sworn into office as Governor of Minnesota. To Merriam, any consideration of parole for the Younger brothers was *personal.*

"Edwards did a nice job for Buck and now he's written a good piece for us," Cole told his brothers.

"More of his nonsense about us being noble victims of circumstance?"

Bob may have once believed that but he didn't any more. Like he should have done with Maggie, they could have walked away from it at any time once the War was over. Left Missoura and headed west. Look at what his love of that state had wrought. God, he wished he believed that fantasy....

"The man is a windbag," Jim dismissed.

"You boys need to be more appreciative." Their attitude about Edwards was annoying. "He's one of the best friends we have right now. Someone goes out of their way to help us and you insult him?"

They knew Cole was right. They needed all the friends they could get.

"Do you want to hear about it or not?"

"Sure, Cole," Bob nodded. "What's he got to say?"

"It's not what he has to say but what he's done. He wrote a damn fine document asking for our parole. Not only that, but he has the signatures of twenty-eight members of the General Assembly of Missoura attached to it."

Jim nodded. That was impressive. He never imagined they would have that kind of support.

"How'd he do that?" Bob was surprised too. "Why are they coming to the aid of men who robbed their banks and trains?"

"Because they're men of justice," Cole pompously replied. "And regardless of who they think we are, we've paid our debt and deserve to be treated fairly."

Jim and Bob may be perplexed about the support, but Cole felt it his due.

That summer Bronaugh was elated when former Minnesota Governor Henry Sibley wrote a letter stating that *"Minnesota has shown her power to punish malefactors, let her now manifest her magnanimity by opening the prison doors to the men who have so long suffered for a violation of her laws and bid them 'go and sin no more'."*

Now *that* was a mouthful.

Bob acknowledged in a second letter to Maggie that those were pretty words but the proof would be, as they said, in the pudding. He would try to stay hopeful but anything beyond that was out of his control.

CHAPTER 69
1889

Bob continued to keep mostly to himself but that fall he developed a friendship with the Deputy Warden. Jacob Westby liked Bob. He enjoyed Bob's intellect, his observations and his witty approach to his circumstances. He felt that Bob was humble and honest; certainly not traits he had experienced in other bank robbers he had encountered. Bob worked at a table near Westby's office and Westby often invited him in to pass the time at the end of the day. This was one of those days.

"It's nice to see the sun shining through that window, isn't it, Bob?"

"That's probably what I most enjoy about this job," Bob smiled. The window didn't allow for much sunshine but it certainly would do.

"You look tired, Bob," Westby frowned. "Aren't you sleeping well?"

"Oh, you know how it is here, Mr. Westby." He shrugged. He'd gotten used to the constant clomping and clanging.

"You told me last week when I asked you that you were fighting off a chill. Come to think of it, you told me the same the week before that."

Bob shrugged again. "The nights are long in the cells. Even when it's warm there's a dampness to it. Guess it just stays with me sometimes."

"Sounds like you've got a bit of a wheeze. Is your health all right?"

"Well, my lung hasn't been right since one of your fellow Minnesotans choose to pepper it a little back there in the slough when I was surrendering." Bob smiled. He still hadn't gotten over his luck that day. There was little to do except find the black humor of it.

"That was some ill fortune, Bob." Westby shook his head.

"Yeah, well, it was just part of the bad ending to a bad idea."

Westby nodded. There was no response to that.

"I wonder if you ought to see one of the doctors. It seems you're not able to shake what ails you."

"There's a lot of things I can't shake," Bob smirked.

The truth of the matter was that the coughs and the colds weren't going away like they once had. It was so damn damp. He seemed never to throw off the chill he felt. He'd considered seeing one of the doctors but he'd had enough of people poking into his business during those days at Faribault to last him a lifetime.

"I'll be all right," he smiled at Westby. "Thanks for your concern, though. I appreciate it."

A couple of days later Westby brought the matter up again when he noticed Bob bent over his work station trying to stifle a coughing fit.

"Bob, you need to visit the doctor. There's likely something he can give you to help you get rid of that cough."

Yeah, it was time he stopped postponing seeing the doctor. He'd learned how to face up to things and this was something that he no longer could put off. He ached day and night. He coughed all the time. The situation wasn't getting any better, it was getting worse.

"I'll do that, Mr. Westby," he nodded.

He saw the doctor the next day. He wasn't that surprised at what the doctor had to say to him. There are some things that you just know and this was one of them.

"It's phthisis, Bob." The doctor was fittingly somber. "You might know it as consumption."

He nodded. He'd looked it up in a medical book when he started to suspect it. He knew what that diagnosis meant.

"How long?" What else was there to ask?

"It's hard to say."

"I'll accept that answer."

He asked for a meeting with his brothers. He didn't want them to learn of it through the grapevine.

"You'll survive this." Cole chose to be optimistic. "God knows you've survived worse."

"We'll see," Bob shrugged.

"You've got to stay positive, Bob." Jim was overwhelmed. This couldn't be happening to his little brother. Bob was always the personification of good health. Look at how well he handled the destruction of his arm. "You can't let this…"

"*Consume* me, Jim?" Bob joked. He wasn't going to wallow in it. "All the time I thought I was being consumed by guilt, I was being consumed by something else. What do you know."

"Why didn't you see the doctor sooner?" Cole was angry, but not at Bob.

"It is what it is, Cole."

He wasn't going to dwell on that but he did have some ground rules he would ask his brothers to follow.

"I'd appreciate it if you don't talk about it around me. Can you give me that?"

Cole and Jim nodded. They would give him whatever he needed.

"Now I don't want you to think I'm pulling out of this parole drive. I'm still in it. You both deserve to be free of this place. Maybe there will be enough time for me to see Missoura again."

It broke their hearts. As tough as they both felt they were, it broke their hearts.

"Maggie? Retta?" Cole asked.

This might be the biggest favor he had ever asked his brothers.

"Don't say anything to Rett. I'll tell her and Maggie in my own time, in my own way."

His own way was to say nothing to either of them for now. Their emotion had to be centered on the parole drive, not on him. He wanted that to succeed more than ever. If it came in time for him to be released, he could return to Missoura...to Maggie...even if it meant he would be spending his last days there.

He should be bitter. He found that he wasn't. Nor did he receive the diagnosis as his just reward. He felt only sorrow for all the time that was lost. He was just thirty-four years old, but he had lost two brothers and two sisters who were a hell of a lot younger. He had encountered situations that should have done him in before this and they hadn't. Times during the War, during the train robberies, during that God-awful retreat out of Northfield... Hell, ten years ago, when he was told he would serve a life sentence in the Stillwater pen he had even wished his own death. Now, here in this Minnesota prison, he had been handed a death sentence of another sort and he would accept it like he had the first one. He had no one to blame for the stealing of his dreams except himself. There were no regrets that he hadn't already considered and come to peace with except one. He wanted to see Maggie's face again.

Wal Bronaugh was giving it his best. Together with Mrs. Twyman, he had managed to secure letters of support from the Governor of Missouri, past governors of both Missouri and Minnesota, United States senators, Republicans, Democrats, congressmen, three members of the posse, along with Sheriff

Barton, and the past and present wardens of the Stillwater Prison. What more could Governor Merriam want?

What William Merriam wanted was simple: revenge.

Merriam held a deplorable secret and those goddamn Youngers would pay for it, you'd better believe they would. It was his father who had been humiliated at the hands of that arrogant bastard Jesse James and his decadent gang of playmates at Gad's Hill when he had been ordered to strip down to his underwear. The degradation that fine and noble man had suffered... it made his blood run cold.

Well, now the son of that man, he himself, was sitting in the catbird's seat. He wasn't about to reveal his personal motivation to keep the men responsible for that sordid act behind bars for the rest of their goddamn lives. The first mortification was bad enough without the general public being made aware of what had happened along the railroad tracks that day. So he would admit his personal prejudice, but the reasons for it were not something he cared to discuss.

Despite the letters from more prestigious men than himself, Merriam denied the request for parole within minutes. Regardless of the fact that the Youngers were serving a sentence for robbery, in his mind they could rot in prison for their part in an unwarranted and reprehensible practical joke.

"This man is malicious, Cole." Bronaugh was trying to make sense of it all. How could anyone so blatantly defy the powerful men who had requested the Youngers be paroled? "His refusal to even consider parole is beyond reason."

"Having our fate in the hands of one man with a vengeance, whatever it is, is nothing new to us, Wal."

Cole was angry and disgusted but there was nothing he could do about it.

"But for Bob's sake, isn't there something we can do? The kid doesn't have long to live. Can't we at least get him home to Missoura to die?"

"No, no. I don't want it focused on me, Wal."

When Bronaugh presented a plan to center the drive on Bob, Bob didn't want any part of it.

"I don't want to spend my last days having people say 'poor Bob Younger'. Good God, haven't I been humiliated enough?"

As far as he was concerned, if this is going to be the way it was, the only thing left on his plate was to write to Maggie and Retta about his condition. He hadn't yet figured out what to say.

"But this might open the doors for your brothers too, Bob," Bronaugh countered.

That wasn't entirely true, but everyone concerned wanted to do everything they could to keep Bob from drawing his last breath in this desolate environment. If it took a little twisting of the truth, Bronaugh could do that.

"I won't try and fool you and withhold the information that some of your enemies see it as a ploy. They think you might be feigning your illness. Phillips, the man who was president of the Northfield bank at the time of the robbery, wants to send his personal physician to check you out."

"Oh, for God's sake. I just want everyone to leave me the hell alone."

That was exactly what Governor Merriam wanted. Appeals on Bob's behalf fell on his deaf ears. He would in no way entertain it.

Former Governor Marshall offered to act as a hostage of the prison if Bob could return home to die.

Merriam's response was that even if Mrs. Heywood would come back to life and make the request herself, he would refuse to pardon Bob Younger or his brothers. There was nothing more to be done to influence him or make him change his mind.

The focus on his bad health was annoying. Even so, he couldn't go another day without telling Maggie. He didn't want her to read about in the newspaper.

"Dear Maggie," he wrote. *"I don't know how to say this to you with any gentleness so I'll just say it. The cough that I haven't been able to*

shake is consumption. You know what that means. I guess I'm all too familiar with what they say about the best laid plans...I'll write more later. I just wanted you to hear it from me. With all my love, Bob."

She clutched the letter and sank to her knees.

No, she would not accept this. He was not going to die and leave her alone with empty plans for a future without him. She would *not* accept this. She would *not*.

Eventually, word leaked to the newspapers and they began a death watch. Reports of Bob's deteriorating condition began to appear in print. Where they were getting their information was anybody's guess. Bob didn't read the newspapers or grant interviews and neither did Cole or Jim. Like so much written before, the sensational reports were mostly flowery babble.

Bob accepted his fate. There was no way to change or influence his condition. He only felt it was a shame that he had to suffer all those long years in a place like this when he faced the same consequence as he had back there in '77. Had he been killed in that gunfight, it would have saved him a lot of misery. The will of God was indeed mysterious.

He could feel himself growing weaker. There was no chance now that he would be allowed to return to Missoura and Maggie. That's just the way it was going to be. His time had all but run out. The only thing left for him to do was maintain what little dignity he had left.

"We're not giving up, Bob."

Wal was once again in his cell. The Warden allowed Bronaugh the access of an attorney and although he mostly met with Cole and Jim, he sometimes came around to talk to Bob.

"We're racking our brains trying to think of another approach," Bronaugh told him. If anyone had doubts that Bob was sick, all they had to do was look at him.

"I know you did your best, Wal. You did more than any man could reasonably ask. It's just not going to happen."

The guard came to the door.

"Mr. Bronaugh, the young lady has arrived with the papers you requested."

"You've got young ladies working for you now, Wal?" Bob smiled. "Well, haven't you come up in the world? Hitched your wagon to the saga of the Younger boys and look how far it's taken you."

"Please show her in," Wal directed the guard. "I need to talk with Miss Younger. Miss Josie will stay here with Bob, if you don't mind. I'll be back in a few minutes."

And there she was.

There was Maggie.

She said nothing until the guard was out of the room.

"Bobby," she whispered, just as she had when he'd seen her in the Faribault courtroom.

"Maggie..."

She was standing in front of him and she was beautiful still. His heart pounded in his chest just like it had all those years ago when he first laid eyes on her.

He rose as she crossed to him and enveloped him in her arms.

She placed her hands on his face as she used to do and looked up into his eyes.

"I love you, Bobby."

"You shouldn't be this near..." he started to warn her.

Then her lips were on his.

He closed his eyes and drank her in. He felt like he was in a dream. He was holding his Maggie and everything that was his reality was lost in this moment. He was back at their farm. Back at their better days.

"My God, Maggie. I love you so much," he whispered against her mouth.

She laid her head on his chest and just held him. She had dreamed of holding him for so long. How she longed for him.

He was older now and so thin. Where there used to be strong muscle, there was now only bone. But it couldn't be true that he was dying, she didn't believe it. Yet when she looked up at him she could see in his eyes that he did. The tears tumbled down her face.

"Please don't cry," he asked her. "I'm looking at your beautiful face and holding you in my arms. I never thought I would again."

She kissed him again. For so many years she had loved this man, had missed the presence of this man, had thought of little else than being with this man. Now she was supposed to accept that he was being taken away from her a second time. This time forever.

He continued to hold her. He stroked her hair, that incredible red hair.

"Maggie, I wish to God it didn't have to end like this."

"Shhh." She shook her head. She wouldn't hear it. She wouldn't have it. "I'm going to find a doctor who can make you better, Bobby. There's got to be a treatment that will help. There are new medicines, new cures to diseases that were once…"

Wal Bronaugh knocked, then walked back into the room.

"I'm sorry, that's all the time they'd give me."

"There's got to be something more we can do, Wal!" Maggie turned to him. "He's served a reasonable time. What more could they possibly want from him? What haven't you thought of that will get him home?"

Bob turned her head toward him and looked down upon her face, the face that he had hungered to see for ten long years.

"Wal's done enough for me, Maggie. He's brought me you."

"I'm sorry I had to spring it on you like this, Bob. Maggie was adamant that you not be told, in case you didn't want to see her."

"I know what it's like when Maggie is adamant," Bob smiled.

"Just because the doctors here haven't….I'm on my way to Chicago, Bobby." Maggie clutched at his hands. "I'm going to talk to every last doctor there until I find one who will come here, treat you and make you well."

"Maggie."

He knew her love and devotion was causing her to grasp for reins that even she knew were broken and hanging short.

"You need to just accept it. I have."

"I'll never accept it."

She shook her head. Her green eyes flashed. How he had missed that.

"There's got to be someone who can treat you, make you better." Tears once again welled in her eyes. "God, Bobby, you need to come *home*. Home to me. Everything is still there for you!"

"You're *here* for me, Maggie. That's more than I ever expected or deserved. That's all I need."

He brought her hands to his lips and kissed them.

"Always remember what we had, Maggie. But make a life for yourself that brings you contentment. That would make me happy. That's how you could honor our love most."

"My only contentment will be with you. Home in Missouri."

She kissed him tenderly. A kiss that would be their last.

The guard came to the door.

"I'm sorry, Mr. Bronaugh, time's up."

Bob looked deep into Maggie's eyes.

"I love you, Maggie girl."

"I love you, Bob Younger. And I'm *proud* that you are in my life, do you hear me? *Proud* to know the man you are and *proud* to love you. There's nothing more important to me than having you in my life. You are everything I've ever wanted, everything I'll ever need, everything I live for."

He nodded because yes he knew, more than he ever knew anything in his life, he knew she was telling him the truth. He closed his eyes and believed.

CHAPTER 70

Maggie wasted no time after arriving in Chicago; she talked to every prominent doctor she could find to ask them if they knew of any new or advanced treatment that might prolong Bob's life. The very sad fact was that no matter how persistent she was, it was just too late for the man she loved.

It simply was not within her power to alter his destiny.

Bob asked for his brothers and Retta that late afternoon of September 16, 1889. The sun hadn't gone down yet and there was a nice warmness to the room. The end had come upon him quickly; almost as if he had been granted his earnest prayer that Maggie not be with him when it came. He didn't want either of them to face that last, sorrowful goodbye. It was hard enough for his brothers and sister. They'd hardly left his side. When he'd grown uncomfortable with their constant presence they had waited in the hospital's anteroom.

"I need to know that you forgive me," he whispered to his brothers now. There was little left of his voice. He looked from one face to the other. He had never come out and asked them that question, mostly because he had honored their desire not to talk about the subject.

"Of course we do." Cole felt his throat constrict. "But Bobby, Jim and I played our own part. It's not like you forced us. It was our own decision to come up here."

"Fate has never been in your hands, Bob." Jim was going to miss him. God, he was going to miss him. "You of all people know that."

Bob nodded. He guessed that he finally did. And there was nothing more to say about any of it.

"Bob, I know you always felt that you stood in the shade of events that you think I brought to bear, or had influence on."

Cole looked out the window. He wasn't sorry for anything he had done, but it was hard for him to say what he needed to say to his brother. Still, what he needed to say was important.

"None of that matters now, Cole," Bob sighed. It had mattered a hell of a lot for most of his life; had been the obstacle he had never been able to overcome. Cole's actions cloaked his childhood and Cole's reputation complicated his youth. At the core of it, it was because of both of those things that he lay dying in this bed. But for all that, when it came down to this moment, it just didn't matter anymore. He never thought he would feel that way, but as much as those things defined his life, when it came to the time of his death, those things just didn't matter at all.

"I just want to say that I truly am sorry for making an already bad situation worse for you." Cole searched his brother's face. He wouldn't ask for forgiveness but he wanted to know Bob would grant it.

"You did what you felt you..needed to do, Cole. I guess I understand that...more than ever."

"I did do what I thought I needed to do. But I'm sorry I was sometimes insensitive to the toll those decisions had on my family."

"If anyone knows that more than me...I don't know who that would be."

"Seems to be the only trait I passed on to you."

Bob smiled.

"I just want to tell you..." Tears flooded Cole's eyes. "I just want to tell you, Bobby, that bad decisions aside, as a brother? You never stood in anyone's shadow."

Bob took Cole's hand. With all their differences over the years, Cole had given him the kindness of those words when he needed it most. He loved Cole for it. And Jim, blindly loyal Jim, who proved his love by devotion, not words.

And he thought of Dick, his friend, his teacher; then of John, the one who *knew* because he'd been there beside him. God, it all seemed like a lifetime ago. Yet even now he missed them both so much.

He cocked his head when he heard a bird call from outside the window.

"Hear that? If I didn't know better...I'd think it was one of those Cardinals...that used to sit on the fencepost...back home."

Jim had to turn away. This was so painful, unbearably painful. Of all of them, Bob had loved Missoura the most.

"Cole...can you lift me up....so I can see the sky...one more time?"

Cole moved to raise him. Bob looked out the window and smiled.

"Oh....there's a hill. Maybe...my soul will rest on it...for a minute or two."

Retta started to cry. She'd never in a million years expected all this for Bobby. She still didn't understand how it had. He was such a good and kind person. He had *always* been a good and kind person. Why he had made such hideous decisions in his adult life, she would never understand.

"Don't cry Rett." He smiled at his faithful little sister as she took his hand. "Not for me. I've made my peace with the Lord."

All thoughts of mistakes and regret left his mind. He only thought of one thing now. He only thought of Maggie. He had experienced the greatest of pain from the time he was a child but more importantly, he had experienced the greatest of love. With that acknowledgement came the overwhelming gratitude that, if only briefly, he had known the home he had so long sought. It was back in Missoura with Maggie. She had been so right when she'd told him all those years ago that his home was with her heart. That home was one no one could ever take from him.

His home was in her heart.

He motioned Cole over and took hold of his shirtfront to draw him nearer.

Cole, the one whose shadow had been cast over his life for so long, would be the one who would hear his final testament.

Cole bent over so that his ear was close to his little brother's mouth.

"Tell her...I died thinking of her. Will you...tell her that?"

Cole nodded, tears running freely down his cheeks.

Bob closed his eyes and smiled. His extraordinary and intricate life passed on to an environment of tranquility; a place of happiness, a place where he would be accepted for who he was as an individual. He would be home and this home would, at last, be all he ever yearned to know.

PROLOGUE

Maggie was devastated when she heard the news. She knew her place was with him on that final day and not in Chicago looking for an answer that would never be delivered. Yet in her heart, she knew that her absence made it easier for Bob to go and she felt he was entitled to at least that.

It was hard for her to make sense of it all. There had been such extraordinary love and such overwhelming heartbreak. She wondered why Bob had been brought into her life, only to be removed from it so quickly. Yet most importantly, the fact that they had shared what little time they had, made it all worthwhile. They made a home together, however brief, and she felt certain that he ultimately believed in that and treasured it as much as she. She would never know anybody like Bob Younger again. His was, and would always remain, the love that defined her. He would live as long as her heart beat.

They buried him next to his mother in Lee's Summit. It meant a lot to his sisters, although when Retta told Jim, he couldn't help but think that Bob might've preferred St. Clair, next to John. Maybe Bob wanted Jackson County because he was happy with Maggie there. Jim didn't know if Bob had discussed such things with Retta as his burial. He doubted he had. Jim, as always, kept his thoughts to himself. It was only Bob's body, after all. His soul wouldn't be buried at all.

It was an emotional ceremony, one that likely would have made Bob uncomfortable. Maggie was gratified that they honored him, that so many cared. He had served his prison sentence with humility and dignity and no one could possibly say otherwise. She had been afraid that there would be crowds of people who didn't even know him, just there to gawk, but even though there were hundreds, they were respectful. Thank God for that.

Although he likely learned of Bob's character from his sisters, Reverend Francisco spoke of Bob's capacity for love and loyalty. He spoke of Bob's repentance and his contrition and noted that these things had only been discussed with those closest to him as Bob did not want to appear hypocritical. The reverend's final words honored Bob most. In a voice strong with sincerity, Reverend Francisco felt sure that in circumstances other than those in which he was forced to live his life, Bob Younger would have been, like his father and his brother Dick before him, a contributing and honored member of his community. It was another preacher, Reverend Buchanan, who reminded everyone that when it came down to it, Bob wasn't the only one who had made mistakes. "Let him that is himself without sin," he intoned, "cast the first stone."

The parole drive for Cole and Jim continued long after Bob's death. When S.R. Van Sant was elected Governor of Minnesota, the heinous treatment of Governor Merriam was put to rest. The persistent hard work of Wal Bronaugh and Retta Younger, with twists and turns continuing throughout, was finally rewarded with success. By the time of their release, twelve years after Bob's final breath, Cole and Jim had served twenty-four years in the Stillwater Penitentiary.

Continuing the run of irony that seemed to characterize their lives, one of the conditions of their parole was that Cole and Jim go to work for the Peterson Granite Company as tombstone salesmen.

Cole adapted to his freedom and the constrictions of the parole, which forbade them from living in Missouri or any place other than Minnesota. He enjoyed going to the theater and even was a guest at the annual supper of the Railroad Men in Minneapolis. Cole attended religious lectures and a convention of newspapermen men at the Elks Hall. He held a few jobs that he found boring but eventually took a job with St. Paul Police Chief John J. O'Connor. Cole, although he might report differently in his parole reports, was the toast of the town.

Jim, on the other hand, found all of it more difficult than he expected. He complained to his parole official that he was constantly harassed and he found it difficult to hold down a job. Yet his life took quite an unexpected turn when he began keeping company with a reporter named Alix Mueller that he met while he was still in prison. Although Ms. Mueller's family didn't approve, Alix and Jim decided they'd like to get married. Well, even if Jim was indeed in love, he couldn't marry Alix. That was yet another thing he wasn't allowed by condition of parole. Alix petitioned the governor to make an exception in Jim's case and her letter was somehow made public. The ensuing publicity was too much for her family and Alix was summoned home to Idaho. She continued to write to Jim but her absence sent him into a tailspin of deep depression. He buried himself in the study of socialism, women's rights and metaphysics and rarely left his room. He didn't want anything to do with Cole or anybody else.

Only a year since he had walked out of Stillwater Prison, Jim had seen and experienced all he cared to. Once the devoted pillar of his family, Jim had evidently provided all he felt they were entitled to ask of him. He wrote a note that included a clear directive to them: *"All relatives just stay away from me."*

One night in the darkness of his St. Paul hotel room, Jim put a bullet in his brain.

Cole was the only one now. His brothers would have found that ironic. Yet Cole used to say he could weather anything and he ultimately did.

He was finally allowed to return to Missouri. After taking the time to visit with his family and friends, and in need of money, he teamed up with his old friend Frank James as part of a traveling carnival.

Jim and Bob would have been appalled.

Cole's last years were ones of Christian repentance. At least that's what he said. He toured the circuit lecturing on what his life had taught him. Many chose to believe him. Others thought that he was probably the same old Cole, a man who could make any situation work to his advantage. Regardless, it was a good discourse.

Frank James' life finally came to an end. Not even a year later, at the age of 72, Cole took ill and he knew it was the end of the line for him too. On his deathbed he finally revealed, privately of course, that Frank James was the one who shot Joseph Heywood. Even so, the secrets and lies would remain a part of American history that would likely never be told accurately.

Maggie and Jeremy had to live with the fact that Bob would never return to their farm. For those two brief years it had been their sanctuary, their subsistence, their potential. Yet like the mythological Camelot, their happiness had been destroyed by a single self-centered hunger.

It was only a moment in time, a time of indescribable joy, but it would live on in their hearts until the day both Maggie and Jeremy drew their own final breaths.

Some say the pain of living on the farm without Bob was more than Maggie could bear; that she started a new life in California, the place she would have lived had Bob returned to her.

Most others say they never even knew Bob had anyone special in his life. They never heard of anyone named Maggie.

None of that mattered to Maggie. Bob never left her thoughts, no matter where she was. In her heart, they lived open and visible, as a family should. Their lives may have been different than most but that didn't make them any less valuable.

Bob was now at peace with all that had once terrified, anguished, frustrated and defined him. The shadow had been vanquished; its fragments left to lift into the sky, only to dissolve in the incandescent flicker of another phase…another essence… another chapter….

ACKNOWLEDGMENTS

With thanks to those who always care; those who are always there....

Kathie (for the mind-blowing trip to "Hawaii"; who else can validate some of those strange adventures down the rabbit hole?); Dave (the guy who knew which frequency to tune in to find the shy little Valley Girl and whose support through it ALL has been nothing short of incredible); my incomparable Tim (I love you so much and pray that one day you will find your Osage Overlook); Willie (The "Duke of Earl", my early music guru); my delightful sister-in-law Carol; My Kids (the multifaceted John, the inimitable William, the mesmeric Jennifer); Beth (may she ever elude the Stink Eye); my incredible Aunt Jean (who is love personified); My very special nieces, nephews, cousins, aunts and friends (whom I adore and yes, I can tell you a story about each one of them!); Mom (my lifelong cheerleader, my Christian inspiration); Dad (my enduring hero); and Chachi (my Schnooks) – I miss you so, so much. And to Jo, who read more novels than anyone I've ever known; here's that novel that you always wanted *me* to write.

Lastly, but of great importance, thanks to the Younger family. So many of you have shared so much with me over the years and I am forever grateful for your confidence and trust. I treasure our many friendships and you will always hold a special place in my heart.

www.ingramcontent.com/pod-product-compliance
Lightning Source LLC
Chambersburg PA
CBHW020822030726
47496CB00001B/54